Reviews for Barry Maitland's Brock and Kolla series

'An unguessable plot, flowing writing and solid characters – forget the stamps, start collecting Maitlands now' *Morning Star*

'One of the best crafted, best plotted and most convincing British thrillers for decades' *Daily Mirror*

'Unflaggingly lively and amusing … a bravura opening full of zest and confidence' *Times Literary Supplement*

'Maitland has a sure touch, and his story line is complemented by a serious look at the issues of sexism and corruption in the police force' *Sunday Express*

'A thoroughly lively and devious debut which is full of devoted invention' *Sunday Times*

'Solid procedural suspense and a serious subtext concerning the nature of corruption make this new series stand out' *Time Out*

SILVERMEADOW

BARRY MAITLAND

ORION

This edition first published in Great Britain in 2000 by
Orion
An imprint of Orion Books Ltd
Orion House, 5 Upper St Martin's Lane, London WC2H 9EA

A CIP catalogue record for this book is available
from the British Library

Typeset by Deltatype Ltd, Birkenhead, Merseyside

Printed in Great Britain by
Clays Ltd, St Ives plc

*To my faithful supporters' club
Margaret, Duncan and Pip.*

Prologue

On a bleak December morning, the east wind gusting in across the Essex marshes and dousing the city in cold rain, Alison Vlasich decided, finally, to go to the police.

She was standing in her daughter's room when she reached this decision. The silence inside the flat seemed intensified by the muffled moans and buffeting of the wind outside. It was an uncanny, nagging silence, and in her state, both panicky and weary, she couldn't decide whether it was really there or whether it was just a numbness inside her head. Then she realised that Kerri's bedside clock, with its happy Mickey Mouse face and loud comforting tick, was gone.

It had taken two sleepless nights and many hours of fruitless phone calls to bring her to this point. The only time she'd previously rung the police was when old Mr Plum had collapsed outside her front door after he'd returned home to find his flat crawling with pre-teen burglars. Mrs Vlasich's 999 call had produced such an intimidating array of sirens and flashing lights that she was inclined not to repeat the experience. No, she thought, on the whole, the best thing would be to go down in person to the local police station and speak to someone face to face about the fear that was now making her feel quite physically sick. This was how they did it on TV on *The Bill*, she told herself, pouring out their troubles to a big, attentive, reassuring desk sergeant with a name like Derek or Stan, who would then take it upon himself to make sure things got properly sorted out.

She put on a little make-up, noticing with surprise how pale she had become, then zipped up her anorak and stepped out onto the rain-swept deck. She hurried away, avoiding the stairs and lifts at this end of the block, following the zigzag route of the deck as it passed through court after court until she came at last to the big ramps at the

I

south-east corner of the estate. Below her she saw the glow of the Tesco shopfront on the other side of the street, the dark bulk of The Merry Jester by the traffic lights, the Esso station opposite, and the concrete framework of the police station, tucked in between the last block of housing and the primary school.

She had some trouble finding the public entrance to the police station. It wasn't the nice timber and glass doorway that she thought they had on TV at Sunhill, but a brutal aluminium job with wired glass and a closed-circuit television camera mounted overhead that looked as if it had been designed to keep out the IRA or gangs of teenagers.

Inside there was a kind of waiting room with metal seats but no counter, and no friendly desk sergeant. No one at all, in fact. In the far wall was another door with wired glass and no handle. Beside the door was a notice: ONE PERSON AT A TIME ONLY PERMITTED IN THE INQUIRY AREA.

Mrs Vlasich looked through the wired glass and saw an elderly man in a cap leaning on a counter, deep in conversation with a uniformed officer on its other side. She tried to push the door, but it was firmly locked and the two inside didn't notice her. She stepped back and saw a button mounted on the wall with a sign: PRESS FOR ATTENTION. She pressed, and heard a buzz beyond the locked door. Nothing happened. The two men continued with their conversation, the man with the cap gesticulating to elaborate a point.

She pressed the buzzer again, and this time the door clicked open. She pushed at it, but was stopped in her tracks before she could step inside by the policeman's voice.

'Please wait out there until I'm finished with this gentleman,' he said to her, quite sharply, before she had a chance to say anything.

She hesitated, then began to explain how urgent her problem was, but the door had clicked shut again in her face.

She sat down and waited. Five minutes. Ten minutes. The room was extremely depressing, bare but not what you'd call clean. There was a large stain of some brown liquid that had dried under a chair in the corner. She didn't see how people could have had coffee in here. Unless the regulars knew the score and came equipped with vacuum flasks.

Fifteen minutes. Alison Vlasich sighed, got to her feet and looked through the wired glass of the locked door. The old man was still talking, the officer writing out a report. She clenched her fists and walked out.

Ten minutes later she arrived home again. The driving rain had soaked through her anorak, and her shirt was wet. She put on a fresh blouse, picked up the phone and dialled 999.

'It's my daughter,' she said. 'She's been abducted.'

Half an hour after her call two people came, a stern-looking woman in uniform and a man in a suit. They both seemed very young. She was so flustered by now that she didn't catch either of their names the first time, and had to ask them to repeat them: Police Constable Sangster and Detective Sergeant Lowry. They all sat down and she gave them her daughter's name, Kerri, and age, fourteen last birthday in July.

Why had it taken her almost forty-eight hours to report Kerri missing? She bit her lip and twisted her fingers and tried to explain, the effort almost more than she could manage. The flat was empty when she'd got home from work on Monday evening, two days ago. She'd looked in Kerri's bedroom and seen that her daughter had changed her clothes after school, and had then presumably gone out again. When Kerri hadn't appeared by seven that evening, Alison Vlasich had had another look in the girl's room and realised that she had taken her pyjamas and her frog bag.

'Frog bag?' The woman constable looked up from her notepad.

'It's shaped like a frog, bright green, and when she wears it it looks as if there's a big frog sitting on her back.' Alison began to cry quietly.

'So you thought she'd gone to stay with someone for the night?' the woman constable suggested eventually, offering her some tissues. 'A friend maybe?'

Alison nodded and sniffed.

'Without telling you?' the man called Lowry asked, sounding rather bored.

This was the difficult bit to have to explain to strangers, straight out. Kerri had changed so much in the last two years, through the divorce. She had been such a good, obedient little girl before. Now she seemed set on hurting her mother at every opportunity. She had done this before, going off to stay with a friend without warning, knowing Alison would worry and be forced to ring round everyone until she found where she was. To be quite honest, it was a relief (she was ashamed to say it) to find the flat empty when she returned exhausted from the hospital, because then she didn't have to face the sulks, the

3

rudeness, the jibes, becoming more habitual and polished with every day that passed.

'You're a nurse?' the woman constable asked.

'I work in the kitchens.'

She felt that the policewoman was sizing her up, trying to decide how reliable she was, and she fiddled self-consciously with the sleeve of her blouse, glad now that she'd changed into something smart, a reminder of better times.

So Alison didn't ring round her daughter's friends that first evening. The following evening, yesterday, when Kerri still hadn't come home, she started to make the calls, thinking that the girl, to punish her, was refusing to appear until she did so. Nobody knew where she was. Worse, none of her friends had seen her at school that day. The school was closed by this time, and Alison had waited till this morning to get them to confirm Kerri's absence.

'I think her father's got her,' she concluded, any hope that the police could help her ebbing away.

'What makes you say that?' the man in the suit asked. The way he pursed his mouth with impatience, and drummed his fingers, flustered her. His fingers were stained brown, and his eyes kept flicking around the room as if they were searching for an ashtray.

'Stefan wanted custody when we split up. He's never accepted things.'

'Does he have access? Does Kerri visit him?'

Alison shook her head. 'He lives abroad. I won't let Kerri go to him, because I know he wouldn't let her come back.' She reached for her handbag and produced a slip of paper. 'This is his address and phone numbers.'

'Hamburg.' Lowry scratched the back of his head. His hair looked newly cropped, very short, and the way he touched it made her think he was still getting used to it.

'I tried ringing him. There was no answer from his home. The second number is his work. They said he's been away. Abroad, they said.'

'If Kerri packed up things to take with her, she must have been planning to go somewhere willingly,' the woman constable said, in that detached, reasonable tone the nurses used with sick people. 'Why don't we have another look in her room and make a list of exactly what she took.'

The man looked at his watch impatiently. 'I'll leave you to it,' he said.

The uniformed woman, who told Alison to call her Miriam, stayed with her for another half an hour, drawing up a list of missing things, from which they picked out the clothes that Kerri would most likely have been wearing when she left, as well as other belongings – the Mexican silver ring and hair clasp, for example – that would identify her. Alison Vlasich felt herself become calmer as Miriam Sangster talked the matter through with her, discussing options and possibilities. It was only when the policewoman made signs of leaving that her agitation returned.

'Why don't you pay a visit to your GP, Alison?' Sangster suggested. 'You probably need something to help you sleep.'

'It isn't that.' She gnawed at her bottom lip.

'What then? Is something else worrying you?'

She hesitated, then nodded. 'If she hasn't gone with Stefan . . .'

'Yes? Is there another possibility?'

'I keep thinking . . . It makes me sick, thinking of it . . .'

'What?'

'But it couldn't be that, could it?'

'Mrs Vlasich, Alison, look, sit down. What's the matter? What do you mean?'

Alison sank into a chair, keeping her eyes fixed on the other woman's face. 'She has a job, at Silvermeadow.'

'Oh yes? What kind of job?'

'A waitress. In the food court. Only a few hours a week.'

'And was she due to work there this week?'

'Not till the weekend. I checked. I phoned them.'

'Well then?'

'There are stories. About Silvermeadow . . .'

'Ah.' Miriam Sangster nodded. 'Yes, I've heard the stories, Alison. But that's all they are, just stories. We get that sort of thing from time to time. A rumour starts somehow, and then it goes round for a while until people get bored with it.'

'But how can you be sure? People seem so, so . . . certain.' She was becoming quite agitated, tugging at the sleeve of the blouse.

'I'm sure because I checked it myself, Alison, on the computer. There have never been any disappearances from Silvermeadow. It's just one of those fairy-tales that goes round, without any substance at all.'

'You're sure? You're quite sure?' She frowned intently at the policewoman, wanting to believe her.

'Where did you hear the stories, Alison? At the hospital?'

'Yes. And the hairdresser's.'

'Ah.'

'But everyone seems so certain. One of the nurses told one of the cooks. She'd looked after an old woman in the geriatric ward, just before she died, who said her little girl was one of the missing.'

'An old woman in the geriatric ward thought she had a little girl?'

'Oh . . .' Alison thought about it. 'I see.'

'Look, you can put that out of your mind, believe me. It seems to me the worst that's happened to Kerri is that she's having a few days with her dad. And maybe that's not such a bad thing, eh? After they've got over the first excitement of seeing each other again, they may come to realise that the best place for her is here with you. It may clear the air, don't you think?'

I

'I thought I might bring the children up to town sometime before Christmas. Just for a couple of days.'

Brock nodded his head against the handset. 'Good idea.'

He took a gulp from his mug of tea. The table in front of him was a jumble of newspapers and the remains of breakfast. He was still in his old dressing gown, although it was already mid-morning. A weak December sun glinting in through the bay window. He'd slept long and deep, the first chance in weeks, and felt expansive, reborn, completely relaxed.

'The Christmas tree in Trafalgar Square, Hamley's toyshop, Billy Smart's Circus, the Science Museum, pantomime at the Palladium . . . wonderful. They'll love it.' He beamed nostalgically and reached for the last piece of toast.

The voice on the other end chuckled. 'Half those things probably don't exist any more.'

'You may be right. You'll stay here of course.'

'Are you eating something? I missed that.'

'I said, you'll stay here.'

There was a pause. 'No. That's sweet of you, David, but I think not. I've got the address of a little hotel near Madame Tussaud's.'

'Do you know how much hotels in the West End cost, Suzanne? That's absurd. I'm only twenty minutes away in the train. Of course you must stay here.'

A longer pause. 'They're very active, David. You've no idea. You've forgotten what young children are like. Miranda is five and Stewart eight. It wouldn't work.'

'You make me sound antediluvian. I get on very well with them.

You know that. And there's enough space here. They could have the attic room, be independent.'

'Thanks. I'll think about it. And you think about it too. Realistically.'

'You sound tired, Suzanne.'

'I've been run off my feet. The Christmas rush.'

'In Battle?' he asked dubiously, picturing the high street in the little Sussex town. 'Anyway, it's a long time to Christmas yet.'

She laughed. 'For you, maybe. I must go, there's a customer. Speak to you soon.' And she hung up.

He refilled his mug from the teapot and walked over to the big window at the end of the room. Outside, weak sunlight was struggling to penetrate the stubborn morning fog which still blanked out most of the features of the surrounding city: the houses perched up on the far side of the railway cutting, the signal gantry beyond the wall of the lane. He might be anywhere, at sea even, or in the air. His mind returned to the high street of Battle, and he pictured the front of Suzanne's little shop. He imagined the customer closing the door against the cold wind blowing in from the nearby coast, and taking in the treasures that filled the shelves. Suzanne would smile a welcome and begin a gentle interrogation, perhaps, trying to figure out how much was to be spent, and what would really appeal – a Georgian spoon, an Art Deco coffee service, some Victorian lace? He pictured her intelligent face, the grey in the hair untinted but carefully cut, and he experienced a sudden pang.

He turned abruptly away from the window and began clearing up his breakfast things. It had been a rough couple of weeks. He should get out of the city, breathe fresh air, sell antiques. As usual, Suzanne had pretty well got it right.

Brock strode out of the archway into the intermittent stream of shoppers in the high street. He walked briskly with a long, rolling lope, hands in pockets, enjoying the wintry sun dappling through the skeletal plane trees in the street. It seemed very quiet for a Saturday morning, and he looked around him with the eye of a host, trying to imagine how the familiar would look to strangers, seeing it for the first time. And it struck him that the place was looking remarkably threadbare, as if the foliage on the trees, now gone, had been masking the underlying scruffiness. Nothing much to appeal to a five-year-old girl and an eight-year-old boy, either. There had been a cinema once, but it had closed down ages ago.

The billboards at the newsagent's door were recycling old headlines, ROYALS BLOW IT AGAIN and OOPS, SAYS TORY MP. He went inside and studied the front page of the *Independent*. MI5's new role caught his eye.

'Not again,' he muttered.

He bought the paper and stepped back out into the sunshine. His eye passed over the electrical goods in the shopfront next door, then scanned the estate agent's, a gloomy little window filled with curling pictures of fading hopes, desperately straining to attract someone to pull them out of the pit of negative equity or divorce settlement. He paused as two elderly people blocked his path, struggling to drag a defective stepladder out of their car, and while he waited for them he watched the owner of the bicycle shop on the other side of the street setting up a rack of kiddies' bikes on the footpath. Apologising profusely, the couple manoeuvred their burden through the door of a DIY shop, stumbling on the uneven pavement. The tree roots had done it, he noticed, and in odd places the council had pulled up the concrete paving slabs around the trunks and patched the footpath with tar. Scruffy.

His next destination lay beyond the unisex hair salon, with its improbably glamorous photographs of stunning heads of hair. Not quite a deli, Butler's was a half-decent grocer's shop with an interesting if unreliable range of goods.

'Morning, Mr Butler.' He nodded, pleased to have the shop to himself. 'Fresh delivery of your steak and kidney pies this morning?'

'I'm afraid they've let me down again, Mr Brock.'

'That's no good. You know I rely on your steak and kidney pies.'

The grocer shook his head sadly. 'Not for much longer, Mr Brock.'

'What?'

'I'm packing it in. Had enough.'

'You can't do that. Are you ill?'

'Not me, but the business is. Got a bad dose of the Sainsbury's. You'll have to get in your car and go down the Savacentre for your pies in future, same as everyone else.'

Brock scratched the crop of his short grey beard. He'd been coming here for years, since the days when it had been a butcher's shop, with a frieze of brightly coloured tiles around the walls portraying the heads of animals – bulls, lambs, pigs, chickens – smiling cheerfully down on the customers engrossed in selecting prime cuts. He'd never tried the Sainsbury's pies, but he was certain they wouldn't be the same.

'Well, I'm very sorry to hear that, Mr Butler, I really am. What's going to take your place?'

'A charity clothes place, so they tell me. Oxfam or some such.'

The shops petered out beyond Butler's, their place taken by insurance offices and car showrooms crammed together. The Bishop's Mitre sat brooding among them, a dour 1950s pub that no amount of half-timbering and geranium window boxes could cheer up. Brock looked at his watch. Good timing. He hadn't had the chance of a relaxed weekend pub lunch in ages. Inside, in the gloom, an off-duty crew from the fire station further up the high street were having a quiet pint.

Brock stood at the bar and opened his paper to see what MI5 were up to now. Before he'd even ordered his ham sandwich and pint, the phone in his pocket started chirping. He recognised DS Bren Gurney's voice.

'I don't think I need this, Bren.'

'A sighting of North, chief. Sounds promising.'

'Really?' There had been a rumour, barely that, that Upper North was back in the country. The possibility killed his appetite.

'You remember Pauline Lewins? The bank job in Ilford. One of the last ones he pulled before the big one in the City. Manager shot dead.'

'Yes of course. I remember Pauline.'

'Well, she works at Silvermeadow now.'

'What's that? A retirement village?'

'Blimey, chief. Where've you been? It's a bloody great shopping centre out in Essex, on the M25. Pauline reckons she saw North there this morning. I've been talking to her, and I reckon it's a possible. If it is him, he seems to have changed his appearance a bit. She's working on a portrait at the moment, and we're going through the security tapes from the shop where she works.'

'Where are you?'

'K Division, the divisional station at Dagenham, Hornchurch Street. Know it?'

'I'll find it.'

'It's on the edge of a bloody great housing estate. Don't go in there whatever you do. There's a security access to the station off the high street. I'll be at the gate.'

'I'll come right over. And Bren, let's keep this as restricted as possible, eh? That includes the locals. The name North doesn't get mentioned.'

'Yeah, that's what I thought. They're up to their ears in their own problems anyway, from what I can gather. There's a WPC who brought Pauline in. She knows what's going on. I'll have a quiet word with her.'

Brock followed Bren's instructions to the AUTHORISED PERSONS ONLY rear entrance to the Hornchurch Street station, where he stopped and spoke into a speaker on the wall. The metal gate rolled up after a moment, and he drove through and down into a basement carpark where Bren was waiting for him. They went up to a room on the third floor where he recognised Pauline Lewins sitting with a uniformed woman whom Bren introduced as PC Sangster. Pauline smiled weakly in recognition at Brock, as one might at a surgeon whom one had fervently hoped never to see again. He sat and they talked quietly for a while.

She explained to him that she loved Cuddles, and he, noticing that she had put on some weight over the years, thought that she, plump, soft and friendly, was perfectly suited to a job in a soft-toy store. Despite her recent shock, she still had the warm, rather shy smile he remembered, made all the brighter, he noted, by new front teeth. In answer to his enquiry she explained that, although she still sometimes became weepy without any apparent reason, and remained a little self-conscious about the scar on her upper lip, her confidence and happy disposition had largely returned. And this was at least partly thanks to Cuddles, where she had learned to get behind a counter again and deal with strangers without dissolving into hysterics. Cuddles was a reassuring place, she told him, selling delightfully reassuring soft toys, and located in the safest and most reassuring heart of the largest shopping centre in the Home Counties. So when she heard that voice again, halfway through ringing up a pair of fluffy tiger cubs, she had just sort of seized up.

'You remember the voice, Mr Brock?'

'Oh yes, Pauline. I remember.'

And who wouldn't seize up, he thought, hearing it again after all that time?

The first time she had heard it, four years ago, she had been working in a bank in Ilford. One morning she had opened up the front door for business as usual, and was immediately confronted by three men who pushed their way in, locking the door behind them and pulling masks over their faces. One of them took hold of her and rammed the muzzle of a gun into her mouth, so violently that it knocked out her front teeth and split her lip. Using her as a hostage, they had forced the other staff to hand over money and then lie flat on the floor. No one offered any resistance, but the robbers maintained a violent and aggressive manner, especially the one holding Pauline, who seemed to be the leader of the gang. He was very agitated and excited, screaming at the bank staff to try making trouble so that he could show them what he would do to them. His ranting terrified the staff and several of the women began to cry. Finally the branch manager – Fairbairn, Brock remembered – had felt obliged to try to calm the man down. He had looked up from his position on the floor and told the man to kindly stop shouting and be reasonable.

There was immediately a terrible silence. All the witnesses subsequently commented on it, as if this was a signal of some kind that the robbers recognised. The man holding Pauline went very still, then smiled down at the manager, withdrew the muzzle of his pistol from Pauline's bleeding mouth, bent down, held it six inches from Fairbairn's upturned face and pulled the trigger.

The three men then calmly walked away, locking the front door behind them. Because of the masks, the other staff weren't able to identify the gunmen, but Pauline had had a clear view of their faces at the moment they had pushed in through the front door. She gave a particularly vivid description of the man who had held her, his wild unblinking grey eyes, the smooth pink skin on his left temple and cheek where it looked as if he had been burned, the belligerent thrust of his mouth. And she described his voice, a hoarse voice, naturally soft but made to sound big by straining his throat, like vegetables forced through a grater.

The task force from Serious Crime, led by Detective Chief Inspector David Brock, had known exactly who she was talking about, and she had immediately identified the photographs of Gregory Thomas North, a professional criminal with a record of violent armed robberies, known as Upper North because of his dangerous habit of psyching himself up with amphetamines before a job.

'You heard the voice, Pauline,' Brock said gently. 'And you saw him?'

'I . . . think so. I looked up as soon as I heard it, and I saw a man walking past behind my customer, talking to a little girl he was holding by the hand. He didn't look at me. He just walked on out of the shop, and I . . . everything went blank.'

'She fainted, sir.' PC Sangster spoke. 'Two of the other sales assistants went to help her, and when someone saw me passing by in the mall they called me in to help.'

Brock turned to her. 'I don't suppose you happened to notice this man and the little girl?'

'No, sorry. The place was packed out this morning.'

Brock picked up from the table a copy of an image of a man's face, based on photographs of North, modified on the computer to Pauline's instructions.

'A bit older – like all of us, eh, Pauline?' Brock said. 'And wearing glasses now. Suntanned?'

'Yes, I think so. But I couldn't see the scar. At least, I don't remember it.'

'It was the left side of his face you saw?'

'Yes.'

'But apart from that, you're pretty certain?'

'I heard the voice, Mr Brock.'

'Yes. What about the child?'

'I hardly saw her. I just had an impression of a little girl. I can't remember how she looked.'

PC Sangster said, 'I took statements from three of the other shop assistants, sir. One of them had served the man. He wanted to know if they had a particular kind of stuffed animal toy, a badger.'

Brock looked sharply at her, wondering if this was some kind of joke. Brock the badger. She blushed and consulted her notebook.

'Yes. He wanted a big badger for the little girl. She was about three or four, blonde curls, wearing a red coat. He was wearing a black bomber jacket and jeans, white trainers.'

'Did they have a badger?' Brock asked.

'No. He'd apparently been there before, because he said he'd seen one there, and the assistant said it'd been sold, but they were getting more in next week.'

'I don't suppose he left a name?'

'No, nothing. He just asked about the badger and then they walked out of the shop, the little girl holding his hand.'

Later, after Pauline had been taken home with advice to get a doctor's note to stay off work for at least two weeks, they played part of the video tape taken by the security camera in Cuddles, from which they had identified the man and child Pauline had seen. Brock sat forward, peering at the screen as they replayed the sequence, then he got to his feet and began pacing up and down the cramped room.

'What do you reckon, Brock?' Bren asked.

'Looks very like him, doesn't it? Same build, way of holding himself. And she was very sure about the voice.'

He stopped and turned to PC Sangster. 'We appreciate your help, Miriam. Did Bren speak to you about keeping this to yourself?'

'Yes, sir. I did report to my inspector, Inspector Rickets, and he was the one who notified the Yard. Other than that I haven't spoken to anyone.'

'Good. If it was him, we don't want a hint to get out that he's been spotted. Don't want to frighten him off.'

'I understand, sir.'

Brock picked up the computer simulation again. It was him, no question. North had returned. They were being given one more chance to put him away. Why had he come back? And for how long?

As Miriam Sangster turned to leave, Brock asked suddenly, 'Is this Silvermeadow on your regular beat?'

'Oh no, sir. We don't patrol there. It's private property, and they have their own security. I was following up another inquiry, a missing girl.' She hesitated, but he seemed to want to know more, so she went on. 'She lives close by here, and hasn't been seen since Monday at school. Her mother reported her missing on Wednesday. The girl had a part-time job at Silvermeadow, and I was just checking with her employer there. It was an accident, really, that I was there at that time.'

'Ah. Lucky for us then.'

At the door she stood back to let two men come in, uniformed and with rank. One announced himself as the divisional commander, Chief Superintendent Forbes, and introduced the other as Inspector Rickets.

Brock thought he remembered the name Forbes, but the face meant nothing: fleshy, large ears, with hair growing on the cheekbones. They shook hands formally.

'They call you Brock, don't they?'

Brock nodded. He had no idea what they called Forbes, apart from sir.

The chief superintendent looked ill at ease, Brock thought, as if he wasn't used to being in rooms like this. It was one of those spaces belonging to no one, windowless, soulless, a dozen chairs around four tables pushed together, all bottom-of-the-range office furniture, a few cigarette burns along the edges. Forbes's smart leather document case looked as out of place as he did.

'We did meet at Bramshill six or seven years ago, a senior officer management course. You gave a paper on streamlining case management. Quite inspiring.'

Brock didn't remember. Had he really spoken on a subject like that? Inspiringly?

A sudden violent burst of noise echoed through the building, like a jackhammer being applied to a concrete frame.

Forbes pulled a face, gritting his teeth. 'They're doing some repair work downstairs,' he said loudly to make himself heard. 'It's been going on all morning.'

Brock wondered if he was making the point that he had been there all morning, at his desk, on the weekend.

They waited for the noise to stop, then Forbes continued. 'Inspector Rickets tells me we may have Gregory North on our patch.'

'It seems possible, sir. We know the principal witness, and she's reliable, I think.'

'I see. At Silvermeadow, I understand. Well, half the population of London goes through Silvermeadow at this time of the year, I suppose. So you'll be wanting to mount an operation there? Shop to shop enquiries, posters, leaflets, information desk . . . ?'

'Well, no,' Brock said. 'The opposite, really. We'd heard rumours that North might have returned, but so far this is the only sighting. It seems that the man at Silvermeadow had visited that shop before, and may do so again, so the last thing we want to do is frighten him off. There's also the question of the safety of the witness. So I would like this whole business treated in the utmost confidence. I've impressed that on PC Sangster. We'd be grateful if you'd leave it entirely with us.'

Forbes looked disappointed.

'If it's a matter of credit . . .' Brock began, but Forbes dismissed the idea with a wave of his hand.

'No, no. Tell me, do you think it possible that North is planning something at Silvermeadow?'

'It's possible I suppose. We have no indication as yet.'

'But it is possible. You see, I wondered if some co-operative arrangement between us, a sharing of resources, might not be appropriate.'

'To be honest, sir, the fewer of your officers seen at Silvermeadow over the next few weeks the better.'

'Ah, but I'm afraid that may not be practicable, Brock.' Forbes leant forward across the table. 'We have our own investigations to pursue, and one of them seems very likely to be focusing on Silvermeadow.'

Brock wondered where this was leading. There was something very calculated about Forbes's manner, an experienced committee man negotiating his way into a position of relative advantage. What it had to do with catching villains he wasn't sure.

'Is that the missing girl investigion?' Brock asked.

Forbes looked startled. He turned to Inspector Rickets, who glanced at Brock. 'PC Sangster briefed you on that, sir?'

'She mentioned that was why she was at Silvermeadow in the first place.'

'Yes, well, she won't be aware that there have been further developments in that case, sir. A body has been found.'

'At Silvermeadow?'

'Not quite. But there seems to be a connection.'

'And that being the case,' Forbes broke in, 'we may well find ourselves conducting an Area Major Investigation right where you want to be discreet and inconspicuous. Hence my thought that some measure of co-ordination, co-operation . . .'

Brock had a distinct feeling that he was being manoeuvred, though he couldn't yet see the point. 'Do you think that's going to be called for?' he asked dubiously. 'An Area Major Investigation?'

'We're not sure yet. The status of the case is currently being reassessed. But it has some disturbing, not to say intriguing features, Brock. And I was wondering if we might possibly prevail upon you, with your considerable specialist expertise, to lend us an hour or two of your valuable time to give us your own assessment. It might just avoid a great deal of unnecessary difficulty further down the track.'

Insurance, Brock thought, that's what he's after, in his pompous, roundabout way. Fireproof me with your considerable specialist expertise or I'll get in your way and stuff up your case.

Perhaps it was an uncharitable thought, and in any case, Brock had never been one to walk away from a murder with disturbing, not to say intriguing features.

'DS Gurney has some homework to do,' Brock said, 'reactivating Criminal Intelligence records on North's connections in this part of the country. While he's doing that, I'd be glad to offer whatever assessment I can on your other case. Only I missed lunch. Any chance of a sandwich to eat on the way there?'

Forbes beamed. 'You shall have the best our canteen can offer.'

He turned to Rickets, who looked doubtful. 'I believe the workmen have cut off power to the kitchen, sir, but we'll do our level best.'

2

Detective Sergeant Gavin Lowry opened the door of the patrol car for Brock as soon as it came to a halt outside Number Three Shed, introduced himself and led him through the tall metal doors into the cavernous interior. Brock had an impression of vast scale, a shadowy Piranesian dungeon lit from high above by a few blinding industrial lamps, whose baleful glare illuminated a cardboard hillside, an unstable-looking avalanche of compacted cardboard blocks with the texture of a giant's breakfast cereal.

'They found her down there, sir,' Lowry said, pointing to one corner, around which the figures of scene of crime officers in white nylon overalls were crawling. 'One of the men was loading the waste onto the back of that truck. The bale split open and she was inside.'

'How long ago was that, Sergeant?' Brock asked, watching the man reach into the inside pocket of his black suit. A sharp dresser, mid-thirties, gel in his hair, after-shave, a smoker. His accent was standard Estuarine, Essex Man, delivered with a cool reserve, anxious to impress, Brock guessed, without showing it. He pulled the wallet of Polaroid pictures from his pocket and offered them to Brock.

'The foreman placed a triple niner at eight forty-three this morning, sir. Reported the discovery of a body.' He looked at his watch and automatically straightened his cuff again. 'I've been here over five hours.' He recounted briefly what steps he'd taken: the disposition of the SOCO teams, photographer, medical examiner.

'The body's been removed?'

'Yes, sir.'

Brock put on his reading glasses and studied the photographs, peering at the strangely distorted figure coiled tight, pale and naked, inside a clear plastic wrapping, disconcertingly like some pre-packaged meal, a chicken leg perhaps, all ready for the microwave.

'What did the FME have to say?'

'Naked human, probably female, probably young, possibly adolescent, five to seven stone, between four six and five six, shoulder-length fair hair. No indication of cause of death, or time.'

'Couldn't get much vaguer than that.' Brock turned to get more light onto the square glossy images.

'She's inside a heavy-duty clear plastic bag, as you can see, sir, and the doc didn't want to open it up here. He reckoned she'd been crushed in a machine.'

'A machine?'

'Yeah, a compactor. The guy who runs this place is over there. He'll explain the technicalities.'

'No identification, then?'

'We could see a ring on one of her fingers. It matches the description of one worn by a missing person, Kerri Vlasich, age fourteen, disappeared Monday, sir.'

They walked towards an incongruously dressed figure: bright yellow yachting jacket, white slacks and espadrilles, a navy peaked cap on his head.

'This is Mr Cherry, sir. The manager of the plant,' Lowry said.

'FD, facilities director,' Cherry corrected tersely. He looked impatient and tense.

'Perhaps you could tell me what's going on here, Mr Cherry?' Brock asked.

'I've already explained it half a dozen times.'

'For my benefit, if you don't mind.'

Cherry pursed his lips with frustration, then spoke rapidly. 'This is one of four WTE plants . . .' He saw the look on Brock's face and checked himself. 'Waste-to-energy plant,' he said. 'Two thousand TPD rating, mixed WTE facility with front-end processing of mixed MSW . . .'

He spoke hurriedly, as if preoccupied with some overwhelming inner problem, so that the incomprehensible acronyms spilled out of their own accord.

'TPD? MSW?' Brock interrupted mildly.

'Tons per day,' Mr Cherry replied automatically. 'Municipal solid wastes.'

A phone began sounding from an inside pocket of his jacket, and he snatched it out. It was the same bright yellow colour as his coat. 'Christ! What now?' He hunched away from the police and barked, 'Yeah? No, no, no, don't do that, sweetheart . . . Just be patient, yes? Please . . . Hang on . . .'

He turned back to Brock. 'How long, you reckon? Before you'll be through with me?'

'Hard to say, Mr Cherry.'

'Shit.' He turned away again, tucking the phone into his shoulder for privacy but making the gesture futile by raising his voice. 'There's some chicken and stuff in the galley, sweetheart . . . no, the *kitchen* . . . and a bottle of bubbly in the fridge . . . Did you? Oh, well, there's more in the cupboard in the corner . . . Lie down, have a rest, eh? . . . How can you be seasick when you're still tied up to the berth? . . . Take a walk outside, sweetheart. I'll ring you back in half an hour.'

He put the phone away, took a deep breath. 'Right. Okay. What do you want to know?'

'Has this happened before, Mr Cherry?'

'What?' He looked alarmed. 'With . . . ?' His voice trailed off. 'Oh, you mean the body?'

'Yes, the body.'

'No, never. They joke about it, the lads, but this is the first time it's actually happened.'

'Maybe if you explained to me in laymen's terms what goes on here, at the plant. You dispose of refuse, do you?'

'In a nutshell, yeah. It comes from all over Essex and east London. We do some front-end processing to the mixed waste for general recovery and recycling in the building near the front gates. The rest goes up the ramp for processing into RDF – refuse-derived fuel.'

'Can we see?'

'Sure.'

He led them out of the shed and onto the roadway leading to a concrete ramp. A light drizzle was falling now and they turned up their collars, hunching against the wind that grew stronger the higher they climbed. Halfway up they were obliged to stop and stand hard against the parapet as a heavily laden truck came grinding past, headlights on. It gave a blast of its horn and continued on up to the head of the ramp. They followed, the view opening up across the surrounding industrial landscape, flat and bleak, the humped profiles of grey factory sheds interspersed with the odd scarlet crane and silver flue.

The truck belonged to one of a number of designated contractors, Cherry explained, whose waste sources were known and whose loads did not require to go through the front-end screening process. They watched as the truck began reversing towards the delivery point, guided by the waving signals of an operative in waterproofs and a hard hat. The back of the truck began to tilt upwards, the load slid with a rumble into the steel maw, and within a minute the truck was disappearing down the exit ramp ahead.

'Nobody actually inspects the load, see?' Cherry said, having to shout now against the wind and the roar of the plant. 'The contractors certify the organic content, and it goes straight in here for processing – shredding, grinding, spin-drying and then into the fuel silos. From there it's pumped to the power plant' – he pointed to a pair of tall gleaming steel chimneys reaching upwards to the cloud base – 'and incinerated. We generate electricity for the grid, and sell the waste heat to a number of industrial plants around here, and to the district heating scheme that serves the Herbert Morrison estate.' He gestured towards a row of grey concrete slabs almost invisible against the dark clouds.

'You're joking,' Lowry said. 'Straight up?'

'Yes, sure. Why?'

'We think that's where the girl came from.'

'Blimey! She could have ended up heating her mum's radiators and giving her a few minutes of Terry Wogan on the telly,' Cherry said softly, and they all stared at the distant housing blocks, looking disturbingly like tombstones in the rain.

The rain was falling with greater density and penetration now, and Cherry said, 'Well, seen enough up here?'

They jogged quickly back down the ramp, returning to the shelter of Number Three Shed where they shook their coats and stamped their feet. The two drivers were back in their machines again, scooping out cardboard bales to the instructions of the SOCO officers. A handler with a beagle had joined them, and the dog was eagerly investigating each new batch of material uncovered. He seemed to be the only one enjoying his work.

'So where does this fit into the process?' Brock asked Cherry.

'It doesn't,' the man said wearily. 'That's the point. We've been having trouble with our emissions. A month ago we were forced to shut down one of the two incinerators while we installed new filters. It's only just been fired up again. Meanwhile we couldn't burn all the material coming in. The RDF silos filled up, and we had to start dumping half the loads in here, as a temporary storage. We've hardly begun to clear it. By rights, none of this stuff should be here. Number Three Shed is due for demolition, to make way for a third incinerator.'

'All this should have gone straight up the ramp?'

'That's right.'

The manager's phone rang again and he clamped the yellow instrument to his ear. 'What's that, sweetheart?' he yelled. 'Where? . . . You threw up where? . . . Oh, Jesus!' He swung round, oblivious to those around him now, staring wildly up into the darkness beyond the floodlights, his mind seized by some vivid mental picture.

Brock walked away, taking the Polaroid pictures from his pocket. The image in the photographs was so bizarre that he wished he'd seen it in situ for himself, the figure coiled inside the cube of compressed cardboard, like a foetus inside an egg. A private, secret foetus that by rights should never have been exposed, should have been delivered straight up the ramp to the shredders and grinders and then incinerated without anyone having a clue. Uncovered by a problem with emissions.

The plant manager seemed preoccupied with an emissions problem of a different kind, Brock thought wryly, watching him thrust his phone back in his pocket.

'Tell me about compactors,' he said.

'Plenty of them about. Factories, supermarkets, anywhere that generates a lot of dry waste. Common type has a two-cubic-yard capacity, four-to-one compression ratio' – he rattled off the technical mantra while his mental eye seemed mesmerised by the vision of his girlfriend vomiting – 'usually linked to a receiving container that's emptied by a contractor.'

Cherry paused, and stared up at the harsh lights. 'Christ, we've had so many fucking disasters lately . . . Stroke of luck for you though, eh? You'll be able to work out where it came from, no bother.'

They spoke to the woman leading the SOCO team, who described their preliminary results from the bale of cardboard waste in which the body had been hidden. The manufacturers' symbols printed on them were those of household names, makers of electrical goods, paper towels, breakfast cereals. Several of the compressed boxes had delivery codes written on them, and one had fragments of a delivery notice inside it, with the sender's name and despatch number, and the destination: a store at Silvermeadow.

When they returned to the patrol car, Lowry held the door open for Brock and said, 'He'll take you to Hornchurch Street, sir. Chief Superintendent Forbes is waiting for you in his conference room on the fourth floor. The driver'll show you the way.'

He was perfectly polite, Brock noted, like a young man looking after an elderly relative who needed direction. Brock rested his arm on the roof of the car and looked him over thoughtfully. 'Where are you going, Sergeant?'

Lowry checked his watch. 'I'd better get over to the autopsy, sir. They said they'd make way for this one, and I'll be needed to establish continuity of identification.'

'I'll come with you.'

'Ah . . .' Lowry's voice became coaxing, the volume low, as if he didn't want the driver to hear. 'Chief Superintendent Forbes is expecting you back there, sir. Area Major Investigation Pool Management has been alerted. I believe there are important management issues to resolve.'

'Bugger the important management issues, Sergeant. I want to see the body.'

Lowry's eyes flicked away briefly, a little smile forming on his lips. The elderly relative was becoming difficult. 'You'll get me into trouble, sir . . .' he began, almost teasingly, then suddenly caught the cold look in Brock's eye and stopped what he was about to say. He shrugged and reached for his phone. 'I'll let them know, sir.'

Brock put out his hand. 'Just get the number for me, Sergeant. I'll speak to him.'

He took the phone and walked away, out of earshot.

She – it definitely was a she – was curiously resistant to their probing, as if unwilling to release her secrets. Her age for a start. Perhaps it was the effect of the prolonged wrapping in the heavy plastic, or simply the result of the brutal compression, but her crushed face appeared old, that of a wrinkled old woman, while some other parts of her body – a thigh, a breast – seemed undeniably juvenile. The juxtaposition was disturbing, and Brock found his eyes wandering backwards and forwards, trying to reconcile a span of sixty years in the one body. In the end the pathologist called for X-rays of the teeth, as the only sure guide, but made an informed guess based on the weight of her organs, especially the liver and the spleen, which of all the main organs experience the greatest growth during puberty, and which in both cases were close to the median weight for a fourteen-year-old of similar build.

How and when she died were also problematic. There were no wounds incompatible with the effects of the compactor, into which, the pathologist was fairly certain, she had been put after rigor mortis was well established. But this was only a guess, he explained, for who had any real evidence of what the relentless hydraulic forces of the machine could do to the joints of a human body, whether stiff with rigor or not? He could only estimate, too, that she had been dead for around seven days, which matched reasonably well with Cherry's conjecture that, from her position in the cardboard mountain, she had probably been delivered to Number Three Shed four or five days before. Maybe. As for identity, the teeth would again most likely provide the most reliable evidence, apart from the Mexican silver ring. It struck Brock as obscene that this little trinket, completely unscathed, should now seem to contain more of her personality than anything else on the stainless-steel table.

When it was over, and they set off again for their meeting with Chief Superintendent Forbes, Brock thought he sensed a certain satisfaction in Lowry that he had kept the senior officer waiting for a couple of hours for so little additional information. But he felt happier. He had, in some way that he couldn't quite define, made contact with the victim, seen what had to be seen. It was the true starting point, from which the axis of the investigation would extend.

The jackhammering was at full volume when they returned to the divisional station at Hornchurch Street. Lowry showed Brock to the fourth-floor conference room and departed. Forbes rose to his feet, smiling, as Brock walked in. This was a much more comfortable meeting room, with high-backed chairs and a long polished timber-board table. The noise was muffled in here, and Forbes waved Brock to a seat. 'So, how was the PM?' he asked.

'Not as informative as I'd have liked. A fourteen-year-old girl, most probably, but nothing much more solid than that. Sorry to have held you up.'

Forbes waved a large hand dismissively. 'Can't stand autopsies. One was enough for me. Had she been interfered with?'

'We'll have to wait for the tests.'

'Mmm. But nasty, you'd agree?' He appeared keen to have Brock confirm this point.

'Yes. Certainly that.'

'A sticker, as my young colleagues would put it, eh?'

Brock nodded. A sticker, certainly.

'Mmm.' He seemed reassured. 'Wouldn't like it said that we'd overreacted.'

Perhaps that was what the insurance was for, protection against some sensitivity in the system to premature approaches to Area Major Investigation Pool Management.

'And an interesting case?'

Again Brock nodded. Interesting indeed.

'No chance of further bodies out there?'

'They haven't found any so far, but they're less than halfway through searching.'

'Ah. So tell me, have you been able to give my proposal any further thought?'

'What exactly did you have in mind, sir? There's no suggestion that North is connected to this other case.'

'No, no. But it has occurred to me since we last spoke that we might be able to come to some arrangement that would suit both our purposes. You want to spend time at Silvermeadow in the hope of tracking North, but don't want it to be apparent, and we need top-calibre people there to support our investigations into the murder of this girl. Now suppose I, or rather AMIP, were to make a request to the Yard for high-level assistance with this murder, and you and your team were nominated. That would give you a legitimate reason to be at Silvermeadow, and of course would be a bonus for us.'

'You would want us to participate in your murder team?'

'Oh, I think that would be essential, don't you? Otherwise people would ask what you were doing there. And, given your . . . status, I imagine people would expect you to play a leading role, at least nominally, yes? And of course, I would express my delight that the Met had agreed to lend us someone so' – he hesitated, searching for the right word – 'distinguished,' he said finally, rather lamely.

Brock was thinking that the insurance Forbes was seeking must be of a more ongoing nature if he wanted him effectively to take over one of his cases. But Brock wasn't averse to that. He wanted to know what had happened to the crushed child he'd just seen dissected on the pathologist's table.

'Yes,' he said. 'I can see possibilities in that.'

'Really?' Forbes seemed almost taken aback at the success of his gambit. 'Excellent, excellent. I'll get it formalised right away. I take it you're happy to work with DS Lowry? Well regarded. Sound. Local knowledge. An asset, undoubtedly.'

Brock noted the sudden abbreviation of Forbes's sentences, and wondered if he might have some problem with this local asset.

'I expect,' Forbes added with a conciliatory smile, 'that you'll want to have your sergeant on the team?'

Brock nodded, acknowledging the etiquette in the balance of power. 'Bren Gurney, yes. But I want him working on the North case. I'll bring in someone else to back up the Vlasich inquiry.'

'Fair enough. Anyone in mind?'

'I've an excellent DS we could probably make available. Name of Kolla.'

'And he is . . . ?'

'She.'

'Ah. Yes, well, good idea. A dead girl – a woman DS should be an asset.'

What a pompous ass he was, Brock thought. 'Her *asset* is that she's a bloody good detective. We've got an excellent forensic liaison officer too, if that suits you. I wonder if I might make a couple of calls?'

'Of course, of course.' Forbes jumped to his feet, reached for the phone, which was sitting on a side cabinet, and hefted it, together with the three Metropolitan Police telephone directories, red, black and grey, across onto the table. He set the books down beside the phone, pointedly placing the black volume, covering headquarters branches, on top.

'Be my guest. Just give me a shout when you're finished,' he said. 'I'll organise tea and biscuits. How do you take it?'

'White no sugar, thanks,' Brock said, and Forbes moved rapidly to the door.

Five minutes later there was a knock and a constable stepped in cautiously with a polystyrene cup.

'The chief super asked me to tell you to ring him on this number when you're finished, sir.'

Brock took the note she offered and lifted the cup as she left. Coffee, sweet. He grimaced.

His first phone call had reassured him that there was method behind Forbes's manoeuvrings. There was a political climate to be appeased, and Forbes had probably acted wisely, both in terms of self-insurance and the greater good. Child murder, if that was what it was, was the number one priority of the day.

He put down the cup and rang a second number.

A woman's voice answered after a couple of rings. 'Hello?'

Brock looked at his watch. Six p.m. on a cold, wet, wintry Saturday night. 'Kathy, it's Brock. Am I intruding?'

'Just washing my hair.'

'Going out tonight?'

'Yes. Nicole Palmer in Records. Know her? She and her partner are throwing a celebratory dinner party.'

'Ah. A baby?'

'No. A Harley Davidson, actually.'

'Very wise.'

'They've got a friend, a male of uncertain marital status. I think that's why I've been invited. Maybe if things go well we might end up having a little motorbike together. But I'll probably never find out.'

'Why's that?'

'Well, I suppose you've got something more interesting on offer?'

'Fourteen-year-old girl, found inside a compressed block of cardboard at a waste disposal plant out in Essex. By rights she should never have been found – should have gone straight into the incinerator. Area have requested our help. But look, I could get somebody else . . .'

'I'll be there. Give me the address.'

Forbes returned with Lowry in tow, the sergeant looking subdued. Brock wondered how he'd taken the news that his case was being handed over to someone from outside.

'I thought Gavin might brief us quickly on the Vlasich case, Brock, and then' – he glanced at his watch – 'then, I really must be on my way. Gavin?'

'Sir. Last Wednesday morning PC Sangster and I interviewed a local woman, name of Alison Vlasich, from the Herbert Morrison estate next door here. She was reporting a possible abduction, her daughter Kerri, age fourteen. The physical description – colour of hair and eyes, height and weight – matches the girl at the incinerator. And she had a silver ring, from Mexico, that she liked to wear.' He opened a file he'd brought and passed Kerri's photograph across to Brock. A pretty girl, with a cheeky smile. No longer, it seemed.

27

'How far did your investigation get?' Brock asked.

'When we interviewed Mrs Vlasich there were several things about the case that didn't seem to add up. In the first place, the girl had obviously planned to go away for a while without her mother's knowledge. She'd filled a backpack with a number of personal things that suggested more than just an overnight stay with a friend. Here's the list we drew up with Mrs Vlasich's help: change of clothes, underwear, favourite CDs, an alarm clock, toiletries, and her passport.'

'Passport?'

'Yes. The parents divorced over a year ago, and the father, Stefan Vlasich, went over to Hamburg, where his brother and mother live. Custody was a big issue, and Mrs Vlasich has always been afraid that the girl's father would try to take her away from her. On top of that, the two of them, mother and daughter, haven't been getting on lately. She described it as a phase Kerri was going through: rebellious, rude, uncommunicative – you know, teenage stuff.'

'Indeed I do!' Forbes said with feeling.

'When she realised that the girl hadn't just gone to stay with one of her friends, Mrs Vlasich tried to contact her former husband in Germany, and was told that he was abroad. She thought he must have come to the UK to pick up Kerri and take her back with him. It seemed like a reasonable assumption, and we initiated a check on ports and airports for the pair of them.'

'Hmm. What's the legal situation?'

'Messy. If the father had been a German national, the pattern would be to get the girl before a German court as quickly as possible, sir, before the wife could act. The court would put the child's interests first, regardless of what the UK court had ruled. If the girl stood up and said she felt herself to be a German and wanted to be brought up as one, the court would give the father custody, end of story. That's the way it goes. However, he's a Yugoslav citizen, apparently, and so it's not at all certain how a German court would rule. Anyway, the point is, as far as we know, there's no evidence that she ever reached Germany.'

Lowry paused as a renewed burst of hammering vibrated through the building.

When it finally stopped, Forbes said, 'What in God's name are they doing, Gavin? At six-fifteen on a Saturday evening?'

'Some kind of emergency, sir. A gas leak, I believe.'

More pounding, louder than ever. There was a knock on the door.

Forbes called 'Come!', but he was apparently inaudible to the person outside, for a second knock was heard. The hammering abruptly stopped just at the moment when Forbes bellowed 'YES!' at the top of his voice. A uniformed policewoman put her head tentatively into the room. 'Message for DS Lowry, sir. You asked to be informed.'

Lowry got to his feet. 'I'd better chase this up, sir.'

'Yes, yes.'

When Lowry had gone, Forbes looked at his watch. 'I'm afraid I've got a dinner engagement this evening, Brock,' he said. 'Rotary people . . . networking, really. Otherwise I'd . . . Maybe you'd care to join us?'

'I'll stick with this, thanks, sir.'

'Hmm.' The chief superintendent caressed his calfskin briefcase with the tips of his fingers, frowning. 'Look, I put a call through to Area Major Investigation Pool Management just now, Brock. And it appears that they have a general AMIP policy that the SIO should be at chief super level, do you see?'

'Oh yes?' Brock wondered how many murder inquiries Forbes had been senior investigating officer on.

'Look, I know it doesn't really make much sense for me to be leading someone like you on this, Brock, but it seems . . . it may just work out that way.' He shrugged apologetically. 'I'll keep out of your way as far as practicable, of course. Leave all the day-to-day decisions in your hands. Give you all the support I can, and all the credit, goes without saying.'

We'll see, Brock thought, but said nothing to ease the awkward moment.

Lowry saved Forbes further embarrassment by coming back into the room, reading from a sheet of paper. 'Purfleet Electrical have traced the batch to their store at Silvermeadow.' He looked up. 'The centre has three compactors, apparently.' He gave Forbes a moment to make enthusiastic noises, then continued, 'Another of the compressed boxes, formerly containing packs of sugar, also seems to have come from Silvermeadow. And the Vlasich girl, as we know, had a part-time job there. We didn't follow that up, though, because of the things she'd taken from home, and also we were put off by her school friends, who said they didn't believe Kerri had planned to go there on Monday evening.'

'What changed PC Sangster's mind?' Brock asked.

'Sir?' Lowry looked puzzled.

'She was there this morning, checking with the girl's employer apparently.'

'I didn't know that. She didn't discuss that with me.'

'Anyway, Silvermeadow seems to be our crime scene,' Forbes said enthusiastically, looking as if he might have been a little premature in promising Brock the credit on this one. The way Lowry was going, they'd have no need of the Yard.

And Lowry was evidently still way ahead of them, for he continued, 'I have my own contacts at Silvermeadow, sir. The head of their security, Harry Jackson, was a DI at West Ham when I was there.'

'Really? They have a big security outfit, do they?' Forbes asked.

'Oh yes. He's probably got more staff than you, sir.' Lowry grinned. 'Well, better equipped, anyway. All right if I give him a bell, get him to line things up for us?' He directed this at Brock, who agreed. They also agreed that Mrs Vlasich would be unlikely to be able to make an identification from the ruined figure in the bale, and that her attention at this stage should be confined to the ring.

Forbes made renewed apologies and departed. Brock accepted Lowry's suggestion to go down to the canteen for something to eat while they waited for Kathy to arrive. The emergency building work had cut off the gas supply to the kitchen, however, and disgruntled groups of uniformed men and women sat at the tables poking at solitary-looking sausage rolls and pasties. Brock ordered an improvised toasted sandwich and mug of tea, without sugar.

While they ate, Lowry maintained a courteous but careful conversation. He knew Bren Gurney, it transpired; they had played rugby together for the Met, Bren in the pack and Lowry, leaner and slighter of build, at fly half. He mentioned this a little too casually, Brock thought, as if implying that he had a wide circle of contacts in the force and wasn't in any way overawed by an attachment from SO1. Or maybe it wasn't that at all. The man was certainly sharp and it was too early to judge him. Brock tried to discount the uncomfortable impression that everything Lowry said had a hidden agenda, as if he was testing everyone in some way.

After half an hour Kathy appeared in the canteen. The sight of the familiar face looking around the room, fair hair glistening with rain, her grin when she spotted him, cheered Brock considerably. He waved her over, introduced her to Lowry, and gave her a rapid briefing.

When he was finished Lowry led them out to his car. He took them first to the far side of the Herbert Morrison estate, leaving his car under a street light on the main road rather than on the estate roads that led through the large courts. These courts appeared to Brock to be identical, so that although the layout seemed simple, it was easy to lose a sense of direction once landmarks on the surrounding streets were left behind. Lowry, leading the way, soon became a victim of this effect.

'I think we've been through this one before,' Kathy said after a few minutes. 'I remember that tree in the middle, with the broken branches.'

'Hell.' Lowry looked around in frustration at the bleak, darkened concrete grids. 'We want Primrose Court. They're all named after spring flowers: Bluebell, Jonquil, Tulip . . . Bloody tragic, isn't it?'

There was no one about, the shadowy decks deserted, the courts silent except for the dripping of the rain, a burst of TV from an open window, the muffled sounds of traffic somewhere beyond. Lowry was eventually obliged to ring a doorbell. After a rattling of a chain a nose appeared cautiously in the crack. The minimum of information was hurriedly exchanged and they went on, coming finally to Alison Vlasich's front door. Although the decks were identical bare concrete throughout the estate, Brock had noticed that many of the residents had put small rectangles of carpet or vinyl floor-covering outside their front doors to individualise their address, or perhaps because they too had trouble finding their own front doors. Mrs Vlasich's threshold was marked by a piece of flowery Axminster, an offcut from her living-room carpet, as they soon discovered.

It was immediately clear to Brock that she felt uncomfortable with Lowry. She avoided his eye and when he opened the conversation, introducing him and Kathy, she turned away and asked what had happened to Miriam, and when he said that PC Sangster was no longer working on this investigation she looked anxiously at Kathy.

'Are you on your own, Alison?' Kathy asked, as they sat down.

The woman gave a little nod.

'Is there anyone we can call, to be with you?'

They watched her reaction, numbness spreading through her. 'You've found Kerri?' she asked, very slowly. 'Is that it?'

Lowry took the plastic bag containing the ring from his pocket, and handed it to her. She stiffened and nodded immediately.

'You're sure it's hers?'

'Yes.' Her responses were becoming slower and slower, as if she might save her daughter by delaying their news.

'Might she have given it to someone else? Swapped it with a friend?'

'No, that's impossible. Her father sent it to her, for her last birthday. She's worn it constantly since.' Alison Vlasich stared at the floor in front of her, at the flowery Axminster, and added dully, 'Have you come to take me to see her?'

'No,' Brock told her gently. 'We have found someone, a girl of Kerri's age, with this ring. She seems to have been involved in an accident. It would be better if we make sure who she is before you see her. Has Kerri been to the dentist recently?'

The question made no sense to her, but Mrs Vlasich answered anyway, giving the name of a local practice.

'Is she dead, this girl?'

'Yes.'

'Where . . . where was the accident?'

'We're not certain. But it may have been at Silvermeadow . . .'

The name had an effect like an electric shock. She went rigid, staring at Brock for an instant, then folded abruptly in half, her hands over her face, sobbing hysterically.

It took a little while to organise a neighbour to stay with Alison Vlasich before they headed off again along the deck around Primrose Court. Their visit had stirred activity. Voices could be heard in the cold night air, and from time to time the patter of running footsteps on the upper deck above them. They took a staircase, comprehensively tagged with graffiti, to the ground. Lowry was ahead of them, hurrying, and as he stepped out into the open a weird sound of whistling made him stop and look up. Out of the darkness overhead Brock was briefly aware of a black object tumbling down through the rain. Before Lowry could move, it smashed to the ground beside him with a shattering explosion. He leapt away and stood staring at the debris.

'A television set,' he said, breathless. 'A fucking TV!'

From overhead they heard a shout, some laughter, then running feet again, like the sound of scurrying rats.

Light suddenly flooded out from one of the front doors and the small figure of an old man lunged forward, bellowing, 'What? What did they use this time?'

Lowry told him, 'A TV.'

'Oh, you're lucky, mate! Last week it was a bleedin' dog. From the top deck. What a bleedin' mess that was!'

'Who?' Lowry asked. 'Who was it?'

'Kids,' the man said dismissively. 'They'll have calmed down in a year or two. Be full of 'eroin by then, eh? That'll keep the little bastards quiet.'

There was a further delay while Lowry reported the incident on his phone, demanding a full-scale raid on the estate from an uncooperative duty sergeant.

While they waited, sheltering under an overhang from the sleeting rain, Kathy said to Brock, 'Two things. The way she reacted to the name Silvermeadow.'

Brock nodded. 'And the other?'

'PC Sangster. I'd like to talk to her.'

'Good idea.' He rubbed a hand across his beard. 'Never mind, Kathy. It could be worse. You could be stuck in some hideously comfortable room, eating and drinking too much, being chatted up by a ridiculously handsome merchant banker with a yen to get you across his pillion.'

'An airline pilot. That's what he was. But it would never have worked. I don't have the leathers, see.'

3

Traffic was heavy on the motorway, the freezing rain continued to gust in across the Essex flats, and Kathy had difficulty keeping Lowry's tail lights in sight through the sluicing water. Along the way Brock briefed her on North, the real reason why they were there. She felt a disconcerting sense of having been through this before, for in her first encounter with Brock he had been doing exactly this, using the cover of another murder investigation in order to get a lead on this same elusive North. It had been her first murder case as investigating officer, and she had been both flattered and intimidated to have a senior Yard detective like Brock looking over her shoulder. After she got used to him he had seemed benign, fatherly and harmless. Later she had discovered that he had been trying to track down whoever it was in her division who was supplying information to North's lawyer. Since she was having an affair with the lawyer at the time, she had been the unwitting prime suspect.

She wasn't sure how far back Brock and North went, but they were already long-standing adversaries at that time, four years before. Brock had led a team drawn from the Serious Crime Branch and Robbery Squad to hunt North following a series of violent robberies in the London area, culminating in what the tabloids dubbed the 'City Securities Slayings', in which two young police officers had been shot dead by the escaping gang. North had fled abroad, but had been lured back to the UK and arrested by Brock, only to escape again while in transit between prisons.

'You say he was with a little girl?' Kathy asked.

'Yes. That's a mystery. He had a wife and a six-year-old boy when he escaped abroad, but we've kept an eye on them over the years and there's been no hint of contact from him. The wife said she'd had enough of him, and eventually we believed her. She and the boy are living in Southampton now. If he had a girlfriend at that time we didn't know of it.'

'The girl might just be cover, someone he borrowed for the day.'

'Maybe.' Brock looked unhappy. 'But who would lend their child to an animal like North, for God's sake?'

It was a chilling thought. Kathy said, 'And Lowry and the others, they're in on this?'

'No, only those that already knew – Forbes, PC Sangster and her inspector. We've asked them to keep it to themselves. Simpler that way. As far as Lowry and the rest are concerned, you and I are investigating the disappearance of Kerri Vlasich. And we will do that, while Bren and his team get on with hunting North. The priority is to sift through the security camera tapes from the centre to get any further sightings of him. If we are very lucky there might a shot of him using a credit card, or getting into a bus or a taxi or car. We're putting a couple of women officers in shifts into the shop where he was seen, in the hope he might return.'

After a while they saw the sign SILVERMEADOW and followed Lowry up the exit slip road to an overpass bridge. From the top of the embankment the view opened up to the west, the blackness of the night fractured by tall lighting masts illuminating a vast carpark with the brilliance of a football stadium. Beyond the cars, thousands of them, lay the indeterminate outline of a huge building which might have been an assembly plant, or a large warehouse complex. Only the electric hype of the entrances, lit up like pinball machines, signified that this was a place at which the public was welcome.

They parked as near as they could to one of the beckoning entrances, beneath a sign which said REMEMBER! ORANGE CAR PARK, AISLE K4. They hurried through the rain towards the brilliant orange neon WELCOME TO SILVERMEADOW sign. Beneath it, silhouetted against the glass doors, stood a group of motionless figures, waiting. As they hurried closer, Kathy could make out uniforms.

One of them, the oldest and tallest, was in a suit, an identity card clipped to his belt. He stepped forward and shook Lowry's hand warmly, Kathy noted, then turned to be introduced to them. Grizzled, but looking fit and tough, he gripped her hand firmly and looked steadily into her eyes, like a general receiving a delegation at the frontier of his command, she thought. The others held back and were not introduced, two men and a woman, all dressed entirely in black, in American cop-style caps and leather blouse jackets with insignia on their arms and identity cards on their left breasts.

'Is this the lot, Gavin?' Harry Jackson asked, sounding mildly disappointed, as if he'd been expecting an armoured division at least.

'We've got a scene of crime team coming to look at the compactors, Harry. I told them to go to the service road entry, like you said.'

Jackson glanced at one of the uniformed men and inclined his head. The man turned without a word and marched off into the night.

'Right then, let's get you into the warm, for a start.' He stretched out an arm in a gesture of welcome, and the automatic doors, picking up the movement, slid obediently open. Kathy breathed in the warm, scented breeze that billowed out.

'And may I say, Mr Brock, that it's a pleasure to meet you at last.'

'Have we met before, Harry?' Brock asked. 'Your face looks familiar.'

'Don't believe so. I was at West Ham most of my time in the Met. Were you ever there?'

Brock shook his head.

'Maybe you saw Harry win the Met snooker championship in 1988, sir,' Lowry offered. 'That's his main claim to fame.'

Jackson chuckled. 'What a night that was! Hardly get the time to play at all these days, which says something about working in the private sector I suppose. There again, the game always got me into bad habits – smoking and booze. At our age we've got to be more careful with our bodies. Am I right?'

Having established a certain level of parity and bonhomie, Jackson took charge. 'I've arranged for you to meet our boss, the centre manager, first, for an initial briefing. Then we'll inspect the compactor site. Your SOCOs should be here by then. Suit you?'

'Fine. I'd be interested to see your set-up, too, Harry. Gavin tells me you're state of the art, is that right?'

'Well, we do our best. Of course our needs are more modest than the Met's. Up to now this has been a relatively crime-free environment. That's really what we're on about. Prevention.' He turned and waved through the window of a building society office at a young woman behind the counter. She smiled and waved back. 'This is a safe community, Mr Brock,' he went on. 'That's why Gavin's phone call was of such concern to us. You'll find us completely co-operative, believe me.'

The uniformed couple fell into step behind them as they set off into the mall.

Kathy's first reaction was of disappointment. She'd expected something spectacular and instead thought it rather plain, with its white polished terrazo floor and mirrored ceiling strips, and standard shopfronts, but this was only a side mall, relatively quiet and restrained. Soon they reached the main mall, and here the space opened out dramatically, golden light flooding down from above. White steel columns arched up between the shopfronts which lined the broad route, and branched and met overhead, so that the view down the long mall resembled a tree-lined boulevard in winter, all sparkling white and silver, but bathed in the golden light of perpetual summer. Christmas music interspersed with birdsong drifted down from the steel branches from which scarlet banners were suspended between glittering fairy lights. YULETIDE AT SILVERMEADOW they proclaimed, CHRISTMAS IN THE MALL. It was surprisingly busy for the late hour. Throngs of people slowly flowed past the glowing shopfront displays, many in light clothes, despite the December cold outside, for in here it was always warm and balmy. Soon they came to Plaza Mexico, where the shops were of adobe and the plants yucca and giant cactus, and a little later they glimpsed the sails and rigging of a half-scale pirate galleon moored at a seventeenth-century wharf in a side mall.

It was partly the effect of contrast, Kathy thought, having come directly from the Herbert Morrison estate, that caused the sense of disorientation that gradually filled her, as if somehow, while no one was really looking, the city had polarised into two grotesque extremes: one a concrete nightmare, the other a luminous fantasy, all make-believe and impossible sweetness and light.

They moved on through the crowded mall, weaving between pushchairs, bulging carrier bags and clusters of seats and café tables, towards what appeared to be the end. But when they reached the place they realised that it was another town square marking a change in direction, and beyond it the mall continued, far into the distance.

'It's huge,' Kathy murmured, 'like a self-contained city.'

'Or an airport,' Brock grunted, sounding determinedly unim-pressed.

To their left the line of shopfronts swept away around the square, with balconies looking down over a lower level occupied by the trees of a tropical rain forest, among which dozens of tables and chairs were visible below. The music and birdcalls had changed, 'Jingle Bells' giving way to Polynesian guitars and the sound of parrots. Crowded escalators and a glass lift carried people up and down between the two levels.

Jackson stopped briefly here to point out the food court below with its Tastes of Five Continents, the entrance to the Grand Bazaar, and, a particular delight, a miniature volcano in a lagoon half hidden among the trees. 'Our very own Mount Mauna Loa. Erupts every hour, on the hour. You'll want to see it.'

Kathy didn't think she would, but didn't argue. She watched a family stroll past, husband, wife and little boy. The boy was wearing a dressing gown and shuffling along in a pair of slippers, his teddy bear tucked under his arm, looking for all the world as if he'd stepped straight out of his bedroom.

'Kerri Vlasich had a part-time job in the food court, Harry,' Lowry said.

'Is that right? Which one, any idea? There are twenty-six outlets down there.'

Lowry shook his head. They could make out knots of teenagers gathered under the rain-forest trees, lounging, swaggering, eyeing each other, older people detouring around them.

'Never mind. I'll find out for you.' He turned away and spoke to the uniformed woman, at whom the small boy in the dressing gown was staring, bug-eyed.

They resumed their journey, past a bamboo thicket in a stand of elaborate planter boxes incorporating seats, litter bins, a small pool, and, half hidden among the foliage, a fearsome-looking gorilla.

Kathy felt uncomfortably warm now in her outdoor coat as they made their way past a queue of small children waiting to meet Santa Claus beneath a huge Christmas tree. Jackson went over and gave Santa a pat on the shoulder as he passed, and the old man playing the role gave a cheery wave and cried, 'Ho, ho! Hello there, Harry!'

Beyond the tree Jackson paused to let three long-legged girls cross his path, with shorts and damp blonde hair and rolled-up towels looking as if they'd just wandered off the beach at Malibu or Bondi. Kathy saw him wink at Lowry as he led them on into a side corridor off the mall, where they came to a glass door labelled CENTRE MANAGEMENT.

A young black woman was in the front office, stacking a pile of brochures and promotional literature on the receptionist's desk. She looked up as they came in and gave them a flash of brilliant white teeth. Jackson introduced her as Bo Seager and she shook their hands in turn and led them through to an inner office where she took their coats and invited them to sit down around a coffee table.

'Can I offer you anything?' she asked. They declined. She leaned back against the edge of the large desk and said, 'Now, how can I help?'

Kathy caught the look of surprise on Brock's face. So did Bo Seager. 'Yes, I'm the manager of this place, Chief Inspector. You thought, female? black?'

'Young,' Brock replied. 'You seemed too young.'

She smiled very briefly. 'Is there any possibility that you've made a mistake about this, about the compactor?'

'I'd say we're eighty per cent certain at this stage,' Brock said. He handed her a list of identification marks from eighteen of the boxes found crushed in the same bale as the girl's body. 'So far only two of these have been definitely linked to Silvermeadow shops. We're working on the rest.'

She stared at the list, mouth puckered with concentration. She was elegantly dressed in a dark business suit and cream silk blouse, simple gold accessories, her hair pulled tight to the back of her head. After a moment she exchanged a look with Jackson and nodded. 'Yes, these could all have come from units in the middle section of the centre that would use the blue compactor. Purfleet Electrical backs right onto the blue compactor area.'

'We'll have to check all three compactors,' Brock told her.

'What, dismantle them?'

'Probably. I'll leave that to the experts.'

'This is Christmas, you know. The whole basement'll fill up with rubbish in no time.'

'I thought Christmas was a couple of weeks away,' Brock said mildly.

She looked at him incredulously. 'Your wife does the shopping, right?'

'I'm afraid not. But I do tend to avoid it whenever I can.'

She took a deep breath. 'Maybe I should say a little bit about this place. Just so you understand our *perspective*, Chief Inspector.'

'I wish you would, Ms Seager. Are those the plans of the centre?' He pointed to two large coloured diagrams mounted on one wall, between framed certificates awarded by the International Council of

Shopping Centres, the Havering Chamber of Commerce, the Ronald McDonald Charity Appeal, and many others.

'Yes. When was the last time you were in a modern shopping centre?'

'Ages ago. The one at Croydon, probably.'

'Right. Before it was upgraded, I guess. A windy, open pedestrian street below the tower blocks. We don't do it like that any more.' She spoke rapidly, as if time was very precious, her accent distinctly North American. 'You haven't been to Brent Cross? Thurrock?'

Brock shook his head.

'OK, well, Silvermeadow isn't just a couple of rows of shops strung between a few anchor stores. It's a whole leisure experience. It has everything in it you'd want to visit a town centre for and more, all climate-controlled, under one roof. It's what retailing is all about these days. We got the industry award for best new European centre last year. And it's big, over a million square feet of trading area, the third biggest retail mall in Europe, probably the best integrated retail and leisure facility this side of the Atlantic. There are two hundred and sixty-eight shops and food outlets, not to mention the cinemas, fitness centre, leisure pool . . .' She pointed to coloured rectangles on the plans of the two levels. 'At peak times, there are over a thousand employees and fifty thousand visitors under this one roof, and they've come from all over, not just this area of London and Essex, but the whole of the south-east and from the Continent too: France, Belgium, Holland, Scandinavia. We're more like a small city than a department store. So when you talk about closing down our compactors, or sealing off the service road, or whatever, just bear that in mind, OK? This is one big beast.'

Brock's frown had deepened as she had described the huge catchment area, and Kathy could imagine him thinking that North might have come here from almost anywhere. He sniffed and said, 'And a beast that has a particular attraction to school children?'

'Well sure, the kids like it here. It's warm, it's cheerful, and plenty of them get part-time work here. They love the shops on the main mall, of course, and then there's the food court and the Hawaii Experience, the leisure centre, the grunge stuff down in the Bazaar, the multiplex cinema. But more than that, it's where the people are. It's where the other kids come and hang out. You know what the most popular activity is in the mall? People-watching. Kids are like everybody else, they're attracted to buzz, to life.'

'In this case the opposite is what we fear.'

The centre manager pursed her mouth. 'Look, I'm not being insensitive or casual about this kid, Chief Inspector. I'm trying to explain. This place has a magic of its own. The kids flock here. And where the good people come, the bad people will surely follow, like sharks following the shoals. We do all we can to make this place the safest it can be – our reputation depends on that. But you can't keep out human nature. Every now and then some sick character will wander through our doors, and we can't stop him. All we can say is that we invest a lot of money and effort in security, and the chances of a child meeting trouble here are a lot lower than they would be in your average high street.'

The phone rang discreetly and she reached back over her desk to answer it. 'I'm busy right now . . . okay, two minutes only.'

She put down the phone and said, 'Harry, will you talk about the layout of the place for our visitors? I have to deal with something.' She shrugged apologetically at Brock. 'Sorry, but Christmas is only about five minutes away in our calendar.'

Jackson stepped forward as she left the room, and began to describe the features of the plans. They were shaped rather like a coat hanger, the long mall bent in its centre where the food court was located in the main square, with other attachments along the arms. Kathy was reminded of the diagrams of futuristic space stations, bits plugged in all over the place because there was no atmosphere or gravity to make them conform to some specific shape. The security chief explained, however, that the bent form came from the fact that the centre was wrapped round the north slope of a low hill, one of the few in this part of Essex. The hill had been remodelled with earth-moving equipment so that – and this was the cunning bit, he explained – the carparks on the flattened hilltop fed people directly into the upper mall level from the south, while the carparks on the lower, north side fed into the lower mall level. In this way, both shopping levels were equally accessible to shoppers, and the flow of people to both was maximised.

The south side of the lower level was buried against the hillside, and it was along there that the basement service road was run, providing secure, enclosed access to the loading docks and storage areas of the shops, as well as to the three compactor areas which they used to dispose of their dry waste.

Jackson yawned and scratched his bum. He wasn't a great public

41

speaker, Kathy thought, and his account was laboured and repetitive. He pointed out other features – his security centre located at the entry checkpoint to the service road, the leisure pool and fitness centre on the north side, the cinema complex – but then ran out of steam. Brock and Kathy got up to examine the plans more closely.

'There's a profile of your boss in here, Harry,' Lowry said. He waved a newspaper, *Silvermeadow News*, at them. 'Born in Trinidad, daughter of an English father and Trinidadian mother, thirty-six-year-old Deborah 'Bo' Seager is the high-flier who leads the Silvermeadow management team. Educated at schools in England and at university in the US, Bo honed her shopping-centre management skills with the big players in the US and Canada – Trizec, Cadillac Fairview and Olympia & York – before coming to the UK. Bo admits her private life—'

'Is shit!' Bo's voice preceded the door slamming behind her as she marched back into the room and threw some papers onto the desk. 'Sorry about that. Harry, your trooper asked me to let you know that Kerri Vlasich worked in Snow White's Pancake Parlour, usually two shifts a week. They haven't seen her the past week.'

'Right, boss. I'll take our visitors there when they're ready.'

'What bugs me,' Bo Seager said slowly, 'is how they could have got her to the compactor.'

'How's that?' Brock asked.

She seemed almost reluctant to explain, then came and stood between him and Kathy in front of the plans. She placed a carefully manicured nail over the blue compactor position. 'The general public aren't welcome in the service areas, Chief Inspector. There are service corridors connecting the rear of the shops to the delivery loading bays, and service lifts to take goods up to the upper-level shops, but all these corridors are out of bounds to the general public. True, there are passages that connect the rear areas to the main mall' – she pointed them out on the plans – 'and in the event of a fire the public could escape down these passages and out through the service road. But there are security doors blocking these corridors, controlled by locks which open automatically in the event of a fire alarm. These locks are also controlled by keypads, and traders and staff are allocated security numbers to open the doors in case they need to have access that way. What I'm saying is, the only ways into the compactor area are through the rear service door of a shop unit or down a common service corridor protected by a security code.'

'An inside job, you mean?' Brock said quietly. 'Someone on the staff?'

She frowned and bit her lip.

'That's not quite true, boss,' Jackson said. 'There's the people who come in through the vehicle entrance – the delivery drivers.'

'Oh yes, of course!' Bo's face brightened.

'She could have been picked up and murdered somewhere else entirely,' Jackson said to Brock. 'Then brought here in a delivery truck, and dumped in the compactor when the coast was clear. That would be my bet.'

'Yes, Harry!' She nodded vigorously. 'That *must* be it!'

'Interesting,' Brock said, 'but we're running ahead of ourselves. Ms Seager, unless something breaks quickly, it sounds as if we're going to be involved in a lot of checking and interviewing. It's possible that we'll have to bring a number of officers here for a while at least. We could bring our own mobile offices onto the site, but if you've got anywhere suitable it might be more discreet.'

'How about unit one-eight-four?' Jackson suggested.

'Yes,' Bo Seager agreed. 'It's on the next side mall, and vacant right now. The shopfitting for the next tenants doesn't start till after Christmas. There's a phone line and a staff toilet.'

'Sounds ideal. What time do you close tonight?'

'Ten o'clock. Another half an hour or so.'

'Then I think we'll have a quick look at the compactors now.'

Bo Seager held out her hand, and Kathy now noticed the lines of fatigue round her eyes. 'I've told Harry to help in any way he can, Chief Inspector. These things happen, I guess, even in the most carefully planned set-ups. It's an aberration, a glitch. Let's get it cleared up as painlessly as possible, huh?'

Brock smiled and took the offered hand. Kathy could guess what he was thinking. She hadn't seen the aberration herself, the smashed figure, so the sentiment was understandable, given her perspective.

Jackson led the way out of the management offices, on the way picking up a handful of glossy brochures with maps of the centre and dispensing them to the detectives like a tour guide. They followed him to the locked fire door at the end of the service corridor, where he demonstrated the security procedure, tapping his code into the keypad before opening the door and ushering them through to a bare concrete stair landing.

'Is that recorded at all, Harry?' Lowry asked. 'Your opening the door?'

'Oh dear me yes, Gavin. All the security doors are networked. The computer records the PIN of anyone opening a door, with time and location. We can provide a printout of all that.'

'Does every employee have a separate number?' Brock asked.

'Not everyone, no. Each tenant applies to us for numbers for their staff, usually senior staff only. They don't bother to get one for every salesgirl and cleaner.'

'So, if a manager was busy, say, and needed to send one of the lads down to the service bay to pick up a delivery, what would he do?'

Jackson was ahead of them on the stair, his voice echoing back up as he replied. 'Get someone with a code to go down.'

'Or give the lad someone else's number,' Brock suggested.

'Strictly forbidden!'

'Still,' Kathy heard Brock murmur. 'It is Christmas . . .'

They reached the bottom and pushed the bar on another fire door and found themselves on a loading platform on the edge of the service area, the air suddenly humid and sharp with the stench of diesel fumes. High overhead the underside of the concrete slab was strung with colour-coded pipes and ducts, and somewhere in the background, out of sight, they heard the growl and warning signal of a truck reversing. With an athletic hop Jackson jumped down to the roadway, keeping up his tour-guide commentary of Interesting Facts.

'Strong, eh?' he said, sniffing the air, keeping a watchful eye on their descent to the slab, wet with the trails of truck tyres coming in from the outside. 'We've had a lot of traffic down here today. Diesel fumes are heavier than air, right? So most of the big extract ducts are at low level.' He pointed to grilles in the face of the wall below the edge of the loading platform. 'Even so, it can get a bit thick on a busy day.'

'Where's the blue compactor from here, Harry?' Lowry said, turning the plan in his hand as though trying to orient himself.

'Round that corner. Not far.'

'Security cameras down here?'

'Only at the entrance to the service road. Not in this area, unfortunately. Not normally considered a hot spot, see? All the shop units backing onto the service road' – he waved a hand at the row of blank doors along the length of the loading platform – 'are alarmed, and we've never had a break-in attempt from down here.'

They marched briskly along the service road to the corner, where the space broadened out into a manoeuvring area. The reversing truck was ahead of them, along with several others backed against delivery bays on the far side. To their right, three figures in white overalls were stooped behind a crime scene tape examining the control panel on a large blue steel box.

They got to their feet as they saw the group approaching, one of them nodding at Gavin Lowry. 'Don't reckon much on trying to take this thing apart. It's got hydraulic lines, compression springs ... Reckon we could do it, or ourselves, a bit of damage if we tried. We need an experienced mechanic.'

'I can arrange that,' Jackson said. 'We have a maintenance contract with the suppliers. Don't know about tonight, though.'

They agreed to leave the compactors until the morning, the SOCOs moving off to search the surrounding roadways and access corridors.

Kathy stared at the mute blue box, trying to imagine how it would have been done. A loading platform ran down its far side and across the back end, providing the height from which waste could be hoisted into the feeder scoop on the top of the machine. The platform had a ramp connecting it to the roadway, so that laden trolleys could be rolled up. And the girl had been light, only eighty-eight pounds Brock had told her. One man could have managed it without difficulty, and probably quite openly, with her packed inside the plastic bag inside a cardboard box. The box itself would probably tell them nothing – next to the compactor was a big wire trailer full of loose boxes waiting to be loaded into the machine, any one of which would have done.

Brock walked up the ramp, pulled a large box out of the trailer and took it to the scoop on the machine. It fitted easily through the opening. 'Then what?' he called to Jackson, looking up at him from the roadway.

'Hit the green button.'

He did so. The machine gave a slight lurch and a snort, as if waking from a nap. An amber warning light on its top began flashing, a steel cover slid automatically across the feeder opening, and with a deep throbbing the motor cut in. After a moment's pause the compactor began vibrating with the passage of the hydraulic ram down its interior. There was a sound of crackling and crunching as the material inside was crushed harder and harder against the far end. Then a moment of heavy, throbbing consolidation followed by a long, deep sigh as the hydraulic pressure was released, the ram withdrawn slowly. When that was complete, the light and motor switched off and with a final shudder the machine went back to sleep.

They walked back with a cold breeze fanning their faces, refreshing in the humid, fumy fug of the service road, until they saw a striped barrier across the way ahead, controlling access at the foot of the entry ramp, a guard visible at a control window to one side.

Jackson led them into a large, brightly lit room glittering with VDUs, computer screens and zoned alarm panels alive with winking multi-coloured lights. As he described the functions of the pieces of equipment and introduced them to his operatives, Kathy noticed that Harry Jackson had relaxed.

'Nothing like a bit of technology to make everyone feel more secure, eh?' he said. 'That's what people want to keep the bogeyman at bay these days. In the States the latest thing is to have your security centre right up there, in the mall, where everyone can see you behind plate glass, with all your computers and communication equipment, and they can all feel safe in the knowledge that Speedy there is keeping his beady little eyes on everything on legs.' He nodded at one of the figures watching the VDUs, a pony-tailed man who raised a hand in acknowledgement without turning away from his flickering screens, his jaw muscles working on gum. 'Although it wouldn't be Speedy sitting there, nor me come to that, because we're not photogenic enough.'

He gave a laugh, and raised a smile from Lowry.

'Straight up, Gavin, it's true. You should see the girls they have on mall patrol in some of those places in Florida! They look like Hollywood film extras. Leads to a glamourisation of the industry, see?' He shot a quick glance at Kathy to see if he'd said something inappropriate. Or perhaps her silence was beginning to bother him. 'I suppose it'll come to us all, eventually.'

'You keep yourself in pretty good shape, Harry,' Lowry said. 'You've lost a bit of weight since I saw you last.'

'I do my best, Gavin. At my age you've got to take care of yourself. And we've got everything here at Silvermeadow, you know. I work out at the gym three times a week, and have a swim most days.'

'What sort of crime do you get here, Harry?' Brock asked.

'Shop theft's the main thing, as you'd expect. We work closely with the tenants' own staff on that. Mostly it's pathetic or perverse – old ladies or kids from well-to-do homes. Once in a while we get the professionals trying to hit the place, and that's when we particularly value help from the local CID, of course, like Gavin here. After shoplifting comes car theft from the carparks outside. Again, both amateurs and pros.

'We have, on occasions, had our more exciting moments.' He smiled grimly. 'An armed robbery at the bank, and two ram raids last year – stolen vehicles were driven through the glass mall doors and smashed into a shopfront inside. One, a jeweller's shop, was during shopping hours, and a shopper got run down as they drove back out again. We've put bollards at all the mall entrances now to combat that.'

'What about violence against individuals – robbery or assault?'

He shook his head. 'Very little. Too chancy, really, with having to make your escape out of the building on foot, and patrols in the mall. Occasionally we get complaints of handbag theft, or some kid comes out of bodybuilding all pumped up and knocks an old geezer in a walking frame. That's the main thing, really. There are so many different types come here, you're bound to get some accidental conflict. We're as much babysitters as watchdogs. We're all trained in CPR and first aid, and we're much more likely to be called out for a heart attack or a mislaid toddler than for a crime. Know what I mean?'

'I'd like a complete list of all reported security incidents since the centre opened, Harry,' Brock said. 'Can you manage that?'

'No problem.' He nodded. 'It's all on the computer.'

Lowry said, 'Sounds boring, Harry.'

'Depends what you're after, Gavin. Far as I'm concerned this is what policing should be like, how it used to be. We get to know our public. We open up early two mornings a week so the over-sixty power-walkers can do their six lengths of the mall before the rest of the customers arrive, and we make sure the kiddies and the pregnant mums get front-row seats when Mount Mauna Loa erupts for the Hawaii Experience.' Jackson beamed – the rosy-cheeked village constable, Kathy thought.

The closed-circuit television screens were of most immediate interest to Brock, two banks each of six screens, each screen split into four images that continuously flicked from scene to scene. Brock went over and stood between the two people monitoring the screens, seated in shirtsleeves, their leather jackets slung over the backs of their chairs, one Speedy and the other, introduced now as Sharon, the young woman who had been in the reception party at the mall entrance. Brock leant forward, asking questions, and they showed him how their control panels worked, selecting individual images, freezing, zooming, panning.

Harry Jackson turned to Kathy, trying to include her. 'Ever worked in this part of the country, Kathy?'

'A little. I was in traffic for a while before I joined CID.'

'But never in Two Area, eh? I think I'd have remembered if I'd come across you.'

She shook her head. 'I was in Eight Area before I went to SO1.'

'Ah.' Jackson seemed satisfied, the genealogy established.

'Gavin and I go way back. We were at West Ham together,' he said to her. 'When did you arrive, Gavin? Eighty, was it?'

'Eighty-one,' Lowry said.

'Then you moved on to Dagenham. And who's your chief now?'

'Forbes.'

'Old Mother Forbes? What's he now? Going for commander, last I heard.'

'No, no, no.' Lowry shook his head dismissively. 'No way. Chief super still. He should do what you did, Harry. Get out.'

Jackson chuckled at that one. 'Think anyone would have him, Gavin? Not out here. Not in the real world, mate.' He turned to Kathy, wondering if he'd been tactless. 'Met Mr Forbes, have you, Kathy?'

'No.'

'He's not exactly what you'd call a hands–on working copper. A committee man, not like Mr Brock there.'

'Not any more, Harry. Forbes is SIO on this one.'

'Senior investigating officer! Forbes?' Jackson exploded, then, seeing Brock turn sharply to see what was going on, lowered his voice and murmured, 'I'm sorry to hear that, Gavin. For all our sakes.'

'Harry,' Brock called. Jackson snapped to attention and hurried over. 'Would it be in order for me to brief your people here?'

'Course. Hush everyone! Listen up, please. Chief Inspector Brock from Scotland Yard wants to say a few words.'

Brock cleared his throat, the hum of the machines suddenly loud as the humans went quiet. 'We'd appreciate your help in tracing the movements of a fourteen-year-old girl by the name of Kerri Vlasich, from the Herbert Morrison estate, who was last seen at her school on

Monday, sixth of December. The body of a naked girl matching her description was found earlier today, and it seems probable that it was dumped in the blue compactor here at Silvermeadow.'

This sparked a murmur of interest. Speedy turned from his consoles, and Kathy caught a glimpse of a pale face, jaw working on chewing gum, the screens reflecting in his large eyes.

'We would be interested in any recent sightings of the girl. She had a casual job in the food court, at Snow White's Pancake Parlour, and we shall be distributing photographs and a description of her shortly. She had shoulder-length blonde hair, was slight of build, and when she left home was carrying a distinctive backpack in the form of a bright green frog. Does this ring a bell with anyone?'

People shook their heads. There were so many people going through the mall.

'Your video tapes should help us, Harry,' Brock went on. 'It may take a bit of a search . . .'

'Ah, that would be something. But I'm afraid not.' Jackson shook his head regretfully.

'How can you be sure?'

'Because the tapes are reused almost as soon as they're run through, Mr Brock. Right, Speedy?' Speedy nodded. 'Six-hour tapes, rotated in threes or fours. That's the way the system's designed, with a twenty-four-hour memory, long enough to identify and recover the sort of incidents we meet. *Archiving* just isn't part of our requirement. It's not set up for the kind of situation you're looking at.'

'Seems a bit limited, Harry,' Lowry said.

'No, no. Look' – the security chief spread his hands as if to grapple with this slur – 'the vital thing when you're designing one of these systems is to be as clear as possible about what your objectives really are. You've got to be ruthless about that, otherwise you just end up with tons of hardware, cameras all over the place, wide angle, infra-red, pan tilt and zoom, and nothing integrating with anything else.'

Jackson's voice had taken on the cajoling tone of a devotee, convinced, proselytising. Kathy watched Lowry, trying to figure him out as he listened impassively to the older man. There was something rather patronizing about the way he was handling Jackson, who, playing the old father-figure copper, was making more of their relationship than Lowry seemed willing to acknowledge.

'First you got to make your DIS analysis, right? That's deterrent, investigation and supervision, the three strengths of your CCTV system. How will you deploy them? You got to remember what security is all about, Gavin: establishing the normal, and managing the exception. So we generate the exception list, right? Things like vandalism, store pilferage, pickpockets, ram raids, break-ins, armed hold-ups – the potential list is a long one, right?'

Kathy stifled a yawn. She watched Speedy shove another stick of chewing gum in his mouth, and wondered what he'd done with the last lot. He turned away, ignoring the debate going on behind him, and stretched out his hands to work the buttons and joystick on the control panel on the table in front of him. Kathy watched the expert way he worked the panel without looking down, his eyes glued to the screens, like a kid absorbed in a video game. Perhaps it was this that had made her think him younger than he really was, for when he had turned towards them she had seen the creases of middle-aged skin, his cheek pitted with ancient acne scars.

'So now we link the exception events to hot spots,' Jackson was going on. 'Like, the hot spot for a hold-up will be the cash counter or the ATM, so that's where we need the camera. But now we discover that we've got far too many exception events and hot spots for our system to cover. The system has bottlenecks, see? Like one operator can only monitor six screens at max. And each screen can handle the output from sixteen cameras at max, so that's a total of ninety-six cameras for a single operator system. That sounds a lot, but this is a very big place! So now we have to prioritise our list, and maybe go upstream for some of the items. That means, Gavin, like putting in those bollards against the ram raiders, so as to channel the risk and reduce the hot spots. You follow?'

'I follow, Harry,' Lowry said, sounding unimpressed. 'And you're saying abductions of minors weren't on your exception list, is that it?'

'Too many hot spots, Gavin!' Jackson cried indignantly. 'It could happen anywhere, see? You'd need your ninety-six cameras just to cover that one exception, not to mention the archiving system you'd need to establish a seven-day memory, say, or longer, before you realised that an abduction had in fact taken place. Because one thing you can be sure of, Mr Brock, is that no little girl was dragged kicking and screaming from this place without us knowing about it. If she went, she went willingly, and you'd never even know you'd got an exception on your hands till long after the event. You got me there?'

'Yes, Harry, I understand,' Brock said, weariness creeping into his voice. 'What about your tenants? Banks, building societies, big stores

. . . there must be dozens of CCTV systems in this place apart from yours?'

'True, and all different. But I think you'd be lucky to find anyone now with a tape going back to Monday. But we will certainly help you find out. One thing you will discover, I can assure you, is that my team will be behind you all the way.'

'Many thanks, Harry. As a first step, we'd like to take all your surveillance tapes away for analysis.'

'But Mr Brock, I just explained. They'll only go back to first thing this morning, last night at most. I thought—'

'All the same, Harry, we'd better check them all, just to be on the safe side. Is that a problem?'

Jackson shrugged. 'No, no problem. We've got plenty of new tapes we can use. That right, Speedy?'

Speedy gave a brief nod, and Jackson gave instructions to a couple of his staff to gather up the tapes in boxes.

It was only as they were leaving that Kathy noticed that Speedy's chair had wheels. She said nothing until they were outside in the underground service road, then she asked Jackson, 'Speedy's handicapped, is he?'

'Paralysed from the waist down, Kathy. Motorbike accident, about five years ago. Hence his name. I'd known him long before then. He'd been a bit of a tearaway in the old days, and when I was at West Ham he was a snout of mine for a while. I fixed him up with this job. Speedy Reynolds is living proof that our company's disability action plan is more than just pious words.'

Kathy wondered if he was being sarcastic, but the expression on his face was all sincerity. Harry Jackson was that sort of a bloke, it seemed.

'Hell of a job he's got,' Lowry murmured.

'But it's as if he was born to it, Gavin,' Jackson replied. 'They all take turns at the consoles but he's the best camera control operator I've ever come across. He never loses interest or concentration. I don't know how he does it, frankly. It would drive me barmy.'

As he took them back along the service road, Brock striding ahead, Kathy heard him say quietly to Lowry, 'Here's the number of my mobile, Gavin. Give me a ring direct anytime you think I might be able to help. You don't need to go through the boss upstairs. Especially if you think you've spotted any little problems with the security here, know what I mean?'

Lowry nodded. 'Rough with you, is she, Harry?'

'She's tougher than she looks. Often the way with the ladies these days, eh?' Harry said, and seeing that Kathy was listening to their conversation, he chanced a wink in her direction. 'This way, Mr Brock,' he called out, and led them into a side service corridor, staying this time at the lower level, so that when they finally emerged through a security door into the sudden noise and bustle of the mall they found that they were close to the food court surrounding the tropical forest grove. The thinness of the barrier between the bare concrete and block service areas and the exotic glitter of the public areas was disconcerting, as if to confirm that what passed for reality here was no thicker than a skin of chrome or paint.

It was just after ten and the crowds were now thin, dispersing towards the exits and the wet night beyond. The waitresses at Snow White's Pancake Parlour, identically dressed in laced-front Snow White costumes and incongruously perched on roller skates, were drooping with fatigue beneath their rosy-cheeked, scarlet-lipped make-up as they cleared and wiped down the tables. The manageress confirmed that Kerri Vlasich had a regular shift on Saturday and Sunday afternoons, and had worked both the previous weekend, but, like the girls, could add little more.

While Brock and Lowry spoke to them, Kathy noticed Harry Jackson amble over to two men standing in front of the next unit, a Chinese fast-food counter called the Peking Duck. One of the men was Chinese while the other looked like a caricature of an Italian in a gondolier's striped jersey and red scarf, presumably from Bruno's Gelati next door. She followed, picking up their conversation.

'Two weeks to Christmas, and everybody's going crazy,' the gondolier was saying, with an expansive Latin sweep of his arms. 'It's all very well for Mr Chang here. He can call in half the Chinese population of east London if he needs help, but I have to make do.' He gestured at a second gondolier, a weary man who looked too old for the part, wiping down the tables outside Bruno's Gelati. At closer range the Italian seemed even more theatrical, with a florid complexion, his thick black hair, eyebrows and moustache looking fresh from the bottle.

He caught sight of Kathy moving to Jackson's side. 'Who's your new friend then, Harry?' he asked mischievously. 'New security officer? Bit of an improvement on your usual crew.'

'Not quite, Bruno.' Jackson introduced Kathy to Bruno Verdi and Mr Chang. 'There's a bit of a fuss about a missing girl, worked at

Snow White's. They've brought in the heavy mob. Sergeant Kolla here is from Serious Crime Branch, Scotland Yard.'

The gondolier appeared surprised, his bushy eyebrows rising.

Mr Chang said anxiously, 'They must be real worried. I heard the girls mention that someone had been missing from work today.'

'Worse than that. They found her this morning, murdered.'

Now both men looked shocked.

'Murdered!' Chang shook his head in horror. 'That's terrible.'

'There's been no positive ID on the body yet, Mr Jackson,' Kathy warned.

'Worse still,' Jackson charged on. 'They reckon she may have been killed here.'

Verdi seemed suddenly immobilised, the colour fading from his face. He swallowed before finding his voice. 'What was her name?' he asked hoarsely.

'Vlasich, Kerri Vlasich,' Kathy said, 'and she's still officially only a missing person. I've got a photograph . . .' She went to open her shoulder bag, but stopped at a sudden movement in front of her. Bruno Verdi had slumped back onto a chair, so abruptly that at first she thought he had fallen. He sat rigid, eyes wide but unseeing, his face startlingly white now against the artificial jet black of his hair.

'All right, Bruno?' Harry Jackson looked at him curiously.

Verdi suddenly blinked and shook his head, inhaling deeply. 'Sure . . . sure . . .' he mumbled, shaking his head. 'It's okay . . . it's nothing. I been on my feet all day, that's all. I'm okay.'

Mr Chang looked concerned. 'He has blood pressure. I'll get you a drink of water, Bruno.'

'Did you know this girl, Mr Verdi?' Kathy asked.

'Girl?' He blinked at her, looking puzzled, as if he'd forgotten who Kathy was.

'Kerri Vlasich.' She showed him the photograph.

He stared at the picture for some time, then said simply, 'I recognise her, yes.'

'When was the last time you saw her?'

Mr Chang hurried back with a plastic cup, which Verdi took and put to his mouth.

'I couldn't say,' he said at last. 'They come and go, these girls. Come and go.'

Later, as they left the food court, Jackson filled them in on some of the characters.

'Bruno Verdi is one of our more colourful tenants, and he has a bit of clout, too. He's the chairman of the Silvermeadow Small Traders' Association. Very vocal on security and the like. He'll be useful in helping us organise things, if it comes to large-scale interviews, talking to staff and so on.'

'I've no doubt it'll come to that, Harry,' said Brock.

They were walking around the coral shores of the lagoon that surrounded the volcano.

'What are the centre's opening hours?'

'Normally ten till ten for the general public. Management office nine till five, six days, but Ms Seager's there longer than that. The building shuts down during the night from eleven till six. During those hours the perimeter's secured and an outside contractor comes on call with dog patrols of the outdoor site. Otherwise our security centre is manned all the time.'

'Okay, well I don't think we can do much more tonight. We'll be back tomorrow morning at nine. Maybe you could arrange access for us to unit one-eight-four, so we can start to get things organised. We shall certainly be wanting to go round the shops interviewing staff, and we'll need to organise a search of the centre too.'

'A search, chief?'

He looked worried. Kathy noticed that he had lapsed into the slang of the force, addressing Brock as if he were his senior officer.

'Is that a problem?' Brock asked.

'Not for me, chief, but it's a big job. This is a huge place. How close do you want to look?'

'We need to find where the girl was assaulted and undressed, and we need to find her belongings, her clothes and the frog bag.'

'If—' Jackson began to object, but Brock lifted a hand to interrupt.

'Okay, I take your point about her possibly being assaulted somewhere else and brought in here only for disposal, but we need to check anyway.'

'Sure. Well, you'll need plans of this place for a start. I'll get them organised, shall I?'

'That would be very helpful.'

As she watched them shake hands, Kathy thought that Harry Jackson seemed on a bit of a high. Maybe, she thought, he misses the grubby world outside after all.

★

Towards midnight, Kathy drove home the long way, orbiting London on the M25 round to Junction 25, a Diana King tape playing softly. Too late now to meet up with her airline pilot, who was probably packing his boxer shorts for another trip to LA or KL in the morning. Nicole had thought they might have had a perfect relationship, since he would be away most of the time circling the globe, while she would be equally absent poking about in London's garbage. Ah, Kathy thought, but what about the one weekend in six when they did manage to touch base together? Might they be like the gelati man, unable to handle the shock of reality, discovering that the gloss is only microns thick?

4

Kathy returned to the Hornchurch Street station first thing the following morning, and found PC Miriam Sangster in the canteen, eating a meal after coming off night shift. The building seemed less bleak in the wan morning sunlight, and the emergency seemed to be over, gas supplies resumed to the kitchens and the reassuring smell of deep-fat frying heavy in the air.

Sangster struck Kathy as a brisk, intelligent woman, a wary, sceptical set to her eyes.

'They switched me to nights,' she said, wiping her mouth with a paper napkin. 'Still getting used to it.'

'I hate that shift,' Kathy said, spreading butter on toast. 'Did you hear about the Vlasich girl?'

'Yes, people were talking about it. Gavin . . . DS Lowry's working with you, isn't he?'

'Mm. But you were on your own for some of the time when you saw Mrs Vlasich, weren't you? I thought I'd better go over it with you.'

'Is there a problem?' Sangster asked carefully. 'About what I did? I wrote a fairly full report.'

Kathy sensed the other woman's caution, just as she had with Lowry, in talking to an outsider. 'No, no. No problem,' she reassured her. 'I've seen the report. I just wondered how you felt yourself about the business with the father.'

Sangster shook her head. 'It was hard to tell without seeing him or the girl. There was a lot of fear on the mother's side, as if she'd played it out so many times in her imagination, losing Kerri to the father, that when it actually happened she kept swinging from disbelief to absolute certainty. But the company he works for in Hamburg did

56

confirm that he was abroad in Poland, not the UK, working for them on some pipeline project.'

'Yes, I saw that in your report. But he had other relatives in Hamburg, didn't he? They could have come over for her, I suppose?'

'Yes. And there was a Vlasich in the computer, too, with a sex offence on his record, but that turned out to be a dead end. So without any other evidence it seemed simpler to assume she'd gone on her own, probably hitching, and probably to see her dad – she'd threatened to do it. Course, it's easy to say now . . .' she concluded defensively.

'No, no one's suggesting you should have done anything differently, Miriam. You spoke to her friends, didn't you?'

'I saw two of them at the school, Naomi and Lisa. Mrs Vlasich said they were Kerri's closest friends, but they knew nothing. They said they had no idea she was planning to run away, and they seemed credible to me. Naomi is the brighter of the two, Naomi Parr – I'd start with her if you want to talk to them. They both have jobs at Silvermeadow, too.'

'How do they get over there? It's quite a way.'

'The centre runs special bus services to bring people in from surrounding towns. One runs right past their school and the estate.'

'Convenient.'

'Yes. You've seen Mrs Vlasich, have you?'

'Yes. When we told her the news. She was very shaken up, of course, didn't say a lot.'

'You mentioned Silvermeadow, did you? Did she say anything about that?'

Kathy noticed a certain hesitancy in the way Sangster said this. 'That did seem to shake her, when we mentioned that. It seemed to hit her then. She went to pieces after that. Why?'

Sangster hesitated, then leant forward. 'Did she mention the others?'

'Others?'

The constable frowned and lowered her voice. 'Gavin will say this is rubbish, but there've been stories going round about Silvermeadow: young girls going missing, a monster in the mall, stuff like that. Mrs Vlasich had obviously heard them, and she confided in me, after Gavin had left. The idea really terrified her.'

'Nobody's mentioned this. It's not in your report.'

'No, of course not. It's just another one of those urban myths. You know, like that tattooed man with the hangman's noose who's supposedly been spotted in every other multi-storey carpark between Glasgow and Exeter, or the West African cannibal prince who lives on baby stew and has been seen – really, actually *seen* – with a baby's tibia through his nose, by a friend of a friend of half the population of Leicester.'

Kathy smiled. 'Yes, I know. And you'd heard the Silvermeadow stories yourself, had you? Before Alison Vlasich brought them up?'

'Yes, I'd heard them, not through my job but from my partner. He's a schoolteacher, and he was told about them by the kids in his class. He told them that they were just fairy-tales reinventing themselves, like Babes in the Woods, Little Red Riding Hood. But the kids wouldn't have it. They *knew* the stories were true. They'd heard them from someone who had actually spoken to someone else who was a close relative of someone who had been there at the time. They were so convinced that he told me about it, and I agreed to check the computer. And of course there was absolutely nothing to it. I couldn't find a single missing person report that made any mention of Silvermeadow. I told Gavin about it afterwards, and he advised me to forget it.'

'Had he heard the stories before?'

PC Sangster lit a cigarette, thinking. 'I don't think so, not when I first mentioned it. But he spoke to me again a day or two later. He'd talked to someone he knows at Silvermeadow, one of the security people there, and they'd told him it was nonsense.'

'So they'd heard of it?'

'Oh yes. Gavin said they were really pissed off about it. They even thought one of their competitors might have deliberately started the rumours. That's why he said to forget it. Only' – she exhaled a column of pale smoke from the side of her mouth up at the ceiling extract grille – 'when they told me she'd been traced to Silvermeadow, my blood went cold. Really, it did. I wondered what Mrs Vlasich must be thinking.'

'Yes, I see.'

'Tell me, when did she die? Do they know?'

'We don't know for certain it's Kerri's body yet, Miriam.'

'Oh come off it, Kathy. When did she die?'

Kathy could follow the train of thought, and she looked down to sip from her tea. 'Some time this week. They're not certain.'

'So it could have been Thursday, say,' the constable added softly.

'She might still have been alive when I told her mother that it had nothing to do with Silvermeadow . . .'

'Miriam, you couldn't—'

'And I didn't do a bloody thing to check.'

'You phoned the people where she worked, didn't you? No one had seen her.'

'Yes.' Miriam Sangster crushed out her cigarette with a bitter little flourish and got to her feet. 'Really thorough that was, wasn't it?' She swung away, then stopped and turned back. 'If you can avoid telling Gavin that I told you this, I'd be grateful. We do have to go on working together when this is over.'

'Sure.' Kathy smiled reassuringly. There was something ever so slightly self-consciously casual about Miriam's use of his first name that made Kathy wonder if she and Gavin had ever done more than work together.

At this hour on a Sunday morning the carpark was bare, the building as forlorn as a vast abandoned circus tent in a macadam desert. Kathy parked next to the head of the service road ramp and descended to the striped barrier, where the man at the control window looked up briefly from his Sunday paper, glanced at her ID and nodded her in. She walked along the service road past the first compactor area, its tape untouched from the previous night, and on towards the sound of metallic clanging, men's voices, a dog's sudden bark. Turning the corner she saw the blue compactor taken half apart, white overalls crawling over its loosened panels on the ground, a dog and its handler working further along the service road. The man in blue denim overalls wielding the large spanner was presumably the mechanic, talking to a SOCO with hands on hips, whose face Kathy couldn't see. She was aware of the mechanic registering her, his eyes flicking over to give her a quick appraisal. The SOCO turned to see what he was looking at, and Kathy saw the Indian features and recognised Leon Desai.

There was no reason at all why the laboratory liaison sergeant shouldn't be there. Brock had undoubtedly insisted on it, and Kathy should have anticipated it. But she hadn't, and the sudden sight of him there brought the colour up on her cheeks. The last time she had seen him he'd been in a hospital bed, crippled in the line of duty, and they had parted on bad terms. He had lain there in all his martyred dignity and accused her, quite rightly, of not having trusted him. She could remember his words precisely – *you're so bloody determined to trust nobody* – as if it had been a deliberate policy on her part, a character flaw, rather than a mistake. She had left under a private cloud from beneath which it had taken her some time to crawl.

So by rights he should now have turned away and ignored her, but instead he was walking towards her. He stopped a yard away and looked at her with his steady dark eyes, unsmiling, and said, 'Hello, Kathy. It's good to see you again.'

Was it? Had she gone through all that soul-searching for no reason? He seemed perfectly sincere, genuinely glad to see her. She noticed the small pale scar across his left eyebrow and remembered herself telling him, not entirely unmaliciously, that he would no longer be perfect.

'And you, Leon. Great.'

A smile slowly formed on his face, and she hurriedly said, 'How are things going?' meaning his broken jaw and leg, but he replied, 'Nothing yet. It'll take another hour or more to get this thing apart.'

'Ah.'

'You've come for Brock's briefing? You'll need a security code to get into the centre from here. Do you have one?'

She shook her head.

'Use the one they've given me. Two-one-eight-nine. Want to write it down?'

'No need. That's the last four digits of your phone number.'

'You're right. Amazing memory.' He smiled and turned back to his work.

She went down the service passage they had used the previous evening, using the security code to emerge into the lower mall as before. The emptiness and silence were uncanny, no background music or birdsong, no movement on the escalators, no people on the gleaming terrazzo, but still something, the building's own presence, saying yes, I'm still here even when you're not, I still exist and maybe have secrets.

Then a cleaner came buzzing round the corner on a ride-on floor polisher. The building reverted to background and the illusion evaporated.

Kathy walked up the dormant escalator to the upper mall, past the deserted Christmas tree, and looked for unit 184 in the side mall beyond. She spotted Gavin Lowry outside a shopfront filled with promotional posters for Christmas in the mall, hiding the unit's interior, and assumed this must be the place. He was tugging a cigarette out of a packet, and when he saw her he said, 'It's chaos in there – electricians causing havoc.'

'How long have you been here?'

'Couple of hours. Come on, I need a coffee.'

They found a café nearby, just opening, and sat outside in an area of the mall defined by low clipped hedges in tubs. The café itself was tiled to resemble a Turkish bath house and the waitress who came to their table had her thick black hair tied up in a bandanna, and wore a scarlet blouse that might have suggested something oriental.

'You Sonia?' Lowry said.

'That's right,' she said, suppressing a yawn.

'Harry Jackson told us you'd look after us, Sonia. He said your coffee's the best in the mall.'

'Oh yes. I know Harry all right. Are you in his line of business, then?'

Lowry nodded and showed her his warrant card. 'You'll be seeing quite a bit of us. We're taking over that unit down there for a while. Should be good for business. Our boss is a coffee connoisseur, isn't that right, Kathy?'

'That's nice,' Sonia said warily. 'What you here for anyway? Is it public relations?'

Kathy watched Lowry tell her, show her Kerri's picture, Sonia's look of disgust, thinking how many times they would have to go through this, with hundreds of shopkeepers, thousands of customers. It made her feel depressed, but Lowry seemed to be enjoying it. He ended with something that sounded like a chat-up line.

'You from the exotic east yourself then, Sonia?'

'Yeah, Bermondsey. What's your fancy then?'

Looking up through the tinted acrylic vault high above their heads, Kathy caught the glimmer of sunlight on cloud, too weak to compete with the warm intensity of artificial sunlight in the mall. A group of elderly people bustled past, kitted out in tracksuits, sweatbands and dazzling white shoes as if they really meant business. The pace was set by the joggers, moving marginally more slowly than the walkers, though with greater show. On their backs they bore the motto SILVER MEADOWLISTS.

'Weird sort of place, isn't it?' Lowry said, blowing smoke after them. 'Connie raves about it.'

'Your wife?'

He nodded.

'You have kids?' Kathy asked.

'Last time I looked,' he said, off-hand. 'They hated it here, for some reason. Now Connie comes on her own, when they're at school.'

'And you know Bren Gurney.'

Lowry turned back from watching Sonia making their coffees behind the counter. 'Yeah. Used to play rugger with him. And we went on the inspector's course together. He came out top, and I was second. We've got a lot in common, I reckon.'

Kathy doubted that, but said nothing.

'How do you work with him, the old man?' Lowry continued, voice becoming more intimate. 'Your boss. Keeps a close eye on you, does he?'

'Not really.'

'Cunning old bugger, Bren said. Close.'

'Did Bren say that?'

'Something like that.'

With a soft clash of seraglio bangles Sonia appeared with their coffees, a thimbleful of espresso for Kathy, caffè latte for Lowry.

'Thanks darling,' Lowry said, then to Kathy, 'You haven't met our SIO, have you?'

'Forbes? No, never heard of him before. Harry Jackson didn't seem impressed. You don't like him?'

Lowry smiled grimly. 'Orville M. Forbes. Old Mother Forbes. Doesn't matter whether I *like* him, Kathy. The problem is, as everybody's so well aware these days, there are just too many chiefs in this force and not enough fucking Indians. So the people who are paid to think about these things imagine they can recycle old paper-shufflers like Forbes into born-again coal-face detectives and leaders of major investigations.' He shook his head grimly. 'Snowball's chance. He wouldn't have the faintest idea where to begin. And he knows it. That's why he's persuaded them to bring in your guv'nor, to save his skin.'

'Do you think so?'

'I'm certain of it. He's scared shitless that he'll screw up his first major crime investigation with the eyes of the world focused on him. He told me once he has a recurring nightmare. He's a schoolboy again, playing cricket, standing in the outfield with a long easy catch coming straight at him, and he drops it and loses the match, and all his friends and teachers and family are there to see it.'

They watched a tall elderly man, bewhiskered, stiff-backed, marching by. He was wearing a heather-green Harris tweed jacket and matching cap, and swinging a gnarled walking stick, a laird taking a brisk constitutional through his glen. As he passed he doffed his hat to them.

'Jesus . . .' Lowry muttered. 'This place is full of weirdos.'

'Does it matter, about Forbes? As long as he keeps out of our way.'

'But he won't, he can't. He's petrified by failure and greedy for success. He'll worry, and dabble, and interfere, and stuff us up. People like us have got to persuade people like Forbes, the grey crust through which we must eventually rise if we are ever to achieve seniority in this lifetime, that they should pack it in and bugger off to Bognor.'

'How do we do that?'

'By subjecting them to stress. They don't like stress. Can't take it any more. If you load them up with stress, they soon begin to dream of early retirement . . . or something else.'

'Something else?'

Lowry stretched his arms out and ran the flat of his palm down the short hair of his nape. 'My last boss passed away on the job, Kathy. His secretary came in with his coffee one morning, and there he was, stretched out across his desk, cold as yesterday's toast. Stroke, probably down to stress, the doctor said.' He paused, glanced at Kathy, then picked up the glass of creamy liquid that Sonia had placed in front of him. 'I like to think that was my personal contribution to resolving the unbalanced staff profile of the Metropolitan Police.'

'You killed him with stress?' She stared at him, trying to decipher his expression.

Lowry licked his lips, then allowed them to form a little smile. 'He didn't realise it, of course. He thought I was trying to help.'

Kathy decided this was some kind of test of her sense of humour. 'Well, well. So now you want to kill Forbes the same way?'

He nodded thoughtfully.

'Brock knows, you know,' Kathy said.

That made him sit up. 'What?'

'That you've been told to report directly to Forbes. Without telling Brock. Forbes did tell you to do that, didn't he?'

Lowry stared at her for a long moment before the little smile reappeared. 'What made you think of that?'

'It occurred to me down below last night, when Jolly Harry asked you to bypass his boss in the same way.'

Lowry's grin broadened. 'You've got the advantage of being a woman, Kathy. You'll have your own way to get through the grey crust. They'll pull you up in the name of gender balance. But that doesn't mean we can't give each other a helping hand, does it?'

Kathy sipped at her coffee, watching the early shoppers now drifting along the mall. Across the way was a bookshop, and outside it a small boy studying a pyramid of books about Manchester United. He didn't look like the type you'd usually find near a bookshop: baseball cap reversed over longish black locks, baggy jacket and pants, dark eyes watchful in a thin pale face. And a mobile phone clipped to his belt, of course. The essential teenage fashion accessory. She wondered if she might be witnessing one of Harry Jackson's 'exception events' in progress, and she looked around for a 'hot spot' camera, imagining Speedy in the basement silently panning in on the boy. Maybe all this time he'd been watching Lowry and herself, reading their lips.

'What about Brock, then?' Lowry said.

'You want to kill him too? I don't think he'd fold so easily, Gavin.'

'Getting a bit old for this lark though, isn't he? Why isn't he higher than DCI?'

'He's what he wants to be. He doesn't want to spend his life chairing meetings.'

'Bollocks. People only say that sort of thing when they haven't been given the option. Maybe he did something naughty once . . .' He sat back, musing, stroking the back of his head. 'Something they buried. Something that might come to light again if he tried to go higher . . . Maybe we should look.'

Kathy shook her head, suddenly tiring of this. She had thought of asking him what he thought of the possibility that Kerri Vlasich might not be the only one to have disappeared through the blue compactor, but now she decided to say nothing. 'Forget it, Gavin. Come on, we'd better see how things are going.' She got up and went to the counter to pay Sonia.

They found Brock seated at a desk at the back of the unit, his jacket off, sleeves rolled up, talking into a mobile phone while he signed a requisition form on a clipboard that a clerk held out for him. All around him unit 184 was being rapidly transformed, and Kathy had to step back to allow furniture removers to pass by with desks and chairs. The patterns left by shelving and display racks stripped from the pinboard walls were being obscured by enlarged plans of the centre and of the surrounding area, schedules and gridded roster sheets. A couple of electricians were working on ladders up in the suspended ceiling void, other technicians were setting up computer workstations. A dozen uniformed men and women were already there, standing chatting together, and a second group had followed Kathy and Gavin Lowry inside.

Brock nodded as he saw them approach, finished his call and said, 'Gavin, help our action manager organise the search teams over there, will you? We need to get these characters moving. Kathy, you haven't seen Leon Desai by any chance?'

'Yes, ten minutes ago.'

'How's he doing? I can't raise him on his mobile – there seems to be a dead spot down there.'

'He thinks another hour before they've finished dismantling the machine. I don't think they've got anything yet.'

'Hmm. OK, well, we can't wait. Let's get this thing moving.' His brow furrowed, a last moment of uncertainty. Kathy had seen that look before. 'Always difficult to be sure,' he said. 'Go in too early and you don't know what questions to ask, too late and the trail may be cold, the answers faded away. I'd like to have given them pictures of the girl's father to take round with them, but I don't think we can wait.' He grunted and shook his head, as if to shake the doubts away, then got to his feet and called for their attention.

He was good at this, Kathy thought, striking the right balance between recognising the sombre mood of a murder inquiry and giving them the taste for a hunt that might last a long time. He announced that the pathologist had now confirmed the identity of the body as Kerri Vlasich, through her dental records. He then gave a very brief account of the background, with the calm of someone who had been down such tracks many times before, and spoke of the incinerator and compactor with just an edge of outrage in his voice, so that the frisson would be implanted and maintained, even though they were forbidden from mentioning these details to the public, and above all to the press.

They would begin by dividing their forces, Gavin Lowry taking some to continue the search begun by the SOCO team, spreading out through the huge centre and beyond into the surrounding carparks and service areas, the remainder interviewing the staff in the shops. The questions: names, addresses and phone numbers of all employees; names, addresses and phone numbers of all suppliers who made deliveries between the nominated dates; possible sightings of the girl in the photograph during this period or before; accounts of any unusual incidents in or around the shop during the period; accounts of any unusual incidents in the service road areas and service corridors during the period. Questions with both open and hidden intent, hoping to draw out witnesses, observations, insights, but also designed to sniff out discrepancies, and to harvest names to match against the roll-call of known offenders.

Then Brock asked Phil, their action manager, to distribute the plans provided by Harry Jackson, and to read out the lists of officers' names and the sections of the centre each would cover. Later there would be an exhibits officer and a statement reader and all the other stock characters from the cast of a major investigation, if indeed that was what this was to be. Because of course it could still turn out to be something altogether simpler and cruder than they were assuming. A tiff, a rape, even a mugging, done on impulse and readily uncovered, the compactor a panicked improvisation.

As the briefing broke up, Lowry said to Brock, 'Could I have a quick word, chief, off the record?' He sounded uncharacteristically tentative.

Brock looked up. 'Certainly.' He raised his eyebrows at Kathy beside him, who began to move away.

'No, I don't mind Kathy hearing it. In fact I'd prefer if she did.'

'All right. I know the problem. You haven't got enough men to do a thorough search.'

Lowry shrugged. 'That's true.'

'Do what you can, Gavin, and as quickly as you can. If the killer took that much trouble to dispose of the body, the chances of him leaving her clothing behind are slim. It also seems unlikely that there would have been blood stains. Our best chance is that someone noticed something unusual, so I want your team to do a reasonable search as fast as possible, then join the others interviewing staff.'

'Sure, I understand. That wasn't what I wanted to ask you. It's awkward really. I'm in a slightly difficult spot.'

Lowry stared at his shoes. Brock said nothing.

'Mr Forbes has asked me to report to him, on a daily basis, chief. On the progress of the investigation. Without reference to you. I don't feel comfortable about it.'

'I see.' Brock looked annoyed. 'Did you tell him that?'

'No, sir. At the time I didn't think too much about it. We've known each other a few years, him and me. But I can see now that I'd be putting myself in a false position. Like a spy.'

'Yes . . . well, I'll speak to him. All right?'

Lowry hung his head. 'Thing is, he'll be annoyed I mentioned it to you. I wondered if you might put it to him that you brought the subject up first – asked me straight out if I'd been asked to report independently, and I had to admit that I had.'

Brock gave a little snort. 'All right,' he said. 'I'll do it tactfully.'

'Thanks, chief. Thanks a lot.'

Lowry nodded and left. When he was behind Brock he glanced back and gave Kathy another of his guarded little smiles.

'Well,' Brock grunted at Kathy. 'What do you make of him?'

'I think we're making him nervous. Bren knows him, apparently. Maybe you should ask him. Lowry thinks they're very alike.'

Brock caught the intonation, raised his eyebrows and turned back to his paperwork.

Behind him the room was emptying, men and women, both uniformed and plainclothes, collecting clipboards and interview kits as they went out to find their designated areas.

Kathy returned to the Herbert Morrison estate after the briefing, her task to find out more about Kerri Vlasich. She parked in one of the visitor parking spaces inside Primrose Court, skirted the exploded TV set on the ground and walked up to the first deck level. A woman she didn't recognise answered the door, a neighbour, and led her inside.

Alison Vlasich was seated in an armchair, motionless and very pale. When she lifted her face to Kathy her expression was blank, the empty stare signifying that nothing mattered any more. She didn't even recognise Kathy, who had to explain they had met the previous day. After ten fruitless minutes Kathy got to her feet. The neighbour could tell her nothing useful, and she left.

She made her way along the access deck to the next court, Crocus. Naomi's front door was decorated with a Christmas holly wreath, the effect of its bright red plastic berries and sparkly message, YULETIDE GREETINGS, marred somewhat by the signature of the YOBS graffiti gang sprayed in black aerosol across it.

The woman who answered the door responded immediately to Kathy's ID, as if she'd been expecting her. She was in her sixties,

Kathy judged, hair pulled hard back from her face and thin framed glasses giving her a serious, slightly strained appearance.

'Do come in,' she said, speaking softly. 'We wondered if you'd come again, after we heard.'

'You know about Kerri, then? Mrs Parr, is it?'

'No, Tait's my name. I'm Naomi's grandmother.' They shook hands. 'Yes, we heard about Kerri's ring last night. News like that travels fast round here. Lisa's mother knows the Vlasich's neighbours. Lisa came straight round here, and she and Naomi were comforting each other till late. In fact Lisa stayed the night, and she's only just gone home. So upset they are. It's just so hard to believe. Kerri was such a lively girl, so full of life.'

She showed Kathy into a living room, full of old but comfortable furniture, and introduced her to her husband, who struggled to his feet as they came in. His right arm was stiff and held to his side, his right eye watery.

'It's the police, Jack, just as we thought,' Mrs Tait said, and he grunted and gestured at a chair for Kathy. 'If you're wanting to know,' she went on, patient and well-practised in her explanation, 'Naomi's mother, our daughter, passed away a couple of years ago—'

'Two years ago this Christmas,' her husband interrupted, scowling at his frozen hand.

'And we took responsibility for the three girls. Naomi and her small sister live here with us. Her older sister, Kimberley, is away at present. So that's why you find us here with Naomi.'

Kathy nodded with a sympathetic smile. She could imagine how many times this explanation had been necessary – to social security, the doctor, schools, inquisitive neighbours, parents of friends of the girls. 'I'm sorry to bother you, Mrs Tait. I would like to have a chat to Naomi if it wouldn't be too upsetting for her. You knew Kerri yourself then?'

'Oh yes. Kerri was round here often.'

'The three mouseketeers,' Jack offered. He had a newspaper beneath his good hand on the arm of the chair, folded to the racing section.

His wife smiled weakly at him. 'They did a fancy dress once, the three of them, Kerri, Lisa and Naomi. They were close. And how is poor Alison Vlasich coping?'

'Not too well at present.'

'I must go over and see her. We know what it's like, to lose a child.'

'Give her a bell. Ask her to come here,' Jack said. 'You know I don't like you going over Primrose. Rough buggers in that court. It's not safe.' He glared at Kathy, ready to argue the point if she cared to deny it.

'Kerri was a lively girl, you say?'

'Oh yes, very lively, full of beans.'

'A handful,' Jack offered.   :

'Yes,' Kathy agreed. 'Mrs Vlasich gave me the impression that Kerri was being a bit rebellious lately, not telling her where she went and so on.'

'I wouldn't be surprised. It's not easy for a woman on her own to cope with a lively teenager.' Mrs Tait looked sadly at a group of four framed portrait photographs mounted on the wall. 'Our daughter had three girls to bring up on her own.'

'Would you say she was adventurous enough to take off by herself to see her father in Germany?'

Mrs Tait gave it a little thought. 'I wouldn't be surprised. It's the sort of thing she would do.'

'Pain in the neck,' Jack Tait said grumpily.

'Don't say that, Jack. Not now.'

He looked sheepish and cocked his head to one side to acknowledge the scolding.

'She liked to tease Jack sometimes,' Mrs Tait explained. 'It wasn't cheek, really. More high spirits. Is that what happened, then? She ran away to find her dad?'

'We're not sure yet. Had she mentioned him to you recently? Maybe plans to see him for Christmas?'

'No, not to us. But Naomi would be the one to ask. She would know. Shall I get her for you?'

While she went to fetch her grand-daughter, Kathy said, 'It must be difficult for you, Mr Tait, taking on a family again.'

'We manage,' he said stiffly. 'Don't you worry about that. And we're not the only ones. You'd be surprised how many of us there are, grandmums and dads, lining up to collect the kiddies from playgroup and school. That's the way it is these days.' He looked grimly at the photograph of the lost daughter. 'Something seems to have happened to the generation in between. Do you know what it is?' He glared at Kathy, who wasn't sure if he was really asking for her opinion.

'No . . . not really. What do you think?'

'I haven't got a clue. Not a bleedin' clue.'

He shook his head, baffled. Kathy got to her feet and went over to look at the photographs on the wall. They formed a triangle, the Taits' dead daughter at the top, her three girls below her.

'Is this Naomi?' Kathy asked, pointing to the eldest, a bright, cheerful-looking girl with long black hair, very like her mother, kneeling between two panting golden retrievers.

'No, that's her big sister, Kimberley. Naomi's the middle one.'

She had square, plainer features, her dark hair cut short like a boy's, a stubborn set to her mouth. And as Kathy looked at the picture the girl herself came into the room behind her and said hello at her grandmother's prompting. Then she sat down, face pale, eyes lowered, and Mrs Tait said softly that she would make them all a cup of tea.

'Are you feeling all right, Naomi?' Kathy said. 'It must have been a terrible shock.'

The girl nodded, not looking up.

'We very much need your help, to find who may have done this.'

'Done . . . ?' The girl raised her eyes to meet Kathy's, her voice little more than a whisper.

'We're still trying to work out the details of what happened, Naomi, but it seems likely that Kerri was murdered. Probably at or near the Silvermeadow shopping centre.'

'How do you know that?'

Kathy frowned, surprised by the question. There was something obdurate about Naomi, as if determined to believe nothing without the hard evidence under her nose.

Her grandfather had caught the tone of scepticism in her voice too, and said, 'Don't you be cheeky, young lady.'

'Well, that's the best indication we have so far as to how she met her end,' Kathy said. 'Why? Does it surprise you?'

'Only, we were at Silvermeadow that afternoon, the Monday she went missing, and we didn't see her there.'

'We?'

'Lisa and me. We caught the four-fifteen bus. We didn't see Kerri.'

'You'd seen Kerri at school that day, hadn't you, Naomi? How did she seem?'

70

Naomi frowned at her feet. 'We didn't talk much.'

'Did she seem different from usual in any way?'

A shrug.

'Speak up, girl, when the detective asks you something,' her grandfather grumbled.

'Wouldn't she normally have gone to Silvermeadow with you?' Kathy went on. 'Didn't she give a reason for not going with you?'

The girl's expression had become a scowl, fixed on one toe. 'We were going to work. She wasn't on that afternoon. I dunno.'

'Where do you two work then?'

'Lisa wipes the tables in the food court, and I help in the sandwich bar, on the preparation mostly.'

Kathy wondered if it was accidental that Kerri, the pretty blonde, was out front with the customers, in her short skirt and roller blades, while the stolid Naomi was back in the kitchen. 'The thing is, Naomi, she went home that afternoon and packed a bag as if she was planning to go away somewhere. You'd think, wouldn't you, that she would have said something to her closest friends. Some hint, surely?'

Silence.

Jack Tait said, 'Speak up, girl,' rapping his fingertips on the newspaper.

Mrs Tait had come into the room with a tray. She set it down and stooped beside Naomi and put an arm round her shoulders. 'Come on, love,' she urged. 'Do try to think.'

The girl relented, gracelessly. 'Yes. She told us. She said she was planning to go away.'

Mrs Tait drew back, looking worried.

Kathy said, 'That isn't what you told the officer who came to see you before, is it, Naomi?'

'She made us promise not to tell anyone, see. She said she was going to Germany to stay with her dad.'

'Oh bleedin' heck,' Jack Tait muttered. His fingers abruptly stopped tapping the newspaper.

'Well, what else could I do?' Naomi glared defiantly at him, and Kathy caught a glimpse of his eye meeting his grand-daughter's and then sliding away, so that for a moment she seemed the adult, the one with the difficult responsibilities to deal with.

'Had she arranged this with her father?' Kathy asked. 'Was he going to meet her somewhere?'

71

'I don't think so. She said it would be a surprise. She said she'd saved enough money to buy a ticket for the Channel ferry.'

'Just the boat? Was she going to hitch-hike?'

'I think so. But she wouldn't tell us what she was planning exactly, like it was a secret. Just that she was going to see her dad. But we thought that was what she was planning to do, hitch-hike.'

Her grandmother shook her head sadly. 'Oh, that's terrible, Naomi. A young girl like that on her own! Didn't you try to stop her? Promise me you'll never do anything so stupid.'

Naomi ignored her. 'She said, after she got to Germany and sorted things out, she'd ring her mum and put her mind at rest. But we weren't to say nothing, not to nobody.'

Mrs Tait passed round their cups of tea, fussing slightly, mollifying, removing her husband's newspaper and positioning his saucer securely on a special rubber mat attached to the chair arm. 'They're good girls. They work hard and do their best, Sergeant. You can't blame them. But I just wish you'd told us, love. I really do.'

The girl lowered her head, bottling up any reply.

'Anyway, you want to help us now, don't you, Naomi?' Kathy said.

'Of course she does!'

Naomi gave a reluctant little nod.

'I'd like to take you, and Lisa too, over to Silvermeadow, and get you to show me round. Show me the places you and Kerri liked to hang out, the people you know there. Will you do that?'

'Okay.' The idea seemed to perk her up a little.

'Of course she will!' Mrs Tait passed round the shortbread, eager for Naomi to have a chance to make amends.

'What about Kerri's bag, the one like a frog, do you know where she got that from?'

'Yes, a place in the mall. A bag shop.'

'Good. Maybe you can help me find another one like it.'

'That's the way, old girl,' Jack said, a little restored, lifting his cup to his mouth and blowing on his tea.

Lisa lived in Jonquil Court, distinguished from Crocus by the wrecked children's play equipment corralled within a high chain-link fence in one corner. She was a paler, less confident version of Kerri's picture, with the same length of fair hair cut in the same way, almost as if she had modelled herself on her friend. She confirmed Naomi's account practically word for word, and agreed to come to Silvermeadow on condition Naomi was going too.

As Kathy took the girls back to her car she turned it over in her mind. Both of them seemed certain that Kerri had planned to surprise her father. Or perhaps to *test* him, Kathy thought, picking up on something Lisa had said, that Kerri idolised her dad and made excuses for his absence. For the girl would know, as soon as he opened his front door and saw her standing there, she would know from his expression if he really loved her. What if he'd got wind of it beforehand? Maybe she'd written, hinting at what she intended, and he'd tried to stop her. Or maybe she had reached him and he had tried to bring her back.

But the Hamburg police had confirmed that the company he worked for was quite certain that Stefan Vlasich was in Poland all through the period Kerri was missing. He was still there, waiting for a plane that would now bring him over to bury his daughter, and they would have their chance to interview him when he arrived. A simpler explanation was that she had started hitch-hiking, and had been picked up by someone on their way to make a delivery to Silvermeadow. Someone who had murdered her and then used the simplest and most anonymous disposal method available.

Kathy was about to set off with the two girls when her phone rang. It was Miriam Sangster.

'Can I talk to you again?' the constable said.

'I thought you'd have gone off duty by now, Miriam,' Kathy said.

'I'm still here. There's something I wanted to tell you. It won't take long, but it's quite urgent.'

'I'm not far away now, but I've got the girls in the car with me, Naomi and Lisa. I suppose I could call in at the station.'

'No, don't come in. I'll meet you round the corner in the high street, near the pillar-box outside the post office. It'll be quicker for you. I'll only take a minute.'

Kathy found the place and parked on a double yellow line, making desultory conversation with the two girls in the back. She asked which of them had the best job, and they explained, reluctantly, the good points and the bad. Kerri's had seemed the most glamorous and the most fun, in her costume and make-up, talking to the customers, whizzing about on her skates. But the skates were hard on your legs after a while, and sometimes she'd get a customer who would hassle her. No, no one special, just sometimes she'd get a troublemaker, whereas Lisa and Naomi didn't have so much of that.

Then Kathy spotted Miriam Sangster, out of uniform now, crossing the zebra up ahead and hurrying towards the car. She got out and walked up to meet her in front of the post-office window.

'Sorry,' the constable said. She had the same stubborn, preoccupied look about her that Naomi had had. 'I thought you'd want to know this.'

'Fire away.'

'Okay.' She took a deep breath, then began, speaking low although the street was deserted this cold Sunday morning. 'When I tried to check that rumour, about Silvermeadow, remember?'

'Yes.'

'I was checking missing persons, and there were no references to the centre at all. But this morning, after we spoke, I tried a different line. Obvious really. I called up all the reports we'd had from Silvermeadow. There weren't a lot, considering its size. A couple of ram raids, a few dozen shoplifters they decided to prosecute, some car thefts, some heart attacks, one fatal, that we attended, that sort of stuff.'

'Yes, that's pretty much what they told us. Go on.'

'Then I came across Norma Jean.' She sucked in her breath as if the memory was troubling. 'A right pain she was. Young, under sixteen we thought, and a vagrant. I remember her causing trouble round here a couple of summers ago, begging, soliciting. Then when the weather turned chilly she took a fancy to Silvermeadow and started making a nuisance of herself there. We were called out a couple of times. I attended once – she'd been found in the women's toilets, out cold with a needle in her arm and someone else's handbag on the floor beside her. She was put in a shelter, then juvenile detention. But she kept coming back. The youth offender team took her under their wing for a while, but no one could really handle her. She was like a headache that wouldn't go away. And then one day someone in the canteen said, whatever happened to Norma Jean? And we realised that the headache seemed to have disappeared. No one had heard of her for weeks. It was wonderful.'

'She wasn't reported missing?'

'No way. Nobody gave a damn. I just phoned her last social worker. She said the same thing. Sometime around March, Norma Jean stopped being a bother, and everybody breathed a great big sigh of relief. She'd tried to follow it up, but couldn't find out anything. In theory, Norma Jean is still on her load.'

Kathy didn't say anything at first, not wanting to sound dismissive. Miriam Sangster was clearly taking this very much to heart.

'Yes, all right,' the constable said, 'there are hundreds of Norma Jeans, thousands.'

'She probably just moved on, Miriam. Decided to go somewhere she wasn't so well known.'

'Yes. But still, I thought our records showed that no one had disappeared from Silvermeadow. Now I can't be certain, can I?'

'Tell you what. I'll check her out in the Silvermeadow security records. They may have something on her that we don't.'

'Thanks.'

'And let me know if you find anything else. You said that Mrs Vlasich had heard some stories at the hospital?'

'Yes, but I think she got it confused. A cook had heard it from a nurse who'd supposedly heard an old woman say she'd lost her young daughter at Silvermeadow. Sounded like classic urban myth stuff.'

'Yes, well, frankly I'd forget about it. You've done about as much as you can.'

The other woman nodded reluctantly, relieved all the same. 'I hope you get something soon.'

The girls seemed to brighten a little once they were under the dappled artificial sunshine of the mall, as if this was where they were most at home, whereas Kathy felt the same sense of disorientation as before. It was full of people again now, not as in a city street hurrying past without eye contact, but a relaxed crowd such as one might find at a fairground, perhaps, or a fête, sharing some implied sense of community and well-being. Yet there seemed no substance to it here, no relationships and ties that one might hope to uncover between people in a real street or town. Here everyone was afloat, gliding through a fantasy. She recalled Bo Seager's remark about sharks following the shoals. A shark could easily pass unnoticed here.

They walked down the main mall, the girls pointing out the stores where they liked to window shop, the characters they knew by sight or reputation, and gradually the shock of Kerri's murder seemed to fade from their minds, as if time and reality were suspended in the magic grove, and all the intractable grubbiness of life dissolved away in the glowing golden light. From time to time their eyes would be drawn to a sparkling shop display, and Kathy would pause with them and find herself drawn into their conversation, checking out some lovely thing that none of them had a use for. Then she would have to turn away, and remember what they were supposed to be doing, and get them moving again. Lulled by the scented air, the music not too loud or too soft but just right, it was hard to imagine that anything unpleasant could ever have really happened here – an abduction, a murder. In here the foetal figure waiting for the incinerator was no more than a chimera, a bad dream.

They stood at the balcony overlooking the food court for a while, listening to the sounds of fountains and waterfalls from the rain forest on this side of the lagoon, and the girls pointed out where they worked, and the other food stalls that formed the perimeter of the court. Between Mexican Pete's and the Peking Duck was the Soda Factory, done up like an American drugstore counter in stainless steel and red leather stools. Then there was Snow White's Pancake Parlour, and they were silent for a moment as they watched the girls on their roller skates, gliding skilfully on long legs between the tables.

They descended on the escalator and came to the shore of the volcanic lagoon. There was a uniformed copper standing there in conversation with one of the locals, who was explaining what happened.

'Yeah, well, first you get yer warning tremors and rumblings see.'

'Right, right.' The officer nodded seriously, as if this was significant evidence.

'Well then yer water starts moving, ominous right, and you 'ear the sound of frightened birds. Then the eruption starts – bangs and roars from the mountain – then smoke and sparks comin' out from the peak, and after a while molten lava starts flowing down the sides.'

'Molten lava! You're having me on.'

'No, right up. Course it's not yer actual molten lava, naturally. It's an illusion, see, made with coloured lights hidden down the sides of the volcano. But it's convincing. Then the water foams up, and that native canoe over there tips up in the air and sinks under the waves, like a whirlpool's sucked it down. You should see it, mate. You'll be impressed. Get your mates down here, on the hour.'

'Yeah.' The policeman nodded thoughtfully. Kathy could imagine the scene that afternoon: small children and grannies complaining that they couldn't see for all the hulking great coppers in the front row.

But Lisa and Naomi were bored by this. They'd seen Mauna Loa erupt so many times. They led Kathy across to the far side of the food court, where an abrupt leap took place from the Pacific to Ali Baba's Arabian Nights. Large pots belonging to the Forty Thieves stood at the entrance of the Grand Bazaar, the name written in Arabic-style neon lettering over the cave-like entry, guarded by a turbaned mannequin with a flute frozen in the act of charming a cobra out of its basket.

'Do they have snake-charmers in Arabia?' Kathy asked, then saw from the look on the girls' faces that the question made no sense.

Inside the Bazaar the lighting levels dropped sharply, small spotlights dazzling like stars overhead against a black ceiling, a theme taken up in many of the shops. These were clearly aimed at the teen market – lurid T-shirt boutiques, a Doc Martens store, pop CDs, an electronic games arcade and a salon offering challenging concepts in hair and the piercing of body parts.

There seemed to be something going on here, voices raised above the general noise. Two uniformed officers, a man and a woman, were talking to the agitated tenant of the games arcade, a black man with dreadlocks.

'Look!' he yelled at them, brandishing his arms, rattling the gold bangles on his wrists. 'You lot think that every black guy wearing a bit of gold jewellery is nicking stuff or selling drugs, don't you? That's what it is, innit?'

'Keep your voice down please, sir,' the male officer said.

'No, I won't shut up, 'cos it's true, innit? I get this all the time, don't I? You think I'm selling these kids drugs, is that it?'

'Are you?' the woman cut in.

All around them in the unit, teenage boys were easing away from the machines they had been playing and slipping away into the mall. Among them Kathy saw the boy she'd seen that morning outside the bookshop. He glanced back over his shoulder, then skipped into a run and disappeared into the crowd.

'Hang on, you stay right there.' The male officer left his colleague and moved over to two boys trying to leave. He bent forward and started talking to them. One of them shrugged and reluctantly began to turn out his pockets.

Kathy didn't know the officers. The woman was trying to make some point with the operator of the arcade, who was now adopting an exaggerated pose of silence. Kathy walked over and showed the woman her warrant card. 'Can I help?'

77

'No, it's okay.' The woman smiled. She seemed calm and in control. 'We've received some information regarding Mr Starkey, and we're just persuading him to close up shop so we can talk to him. We can manage, thanks.'

'What information?' the man shouted. 'What you fucking talking about?'

'Watch your language, Winston,' the woman PC said sharply.

Kathy turned back to the girls, and they continued on through the Bazaar until the dark mall opened into a small square from which another set of escalators led upwards towards light and another abrupt change of scene. Here they were on a gallery with large observation windows along one wall, overlooking the leisure centre and pool. It was busy down there, full of little kids with their dads, grandparents sitting under the palm trees and striped umbrellas on the astroturf waving encouragingly to the bodies in the surf, children sliding down the curling multi-coloured intestines of the water chutes, whooping and screaming silently beyond the glass. And there was surf too, surging from the wave machine at the deep end of the huge pool and spreading out across its surface to lap finally on the sandy beach.

'You come up here do you?' Kathy asked, looking at the benches for spectators along the gallery.

'Sometimes, when we have a break at work.'

'What, to check out the good-looking boys?' Kathy suggested.

Lisa giggled and Naomi glowered disapprovingly at her.

'What's down there?' Kathy asked. To the right she could see the shops of the main upper mall, but to the left the gallery continued across the end of the leisure centre, then narrowed to a set of glass doors.

'That's the gym and fitness centre,' Naomi said, offhand.

'Can we go in?'

'If you want.'

Through the glass doors the public gallery continued as a narrower bridge, with a view on one side over squash courts, and on the other into a gymnasium full of machines. The floor of these rooms was only a few metres below the gallery level here, and the people working out below seemed almost close enough to touch. They stood for a while watching a couple of young women capably thrashing a ball around one of the squash courts, then turned to view a muscular male through the other window, pounding the leather arms of the machine in which he lay. He was almost directly below them, the beads of sweat visible on his body as he lifted and dropped, an expression of intense effort on his face as the column of weights behind his head rose and fell with every grunt.

He stopped abruptly, opened his eyes and sat up. Then, as if he could sense that he was being observed, he turned his head and looked up and gave Kathy and the girls a sly grin. She watched his eyes track down each of their bodies in turn, and she turned away from the glass and they walked back the way they had come. She noticed a red blush on Lisa's cheek, and saw Naomi mutter something in her ear which made the other girl pull away with a complaining, 'Naomi!'

'So, where else do you go?' Kathy asked.

'That's about all,' Naomi replied. 'Sometimes we go to the cinema down on the lower mall, just off the food court the other way. They have eight screens.'

'Ten,' Lisa corrected.

Naomi shrugged.

'Are there any pubs, clubs?'

'Yeah, down past the cinema, but we don't go there.'

'Never?'

They shook their heads.

'Do fellers come into the food court from the pub? Having had too much to drink?'

'The security are very hot on that. Mr Jackson.'

'You know Mr Jackson, do you?'

'He's nice,' Lisa said. 'He gives us sweets, and vouchers for things on offer.'

Naomi rolled her eyes. Big deal.

'What about the shop where Kerri got her bag?'

'Oh yes, it's on this level. We'll take you there.'

Along the way they were stopped by a silver-haired woman wanting their signatures on a petition. Though small, she was formidable and not easily bypassed. Pinned to her cardigan was a printed identification which covered a significant portion of her chest on account of the length of its message and the size of the letters: HARRIET RUTTER, PRESIDENT, SILVERMEADOW RESIDENTS' ASSOCIATION.

The woman beamed up at Kathy. 'We are petitioning for significant improvements in the choice of music which is played here in the centre,' she said briskly, with a piping Home Counties accent. 'It is currently repetitious and bland, and we are pressing the management for a more enlightened choice, encompassing a mixture of classical and popular works, selected by a democratically elected committee.'

'A residents' association?' Kathy said. 'Do people actually live here?'

'Aha, well, no, not exactly. We had a great deal of debate over that word. A *great* deal.' Mrs Rutter raised an eyebrow and pursed her lips in a way that managed to suggest that there had been a great deal of foolishness spoken before her own view on the matter had prevailed. 'You see, there's really no appropriate word for what we are. We don't *live* here, no, of course not. No one could *live* here.' She looked about her with a smile at the absurdity of the idea. 'We come from all around, many from miles away. On the other hand, we are not just *customers* or *consumers* or *users* or *stakeholders* – such dreadful terms! We don't come here just to buy things, you see. We toyed with the Friends of Silvermeadow, but that makes it sound like an orphanage, don't you think, or a zoo. We're simply concerned citizens, for whom Silvermeadow has become a kind of focus in our lives, and it occurred to us, after we'd bumped into each other in repeated encounters such as this, that we should form an association.'

'I see,' Kathy nodded, thinking that this might have its uses. 'And you're the president.'

'Yes. Here, let me give you one of our leaflets. You may be interested in joining us. You'll find our mission statement on the second page, and an application for membership section at the back. We've won a good many victories for improvements here over the past eighteen months, and enjoyed ourselves enormously in the process.' She chuckled combatively and thrust a leaflet into Kathy's hand. 'And the petition?'

'I'll think about that,' Kathy said. 'I haven't really formed a view about the music.'

'We'll sign,' Naomi said. 'The music's crap.'

'Oh.' Mrs Rutter was startled, but only for a moment. 'That's nice, dear. Here you are.'

They moved on to the bag shop, in which they found one last remaining frog bag, identical, so the girls said, to the one Kerri had bought on her last birthday with money sent by her father. Kathy bought it and they went back out into the mall.

'Okay,' she said. 'Now I'd like to take you to meet my boss, Detective Chief Inspector Brock.'

Their faces fell.

'What's the matter? You'll like him.'

'We're not in trouble, are we?' Naomi said.

'No, it's all right. I think he'll understand why you did what Kerri asked. But he'll want to hear it from you.'

'He's a big wheel, is he?'

'Yes. He's one of the top detectives in Scotland Yard, Naomi. If anyone's going to find out what happened to Kerri, he will.'

'I feel sick,' Lisa said, and looked it.

'She felt sick last night,' Naomi said. 'It was hearing about Kerri. She hasn't eaten since. Neither of us has.'

'Well look, why don't you come with me to meet Mr Brock, and you can sit down there, and we'll get you something nice to eat and drink, and you'll feel a lot better.'

Phil, the action manager, was now firmly established at a desk just inside the front door, so that no one could come or go without being checked off on his spreadsheets and schedules. Kathy reported to him with the girls in tow, staring wide-eyed and intent at all the activity inside the shop unit. She sat them down beside Phil and got a paper cup of water for Lisa, then went through the unit to Brock's table, now looking considerably more cluttered. He looked up from the papers he was reading and waved her to a seat.

'Progress?' she asked.

'Six staff so far with records, one promising.' He passed a fax across to her. 'Eddie Testor, six months for assault and criminal damage two years ago. Road rage – he forced the other driver to pull in, then battered his car to a crumpled heap with a couple of five-pound hand-weights he happened to have with him. Offered steroid abuse in mitigation. He's been working at the leisure centre as a lifeguard and swimming instructor, based on false references and credentials. Gavin Lowry's interviewing him at Hornchurch Street now.'

'Has he finished the search here?'

'Pretty much. A few of them are still checking outside.'

'That was quick.'

'Yes, he doesn't waste time. I'm on my way over to see how he's getting on, but I'd like to talk to Kerri's friends, see if she ever took swimming lessons from this character.'

'I've just brought them in,' Kathy said, 'Naomi and Lisa.'

'They're here? You must have read my mind, Kathy.'

She told him about their change of story, showed him the green frog bag and mentioned Lisa's physical similarity to Kerri. 'I thought, if we wanted to stage a reconstruction . . .'

'Yes, yes. Good idea.' He thought for a moment. 'I'll talk to them.'

'They're a bit overwhelmed at present. I might organise some lunch for them.'

She led them over. Naomi shook Brock's hand solemnly, but when he leant across the desk to take Lisa's she began making little gulping noises, and with a sudden jerk of her head ejected a bolt of mushy material onto the middle of his desk. Cornflakes and toast, Kathy noted. So she had had breakfast.

'Oooh . . .' the girl wailed, and Brock, looking benignly unconcerned, as if this was always happening, murmured, 'There, there. Don't worry.' He refrained from wiping the splashes off the front of his shirt and trousers while Kathy sat the girl down and gave her tissues.

'Maybe we should take Lisa home,' Kathy said.

5

Kathy was beginning to feel that she was condemned to repeat this journey backwards and forwards endlessly, between two worlds, Silvermeadow and Herbert Morrison, that couldn't possibly coexist, like whoever it was, the god of thresholds, who looked both ways at once. Or the ferryman who took the dead across the river to Hades. Question was, which of them really was Hades, in this case?

She saw Lisa safely back to her flat, whose threshold mat proclaimed BASS, and looked very much as if it had been acquired from the local.

Then she went to Hornchurch Street to see how DS Lowry was making out with the hammer man. Gavin was taking a break from his exertions when she arrived, supping from a polystyrene cup of tea and looking introspective and thoughtful, especially when he caught sight of Kathy.

'He's a nutter,' he observed without malice. 'You don't realise it at first. But then the signal lights start flashing: the repetitions, the forgetfulness, the displacements.'

'Displacements?'

'Yeah. Like, now he comes to think of it, there is this *other* guy he's seen eyeing up the girls, this *other* body builder, this *other* steroid junkie. Not him of course.'

'Ah. Well, Brock should be along shortly. He's talking to one of the girl's school friends. She may know something about this bloke.'

'Hmm. And what about you? What've you been up to?'

'Just that. The school friends. They admit now that Kerri was planning to run away to see her father.'

'So how did she end up in the Silvermeadow compactor?'

'Exactly.'

'Anything else I should know about?' he asked, and drained his tea slowly.

'Don't think so.'

He gave a weary sigh, crushed the cup in his fist and tossed the bits into a bin. 'Oh well. Such is life.' He turned and walked away.

Kathy shuttled back, along quiet Sunday streets, then the link road to the motorway, the motorway itself busy now with weekend traffic, and finally the Silvermeadow turn-off and the expanse of carpark getting fuller all the time, drawing life in from the highways. She went in by way of the service road ramp again and found the blue compactor reassembled and in use, the SOCO team having moved on to the orange machine deepest inside the basement.

They'd taken their overalls off and were sitting together on the edge of the loading dock, eating pizza, and the smell made Kathy feel hungry.

'Pepperoni,' Desai said. 'Have some. We won't finish this. If you don't have it it'll just end up in the compactor.'

He gave her a slice.

'Any progress?' she asked.

'We're getting the hang of it now. By the time we get to the third one we'll be stripping it down in no time. But I don't know if we've got anything useful. Dozens of samples, but who knows what of?'

He took her over to the compactor, its bright orange panels half-dismantled, and showed her where the deposits had gathered in the corners and seams of the compression chamber. 'Oil, hydraulic fluid, fibres, gorgonzola cheese, who knows?' He straightened and added, 'What's it like outside?'

'Cool, dull.'

'I wouldn't mind some fresh air. You want a stroll?'

They walked back along the service road to the ramp, then up into the grey December afternoon and began to follow the pavement that skirted the perimeter of the building.

'Getting on all right with DS Lowry, are you?' he asked suddenly.

'Not too bad. Why? Do you know him?'

'Not personally. But the guys I'm working with do. I've been listening to them talking about him. He's ambitious. Looks after number one. Maybe you should watch your back.'

Kathy looked at him sharply, wondering if he was having a dig at her. The question of trust.

'Well,' she said, 'you know me. Trust nobody.'

He gave a wry smile. 'I haven't forgotten,' he said softly.

'I'll bear it in mind. Thanks.' They stepped aside for a couple pushing twins in a double stroller, then Kathy added, 'I didn't think you'd speak to me again, when I saw you down there this morning.'

He shrugged and gave a sigh that formed a small cloud of breath in the cool air. 'Oh, look, that was months ago, and you know how it is when you're lying in a hospital bed, feeling fragile and sorry for yourself . . . or maybe you don't.'

'You didn't sound fragile, Leon. You sounded lucid and angry, and I deserved it. So thanks for talking to me again.'

They walked on in silence, thrusting their hands deeper into their pockets and hunching up their collars as they rounded a corner and met the north-east wind head on. The contours of the hill, carved up by the earthworks for the shopping centre, dropped sharply here to the lower half of the site. A derelict corner lay below them, a couple of deserted builders' huts in a wire compound, weeds struggling up through raw clay, a battered sign announcing the next development phase.

Desai laughed softly.

'What's funny?'

'I was just thinking, about that time. The thing that really pissed me off, lying there with tape over my eyes and mouth in that derelict flat with Sammy Starling and his gun, the thing that most bothered me . . . Well, no, the thing that *most* bothered me was that I might be sick and choke myself, like that bloke last year. But after that, the thing that annoyed me was the thought that you would go to my funeral thinking I was gay. You remember, the conversation in the pub?'

Kathy smiled. 'When I discovered you were living with your mum, and that you'd taken me for a quiet drink to a pub where all the most glamorous girls turned out to be fellers. Yes, I remember. I did wonder. But I decided you probably weren't.'

They turned about and began to retrace their steps, walking slowly.

'When you're in a situation like that,' he went on, 'you tend to rethink your priorities. When I was lying there, and I realised how much it *did* bother me what you thought, I decided that, if I ever got out of it and saw you again, I'd make sure you knew exactly where I stood, regardless of what Bren had said. But of course it didn't work out like that. Instead I got stuck into you for not trusting me.'

His phone rang and he cupped it to his ear while Kathy stood there wondering what on earth he was talking about. Where he stood? What Bren had said?

'Yes Phil, she's here with me . . . The reception's better because I'm outside in the carpark, that's why . . . Yes, I'll tell her . . . Fine.'

A savage little gust of wind whipped the hem of Kathy's long coat and ruffled Desai's black hair like raven's feathers, and she thought there was something different about him now apart from the little scar, something easier, less arrogant, not quite so anally retentive, as Bren used to put it, as if his experience had reconciled him to himself in some way.

'Phil checking up on you,' he grinned. 'Brock has left some document from the security manager on his desk, and would like you to have a look at it. If you go in this entrance here you're only fifty yards from our unit.'

'Leon, what did you mean just now, about telling me where you stood, regardless of what Bren had said? What had he said?'

'Oh . . . that's all in the past, Kathy. Water under the bridge. Evocative, that expression, don't you think? It's one of my father's favourites. I remember he took us to the Victoria Falls one year, when I was a very small boy, before we got kicked out of East Africa, and we all stood there watching the water thundering below us, and he said, now *that's* what I call water under the bridge.'

'You're being whimsical and evasive. What did Bren say to you?'

'He spoke in confidence, Kathy, and he would be embarrassed if I told you. He's very protective of you, you know. He's a good friend.'

'Yes, I know that. But I still want to know.'

He frowned down at his trainers. 'Now I'm embarrassed, Kathy. This is all in the past. He . . . he was aware of a certain interest on my part . . . a certain leaning, and he felt obliged to put me right.'

'I don't know what you're talking about.'

Desai spread his hands, exasperated, as if she was being obtuse. 'All right, if you're going to give me the bloody third degree, he told me about your continuing obsession with this lawyer chap, whatever his name is, Connell, and advised me not to waste my time. *Get a life, Leon* were his exact words – rather ironic, I thought later when I was lying on Sammy's floor with a gun at my head.'

Kathy stopped dead and stared at him. 'Bren told you *that*?'

But Desai was already on his way. 'Better get on,' he called back over his shoulder. 'Got to get this job finished. See you later.'

★

Phil called out to her as she walked passed his desk. 'Oi! Kathy! Keep me informed of your movements, eh? I run a tight ship, all right?'

'Yes, Phil.'

'You okay? You look a bit peaky. Haven't caught something from that kid you brought in earlier, have you? Only if you're going to throw up somewhere I'd advise against the DCI's desk. Once is enough for one day.'

'Very funny.'

She sat down at Brock's desk, which did still reek mildly after Lisa's accident. At an adjoining table two clerks were working their way through a print-out of the door access codes used during the period Kerri might have been taken to the service road, and putting names against them from a second print-out listing authorised code users. Kathy barely registered what they were doing, thinking instead of what Leon Desai had said. She shook her head and forced herself to concentrate on the report lying on Brock's desk from Harry Jackson, itemising incidents at Silvermeadow.

It was an impressive document, with spreadsheets and dot points and 3D pie charts of incidents by type, and participants by postal area, age and gender, and coloured AutoCAD plans of the centre with numbered stars for locations, and even a couple of scanned crime-scene images for those readers with a short attention span. All in all, considering the time available, it was a tribute to the computer facilities and skills of Harry's team. But it only went back six months, and for all its apparent wealth of data it contained no real details, such as names.

'Security centre, Phil,' Kathy said as she passed his desk. 'Going to talk to the staff. Is Harry Jackson around, do you know?'

'I believe he's salvaging what's left of his weekend.'

'Good.'

Sharon was there, however, keeping an eye on the screens. She was more confident and chatty without the men around, and she made a cup of tea for them both.

'I've been reading the report that Harry prepared for DCI Brock,' Kathy said. 'Really impressive.'

'Oh yeah, it's good isn't it? He and Speedy were at it till late last night. The data room was a mess this morning.'

'Where's that? I don't remember seeing it before.'

'It's just through there . . .' Sharon showed Kathy a small windowless room off the main office crammed with computer equipment. 'Speedy's the ace with this stuff. The rest of us don't know how to use half of it. He does special jobs for Ms Seager, like her business reports and stuff, and for the maintenance engineer too, circuit diagrams and I don't know what.'

'So Speedy's pretty bright, is he? He doesn't just stare at the screens all day.'

'Oh yeah, he's good. He says you don't need legs when you can drive this stuff.'

They returned to their tea.

'So do you enter an incident onto the computer yourself, if you've got something to report?' Kathy asked.

'No, we've still got the daybooks for that, I'm glad to say. Computers aren't my strong point. Harry's a great stickler for the daybooks. I reckon it's what he grew up with in the force, isn't it?'

'Show me.'

They were a collection of thick red hard-bound A4 books of blue lined pages, numbered in sequence, each covering about six months, and they contained the terse reports, handwritten in ball-point, of each incident recorded by the attending security staffer.

'Here's my last one,' Sharon said, opening the most recent book. 'Here. I like to use green ink. Three days ago: seventeen-oh-six hours; fire started in rubbish container opp. unit two-one-five; perp unknown; S.W. attended; no action. Harry likes us to keep it short and sweet. Just the bare facts. Then at the end of the week Speedy enters them in his database.'

'That's fascinating,' Kathy said.

'Don't you have that in the force?'

'Yes, something like that. But this is much more detailed, every little incident recorded.'

'That's Harry – Mr Zero Tolerance, that's what he is.'

'My boss wanted me to check the details of a couple of things in Harry's report, so I suppose the daybooks would be the place to look?'

'Yeah, help yourself. I'd offer to help but I'm meant to be keeping an eye on the screens.'

'No, that's fine. I'll manage. How long have you been here, Sharon?'

'Just on a year.'

Kathy started four books back, in the previous year. After a while, scanning through the plethora of small crises, she hit upon the first reference to Norma Jean X. There were two other mentions in that month, six in the next, and then a cascade of Norma Jean incidents. The reports came from a variety of security staff, whose developing mood could be sensed both in what they wrote – 1042: NJ warned about loitering . . . 1155: NJ escorted AGAIN – and in the increasing force with which their ball-point messages had been scored into the pages of the book. There were gaps for a week or two, when presumably she was being detained elsewhere, but then she was back again, like the daughter from hell, grazing in the aisles of the food stores, shoplifting in the boutiques, embarrassing sheepish dads with offers of her body for cash, pinching their wives' handbags, shooting up drugs in the toilets, falling asleep on the mall benches, and the daybook reports came to sound more and more like the comments of angry and frustrated parents, underlined, capitalised, and even, when things got really bad, containing words which Harry Jackson had felt obliged to obscure and initial with his stern purple fountain pen. Norma Jean's assault lasted, off and on, for almost five months, and then, mysteriously and without comment, it ceased.

Brock scanned the file on Eddie Testor that had been couriered down, and watched Lowry interviewing him on the video screen for some time before he joined them. The man seemed very alert, almost eager in his manner, answering Lowry's questions rapidly and without hesitation. He admitted misrepresenting his background to his present employer, but said he'd been forced into it in order to get a job, and had been helped to massage his CV by a professional employment consultant, whom he named. His record at work had been described as very satisfactory by the management of the leisure centre. He had one caution on his employee's file, a note of a verbal warning from a supervisor that his behaviour with some small boys in the surf – 'larking about' – was inappropriate.

His manner changed somewhat when Brock came into the room. Brock noticed the shift, an avoidance of eye contact, a small hesitation at the start of each reply, and then a developing surliness whenever Brock spoke.

'Tell us again,' Brock said, placing Kerri's enlarged portrait photograph on the table between them, 'about the man you saw talking to her.'

'May not have been her. Lots of girls look like that. Could have been anyone.'

'Yes, all right. Recently?'

A shrug and a scowl.

'Try to picture them talking together,' Brock said softly. 'Never mind the girl, concentrate on the man. Picture the man. Does he look a bit like you, Eddie?'

'No! Not like me at all. He's a smoothy.'

'A smoothy? What does that mean?'

'Smooth. Slippery smooth.'

Later, outside the interview room, Brock rubbed his palm backwards and forwards across his jaw, scratching his beard, thinking.

'He claims he was working between five p.m. and nine p.m. on the Monday, after an hour meal break. We're waiting to hear from the manager at the leisure centre.'

'Did you get a chance to look at his file, Gavin?'

'A fairly quick scan, chief, during our last break. But I've met him before, this one.'

'Did you read the parole psychologist's final report?'

'Not in detail.'

'Worth a look.'

'He's a nutter, chief.'

'Yes, but they come in different shapes and sizes. This one doesn't seem to have any interest in women. He doesn't hate them, or like them, or respond to them in any way. Remarkable, eh?'

'He's got bits missing in his head.'

'Did you notice the way his mood changed when I came into the room?'

'Yes. I wondered if you two had met before.'

'No, never.' Brock turned the pages of the file until he came to a photograph of the car that Testor had attacked. It was spectacularly beaten flat, a crumpled metal pancake, like a cartoon car that a cartoon elephant had sat on.

'Like what happened to Kerri,' Lowry said.

'Mmm.' Brock rubbed his chin again. 'A Jaguar, almost vintage, British racing green. It's the same type and colour as the car that was owned by the man who ran the home he spent five years in when he was a little boy. He didn't mention that at his trial. It came up almost by accident when the prison psychologist was interviewing him for the parole board. And the man driving the flattened car was elderly. He had grey hair, like the man who ran the home. Like me. It was at the home that he had the accident to his head.'

A uniformed man looked round the door with a message for

Lowry, who read it and cursed softly under his breath. 'The manager has confirmed the times of Testor's shifts. He was at work from five p.m. all week. Hard to see how he could have fitted it in.'

Brock closed the file and handed it to Lowry. 'I really wonder whether Testor isn't more of a danger to me than to girls like Kerri, Gavin.'

'Fine,' Lowry muttered as Brock turned to leave. 'I'll let the bastard loose.'

Towards five that afternoon, seated again at his table in unit 184, Brock received, not a summons exactly, but an invitation, firmly couched, to meet with Bo Seager and some of her senior management team at six, to report on progress. There was a hint of coolness in the way the invitation was delivered that suggested all was not well. There were times, Brock reflected, when a potentially hostile committee could be best handled by a lone figure, vulnerable and outnumbered, but also, for that very reason, at an advantage; there were other times when a show of manpower worked better. He thought about that and about the formidable Bo Seager, and asked Kathy and, when he checked in soon after, Gavin Lowry to accompany him.

Finger food had been sent up from Penelope's Pantry, and a couple of bottles of chilled Chardonnay opened for the occasion. Harry Jackson had reported back to hear the briefing and pour the wine, and there was another man there also, a thin-faced unsmiling man with rimless glasses and a tumbler of mineral water who was introduced as Nathan Tindall, finance manager. For a fleeting moment as they sat down, Brock was reminded of a medieval court, the queen flanked by her ministers, the ascetic chancellor and the bluff knight.

'Are we to expect Chief Superintendent Forbes?' Bo asked silkily, raising her glass.

'He's otherwise engaged at present, Ms Seager,' Brock said. 'I'm sure he would have wanted to be here if he'd had more notice.'

'That's nice. I'll look forward to meeting him one day. Harry tells me he's actually running the investigation, is that right?'

'He's the senior investigating officer, yes.'

Bo sipped her wine. She sounded amused rather than antagonistic. 'Hmm. Well, so how—'

'Excuse me,' Tindall interrupted. 'Sorry, Bo, but just before we leave that point, can I be absolutely clear about this. I'm not really familiar with police ranks, but I take it that a chief superintendent is much more senior than a chief inspector.'

Brock nodded.

'Considerably so?' Tindall pressed. He had an angry nasal Lancastrian accent.

'Two steps above,' Brock replied. 'Although the rank has actually been abol—'

'Well, why *isn't* he here then, if this is the focus of your investigation?'

Brock stared at him for a moment before replying. 'We're running this investigation as we think best, Mr Tindall.'

Tindall stared right back, gave a little shake of his head, and said, 'But is that good enough, Chief Inspector?'

'If you have any problems with what we're doing, I hope you'll let us know.'

'Well we do have problems, as it happens.' He turned away with a dismissive shrug, as if he had no intention of spelling out what they were.

Brock waited, and the bluff knight leant forward to take up the point.

'Several problems this afternoon, in point of fact, Mr Brock,' Harry Jackson said gravely. 'An accusation of racist harassment by one of our tenants, a black gentleman, against two of your officers. I have the details here.' He handed a sheet of paper across to Brock. 'Also a general complaint from a number of our tenants that the presence of your officers in their premises has been disruptive and has generally interfered with the carrying on of their business. I'm surprised, as a matter of fact, that we haven't had a deputation already from our Small Traders' Association. Their president, Mr Verdi, whom you met last night, is usually jumping down our throats at the slightest hint of trouble.'

'The accusation of racism is a serious matter,' Brock said calmly. 'I can assure you that it will be taken very seriously. As for the other business, this is a murder inquiry, not a sales promotion. Your tenants have an obligation to help us, and I haven't heard of any of them wanting to do otherwise. Have you, Gavin?'

'No, sir.'

Now Bo Seager took charge of the discussion. 'I'm sure they're anxious to see this thing resolved as soon as possible, Chief Inspector, as we all are. Why don't you bring us up to date? I take it you have the authority to do that? We don't need Chief Superintendent Forbes here for that?'

And that, Brock assumed, was what the opening skirmishes had all been about, to put him in a position where he would feel obliged to tell them exactly what was going on. All in all, not much of a plan.

'I have that authority, Ms Seager,' he smiled, unruffled. 'And I shall exercise it just as far as I feel appropriate, believe me. As far as our enquiries at Silvermeadow are concerned, you'll be aware that our officers have almost completed interviewing tenants and centre staff. We've also finished our forensic investigation in the service road area for the time being.'

He reached for a tiny asparagus and prosciutto roll.

'Is that all?' Bo Seager said.

'All?'

'What about outcomes? What's happening?'

Brock savoured the roll, then took a sip of wine. He felt sympathy for her, despite her attempts to manipulate him. She was obviously under some pressure to make things happen, presumably from this Tindall, whom she clearly didn't much like. 'There's not much I can say about outcomes just at present, Ms Seager.'

'How about the compactors, Mr Brock?' Jackson broke in impatiently. 'Have you got a positive link with the girl?'

'We've got a stack of laboratory tests to be completed first, Harry.'

'But no forensic proof of a connection so far?' Tindall insisted. 'So the whole basis of your enquiries here may be completely flawed.'

'It seems unlikely, Mr Tindall, from what we know.'

'And what exactly is that?'

'Nathan . . .' Bo Seager began.

'No, sorry, Bo, bear with me, please. I just want us to be absolutely clear about this. As I understand it – correct me if I'm wrong, please – you have found a young woman's body several miles away from Silvermeadow, and near it the remains of packaging probably originating from Silvermeadow stores. Is that right? Well, I'm not familiar with police procedures, but simple logic tells me that that really doesn't prove that she was ever at Silvermeadow, does it?'

'Mr Tindall,' Brock said as patiently as he could, 'your desire for absolute clarity is understandable, but in my experience it's a rare commodity at the beginning of a murder inquiry. In this case, the circumstances in which the body and the packaging were found make it highly likely that both were processed through one of your

93

compactors some time between the sixth and eighth of December. We haven't spent all day taking them apart for fun, believe me.'

'Have you any other evidence at all about where she went after she left her home?' Tindall insisted harshly.

'It seems she was planning to hitch-hike to her father in Germany.'

'Well then!' Tindall looked around the room, eyebrows raised, hands spread. It occurred to Brock that he'd probably picked up the posture from watching courtroom dramas on TV. 'Rather makes my point, doesn't it? Why would she have come here?'

'She might have been brought here by whomever she got a lift from. That's why we've been particularly keen to identify people who made deliveries here during the period. Or there could be another explanation. You're on the M25 here, a good place to pick up a lift to the coast. Ms Seager pointed out to us before that your customers come from all over, including the Continent. Kerri could have picked out a suitable car in the carpark with Belgian or German plates, and approached the owner for a lift. Better that than standing thumbing on some motorway slip road in the rain. Or she may have met someone previously, someone who calls in at Silvermeadow on their way to the Continent, a regular traveller, someone who comes to the food court for a meal before heading down to the coast, maybe.'

'But someone like that couldn't access the service areas, Mr Brock,' Harry objected. 'They wouldn't have the code.'

'But *she* did, Harry. She had it. She'd been sent on errands back there more than once, and the Snow White's Pancake Parlour code was used several times on the afternoon and evening of the sixth, and subsequently.'

He let that sink in, then added, 'So that's why it's important to trace any sightings of Kerri here on that day, and to do that we intend to hold a reconstruction, or rather a walk-through in the mall with a girl similar in appearance and clothing to Kerri, as well as a leaflet and press campaign. Monday, the same day of the week, would be ideal for the walk-through, but there's no reason why we shouldn't run it on Tuesday as well.'

'No reason!' Tindall exploded.

'It's a perfectly normal procedure, Mr Tindall.'

Tindall's face flushed darker, but before he could respond, Harry Jackson cut in with a conciliatory flutter of his big hand. 'I think you could say that there's a slight conceptual problem here, Mr Brock. By which I mean that you may still be thinking of Silvermeadow as some kind of super high street, a public thoroughfare with shops down each side and a bit of a roof overhead. But it isn't that, not really. The mall here is more like a living room than a street. It's private property, it's looked after as well as if it were your own house, and it's as safe. Think of it that way. How would you like a crowd of coppers marching through your living room and staging a walk-through, eh?' He chuckled.

Tindall clearly found Harry's homely little clarification irritating. 'You might as well put up a sign in flashing lights, "Beware – this place is dangerous",' he grated. '"Serial killer on the loose".'

'This is important,' Bo Seager came in. 'Our whole ethos is built around this, Chief Inspector. People must feel completely comfortable and safe here. What you're suggesting simply isn't acceptable. It would create a perception, perhaps even panic.' She closed her mouth firmly, as if the point were settled.

There was something very irritating about all this, Brock felt, as if the team had been on some management course together – How to Get Your Way in Meetings – and had worked out beforehand how they would tame him, while Lowry and Kathy were left to sit in silence on each side of him like a pair of china dogs. Kathy might have read his mind, for she broke her silence.

'That's an interesting choice of words, Mr Tindall,' she said. The finance manager glanced at her in surprise, as if she should know that she didn't have a speaking part. '"Serial killer on the loose". Has there been any suggestion that this may have happened before?'

Brock saw a look of shock flare briefly on Tindall's face, and also a rapid exchange of looks between Jackson and Lowry.

'What the hell do you mean by that?' Tindall snapped, recovering himself.

'The victim's mother, Mrs Vlasich,' Kathy continued, 'mentioned in interview that she was frightened for her daughter's safety if Kerri had come to Silvermeadow, since she had heard rumours that girls had disappeared from here in the past.'

Jackson and Tindall immediately began protesting together, shaking their heads in disgust, while Bo Seager looked merely irritated, Brock thought, and Kathy expressionless, watching them. He couldn't see Lowry's face, but it was he who restored calm, speaking without raising his voice.

'We were aware of that,' he said, addressing himself alternately to Brock and Bo Seager. 'One of our officers checked out the stories when Mrs Vlasich first raised it. We found no basis whatsoever. It's just hysteria.'

'Yes,' Jackson nodded. 'We did the same. Nothing to it. Rumours, hysteria, like Gavin says.'

Bo leant forward intently towards Brock. 'Well, it just confirms how important it is to avoid encouraging ideas like that.'

'Rumours grow on secrecy,' he replied. 'Far better to have it out in the open and eliminate the possibility if we can. I'm afraid I'm going to have to insist on our plan.'

For a moment it looked as if Bo was going to fight, but then she shrugged and conceded with a smile. 'Okay, but let our publicity people work with yours on handling the press, please?'

'Certainly.' Brock got to his feet. 'Thanks for the snack, and for your co-operation, Ms Seager. We do appreciate it.'

She laughed out loud at this. 'Just so long as we can speak frankly, Chief Inspector.'

When they reached the front door Lowry hung back to speak to Jackson, and Kathy and Brock went out alone into the mall crowd.

'That was news to me, Kathy – the serial killer.'

'Yes, sorry. I wasn't going to mention it until I'd done some more checking. I just thought they needed shaking up a bit.'

'Well, it did that all right. I thought Gavin sounded rather defensive. Do you think there could be anything in it?'

'Probably not.'

'Mr Brock! Kathy!'

They turned round and saw Jackson weaving through the throng. 'Just wanted to say, no hard feelings, eh? Mr Tindall likes to sound like he's well hard, but they both know you've got a job to do.'

'Of course, Harry,' Brock said. 'We'll work with you on the walk-through. You'll help us, will you?'

'Course, course. And Kathy, that stupid rumour. Maybe it would put your mind at rest if you had a look through our security daybooks, eh? We record every little incident in there. If anyone had been aware of anything weird going on, it'd have to be recorded there. Okay?'

'Thanks, Harry. Yes, I'd like to borrow them for a day or two if that's all right.'

'No bother! I'll send them up tomorrow first thing. Night.'

'Good night, Harry,' Brock said, and they moved off again through the strolling crowd. 'Well, that's more like it, Kathy. The books will be more use than that glossy report he did for us.'

'Yes,' she agreed. 'They are. I photocopied most of them this afternoon while he was out.'

6

Leon Desai was in unit 184 when they returned, chatting to one of the clerical staff. Seeing him there, unexpectedly, Kathy got that little jolt she'd experienced seeing him that morning. He looked good, very trim and sleek in his black leather jacket and jeans, she thought, with his brown skin and blue-black hair. She saw a couple of the women eyeing him and thought yes, you wouldn't mind being seen with that.

'Hi.' He grinned at them both.

'Hello, Leon,' Brock returned. 'All done?'

'Yes. Even had a shower and a swim downstairs in the pool. Feel a lot better than I did after I'd finished crawling around on concrete and grease all day. I just wondered if anyone could give me a lift in to a tube station. The guy who brought me out here this morning has gone.'

'Certainly—' Brock began.

'I'll do it. I'm going north of the river.'

'You sure, Kathy?' Leon asked. 'Anywhere I can pick up a tube.'

'Not a problem. I'll just get my coat.'

They ran across the rain-swept tarmac and Leon held his umbrella over her as she unlocked the car. As they got in it occurred to Kathy that there is that moment when a couple, getting into a car together on a wet windy night, slamming the doors shut, experience a sudden compression of space, as the world shrinks to the intimate cabin around them. After a few seconds the effect fades, the mind adjusts to the new dimensions, and normal service is resumed. But for that moment they may be caught unawares, their mental-space reference tricked, and their sense of the proximity of the other dramatically heightened. At that moment, she thought, if there is the potential for something to happen, it probably will.

She glanced across at him, and found that his dark eyes were fixed on her. Unnerved by that look, Kathy said lightly, 'I can't believe Bren told you that, about Martin Connell. I haven't seen him in ages.'

'He didn't say you were still seeing him, just that you were still obsessed with him.'

She flushed at the word 'obsessed'. 'That's ridiculous. How would Bren know, anyway? And, come to think of it, Bren was the one who first put the idea in my head that you might be gay.'

'Naughty Bren. Let's go round to his place and beat him up.'

She smiled. 'Better not. He's bigger than both of us.'

'Why would he do that, though? Does he fancy you?'

'No, of course not.'

'I wouldn't say there's any "of course" about it, Kathy. It's not that hard.'

She looked away, got the car going with quick, hard gestures and drove off. She felt quite absurdly unsettled and she couldn't imagine how they were going to get through a long car ride together. As they approached the edge of the carpark, she recalled that she had been in this situation before with Leon, and had evaded its possibilities and regretted it afterwards. And she had a sudden sharp sense of how much she would regret doing that again. She braked hard and switched off the engine.

'Let's just think this through,' she said, as if this was some practical sort of project. 'You have to ask why we let Bren put us off, don't you? I mean, we didn't exactly struggle against his guiding hand, did we?'

'Ah, it was the colleague thing,' Leon said. 'You and I, we don't really approve of the colleague thing, relationships with people at work, do we? We're embarrassed by it. It gets in the way, it's messy.'

'Yes, that's true. That was one of the disastrous things about Martin, that he was connected to my work. Also he was married, and he was a total bastard.'

'Was he really?'

'Oh yes. You're not married though, are you, Leon?'

'No.'

'And you're not a bastard.'

'It's sometimes hard to know. Maybe everyone is.'

'No, you're not. But you are a colleague.'

He nodded, turned away, as if accepting that she wanted him to keep his distance.

'Oh . . .' She looked at his profile, the light from the tall mast floodlights rippling in the rain. 'Bugger the colleague thing,' she whispered, and undid her seat belt.

'What did you say?'

'I said, the windows are greasy. Hang on.'

She grabbed the cloth from the door pocket and jumped out of the car, feeling a great need for cold air and rain on her face and space around her. 'Heck,' she muttered to herself, rubbing the glass furiously. 'Get a grip, girl.'

She heard the other car door open and was aware of Leon walking round to her side of the bonnet, then the shelter of his brolly over her. She put down the cloth and they looked at each other, that same look again, and the space beneath the umbrella closed around them as they kissed.

After a few minutes they broke apart and she said, somewhat stunned, unable to recall quite how it had happened so decisively, 'We'd better go before we become an entry in Harry's daybooks.' They got back in the car and drove away.

She took him to her home, a small flat on the twelfth floor of a tower block in Finchley. They were prickly with the dampness and the car heater, and when they got into the flat they peeled off their coats and then everything else, and made love under the shower. Then Kathy led him to her narrow, cold bed, and they curled up tight together there and made love again, at a more leisurely pace.

In the grey light of dawn she slipped out of bed to try to forage for something for them to eat. They had missed dinner, and she soon realised that her fridge and cupboards were bare. The whole place was bare in fact, like a nun's cell, she realised, looking round at it as a stranger might – as he would. She'd made no effort to make it comfortable at all. The washing machine was old, and there was no tumble drier, so there wasn't much she could do about his clothes. The TV was on the verge of packing up and she rarely watched it because there was no video and she was never there when the programmes she wanted to watch were on. The furnishings were uniformly spartan. Not much of a love-nest. Probably about as far from Mrs Desai's cosy home in Barnet as you could get.

At least the central heating worked, which was just as well, because she didn't have anything he could use as a dressing gown, so he was naked when he slid up behind her and put his arms around her.

'I'm sorry,' she whispered. 'I haven't got a thing to eat, and the milk's gone off.'

They had a big breakfast at the station café before Leon got a train into central London for meetings at the forensic science lab. She went onto the platform with him and kissed him goodbye when the train came in. It was crowded, and he got in last so that he could stand crushed against the door and they could look at each other with goofy little smiles as the train began to pull away. Kathy noticed people at the adjoining windows looking at their sleepy faces and guessing what was up, turning back to their morning papers with nostalgic grins.

There were arrangements for the walk-through to be confirmed, publicity material prepared, press statements cobbled together, liaison meetings attended, and a mountain of reports to sift, but Kathy didn't feel much like any of it. Harry Jackson's daybooks were delivered to unit 184, marked for her attention, but she didn't feel much like immersing herself in them either. Instead she picked up a wad of information leaflets and interview kits and told Phil she was going to chase up some loose ends from the shop interview reports.

She stopped outside a large household furnishings store on the lower mall, and gazed idly at the ranks of beds disappearing off into the distance. So many! What on earth was the difference? She strolled in, and a young man immediately came over.

'Morning, madam. Can I help you?'

'It's okay, I'm with the police team, following up the visits yesterday. But I was just looking at your beds. I need a new one, actually.'

'Well, you've come to the right place here.'

'But what's the difference between them all?'

It took him a little while to cover just a bare overview of the intricacies of inner springing and foam, orthopaedic and lumber support, and during the course of it she was persuaded to try a few of the mattress types, which she did, a bit cautiously at first, imagining herself being spotted by colleagues in the mall as she slipped off her shoes and lay down and bounced. But the mall was quiet this Monday morning, and she soon entered into the spirit of the thing, and actually did decide which one she would have got, if she had actually been intending to buy something.

'I can do a special on that one,' the young man said, and quoted quite a decent discount price.

'That's good,' she said. 'I'll think about it.'

'Not for too long though,' he said. 'This is a special for the run-up to Christmas.'

'Oh, I see. But it would be difficult,' she said.

'How come?'

'Well, for a start, I live on the twelfth floor of a block in Finchley.'

'Not a problem. Finchley? We're delivering that way this afternoon.'

'But I won't be there.'

'Neighbour?'

There was Mrs P in the next flat, for whom Kathy often did favours, and who had a key.

'But I have an old bed I'd have to get rid of first.'

'We'll take it away for you. No charge.'

'Really?' That easy. 'Maybe I could . . . but then I'd need bedside cabinets, and reading lamps.'

'I'll show you our range: modern, traditional, cottage style.'

'And new bedding, of course. I'd need completely new bedding.' And about time, she thought.

'Pop into Davis's next door. They've got a huge range there. Pick out what you want and tell them that we're delivering for you this afternoon. We'll fix it up with them.'

Half an hour later Kathy left Davis's feeling rather numb. It was all so amazingly easy. This wasn't like battling through the supermarket or the chain store in the high street on a Saturday morning. This was *shopping*. She felt she'd never really understood before.

There was a vast electrical goods shop further along the mall. There seemed no harm in wandering in, just to get a preliminary idea of what was on the market these days. She had the place to herself. This time two sales assistants fell over each other to serve her. When she came out again, tucking her hot little credit card back in her purse, she made another call to Mrs P, to let her know there would also be a delivery of a new combined washing machine and drier, to be connected on delivery and the old machine taken away, as well as a video/TV, same deal. Oh, and the hair drier and toaster, her old ones being practically antiques. And the waffle maker. She detected a certain avid curiosity from Mrs P, who asked if she might have first refusal on the old stuff.

It was a heady combination, she decided, sex and shopping. She felt oddly elated and exhausted, and thought she'd better sit down calmly somewhere and have a cup of coffee.

She was so dazed that she didn't realise at first that the couple sitting at the next table in the Café de l'Opera were making surreptitious little signals to her. Then she recognised them: the woman with the petition about the music in the mall, together with the tweedy old gent who'd doffed his hat to her when she'd been drinking coffee with Gavin Lowry.

'Oh, hello,' she smiled.

'Would you care to join us?' the little woman asked, and Kathy, remembering the residents' association, thought, why not? I might as well look as if I'm working, instead of daydreaming of Leon naked in that bloody great bed.

'Robbie was just telling me that he'd seen you at the weekend with your husband,' Mrs Rutter beamed, 'and I said that I'd met you with your children, and so we thought, aha!, a new family we should get to know. This is Robbie Orr, by the way, and I'm Harriet Rutter.'

'Kathy Kolla,' she shook their hands, 'and I'd better explain about the family.'

They looked grave but also extremely interested by what Kathy had to tell them.

'Ah!' Mrs Rutter nodded at her companion. 'Of course we saw the officers here yesterday, but there were conflicting rumours going round as to what they were doing, and I was rather too busy with my own work to question them directly.'

'We'll be holding a reconstruction later today, and giving out information to the public. I have some leaflets here, and I wondered if you might like to take them for your members.'

'Of course.'

'Shocking business,' Orr said. Beside Mrs Rutter he looked lanky and craggy and slightly manic, tufts of grizzled hair sticking out of his ears and nostrils and forming the little beard which bobbed up and down as he spoke. 'Was she seen here, then, on the day she disappeared?'

She had his accent now, clipped, Scottish east coast from Edinburgh or Fife.

'That's what we need to establish, Mr Orr. It seems probable from what else we know that she did come here on that afternoon or evening, but we need witnesses.'

'Professor,' Mrs Rutter said.

'Pardon?'

'Robbie is *Professor* Orr,' Mrs Rutter beamed. 'I thought I should let you know, but you must call us Robbie and Harriet.'

'Oh. Thank you.'

'A *highly* distinguished man. A professor of archaeology.'

'Former professor of archaeology, now retired,' he said. 'A mere amateur historian now, and thorn in Boadicea's flesh.'

Harriet burst into more trilling laughter. Kathy guessed that this was rather excessive for her, brought on by Professor Orr's presence.

'I'm sorry, Kathy. You must excuse us. This is one of our little in-jokes. Boadicea is our name for the manager of this shopping centre. A harridan of a woman, whom Robbie puts securely in her place.'

'Her ambition, do you see,' Orr added, acknowledging the compliment with a smile that made his beard jump, 'is to do, in shopping terms, to London and the Home Counties pretty much what Queen Boadicea did to Roman Britain – which is to say, lay it waste.'

More appreciative laughter.

'Boadicea – Bo Seager; yes, very good.' Kathy smiled.

'You know her, do you?' They looked at her in surprise.

'I've met her, yes. And I can see what you mean.'

'Robbie was here before any of us, fighting the good fight. Before the centre was even built.'

'It was my last major project, Kathy – may I call you that? Sergeant seems wrong somehow. Whenever anyone uses the word sergeant I immediately picture my old drill sergeant, the most terrifying man in all the world. Conditioning, I suppose. You're not too terrifying, are you, Kathy?'

His beard gave a playful little leap and Kathy thought, you're a bit of a lad, aren't you, Robbie?

'*Well*, tell Kathy about your work here, Robbie,' Mrs Rutter scolded him.

'Ah yes. Well now, would you be aware of the reason for the name Silvermeadow, Kathy?'

'No, I'm afraid not.'

'It's like this. Do you know that great big ugly structure out there in the upper carpark, with illuminated advertisements for the films showing at the picture house and so on?'

'Yes.'

'It's hard to believe it now, but that used to be the edge of a small wood, a copse really, on the crest of the hill. And one hundred and seventy years ago, a farmer who was ploughing up there, extending his field into the wood, unearthed a hoard of Saxon silver.'

'Really?'

'Aye. It's believed that it was buried by a nobleman fleeing from the Battle of Maldon, which was fought twenty miles east of here. Would you be familiar with the Battle of Maldon from your schooldays, Kathy?'

'Er, don't think I am. Must have been asleep during that one.'

'Shame on you!' he teased. 'Not a huge battle by modern standards, of course, but a great battle for its time all the same, between the Saxons and the Viking horde. I'm talking here of the *true* Battle of Maldon, of AD nine ninety-one, not the *legendary* battle of nine ninety-four, said to have lasted for fourteen days.'

'Right.'

'Aye. Well, anyway, these shopping centre people had no knowledge of the origin of the name. They merely noticed it on their maps as Silvermeadow Hill, and I suppose the combination of images that it conjured up, of hard cash on the one hand and a pastoral fairyland on the other, must have had a strong appeal to them.'

He arched one bushy eyebrow at her, a slightly manic gleam developing in his eye as he made the point. 'Their choice of name was completely cynical, of course, suggesting that their monstrous new construction had some sort of connection with this place. I'm quite sure they never even considered whether this miserable little hill might have had a history at all. To them, it was merely a suitably positioned piece of real estate that might as well have been in Illinois or Manitoba.

'But the place did have a history, you see. For after the battle one of the Saxon noblemen and his party were pursued here by the victorious Vikings, as rapacious for silver as the developers of this shopping centre. Indeed, I have no doubt there is a strong genetic connection.'

'What happened?'

'The Saxon party arrived here in the late afternoon, exhausted and demoralised, and buried their precious silver in the wood. Then they came down here, where we are now, in the lee of the hill, and made a fire and a camp for the night. They must have thought themselves safe from pursuit. But the Norsemen had not given up, and with the first dawn light they swept over the hill and descended on the Saxons like wolves, slaughtering them, every one.' Orr paused for effect, sweeping his hand about him. 'Eight men and boys, all murdered here, their corpses buried on the spot. Here they lay, undisturbed, for precisely one thousand years.' He leant towards Kathy and fixed her with a wild stare. '*Precisely*, mind you, that's the uncanny thing. One millennium, to the day, perhaps the very hour, until they were disturbed by a bulldozer beginning the construction of this place.'

Kathy nodded, imagining the effect of his theatrical story-telling on his lady admirers in the Silvermeadow Residents' Association.

'Well, they had to stop, of course, as soon as the skeletons came to light. A proper archaeological assessment had to be made. I was nearby, at the local university, and this was my period, the Viking incursions. I lived here on the site for months, in those site huts you can still see round the east end of the building, with a team of volunteers, students and young people from all over, trying to establish what else was here before they chewed it up in their great machines.'

The imagery struck Kathy as oddly apt, given what had happened to Kerri Vlasich. But then the whole of Orr's tale, with his rather exultant account of past murder, had an uncomfortable resonance with Kerri's death.

'And was there anything else?'

'No. Oh there were a few surprises beneath the ground for them – a hidden spring, a pocket of sand – but nothing for me. My volunteers left at the end of that first summer, but I returned, from time to time. The construction workers got to know me, the mad professor.' He chuckled, eyes twinkling. 'They adopted me, like a mascot, an old goat.'

'And now he's one of us,' Mrs Rutter said. 'One of our most distinguished members.'

'Oh now Harriet . . .' he admonished her.

'You must enjoy coming here,' Kathy said.

'I should describe it as a love-hate relationship,' she said. 'It's terribly convenient, and comfortable, and we meet all our friends here. But it's also very crass, of course, so *commercial*.'

'It's worse than that, Harriet. It's deadening, it feeds on life.'

'How do you mean?' Kathy asked.

'I mean that it feeds on all the real places around here, all the real towns and villages that have been steadily growing and developing for a thousand years, and are now having the life-blood sucked out of them by this great hulking *parasite*!' His eyes blazed at the word. 'And I also mean that it takes the life out of people, too. It is an offence against our natures, Kathy. It sanitises us, deodorises us, and turns us into shadows. Look at them!' he roared, sweeping an upturned hand like a claw towards the shoppers meandering past. 'It's turning a warrior race, the hammer of the Scots, the butchers of the Welsh and Irish, the ravagers of half the globe, into a docile herd of consumers who care for nothing but woolly jumpers and soft music.'

Harriet Rutter gave a delighted chuckle. 'And yet we keep coming back, do we not, Robbie?'

'Aye,' he nodded, calm again, wiping some spittle from his chin. 'We keep coming back. The only thing that can be said for it is that: just as it has no past, so it also has no future. It didn't grow out of anything that was here before and nothing will grow out of it; it will not age or acquire the patina of time, and no archaeologist will ever excavate its ruins; for when its usefulness is over its owners, caring nothing for it, will simply bulldoze it, sweep it away, and not a trace of it will remain.'

Brock was taking an early working lunch, munching a pie while he worked through the piles of reports covering his table. Kathy spotted a Sainsbury's bag by his chair.

'I'm getting bogged down, Kathy,' he complained. 'Buried in paper.'

'Sorry, you should let me do that,' she said, guilty at her morning lapse. She still couldn't quite believe that she'd bought all that stuff. On impulse.

'No, no. I want you out there, finding out about the girl. There's a lot about Miss Kerri Vlasich that we don't know, I'd say. You all right?'

'Yes. Why?'

'Just thought you looked a bit . . . distant. Phil thinks you might be going down with something.'

Going down with something. Well, it did feel a bit like that.

'No, I'm fine, really. Why don't you get Gavin Lowry to do it then?'

'He's the one shovelling most of it onto my desk,' Brock said, thoughtful. 'Yes, you're right. He can do this. He elected himself to meet the father at Gatwick this afternoon, but we should go. We'll bring him here for the walk-through. Watch his reaction.'

'Good idea.'

'You missed our SIO's visit,' Brock said dryly.

'Oh dear.'

'Never mind. You'll see him on TV tonight. He's made a public statement, appealing for information. You do have a TV, don't you?'

'Yes, of course. Gavin isn't loading the chief super down with paperwork, then?'

Brock smiled. 'Too nimble on his feet for that, is our Orville. I get the impression he knows Gavin pretty well. He was highly amused when I brought up Gavin's little worry about reporting direct to him. Said he'd only asked him to let him know if we were short of anything. Didn't want me to get the impression they were penny-pinching.'

Stefan Vlasich showed little reaction to anything when they picked him up at the airport. He had broad, impassive Slavic features, and seemed determined to show no signs of emotion. He'd been working in the forests near Jaroslaw in eastern Poland, near the Ukraine border, he growled, staring stolidly at the Surrey countryside flashing past the patrol car window. Communications had not been good. It had taken longer than it should have to get him back to Warsaw and catch a plane. How long had he been there, in the forests? He swivelled his blank eyes round at Brock and said, 'Four weeks. Almost five. Living night and day in a camp with twenty others, laying pipeline. The police spoke to the supervisors. They confirmed it, didn't they? What, you think I came over here and killed my own daughter?'

'We'll have to go over all this in a formal interview, Mr Vlasich,' Brock said. 'I'm sorry, but it's necessary for the record. But tell me now, will you? I'm curious. You really had no idea at all that your daughter was planning to visit you?'

Kathy was in the front passenger seat, next to the police driver, Brock and Vlasich in the back, Vlasich directly behind her so that she had to swivel right round to see his face.

'No. No idea,' he said, and turned away to watch the slip road curve onto the M25.

They crossed the Thames through the Dartford tunnel and emerged into the flat industrial wastes of Essex, and Kathy tried to imagine an earlier landscape, of marshes and Saxon hamlets, without success.

'Are you taking me to see her?' Vlasich asked heavily.

Brock replied, 'Later, Mr Vlasich.'

They passed Junction 29, and then the driver began signalling his turn, and Vlasich said, 'Where are we?' Then, seeing the Silvermeadow sign, 'What is this?'

'We're calling in here first, Mr Vlasich,' Brock said. 'It's possible that Kerri died here.'

The vast carpark panorama opened up as the slip road reached the crest.

'What?' There was a note of sudden alarm in Vlasich's voice, the more startling after its persistent monotone.

Kathy twisted round in her seat, but her attention was caught by Brock's expression as he studied the other man, watchful, attentive, the hunter's focus in his eyes.

'She worked here, you know,' Brock said, sounding the same as before. 'We're staging a walk-through with someone who looks like Kerri. We'd like you to witness it, if you wouldn't mind. Is that all right?'

Kathy turned to look at Vlasich. He was staring at the long low bulk of the building ahead. 'No . . . I don't want . . . I won't do this. I don't want to go in there.'

'I can understand it might be distressing for you,' Brock said carefully, sounding more curious than sympathetic. 'But your observations might help us. You may recognize someone. Something might jog your memory, about something Kerri might have said, or hinted.'

'No way!' Vlasich said, almost in a panic. 'You turn round this fucking car right now!'

Brock considered him silently for a moment, then turned to the driver and murmured something. The car drew to a halt. 'Kathy,' Brock said, 'you'd best stay here and meet the girls when they arrive. I'll take Mr Vlasich to Hornchurch Street to make a formal statement.'

'Fine,' Kathy said, and looked again at the dead girl's father. His face was as grey as the weeping sky.

Brock had told Kathy of his concern that the re-enactment might be lost among the shopping crowds at Silvermeadow, but it was clear, as soon as the police car pulled up at the west mall entrance, that the radio and poster publicity had ensured this was going to be the big event of the afternoon, if not the shopping week. A crowd of people was waiting as Lisa and Naomi stepped out, like stars arriving for a guest appearance. They walked forward to the doors, then hesitated at all this attention: the people strained forward, a TV cameraman backing away in front of them, lights and microphone suspended over their heads.

Kathy came to Lisa's side and whispered encouragement. She looked very pale as she drew herself up and set off again, face set, striding forward, her hair pulled back in a ponytail tied up in a scarlet and green ribbon, as Kerri's had probably been, the green backpack bobbing conspicuously between her shoulders. There had been doubts about whether Lisa should do this, whether it might be distressing for her to play the part of her murdered friend, but when it had been raised with her she had been adamant. It was her duty to Kerri, she had said through tears. Kerri wouldn't want anyone else to do it.

Once in the mall it seemed to Kathy that the cavalcade took on the character of a royal progress, with lines of shoppers forming up on each side of the route in front of the advancing party, Harry Jackson's security guards forging the way ahead, small kids running along the outside to stir up the stragglers. A second local TV news camera crew joined the procession, then another. Shoppers got to their feet at the café tables as they passed, and lined the balcony rails overhead. Kathy noticed how the girls seemed to become more confident. When they reached the C&A windows they paused, positioning themselves advantageously in front of the cameras, and put on a show of window-shopping while the crowd stood attentively silent all around.

They moved on down the mall and the music on the PA system cut out so that a voice could inform everyone what was happening, the programme notes to a real-life tragedy. The music resumed, an upbeat number, just as it had a week before, and the cavalcade moved forward towards the escalators and surged down into the rain forest and through the food court. It was obvious that the crush would never make it through the narrower spaces of the Bazaar, and the PA system came on again to announce that the re-enactment was now at an end and that police officers would be ready at tables strategically positioned throughout the centre to hear from witnesses, their tables identifiable by enlarged photographs of Kerri's smiling face. At the same time, all stalls in the food court would be offering a ten per cent discount on food purchases made before six p.m., twenty per cent on family specials.

Kathy took the girls back to the patrol car waiting to take them home. Lisa was subdued, but Naomi seemed almost serene as she turned to Kathy at the car door and said, 'Same time tomorrow, then?'

'Yes, thank you, Naomi. We really appreciate it.' And she added, though afterwards she wondered if it had been a bit mawkish, 'Kerri would be grateful too, for what you've done.'

She tapped in her security code at the door to the service area, getting a little buzz from the recollection of Leon giving her his number. So long ago it seemed, before everything happened, before she had even imagined that it could happen. She was impatient to leave, to pick him up in Lambeth as they'd arranged, but there were things that had to be done.

Sharon gave her a wave from her console in the security centre as she came in. Speedy was working at another table, on what looked like a video-editing machine, with images flashing past on the screen in front of him. He spotted her reflection in his screen and turned to her with a big toothy smile. 'Yo, Sergeant!' he called.

'Hello Speedy,' Kathy said, surprised at this welcome, wondering what had put him in such a good mood.

'Your tape's ready, babe,' he said. 'All done.'

'Thanks. We appreciate it.' Bo Seager had arranged for Speedy to compile a tape of the walk-through from his monitors for Brock to view when he returned from Hornchurch Street.

'Ms Seager said if you want you can use the video machine in her office,' Sharon said. 'The office'll be open till late.'

'Great. We might do that. It gets rather hectic in the unit.' Kathy took the tape that Speedy offered her and turned to go.

'Oh, and I've got this as well,' Speedy said, reaching for a second tape in a sealed box.

'What's that?'

'It's some odds and ends I found,' Speedy said, grinning rather wildly. He's on something, she thought. 'Just stuff from the monitors. But I thought there might be something there of use to you. You never know.'

'Really? You think it could help us? Maybe I should leave this for my boss too.'

'Oh, no.' He sniggered as if at some private joke. 'Have a look at it yourself first, babe, before you show him. Decide whether it's worth a wider audience.'

There was something about the way he put it that she didn't like.

Maybe it's a dirty movie, she thought. Maybe this is Speedy's way of flashing.

'Okay. I'll do that.'

'Yeah.' He grinned, and turned away. 'You do that, *babe*.'

She turned to Sharon, who shrugged and gave her a look that said, that's Speedy for you.

Kathy returned to the unit and phoned Brock. He was on his way back, he told her, having spent over an hour interviewing Stefan Vlasich, which hadn't been very helpful. The man's composure had been reimposed, his answers short and unilluminating. When pressed about his reaction to going into Silvermeadow he claimed that he had been unable to face the sight of another child playing the role of his little girl, but Brock knew that his panic had started before he had mentioned the walk-through. There was something odd there all right. Then they had gone to the morgue, where the people had done their best to make one side of Kerri's face presentable. Stefan Vlasich had stared through the window at the small shrouded figure of his daughter without a flicker of reaction.

'What about the walk-through?' Brock asked. 'How did it go?'

'Fine. The girls did it very well. We've had a lot of reports from members of the public who say they knew Kerri by sight, but no one who can be specific about the sixth. The walk-through itself was like a circus. There's a tape of it here for you to see, if you want. There's a machine in the centre management offices, and they say they'll be open till late if you want a bit of peace and quiet.'

'Okay. Why don't you go home now, Kathy? Get to bed early tonight. Boss's orders.'

Kathy hesitated. 'I'd like that,' she said, with a little smile.

She drove into central London, phoning him on the way, so that he was waiting under the arch of the railway bridge when she arrived. He put the carrier bags he was carrying into the back and slipped in quickly beside her, and they grabbed each other as if their whole day had been spent waiting in furious impatience for this moment, which it had.

'God,' he whispered. 'I've missed you. I can't believe how much.'

'Me too. Home?'

'Yes please.'

'What did you tell your mum and dad?'

'I'm staying with a friend. We're thinking of getting a place together.'

'How did they take that?'

'Fine. They seemed pleased.'

'Did you specify the gender of the friend?'

'No, and they didn't ask. Funny really.'

Kathy pulled out into the traffic and turned north, heading for Vauxhall Bridge. 'Have you been shopping?' she asked, nodding over her shoulder at the bags in the back.

'Just a few things for you. Food, a couple of bottles, one or two little things for the kitchen. You're not offended, are you?'

She laughed. 'Course not. What sort of little things?'

He reached back for one of the bags and brought them out: pepper and salt grinders, a corkscrew, two eggcups and a thing for drizzling olive oil.

'*Drizzling* olive oil! Wow.'

'You're sure you're not offended?'

'Not in the least. I did a bit of shopping today too.'

'What did you get?'

'That's a surprise.'

Brock took the video down the mall to the centre management offices. The door was locked, but Bo Seager answered his knock. Her mood seemed much changed from the previous evening, relaxed and welcoming. She took the tape from him and put it in the machine, sat him down and offered him a malt.

'That does sound tempting,' he said. 'Just a small one, thanks, Ms Seager.'

'Bo, please.' She smiled. 'I'm sorry if we sounded kinda belligerent last night. David, isn't it? Frankly, we were nervous about the impact of all this. And I guess Nathan Tindall felt he had to make a point.'

'He did that all right.'

'Nathan believes in covering all the angles. That way he may well end up with my job, if and when I mess things up good and proper.' She said it lightly, as if it was to be taken as a joke. 'Cheers.'

'Cheers. So you feel less nervous now . . . Bo?'

'After the way the walk-through went today, I feel we may have to make a big donation to the police widows fund, or whatever. Oh dear, you're frowning at my tastelessness. Sorry.'

'That's all right. So it didn't put your customers off?'

'Quite the opposite! It seems a murder is a much bigger draw than Santa Claus. Isn't that interesting? I might give a paper on it to the next marketing conference. Look, I'll show you.'

She reached for the remote and sat back, crossing her long dark legs in a way that Brock found momentarily distracting. Then the screen came to life with a scene like a triumphal parade.

'Good grief!' Brock muttered.

There was no doubt that Speedy Reynolds had flair, heightening the drama of the occasion with rapid switches from camera to camera, distant shots alternating with close-ups, panning and zooming like a professional.

'He's good, isn't he?' Bo said. 'Speedy, I mean. He does it really well.'

'Good grief,' Brock repeated, shaking his head as the edited film came to an end.

'What's the matter?' Bo asked him.

'It's a bloody circus!'

'You look shocked.'

He shook his head. 'No, not really. We uncover a body in the woods, or a plane comes down somewhere, and suddenly the lanes are full of cars, like blowflies homing in on the smell of death. But still, this is something, isn't it? Carnival time.'

'Oh, come on! You called them here! You wanted them to take an interest. Then you sit back and call them blowflies!'

He saw that she was teasing him, and he smiled back. 'Yes, well, you don't seem to be wasting the opportunity – ten per cent discounts on food in the food court? And it all seems to be doing great things for your turnover – the carparks look pretty full.'

'Fifty per cent up on a normal Monday evening, I'd say. You're disapproving again, but seriously, I wonder why you object to people showing their interest in their own way? Who's to say what's responsible interest and what's morbid? Me, I prefer to take people just as they are.'

'Then you'd probably make a good copper, Bo.'

'No, a good shopping centre manager – much more rewarding, financially anyway. And more than financially. I don't know how you can spend your life digging about exposing the shit in life. I prefer to wrap it all up in gorgeous gift paper and sell it for a bomb. I guess it's basically a difference of philosophy.'

'Is that so?' he said. 'Philosophy, eh?' He finished his drink and she reached across with the bottle, ignoring his shake of the head.

'Sure. You're a liberal, right? You adore positive logic, and you have a certain political awareness, which maybe is the conscience of the privileged. You want to have things verified, and at the same time help the less fortunate. It's very old-fashioned.'

'Thank you,' Brock grunted. He had heard this lecture before, and wasn't really in the mood for it again.

'Winston Starkey, for instance, the black guy who runs the games arcade, who your officers were hassling.'

'I am pursuing that, don't worry. If they were in the wrong, they'll pay, believe me.'

'Oh, I do. You've been talking to him, yes?'

'I went and had a word with him this morning, yes. You're well informed, Bo.'

'Naturally. But actually he came and told me so himself. He believes that some of the other traders and our security guys – all white, of course – have it in for him. Put your people up to it.'

'He's probably right. What's your point?'

'My point is that you want to believe the best of him, because of what he is: black and gay and kinda dumb. Whereas I don't.'

'Don't you?'

'No. If he's up to anything, and especially if it's drugs, I want you to hit him hard. And I'm black and wear gold jewellery too.'

'Fair enough.'

Bo smiled. 'Your sergeants have a more modern philosophy.'

'Have they really?'

'Sure. They're not like you, they're classless, thank God.'

Brock frowned at his glass, feeling tired.

She mistook his expression and said quickly, 'Sorry, David, no offence to you. I just find this English class thing *so* boring.'

'I know . . .' He decided he'd better let her have her fun. 'I thought I was fairly classless, actually.'

'Sure,' she laughed. 'Middle-classless. I'm not sure whether it's upper-middle-classless or middle-middle-classless, but that's because I'm a foreigner. If I were English I'd know for sure within ten seconds of you opening your mouth which kind of classless you were. Now the tough guy, what's his name?'

'Lowry.'

'Yes. He's a contemporary, post-Thatcher, English type, I'd say.'

'How's that?'

'Oh, hungry, devious, prepared to do whatever it takes.'

'I think that's just style, Bo. Posturing. We all do it, in our different ways. Reassures us that we aren't completely beholden to the chief super' – he eyed her over the rim of his glass – 'or the finance manager.'

She flinched, then smiled and continued, ignoring his little barb. 'Your other sergeant, Kathy, is different. I like her. She's kind of intense, but interesting. Not too politically sophisticated, I'd guess, but she's very keen on catching bad guys. She thinks in her own way. You tell her one thing, she'll try something else. Am I right?'

'Pretty much, yes. Intense, you think?'

'Yes, but I think there's a fairly straightforward reason for that.'

'I work her too hard?'

Bo laughed. 'No. I'd say ... it's just a guess. I'd say she needs a good screw. You look surprised. Am I right?'

Brock took another swallow of his drink while he considered that. 'Quite possibly. I didn't think you'd really seen much of her.'

'Oh, I read people quickly, David. And I have talked to her, as a matter of fact. We bumped into each other this morning. She wanted to know about our archaeologist.'

'Your what?'

Bo laughed. 'One of our local fruitcakes. He first showed up when we started building here. Early on, when they disturbed the ground, they hit something bad.' She leant forward, eyes bright, and whispered, 'Bones.'

'Bones?'

She nodded. 'Human remains.'

Brock sat up sharply, pushing out of his mind the extraordinary way her broad lips formed the first syllable of 'human'.

'Human? How the hell didn't I know about this?'

'They were kind of old.'

'But still . . .'

'Like, a thousand years old.' She laughed. 'It was really bad news, because of course the archaeologists had to be told, and for six months they were here, off and on, digging around the place, getting in everybody's way. We were terrified they'd find a Roman city or something, but all they ever found were those bones. Eventually they all left, all except this local fruitcake, a professor of archaeology, who'd been helping them. He's still here, haunting the place, mainly I think so he can lord it over the elderly matrons of the locality, who fuss over him and give him treats. Kathy bumped into him with one of those ladies in the mall, and came to find out from me what they were on about.'

'I see. She didn't mention it to me. Which reminds me that I've got a pile of reports to read before I go home.' He sighed and got to his feet. 'Thanks for the use of your video, and the drink, and the assessment of my team. It was all most enlightening.'

'You're not cross with me, are you? About the class thing?'

'No, not at all. Although it did make me feel a little old.'

'Well, you know the best way to stay young, don't you?'

He never heard the answer to that because her phone started ringing, but from the look she gave him as he left he guessed that sex came into it somewhere.

Kathy opened her front door with some trepidation, expecting a mess, but between them Mrs P and the delivery men had managed things remarkably well. There, facing them, where the battered old brown box of her TV had been, was an impressive black electronic presence winking a small red light at them to tell them it was alive and ready to go. Over to the left, through the door of the kitchenette, she could see other gleaming new friends, while the transformation in the bedroom was even more impressive.

'When did you manage this?' Leon gasped, astonished.

In the vast spaces of the showroom the bed had seemed quite moderate in scale, but now, in the small bedroom, it looked huge. There was barely room to move around it, or open the built-in wardrobe door.

'Is it too big?' Kathy said, feeling a twinge of loss for her old narrow bed.

Leon shook his head. 'Hell no. What's a bedroom for?'

They unpacked the bedding stacked neatly at the foot, and made up the bed, adjusting to its dimensions. Then Kathy checked her watch and said, 'Let's see if we can get the TV to work. Forbes is making a press statement.'

She was astonished at the clarity of the picture, the subtle flesh tones that made the people on the screen look and sound like humans instead of plastic puppets. And Chief Superintendent Forbes filled these new dimensions like a seasoned performer, voice resonant, gaze steady, as he appealed for public assistance. The pictures of the girl wearing the frog bag, and of Kerri herself, leapt out into the room.

When it was over, they switched off and unpacked the food and wine that Leon had bought.

'I'll get plates and glasses,' Kathy said, and handed the remote to Leon. 'See if you can figure out how to work the video. One of the security guys at Silvermeadow gave me a tape he said I'd want to see. We can try it out.'

When she returned a few minutes later Leon was standing staring at the screen, transfixed. 'Who did you say gave you this thing?' he said.

'Oh, don't tell me it's tacky.'

'Look.' He rewound the tape and began it again as she came to his side.

It was hard at first to make it out: a night scene, the camera dazzled by a car's headlights, then tracking after it, across a dark wasteland. The car stopped, some way away, and the camera zoomed slowly in on it as a figure got out and began cleaning the windscreen.

'Hang on . . .' Kathy said.

A second figure had got out of the car, the picture brightening and becoming clearer as the camera zoomed closer and adjusted to the lighting levels. The second figure moved to the side of the first. They turned towards each other, and after a moment's hesitation they began to kiss. By the time they broke apart, their upper bodies and heads were large in the screen and clearly identifiable.

'Hell . . .' Kathy breathed. 'That's us.'

The picture jumped: a new scene, bright lights, the camera panning across a shopfront, stopping, then zooming in on a woman lying on a bed, shoes off, bouncing, then sitting up with a self-conscious smirk on her face.

'The bastard . . .' Kathy whispered. 'The creepy little bastard.'

The screen went blank.

Afterwards Kathy tried to recall what had gone through her head. She remembered the stories of people who wouldn't let travellers take their photographs for fear that some part of them would be stolen, and for the first time she understood what they meant. She did feel robbed, intruded upon, assaulted, and the fact that she had no physical damage to show for it only somehow made it more insidious. And she also understood for the first time the fuss that people made about surveillance cameras, which up until then had seemed neutral, even benign.

But it was Speedy that most bothered her, the hand controlling the camera, the intention behind the electronic eye. The way he had giggled and squirmed when he handed her the tape, and called her 'babe'.

'I'll knock the bastard's head off,' Leon said.

'That wouldn't look good. He's a cripple, confined to a chair.'

'Why's he done it? He's obviously trying to embarrass you.'

Kathy tried to remember exactly what he'd said, something about looking at it before she decided whether it was 'worth a wider audience', and she felt a cold chill creep over her skin.

'He couldn't exactly blackmail me with it, could he?' she said. 'Just make me look stupid. Bouncing on a bed at the height of a murder inquiry. I *feel* bloody stupid. Imagine if Brock saw it!'

Leon put an arm round her shoulders. 'How many days off have you had in the last month? I don't think you have to feel guilty about buying a bed. I don't think you need to feel guilty about anything.'

'No.' But that was the result all the same. It made you feel guilty, so you'd be looking over your shoulder next time.

It had a dampening effect on the rest of the evening, and Kathy found herself making sure the lights were off, the curtains drawn and the door to the sitting room closed before she took off her clothes and slid under the new duvet with Leon.

Brock, too, felt on edge as he cooked some pasta for his dinner. Partly it was the lonely sound of rain spattering against the kitchen window, partly Bo Seager's conversation, but mostly it was a matter of timing. The machine had been organised and set in motion, so far without result. Data was being amassed, but key pieces were missing, forensic most of all. There would be action soon enough, but not yet. There was no point beating the table about it. It was only a matter of timing. It would come.

He really wanted to ring Suzanne, but thought it might be a bit soon after their last conversation. Not good to sound pushy. And then he thought of Bo Seager's explanation for Kathy's air of intensity, and smiled. If only things were that simple. Kathy was surely driven by deeper demons than that. Although, now he came to think of it, she had seemed different that day. Calm. Almost euphoric. Probably the anticipation of a fresh case.

He opened a bottle of red, drizzled some olive oil on a chunk of bread, and sat down to eat. When he was finished he put his feet up and dialled a number on his phone.

'Suzanne?'

'David! I'm glad you called. I wasn't sure when to ring you, with your new case. How is it?'

'Just getting started.'

'I saw someone on TV tonight. A rather pompous man in uniform, talking about a murdered girl. Is that your case?'

'You've got it. Probably abducted from one of those big new shopping centres.'

'Silvermeadow, yes, I've read about that place. I'd love to see it. Do you like it?'

'Not my cup of tea. Huge place, a sort of shopping fantasyland.'

'*The Ladies' Paradise*.'

'What's that?'

'It's a book. Zola. About a wonderful new department store that takes over Paris. I'll lend you my copy if I can find it.'

'Thanks. How are your plans?'

'Our trip? Well, I've got dates for a pantomime, *Peter Pan*. Will you come with us?'

'Certainly. I always had a soft spot for Captain Hook.'

'Oh. That's interesting.'

'And accommodation?'

'The place I'd had recommended is booked up. I'm trying somewhere else.'

'You're daft. I told you what to do. Stay here. It'll be so much simpler.'

'The children will wreck your calm sanctum, David. You'd hate it. We'd end up fighting.'

'Rubbish. Anyway, maybe I need my calm sanctum being shaken up a bit. You can get too set in your ways, I'm told.'

'Your job does all the shaking up you need. Two small children . . .'

'Bugger the children, Suzanne. I'd like *you* to stay here. Just to try.'

'Ah . . . Well, put like that, so eloquently, I'd have to give it serious thought.'

'Exactly.'

Later, on the edge of sleep, a chain of thoughts passed through his mind. He had to force himself awake to reconstruct it. It went something like this: pantomime – improbable characters (Widow

Twankey, Captain Hook, etc.) – the improbable Italian, Bruno Verdi, in the food court – the joke about Guiseppe Verdi not being such a great composer if he'd been called the English equivalent of his name, plain Joe Green – they were checking Bruno Verdi, but what about Bernie Green? Then he'd fallen deeply asleep.

7

Kathy went straight to the security centre the following morning, wanting to have it out with Speedy Reynolds, but a different man, one she hadn't seen before, was operating the cameras, and Harry Jackson came out of his office to tell her that Speedy wasn't back on shift until that afternoon.

'You get the daybooks all right, Kathy?' he said.

'Yes, great. Thanks for that, Harry.'

'Anything else I can do, just shout. Any results yet from yesterday's bunfight?'

'The walk-through? No, nothing definite.'

'Better luck this afternoon, eh?' He seemed remarkably relaxed and jovial today.

She left him and went up to the unit to start work on the reports that had accumulated from the previous evening. As she entered the upper mall she was aware of something going on, people standing looking upwards, pointing, and when she stopped she saw that a small bird, a sparrow, had somehow got into the centre and was now flitting about distractedly beneath the vault, beating against the glass.

Towards lunchtime she took a call from Leon. They confirmed their arrangements to meet that evening, and then he asked to be put through to Brock. Kathy could tell from his tone that he had something.

'He's at a meeting at the Yard, Leon,' she said. 'We're expecting him back shortly. Can I take a message?'

'Yes, you'll be interested in this, Kathy. We've just got the first toxicology results from Kerri's autopsy back from the lab. They've been having a bit of bother because of the time interval since her death, but this is something. I'll fax the report through now. It's quite technical, but basically it's about her hair.'

Hair, it seemed, provided a special kind of record of the body's chemistry. At its point of growth, it absorbed traces of the body's chemical responses to any antigens that might have found their way into the system. Growing at the rate of around twelve millimetres a month, hair of the length of Kerri's represented a couple of years' record of body chemistry, a print-out of specific bodily responses to antigens, and in particular drugs. Her hair, in effect, provided a two-year record of her drug history.

From this it appeared that Kerri had been experimenting with something, probably Ecstasy, over something like a four-month period before her death. In addition, the millimetre of hair closest to the root showed that in the final days of her life she had taken substantial amounts of an unknown antigen.

'She was drugged?' Kathy asked.

'Drugged or drugging.'

'Will they be able to identify it?'

'The hair doesn't carry traces of the drug itself, only of the body's chemical response to it, so they can't always tell. But they may have something later today or tomorrow.'

Leon's information made Kathy impatient to act, but she thought Brock would want to be involved, and his meeting was lasting longer than planned. While she waited, Kathy moved on from the reports, which held nothing new, to Harry's daybooks, sitting untouched on the table. She began working backwards through the latest one without enthusiasm. Having already skimmed it once she expected to find nothing, but she forced herself to it, almost as a kind of penance for her shopping spree the day before.

Since she had the photocopies she had made in the security room, she used them to mark items of possible interest with a coloured marker as she went, reading from the original books whose entries were more legible. It was only because she used this method that she came across the missing page. At first, when she turned up a photocopied sheet that didn't correspond to the next daybook page, she thought she'd got the loose photocopies out of sequence. But when she checked the dates she found she had two extra photocopied sheets, covering a week in the middle of August, for which there were no book entries. She would never have detected the missing page otherwise, because it had been sliced out with such care, so close to the binding, that its stub was invisible. It must have been removed sometime between Sunday afternoon, when Kathy had photocopied it, and Monday morning, when the books had been delivered to unit 184.

What made it odder was that there seemed to be nothing of interest in the missing entries. They recorded a mild heart attack on the Monday, nothing on Tuesday, two cars broken into in the carpark on Wednesday, a confused woman taken home on the Thursday, and some graffiti sprayed on one of the perimeter signs on the Friday night. All in all, a typical, uneventful Silvermeadow week.

Brock was very interested in Desai's report, and he and Kathy decided to drive over to speak to Kerri's mother again. A social worker was with her this time, and she was much more composed than before, but still very pale and fragile.

'I think it helped, seeing Kerri,' she whispered. 'I knew then that it was true that she was dead. It helped me to face it. Has Stefan been to see her?'

'Yes,' Brock said. 'You haven't seen him?'

'No. I heard he was over here, but we won't see each other, except at the funeral.' She turned quickly away and wiped a hand across her eyes. 'Did you want to ask me something?'

'Yes. It isn't an easy thing to raise with you, Mrs Vlasich, especially so soon, but I think we must.'

'Oh . . .' The woman lowered her eyes to the carpet and waited without expression for whatever was coming.

'Kerri was a sociable girl, I remember you saying, Mrs Vlasich. And I suppose she and her friends would go to parties and so on.'

Alison Vlasich gave an uncertain shrug.

'And I daresay that Kerri was, like all kids, trying things, experimenting, eh? They have to try smoking, don't they, and alcohol? And these days other things too.'

She looked up warily. 'What are you saying?'

'What I'm saying is,' he said gently, 'that we know Kerri had been experimenting with drugs for some time, several months, and we'd like to know a bit more about that.'

Mrs Vlasich put her hand to her mouth, shaking her head.

'It may have nothing to do with her death, but we need to be sure. Can you help us?'

He let her take her time, and eventually she said, 'I didn't know.'

'Not even a guess? A hint?'

She shook her head. 'But I was always afraid. It's what you hear, isn't it? Teenagers, round here especially. I used to ask her at first, when she started going out: do the others take drugs, Kerri? She always said no. She didn't like me asking though, said it was stupid, and so after a while I stopped.' Her voice trailed away. Then she blinked as if an uncomfortable thought had just surfaced. 'She never had any money. She didn't earn a lot at the food court, but I never really knew what she spent it on. She never brought any home.' Another long silence, then, 'You should speak to her friends, to Naomi and Lisa. They might know.'

Brock nodded. 'We're going to ask them. But it's just possible that we may have overlooked something that Kerri left behind here. I know we have already had a good look at her room, but we didn't know then what we know now, so we'd like to check your flat again, with your permission.'

Mrs Vlasich agreed, and they spent an hour going through the place again, but found nothing. If Kerri Vlasich had possessed drugs at the time of her death she most probably had taken them with her.

Naomi hadn't yet returned home from school, so her grandparents invited Brock and Kathy to come in to wait for her.

'They're coping as well as might be expected,' Mrs Tait said. 'Poor Lisa is taking it especially hard. She says she'll never go back to Silvermeadow when this is over. She's going to give up her job there. Naomi doesn't show it so much, on the surface . . .'

'Sterner stuff,' her husband muttered.

'But underneath she's shattered too, I can tell.'

They listened in sombre silence to what Brock had to say, and didn't seem surprised by his suggestion that Kerri had been using drugs.

'I don't think poor Alison can really have been surprised,' Mrs Tait said eventually. 'It's everywhere these days. So hard for the children to avoid.'

'Especially over there in *Primrose*,' Jack Tait growled.

'Everywhere, Jack. We, of all people, know that.' She looked steadily at Brock and said quietly, 'That was how our daughter, Naomi's mother, died, you see. She tried so hard, but she kept going back to it. Things would get her down, and then she would go back to it. You know, don't you? You must see it every day.'

Brock nodded. 'Yes.'

'A scourge,' Mr Tait said. 'A curse.'

'And now Kimberley, Naomi's elder sister, is in the same trouble.' She glanced across at the photographs on the wall. 'The one on the left.' To Kathy it seemed as if the family portraits were taking on the character of a gallery of missing persons, or perhaps a shrine. Brock got up and looked at the pictures dutifully.

'Always like her mother,' Mr Tait said.

'I'm sorry,' Brock said.

'So we can understand how Alison must feel. But was it a serious problem? Kerri was so young. Did it contribute in some way—'

'We're not sure yet. We need to find out as much as we can about it.'

'Yes, well, Naomi may know something.' Mrs Tait stopped and looked fixedly at Brock. 'You're wondering, aren't you, about Naomi? You're wondering if she's in the same boat? Well I can tell you straight away, she's not. Naomi has not touched drugs.'

Brock shrugged. 'Well, I know how difficult it is to be sure—'

'No.' She shook her head determinedly. 'I know. We've been through it twice already. We know the signs all too well, believe me, Chief Inspector. We had it all from our daughter: the little lies to borrow money, the money gone from your purse, the strange phone calls at odd hours, things missing from the house, the moods. We got to know those signs very well. And when Kimberley started we knew straight away, although she denied it till she was blue in the face and convinced everyone else, her sisters included, everyone except Jack and me. And Naomi's seen it too, and she knows what happens. She's not like Kimberley. She won't end up the same way.'

'She never borrows no money,' Jack Tait said, leaning forward to emphasise the point. 'She saves every penny of her work money. Every penny.'

'It must be tough for you both,' Brock said.

'You cope, don't you? You have to. We'd had our dreams of what we'd do when Jack retired, go live by the sea near our friends. But that wasn't to be. We were needed here, to look after our grandchildren.'

'This'll give you some idea what our Naomi's like,' Jack Tait said. He got stiffly to his feet and went over to the mantelpiece and lifted a piece of paper out of a bowl. He handed it to Brock proudly. It was a lottery ticket. 'Once a month she buys us one of these out of her pay from the sandwich shop. She says, one day we'll win, and we'll be able to buy a house in Westcliff big enough for us all. And she believes it too.'

They heard the front door bang and the sounds of Naomi discarding her bag and coat in the hall.

Her reaction to Brock's questions was almost a mirror of her grandparents. She nodded sadly, and said she knew that Kerri had been trying things – speed, she thought, and Ecstasy, which she'd got from boys at parties. Lisa and herself had tried to make her stop, but Kerri said it was exciting, and they were stupid. They'd had an argument over it, which was the reason Kerri had stopped confiding in them about her plans.

'We should have told someone, shouldn't we? Her mum or something. Then maybe she'd have been all right.'

'It may have nothing to do with what happened to her, Naomi,' Brock assured her. 'But we want to check everything. What about these boys? Do you know who they are? Do they go to Silver-meadow?'

Naomi shook her head. Lisa and she had tried to find out, but Kerri kept it a secret.

'You're sure she said "boys"?'

She pondered. 'Boys, or "this boy". I'm not sure. I thought there might be more than one, but I'm not sure. She told lies sometimes, just to wind us up.'

As they got back in their car, Brock said to Kathy, 'This doesn't sound like much. What do you think?'

'I agree. She was trying things, but most of them do. She wasn't exactly a junkie. They never found needle marks on the body, did they?'

'No.'

'I feel very sorry for Mrs Tait, trying so hard to do the right thing, worn out.'

'Mmm. Might be better than being stuck in a cottage with old Jack at Westcliff, though, don't you think?'

Kathy smiled. 'Maybe.'

'So what now? I was really hoping forensic would give us something more concrete to work on.' Brock folded his arms and frowned out of the window as Kathy edged the car into the traffic of the high street. 'The thought of this turning into one of those interminable cases, hundreds of fruitless leads, thousands of interviews, millions of words . . .' He shook his head. 'Have you been keeping in touch with what Leon's been up to?'

She nodded. 'Pretty much.'

'I hope he's giving us his undivided attention.'

'I'd say so, yes.'

'Someone said they saw him laughing yesterday, and *whistling*, for God's sake. Leon doesn't whistle.'

'Maybe he's happy.'

'I don't want him happy,' Brock growled. 'I want him dissatisfied and frustrated, like me. I want him harrying those lab people till they find us something useful.'

'Maybe the samples from the compactors will give us something.'

'That's a long shot. She was pretty well wrapped up. And clean – no semen traces, no foreign hairs, no fibres. We find a body, and then it tells us nothing. They've got equipment can read your life story from a single hair, and all they can tell us is that she was a teenager who experimented with Ecstasy.'

Kathy found Speedy alone at his console that afternoon. She saw him grinning to himself as she came in the room, but he didn't turn round. He continued ignoring her as she came to his side. Kathy looked down at the control panel, at the keyboards, the rotating dials, the sliding knobs, and spotted a simple switch at one end, marked ON–OFF. She reached forward and pushed it to OFF, and all the screens simultaneously went blank.

'Oi!' He blinked at the dead screens, then jerked round as if she'd physically hurt him.

'I'd like your attention, Speedy,' Kathy said softly. 'I'd like to know what you thought you were playing at, making that tape.'

His mouth formed into the smirk again, and Kathy wondered if he'd had facial surgery after his accident. 'Did you like it?' he asked, with exaggerated innocence.

'I asked what you thought you were doing.'

'Just a little present. I thought you'd appreciate a demo, of what we can do. Something personal, just between you and me.' His smirk trembled on the point of becoming a sneer.

'You like making demos, do you? Make a habit of it?'

He held her gaze without answering.

'You're quite a creepy bloke, aren't you, Speedy?' she said. 'What seems strange to me is that you've got all this talent for spying on people, but you can't give us a damn thing about that girl.' She stared at his expression, trying to decipher it, trying to work out if he really meant to look like that, or whether the muscles were damaged and he couldn't do anything else. 'You sure you haven't got any little demos of girls in the mall? Any of her?'

Still no answer.

'I'd tell you to watch your step,' Kathy went on, 'only that wouldn't be appropriate. Just be careful, eh? Or I might have to give you a demo of what *I* can do.'

She pressed the switch back on and turned away as the screens flickered to life, and saw Harry Jackson standing in the doorway, watching them.

'Have we got a problem, Kathy?' he said carefully.

'I don't think so, Harry. Speedy was just showing me how things work around here.'

After the excitement generated by the first walk-through, the second attracted an even larger crowd. Chief Superintendent Forbes, who until now had been reluctant to appear committed to the Silvermeadow connection, had decided to attend, his uniform adding an element of formal pomp to the group waiting at the west entrance in front of the TV cameras to receive the girls.

The moment of their arrival was given some unexpected drama by the sudden eruption of a man from the crowd, who walked swiftly to Lisa's side just as she was stepping out of the police car. Looking like a pale office worker at the end of a long week, in limp dark suit and tie, he had a placard hanging round his neck with the message I AM UNEMPLOYED BUT HAVE NOT GIVEN UP. BUY A PEN £1. He held a bunch of the coloured pens in his fist, and raised them up to the cameras as they recorded his brief moment in the spotlight before two security men bundled him away.

Kathy turned to Sharon at her side and said, 'Know him?'

'Yes, he's one of our regulars. We don't let him inside, but he often hangs around the entrances, looking pathetic, until we move him on. I've never seen him here after dark though. It's this walk-through, it's attracting everyone. Bigger than the *Titanic*, I reckon.'

And that was true, Kathy thought, looking at the crush of people in the mall, straining for a sight of the parade. In death Kerri was bigger than Snow White, Mauna Loa and Santa Claus combined.

As they moved forward, Kathy caught sight of a figure in the crowd she recognised, a boy of about twelve, with long black curls coming out from under the baseball cap reversed on his head, the boy she'd seen at the bookshop on Sunday morning and at Starkey's games arcade. She moved into the crush and worked her way to his side.

'Hi,' she said, slipping a hand under his arm.

He looked up into her face, startled, saying nothing.

'My name's Kathy. I'm with the police. What's your name?'

'Wiff,' he said in a soft whisper.

'Wiff what?'

'Wiff Smiff.'

'I've seen you around the mall, Wiff. You spend quite a bit of time here, don't you? Has anybody asked you if you ever saw this girl?'

He stared at the picture for a long time without speaking. His skin was very white, as if it was never exposed to the sun.

'Well?'

He looked up, a blank expression on his face, and shook his head.

'How old are you, Wiff?'

Wiff gazed at Kathy's face for such a long time without replying that she wondered if he was quite right in the head. Then his eyes flicked to someone behind her, and as if he'd suddenly been switched on he gave a whoop and cried, 'Sherro! I'm coming too!', and before she could stop him he slipped out of her grip and went tearing off up the mall, weaving through the crowd of shoppers until he was lost to sight.

Surprisingly, Orville Forbes and Bo Seager seemed to have hit it off, walking side by side in the wake of the little figure with the green frog on her back, and when the chief superintendent held a further press briefing at the end of the walk-through, the centre manager was there too, the pair of them standing against a backdrop of tropical palms and Christmas fairy lights.

The hope was that on one of these two early evenings someone with a pattern of regular visits to Silvermeadow at the beginning of the week might be able to place her there with certainty. It was beginning to look like a vain hope until Gavin Lowry ushered a young girl and an older woman into unit 184 towards six p.m. They were shown into an area screened off from the rest of the unit, and used for interviews and small meetings, while Lowry briefed Brock.

'I think I've found a positive sighting, chief,' he said, fairly bursting with it. 'They usually come on Tuesdays, and only Tuesdays, only last week they were here on the Monday. I found them down in the food court.'

Belinda Tipping was aged seven, as she immediately informed Brock when they were introduced. Her grandmother, elderly and looking overwhelmed, was her companion.

'Now, you come here every Tuesday afternoon, is that right, Belinda?' Lowry asked.

'Yes, I told you. I come with my gran.'

'Yes, well I want you to tell the chief inspector here, because he's the big chief, all right?'

Belinda looked flirtatiously at Brock. 'I used to come with Wendy,' she confided.

'Ah.' Brock smiled at her. 'And who's Wendy?'

'My big sister. She doesn't come any more, though. Not since she ran away with Mr Palmer across the street. Mrs Palmer won't speak to us any more now.'

Her gran coughed warningly. Belinda ignored her and smiled sweetly at Brock. 'My gran brings me after school. I like to see the fireworks coming out of the top of the mountain.'

'Yes, that's right,' her grandmother confirmed. 'Every Tuesday. Then we go to my son's and I stay the night. Except last week it was Monday, because of my appointment with the specialist.'

'And what can you tell us about this girl?' Brock pointed to the enlarged photographs of Kerri and of the girl with the frog bag pinned on the wall.

'We saw her here last Monday,' Belinda said.

'You're quite certain it was her, Belinda?' Brock queried, sceptical. 'Are you good at noticing things?'

'Oh yes.' The little girl was completely confident. 'I'm very good at noticing things. I noticed the girl, because I want to have my hair in a ponytail like that. It was tied up in a red and green ribbon. And I noticed the green bag, like a frog. I told Gran I wanted one like that for Christmas.'

'Is that right? Do you remember that, Mrs Tipping?' Brock asked.

'I do remember Belinda talking about a frog bag,' she said. 'She talked about it all the way back on the bus. But I didn't notice the girl. I was too busy trying to get us to the bus station before the bus left. It was definitely last week.'

'And where did you see her, Belinda? Was it down in the food court, where you spoke to Sergeant Lowry tonight?'

'No. We had been there. Gran and me usually sit by the side of the lagoon, where the canoe is. They keep those seats for the children. Except . . .' She put her hand to her face and smothered a giggle.

'Except what?'

'Except today, he' – she pointed accusingly at Lowry – 'sat on one.'

Lowry coloured. 'Well, I wanted to talk to people like you and your gran, didn't I, Belinda? Tell us where the girl was.'

'Upstairs, on this level, near the windows that look over the pool, talking.'

'Belinda showed me exactly where on our way here, chief,' Lowry explained. 'She saw the girl as she and Mrs Tipping passed along the main upper mall towards the east entrance where the bus station is. She looked down the side corridor towards the observation deck over the pool. The distance would have been twenty yards.'

'Talking, did you say, Belinda?'

The girl didn't seem to mind their attention one bit, all focused on her and her little voice.

'Yes. To a man.'

Lowry's face split in a grin of triumph. 'Tell the chief inspector what you told me about the man, Belinda. Tell him what he looked like.'

'He was a funny man.'

'Funny? In what way?'

'He had no hair.'

'No hair? You mean he was bald?'

She shrugged and looked at her gran, who said, 'You know, dear. Like grandpa.'

'No.' The girl shook her head. 'Grandpa has *some* hair, round his ears. This man had no hair. His head was like an egg. Mr Egghead, that's what he was.'

Brock and Lowry exchanged a look.

'Was he an old man or a young man?'

Her nose wrinkled up with thought. 'Probably he *was* old. Like him.' She pointed at Lowry, who was thirty-six. 'Only *he's* got some hair.'

She couldn't remember what he was wearing.

'When he was standing talking to the girl, was he taller than her?'

'Oh yes.'

'Where did the top of her head come up to on him, would you

say?' Brock stood beside Lowry and pointed his hand at the level of his eyes, then lowered it as she shook her head. She wrinkled her nose and said 'There!' when his hand had dropped below the shoulder.

'And he had big shoulders,' she added. 'Like the Incredible Hulk. Only not green.'

'What about the time? Can you pin-point the time?'

'Yes,' Mrs Tipping said. 'We'd been watching the five o'clock eruption, as usual. I had a cup of tea, and Belinda an ice-cream.'

'A gelato,' Belinda corrected.

'I was feeling tired, my veins were playing up, and I didn't want to get up. Then I saw the time, almost five-thirty, and I realised we'd have to get a move on or we'd miss the bus. So we got up, went up the escalator and along the upper mall to the east entrance. The bus leaves at five-forty, and we got there with a few minutes to spare. So you can work it out. It must have been almost exactly five-thirty-five when we passed the spot where Belinda says she saw the girl.'

'Good.' Brock nodded. 'And you're sure you can't remember anything else about the man, Belinda? You didn't see if he gave the girl anything, or if he touched her?'

She shook her head.

'Could they have been arguing, do you think?'

'I don't think so.'

'All right. Now we've got a very clever artist here, who can make up people's faces on her computer, and I'd like you to talk to her, and help her to make a picture of this Mr Egghead for us to see. Would you like to do that?'

'Oh yes. I like computers.'

'Well I can see you're a very bright girl, Belinda. Your gran can stay here and have a cup of tea while you're busy.'

By the time she was satisfied with the picture, Belinda had attracted a big crowd of officers, eager to see the result. It wasn't Eddie Testor, not exactly, but it was very close. The girl had seemed to want to exaggerate and idealise the egg-like head shape, like Humpty Dumpty, with a small face, and the police artist had to nudge her carefully towards a realistic result without violating the obviously vivid picture in the girl's mind.

Taken with the bulging shoulders and the location, it was hard to avoid the conclusion that Belinda had seen Kerri Vlasich talking to Eddie Testor at almost exactly 5.35 on the evening of her disappearance. Brock turned away, trying to avoid showing on his face the relief he felt. It would have been better if the girl had been older, and if the grandmother had seen the green bag too, but all the same, Belinda was a convincing witness. Kerri had come to Silvermeadow that night. Now there surely could be no doubt.

He saw Chief Superintendent Forbes entering the unit and went over to explain what had happened.

'Excellent! Exactly what we needed, a witness. Thank God.' The relief certainly showed on his face. The last press briefing had turned out to be an uncomfortable affair, since he had no real fresh information to give the reporters, who were becoming frustrated by the police's reluctance to spell out exactly what evidence they had linking Kerri's disappearance with Silvermeadow. 'Pity we didn't know this an hour ago. Premature to call the media back now, do you think?'

'Let's follow it up first,' Brock said. Seeing Lowry looking their way, he waved him over and told Forbes, 'Gavin was the one who found the witness.'

Lowry accepted Forbes's congratulations with a cool smile, then turned to Brock. 'Pick him up, shall we, chief?'

'Yes, let's do that. You care to come along, Orville?'

The chief superintendent checked his watch. 'I've got something else lined up unfortunately, Brock. I think I can leave it in your and Gavin's capable hands, eh?' He gave them a confident smile. 'You've got my mobile number, haven't you? Keep me in touch. Let's get a swift confession, shall we? I have a feeling in my bones that we're getting close here. An excellent result. Well done again, Gavin.'

But it didn't prove to be that easy. Eddie Testor wasn't to be found at the leisure centre, although he had been scheduled for duty that afternoon. After some enquiries it transpired that he'd phoned in sick the previous day, saying that he'd caught a bug and had been told to go to bed for a day or two. But he wasn't at his home, either, a rented flat above a video store in the centre of Romford. No one in the store or the neighbouring flats and shops had seen him for a couple of days.

Eddie Testor, it seemed, had disappeared.

By the time Kathy got back to unit 184 that evening, after following up a number of reports from the police information desks in the malls, the excitement generated by Belinda and the hunt for Testor had evaporated. Phil, the action manager, still at his sentry post by the door, filled her in in lugubrious detail. 'Best you pack it in for the night, Kathy,' he concluded. 'You're not getting paid for this anyway, not with my overtime budget.'

'Thanks, Phil.' She did feel weary, and thought of Leon.

She went to a phone in a quiet corner and was dialling his number when she heard a familiar female voice in the background.

'We particularly wish to speak with Sergeant Kolla,' the voice said, in a piercing tone. 'We have information for her . . . There she is! We can see her over there. Sergeant! Sergeant Kolla!'

Reluctantly, Kathy put down the receiver and turned to see Phil vainly trying to restrain Harriet Rutter. The use of the first person plural was probably not a case of the royal we, she saw, for the tall figure of Professor Orr was there too, looming in support in the background.

She took them into the interview space and sat them down and tried to look enthusiastic. 'You've got some information, Mrs Rutter?'

'We feel so stupid. You see, we knew the poor girl. We knew her quite well, didn't we Robbie?'

Orr nodded without comment.

'A lively young thing, bubbling with life. I can't believe it's her. It was only just now, when we were passing one of your posters, that Robbie said to me, isn't that our young friend at Snow White's? And I said, good heavens, yes!'

'And how exactly did you know her, Mrs Rutter?'

'Well, we like to get to know the young people who work here. And she was a favourite of ours. Robbie has a weakness for Snow White's pancakes, and I love the milk shakes . . . Yes!' She laughed, slightly shame-faced. 'Milk shakes!'

'Strawberry,' Orr said.

'Quite delicious. I'd never had one before. She persuaded me to try it, Kerri did. She said I must try it at least once in my life, and she said it so mischievously, that I just agreed. And it was delicious. So we made it a regular thing, a pancake and strawberry milk shake. Once a week.'

'On a Monday?' Kathy asked hopefully.

'No, Wednesday. I don't know why. No reason, really. It's just nice to have little habits, to mark the days of the week.'

'Yes?' Kathy smiled, waiting for more, but there didn't seem to be any more. 'So, did you a see Kerri on the Monday? The sixth?'

They shook their heads. 'No. We just thought you'd want to know . . . that we knew her.'

They saw the look that Kathy wasn't quite able to keep out of her eyes.

'Oh, you're disappointed,' Mrs Rutter said, and they both frowned at once, as if she'd reproached them.

'No, no. Not at all. Every little bit of information is useful,' Kathy lied. They just want to find out what's going on, she thought, want to be part of it, like everybody else, play a little role in the drama in the mall. It would probably be humiliating for the secretary of the Silvermeadow Residents' Association not to play a part, to be able to speak as an insider to her committee.

'Have you had a good response from the public?' Mrs Rutter asked stiffly.

'Oh, we've had a lot of reports, yes.'

'But have you had a positive lead?' she insisted, slightly belligerent now, as if she had a right to know.

'Have you got a suspect?' Orr put in bluntly.

'I can't discuss that I'm afraid,' Kathy said, trying to be patient. 'There are a number of leads we're following up.'

Mrs Rutter nodded, as if she'd had her answer. 'We know how you work. Look to the family first, eh? That's usually where the answer lies, isn't it?'

'Really, Mrs Rutter, I can't discuss it.'

'That's all right,' she said, huffily. 'That was our first thought too. That ridiculous little man. She said he gave her the creeps. Well, if it was him . . .' She stopped and changed her mind. 'It doesn't matter. Come along, Robbie. We've taken up enough of the sergeant's time.'

'Mrs Rutter, hang on,' Kathy said. 'What little man? Who are you talking about?'

'Her uncle, of course.'

'Uncle?'

'Well, that's what she called him. Bruno Verdi, I'm talking about, or whatever his real name is. The so-called chairman of the Small Traders' Association.' She said the words with contempt. 'That arrogant, trumped-up little man who presumes to tell the rest of us how this place should be run!'

'You think Mr Verdi is Kerri's uncle?'

They saw the disbelief on Kathy's face and hesitated, as if some long-cherished gossip were coming under attack. 'That was how Kerri referred to him one time,' Mrs Rutter said stoutly. '"Uncle Bruno's watching me again," she said, and we thought it was her nickname for him, but she said, no, he really was her uncle, but they didn't speak, and he gave her the creeps. That's what she said, and I could believe it, because we saw the way he watched her too, from the front of his ice-cream place, watching her and the other girls on their roller skates. It made my skin crawl.'

'You obviously don't like him,' Kathy said carefully. 'But is there anything concrete you can tell me?'

'The man's clearly a phoney,' Orr said. 'He knows about as much about Italy as Harriet's cat. I asked him once where he came from, and he said Rome. So I said, ah Rome, my favourite city, the Ponte Vecchio, the Pitti Palace, the Uffizi, and he just smiled and agreed. Well, you get my point – all those places are in Florence! He had no idea. I even tried a bit of Italian on him. I may be a bit rusty, but he just mumbled something and walked off.'

'*Rude* man!' Mrs Rutter hissed.

'I'd say "gelato" is about as much Italian as he knows,' Orr said dismissively.

After they left, Kathy tried to make sense of what they had said. Clearly there was some kind of feud between the 'residents' and the Small Traders' Association, and some more personal animosity between their two leading figures, but the story of an 'uncle' seemed bizarre. Surely they must have misinterpreted something Kerri had said, and embellished it for Kathy's benefit. Easy enough to check, she thought, and picked up the phone.

It rang for some time before Alison Vlasich answered cautiously. 'Yes?'

'Mrs Vlasich? It's Sergeant Kolla from the police. How are you?' The words came out automatically, and Kathy winced as she said them.

'Oh, you know . . . what you'd expect I suppose.' The voice sounded weary and flat.

'Yes. Of course. I just wondered if there was anything we could do.'

'No, I don't think so. The social worker is very good to me.'

'Oh, that's great. Look, maybe you could help me with something. Is there another member of your family working at Silvermeadow, by any chance?'

There was a long silence. Eventually Kathy broke it. 'Hello? Are you still there, Alison?'

'No,' the voice said faintly. 'No one of my family.'

'Oh, fine. You see, someone told us that they thought Kerri had an uncle working there . . .'

'Yes.'

'Pardon?'

'Yes.' The voice was almost inaudible.

'Yes, she had an uncle?'

Another pause. 'That's right.'

'But I thought you just said . . .'

Every answer seemed to take for ever, and Kathy began to think she'd have to drive over to talk to the woman face to face.

'Not in my family. He's in my ex-husband's family.'

'What relation is he to your ex-husband, Alison?' Kathy said, trying to sound as if it were a matter of no great significance.

'He's Stefan's brother.'

'Stefan's brother works at Silvermeadow? What does he do there?'

Kathy heard her sigh, then, 'He runs an ice-cream shop.'

'And he's called Vlasich?' Kathy persisted.

'Not any more. He used to be Dragan Vlasich. Now he's Bruno Verdi.'

Kathy stared at the notepad in front of her, shook her head. 'Alison, you never mentioned this before.'

'Didn't I? No . . . it didn't seem important.'

And Bruno Verdi hadn't mentioned it either, she thought, nor Stefan Vlasich. What the hell's going on?

'Did Kerri and her uncle get on, Alison?'

'He helped her to get her job,' she whispered.

'But did they get on? Were they on good terms?'

'I'm tired now. I've taken a sleeping pill.' And the line went dead.

Kathy thought. She remembered someone, early on, referring to another Vlasich with a record, apparently unconnected with this family. She went over to the computer and logged in, and tapped her request, and waited, until it came up on the screen: Dragan Vlasich, charged in June 1992 under the Sexual Offences Act 1956, the charge dropped in September of that year.

She tried to ring Brock, but his mobile requested her to leave a message, and she put down the phone and thought some more. Well, that was why they'd kept quiet, wasn't it? Knowing what was on his file, they must be trying to protect him, Alison and Stefan. And surely neither of them would do that if they thought it remotely possible that he could have harmed their daughter. Looked at in that way, their silence seemed to vindicate him rather than the opposite.

She stretched, feeling the tension in her back from crouching over the phone, when it rang.

'Kathy! Hi, it's me.'

She smiled, hearing his voice. 'Hi, Leon,' she said softly. 'Where are you?'

'Your place. And I'm cooking, and if you're not home in an hour you'll regret it.'

She laughed. She'd given him a key, and introduced him to Mrs P. 'Well, I don't want to have any regrets. So I'd better come home.'

But she did detour by way of the food court, not with any intention of approaching Verdi yet, but just to get another look at him. Only he wasn't there, the place was being run by the old gondolier and a youth. Kathy watched them for a while from the upper level, then went down on the escalator and spoke to the man in the striped T-shirt and scarlet bandanna.

'Mr Verdi about?'

'Not tonight,' the gondolier said, with an incongruous cockney accent. 'Mondays and Tuesdays he leaves early.'

'Every Monday and Tuesday?'

'Yeah. Why?'

'I wanted to ask him something. He'll be at home, will he?'

The man took off his boater and scratched his head. 'Don't reckon so. He visits his mother, I think. In a hospital or something.'

'Ah. Doesn't matter. I'll get him another time. Thanks.'

Kathy walked away. She recalled the file entry about Stefan Vlasich, and how he now lived in Hamburg with his mother.

Leon had prepared veal escalopes in a cream and mushroom sauce, with boiled potatoes and broccoli, and was immensely pleased with himself.

'This is wonderful,' Kathy said, as he poured her a glass of wine and sat down.

'I really enjoyed doing it,' he beamed. 'It was *so* nice to be able to cook for someone else. So therapeutic. I forgot about everything else.'

Kathy laughed, then yawned.

'You're tired.'

'No, just relaxed, coming back to this. Thanks.' She took his hand.

'Tough day?'

'Not really. I had a word with Speedy over that tape. He claimed it was just his mischievous sense of humour. Wheelchair or not, I reckon he's pretty good at making people feel uncomfortable. Anyway, looks like we've got a prime suspect. You remember the lifeguard in the pool that Gavin Lowry questioned earlier? We've got a witness that saw him and Kerri together on the evening of the sixth.'

'So she really was there. I'm glad of that, Kathy, because the forensic evidence has been pretty useless so far.'

'Not your fault.'

'Maybe you won't need Alex Nicholson then.'

Kathy looked up from her veal. 'What?'

'You remember her? From the Hannaford case?'

'Of course. The forensic psychologist.'

'Yeah. Well, she's in London, and Brock's arranged for her to come down to Silvermeadow to talk to us. Didn't he mention it?'

'No, I don't think so.' You know damn well so, she thought. Dr Nicholson was young and attractive and on that last occasion had seemed, to Kathy's way of thinking, to have had her eye on Leon Desai. She would certainly have remembered if Brock had mentioned it.

'Do you keep in touch with her, then?' she asked, toying with her broccoli.

'Alex? Yes, now and then. She went to Liverpool soon after the Hannaford case to join the forensic psychology unit at the university. She phoned me last week to say she'd be in London. I told Brock, and he got in touch with her.'

Stop it, Kathy thought. Tell him what you think.

'I thought you fancied her,' she said. 'On the Hannaford case.'

'Did you? Why did you think that?' He grinned, and the way he grinned told her that maybe it was true.

She smiled back. 'I don't know. I just thought that. Anyway, she's going to give us her thoughts, is she?'

'She told Brock she'd be interested to have a look, because of the setting. That interested her, apparently. So I'm glad at least that we've established that Kerri really was there, otherwise it might have been a waste of time.'

Kathy wiped the last sauce from her plate and put down her knife and fork. 'Well, that was wonderful. If you ever decide to run off with someone else – Alex Nicholson, say – promise you'll leave me your recipes.' She thought she got the tone about right – light-hearted banter.

'Kathy,' he said seriously, reaching forward and taking her hands, 'I've still got lots of recipes to try out on you. You've no idea.'

8

The hunt for Eddie Testor resumed the following day. It was spurred on by information given by another employee at the leisure pool, a young man whose shifts ran from Monday to Friday, so he hadn't previously been interviewed. He recalled that he had seen Testor on the afternoon of the sixth. They were both rostered from midday to nine p.m. that day, and Testor had been due for a one-hour meal break from four to five p.m., and this was confirmed by his supervisor. But Testor had wanted his break later for some reason, and had arranged with the other lifeguard to cover for him between 5.30 and 6.30 p.m. The man remembered it particularly because it had messed up his previous arrangements to meet a girlfriend during his break. He also suggested that, although Testor had never confided in him, he thought he might have had a close friend at the Silvermeadow Sports Club and Fitness Salon, where he seemed to spend much of his free time.

'Fitness salon?' Kathy said, taking the note from Phil. 'What's a fitness salon?'

'It's where they make you *look* fit, as opposed to actually being fit, Kathy,' Phil explained patiently. 'Sun lamps and stuff. Liposuction too, for all I know.'

'That figures,' Gavin Lowry growled at Kathy's shoulder. 'That wanker Testor would go for that. I'll come with you.'

On the way down to the lower level, Kathy said, 'Haven't seen much of you recently, Gavin. How's it going?'

He blew his nose loudly, looking out of sorts. 'Bit hung over, actually. Me and a few of the lads went down the pub last night, after it became obvious we weren't going to find that bastard. Drown our sorrows.' In any ordinary town street on a wet December morning his scowling discontent would have seemed entirely normal, but here, in Silvermeadow's perpetual Indian summer, he looked menacing and out of place, and people glanced at him uncertainly as they passed.

'How's your campaign against Forbes going?'

He shot her a mistrustful look out of the corner of a bleary eye. 'Don't know what you mean, Kathy. The chief super has implicit trust. Asked my advice this morning, as it happens.'

'About?'

'About Testor. We decided that it might be a good idea to work up a bit of a media storm about Testor *before* we catch him, so that the result will seem more "meritorious". His word, not mine. He called another press briefing straight away. Rigorous detective work has identified a man the police are anxious to interview, blah, blah, blah. The public are warned not to approach this man who has a record of violent assault, blah, blah, blah.'

Kathy said nothing for a while, then, 'What if he didn't do it?'

'Yeah, well, that's the risk, isn't it? Go public too soon and get egg on your face, too late and miss out.'

'What did you advise?'

'Boldness, grasp the nettle, seize the moment. Christ, I feel terrible. Can you slow down a bit?'

A girl in a tracksuit behind the front counter of the sports club pointed out the tinted glass entrance door of the Primavera Fitness Salon on the far side of the atrium, and they wove towards it through a stream of bustling volleyballers.

A redhead looked up from the schedules she was discussing with the receptionist as they walked in, and gave them a big smile. 'Good morning. Haven't seen you two here before.' Her voice was deep and throaty. 'Kim Hislop, manager. What can we do for you?' The smile faded when Kathy showed her warrant card. 'Oh yes. What now?'

'We'd like some information about one of your customers, Ms Hislop. Is it all right to talk here?' Kathy asked, looking around at the furniture in the reception area, something between a hotel foyer and a clinic.

The manager set her head back on her surprisingly broad shoulders, studying them before she said anything. 'This way,' she murmured finally, and led them into a second waiting room behind the first.

A glass door on the far wall carried the name PRIMAVERA above the stylised figure of Botticelli's Venus wearing a sash that said FITNESS

SALON. She indicated for them to sit, herself perching in her tracksuit pants on the very edge of a seat, projecting herself forward at them.

'Well?'

'We're interested in anything you can tell us about Eddie Testor. Do you know him?' Kathy showed her the computer image.

Hislop glanced at it. 'Is that the best you can do?' She smiled and handed it back. 'We're on performance contracts here. The last thing I need is a reputation for shopping our best clients to the filth, know what I mean?'

'We're anxious to contact him, that's all.'

She shrugged and swept her red hair back from her forehead, her biceps swelling impressively under the brilliant white T-shirt. Then she got to her feet and took a book from a shelf and turned the pages. It was an album of photographs, Kathy saw, of men and women bodybuilders in studio poses. She found the one she was looking for and passed it over to Kathy and Lowry. In it, Testor was wearing almost nothing, his body oiled and gleaming. She traced the outline of the hairless torso with a fingertip. 'This is my work,' she said.

Kathy's reply was drowned by a muffled scream from beyond the Primavera door. Ms Hislop ignored it. 'I wax him,' she said. 'I do most of the regulars myself.'

There was a second scream, a male voice in agony, followed by a string of curses. Ms Hislop shook her head resignedly and rose to her feet in one smooth aerobic movement. ''Scuse me one moment.' She disappeared through the door.

After several minutes she returned and sat down in the same perching position, as if in the middle of a knees-bend exercise. 'Where were we?'

'What was that all about?' Lowry asked.

'God, they're babies,' she replied, shaking her head. 'Men.' She raised an eyebrow knowingly at Kathy. 'It's just so bloody embarrassing when they start to cry. Don't you find that?'

'What are they doing to him?' Lowry asked cautiously.

The Primavera door opened again and a girl in a white tracksuit came out and knelt by Ms Hislop's side, whispered in her ear.

'All right,' she nodded. 'But there's no refund. He knows that.'

She turned back to Lowry. 'Body wax. First time.' She shook her head in disgust. 'The women come in here, pop up on the couch and get it over with without a murmur. But the men . . . God! They want a full consultation first, before they decide. Then they get so worked up thinking about it they're in a panic before we even begin. You can see why God gave the job of having babies to women – if the men had to do it, there wouldn't be any.'

'They're stripping his body hair off with wax?' Lowry looked at her in horror.

'That's right.'

'But . . . why?'

She looked at him as if he was even more stupid than she'd supposed. 'It's the look, isn't it?'

'The look?'

'Yes. Don't you read your wife's magazines?'

'I don't think she has any.'

'Course she does! You take a gander. All the male models have got totally hairless bods. Nobody would touch a hairy model these days. It's the look. Movie stars are the same. When did you see a hair on Arnie Schwarzenegger's pecs? And sportsmen, too, your swimmers and runners and that. Body hair is definitely out.'

'Christ . . .' Lowry's imagination was still coping with the vision of the hair being ripped from his back. 'But still, why bother?'

'Well, it's ecological, isn't it?'

'Ecological?'

'Yeah, you know, clean and green. And anyway, a lot of them, their wives and girlfriends make them do it. They ask why they should be the only ones to have to do it. They expect their men to take equal waxing responsibility.'

This reduced Lowry to stunned silence.

Kathy said, 'How much is it? I might treat him.' She nodded at her fellow DS.

'Men's chest wax is the same as ladies' half leg wax. Fourteen ninety-nine, unless he's very hairy.' She looked at Lowry appraisingly. 'I'll give you a half-price introductory offer.'

'Thanks. Think I'll give it a miss, all the same.'

'So you do Eddie Testor regularly?'

'Yes. He comes in once a month. Has the works. I give him a special deal, as a regular.'

'What, head, body, legs . . .'

'Everything, yes.'

'Everything?' Lowry echoed.

She nodded.

'What's he like?' Kathy asked.

'He never complains. Seems to like it. Ideal client.'

'I meant, as a person.'

'Quiet. Keeps to himself. He comes to the gym regularly, too. To work out, you know.'

'Does he have a friend here? Someone he meets regularly?'

'Not that I know of. He's a solitary sort of bloke.'

'What does he talk to you about?'

'Movies. He just talks about the movies he's been to see. At the multi-plex, usually. He goes to everything that's on: children's films, horror films, comedies, thrillers, everything. That's why the others don't like to do him, because he spoils it for them, tells them what happens, can't help himself. I don't care, cos I never go to the pics. He never mentions friends, or family.'

'What address do you have for him?'

She looked it up on the computer, but it was the same one they had.

'He doesn't seem to be there at the moment,' Kathy said, and then had another thought. 'You didn't see him on the sixth of this month, did you? Week ago Monday?'

'That's the day that girl disappeared, isn't it? Blimey! You think Eddie . . . ?' It hadn't struck her before that this might be why they were there, and she seemed startled by the idea.

'We think he could have been a witness to something,' Kathy told her soothingly. 'That's why we need to talk to him.'

'Ah, well . . .' She checked her computer again. 'No, not the sixth. He was booked in for his monthly the following day, the seventh, four till five p.m.'

As Kathy and Lowry thanked her and got up to leave, she suddenly added, 'Oh, hang on! I just thought of something. Have you been to Carmen's?'

'What's that?' Lowry said. 'A fortune teller?'

Ms Hislop looked sharply at him. 'You should take up the offer on the wax, you know. You could do the sunbed, too. It'd make a big difference to you. Your wife would have a nice surprise.'

'She'd have a bloody heart attack,' Lowry muttered, looking impatiently at the door.

'Carmen's?' Kathy prompted.

'Hair salon on this level, other side of the food court, beyond the multi-plex, through the Spanish market. Everyone goes to Carmen's, me included. And I remember her or one of her girls saying that one of their customers was related to Eddie – his aunty or something.'

'That's interesting,' Kathy said. 'We haven't come across her.' She thought of Kerri's Uncle Dragan. One day, she thought, the computer would have a complete record of the family interconnections of everyone, a map of the hidden blood lines that linked a subject to a second cousin or a step-uncle twice removed who might be waiting in the shadows to provide help, or something else. 'You wouldn't have a name, I suppose?'

'No, but Carmen might.'

The foyer to Carmen's salon was all blonde timber and gleaming chrome, the only indication of its purpose a few discreet displays of bottles under concealed spotlights, like a museum of rare artefacts. Carmen turned out to be a small, dynamic woman with bright, compelling eyes, and a network that seemed to have got somewhat further than the police computer in mapping the human relationships of this area of Essex. She consulted with some of her staff, her technical director (colour), her creative director and her chief stylist, and finally found the nails consultant, who recalled a conversation with a woman who spoke of her nephew (actually, she thought, the adopted boy of her sister's husband's brother and his wife, who'd been tragically killed in a car smash) who was a pool attendant at the leisure centre. The customer, the aunt, was remembered as being in her fifties, blonde, a smoker with problem cuticles, and with an overall style bias described in the private terminology of the salon as 'fluoro'.

'That means brassy, hyper, unsubtle, too much,' Carmen explained.

Together with an approximate date of her last visit, four to six weeks before, the computer came up with three possible names and addresses. Two of the names had bookings arranged for the month ahead, and the receptionist rang their numbers on the pretence of confirming these. As she closed, the receptionist asked if they had a relative working at Silvermeadow, by any chance, since the salon was offering a special discount to centre staff in December. The second one said yes, her nephew worked there, but she didn't want to get him to come to the phone right now, because he was asleep and hadn't been well. In any case, she said with a wheezy chuckle, he'd be the last person to need a booking at a hair salon.

'Carmen, that's brilliant, thanks,' Kathy said as the receptionist rang off. 'I'm really impressed. I wish our information was as efficient.'

Carmen smiled, eyeing Kathy's hair. 'Nice basic structure, love. But you need a better cut. And what *have* you been washing it with?'

Kathy agreed to make a booking once the investigation was over, and meanwhile bought three bottles that Carmen recommended.

When Lowry saw the price on the till display he gave a little gasp. 'Kathy, if you ever meet my wife, do me a favour and don't tell her about this place, eh?'

'Lowry . . .' Carmen frowned. 'I know the name . . . Yes, Connie Lowry, is that your wife?'

'Yeah.' He looked worried.

'Oh, I know Connie. She's nice. She comes here regular. Everyone comes here, Gavin. Even your friend Harry Jackson comes here.'

Lowry looked shocked, as if she'd accused Jackson of participating in some morally questionable practice. 'I wouldn't have thought he'd have had enough raw material for you to work on,' he said doubtfully.

'Oh, you'd be surprised what we can do. You should have come to us for your last cut. Really you should.'

They ran across the carpark through the rain to Lowry's Escort. Kathy was interested to see that whoever took care of his laundry obviously didn't handle the interior of his car. It was full of rubbish: fast-food containers, newspapers, cigarette packets and odd bits of clothing jumbled together over all the passenger seats. He grumbled as he threw things into the back to make room for Kathy, who was shivering by the time she got in out of the rain.

'I'll get the heater going,' he muttered. 'There's a box of tissues somewhere. Look down there.' He began pressing numbers on his phone.

'You reporting to Brock?' Kathy said, groping around her feet.

'Yeah,' he said, but from the muttered words she could pick up it sounded more as if he was calling first for armed support and then, more surreptitiously, with his back to her, speaking to someone about cameras and a news crew. Then he drove off, pulling the car over short of the carpark exit and sitting with the engine running, tapping the steering wheel impatiently while he examined a street map.

A second car appeared on the road behind them and flashed its lights.

'About bloody time,' Lowry muttered, and threw the car into gear.

The address was a modern brick terrace, compact and drab in the rain. The front doors faced a tarmac parking court into which Lowry turned his car, the other following close behind. He switched off the engine and waited.

'Did you call Brock?' Kathy asked. She hadn't seen him at Silvermeadow that morning, and there were things she wanted to speak to him about. She pulled out her phone. 'I'll give him a call.'

'Hang on.' He pointed through the rain-washed windscreen as an unmarked van swung fast into the court and squealed to a halt. 'I told Phil,' Lowry said. He looked at his watch. 'You've worked with the Indian guy before, I take it. Desai?'

The sudden jump in topic threw Kathy. 'Eh? Yes, a couple of times. Why?'

'Like him, do you?'

'What?'

Lowry grinned and pulled a bag of barley sugars out of the door pocket and offered them to her.

'I'm sensitive to these things,' he said.

Kathy undid the paper from the sweet and threw it into the ankle-deep trash. 'Go wax yourself,' she said, and saw another van come to a halt in the street opposite the entrance to the carparking yard. It had a satellite dish on its roof and the logo of a TV channel's news programme on its side.

'Come on.' Lowry jumped out of the car and ran to the back of the first van. As he pulled open the back doors, Kathy saw the outline of men inside with guns.

The woman who answered their knock on her front door was instantly recognisable from the hairdresser's description. Her chemical hair colouring, her glossy orange lips, her lime-green costume jewellery, all vibrated in the dull grey light, working very hard to make the dreary world a brighter place. Kathy immediately understood what 'fluoro' meant.

'Hello.' She smiled at them, taking in the support people hanging back in watchful anticipation. 'To what do we owe this little visitation?'

'Mrs Goldfinch?' Kathy said, showing her warrant card.

'That's me, darling. Call me Jan.' Eddie's aunt appeared unperturbed.

'We want to speak to your nephew, Eddie Testor. Can you tell us where he is, please?'

'Why yes, certainly!' She gave them a little flash of brilliant white dentures. 'He's here! How on earth did you know? Everyone seems to want to speak to him today. Why don't you come on in? I don't think there'll be room for all of you, mind.'

After they'd got Eddie dressed and taken him downstairs to the car with a towel over his head, Jan realised she was almost out of cigarettes, and went back up to Eddie's room to see if he had any. 'What on earth are you doing?' she said from the doorway, staring with fascination at Lowry pulling on a pair of latex gloves.

'Why don't we go downstairs and talk about Eddie, Jan?' Kathy said, steering her back out onto the landing. 'I'd love a cup of tea.'

Aunty Jan was happy to do that, because it was a touching story that she loved to tell. The poor boy had had a very difficult time of it after his parents were killed in the accident, she explained when they were settled in the kitchen. It was divine intervention really that had brought the two of them together after so many years. She had been checking out the sunbeds and spa pools and saunas at the fitness salon at Silvermeadow one day when she had stopped to admire the photographs of the waxed body builders hanging in their golden frames ('Well, Kathy darling, there's no harm in looking, is there?'), and one in particular had caught her eye. It had reminded her so much of her sister's brother-in-law Donald, on whom she'd had a terrible crush twenty years ago, before he and his wife were killed in the accident. So like him, in fact, that she began to think of their little orphan kid Eddie, whom she hadn't heard of for years. And then she'd looked at the signature scrawled across the bottom of the photo and when she managed to decipher the name her heart had gone all of a flutter, for there he was, Eddie Testor, in the glorious flesh.

'It's not that I fancied him, Kathy darling,' she said. 'Not really, cos that would be like incest almost, and anyway I've got a boyfriend, who'll be here any minute actually, to take me to our dancing class, Latin American. But I had to speak to him, and tell him that we were long-lost relatives, and that if he ever needed an aunty I was here. He didn't really take up my offer until last Sunday night, when he showed up in such a state, poor kid.'

'Did he say what had happened? The black eye, the cut lip?'

'Some thugs beat him up, didn't they? He looks a great hunk of muscle, but he's like his dad, a real softie inside.'

'How did he get here?'

'Taxi dropped him off.'

'And he brought a bag with his things?'

'Yes, that's right.'

'So he'd been to his home, then?'

'How do you mean?'

'After he'd been beaten up, he went home.'

'Oh yes, I suppose he did. He was done in when he arrived here. Completely exhausted. He's hardly stirred from his bed since he got here. He's really not been well.'

Lowry joined them in the living room. He was carrying a number of clear plastic bags containing packets and bottles, which he laid on the coffee table.

'What are these, Mrs Goldfinch? Do you know?'

'From Eddie's room?' she said vaguely. 'They'll be his pills. For his body building, you know. He has to take a lot of pills.'

'Where does he get them from?'

'Oh, I wouldn't know that. From his doctor, I suppose, or his friends at the gym.'

'Do you take pills, Jan?' Kathy said.

'Me? Only what the doctor gives me. I'm depressed, see, since Alfred passed away. That's my late husband. But I don't believe in letting it show. You have a duty to add a little sunshine to the world, I always say, no matter if it's raining in your heart.'

Kathy thought that probably explained Aunty Jan's remarkable unconcern at being the subject of a police raid.

'That's your pills in the bathroom cabinet is it?' Lowry said.

'Yes, they're mine . . . Oh!' She looked at him in alarm. 'You haven't touched *them*, have you?'

Lowry shrugged ambiguously.

'Oh no! You can't take *them* away!' Panicking, she looked to Kathy for support. 'You mustn't do that!'

'It's all right, Jan, I'm sure that won't be necessary.' She looked at Lowry, who seemed at first reluctant to co-operate, but then he reached into one of the plastic bags and took out a packet which he handed to Kathy. She made a note of the name and the chemist's label before she returned them to Jan, who looked relieved.

Just then the front door bell sounded and Jan jumped to her feet. 'Oh, that'll be him now, my boyfriend. We're late. You don't mind me dashing off, do you? It's the rumba you see, my favourite. I love the hip movements, don't you? Although my boyfriend has a bit of trouble with them, since his operation.'

★

Kathy and Leon Desai stood at the window, watching Brock and Lowry working on Eddie. Kathy was very conscious of Leon's body at her side and its stillness, observing the exchanges in the other room with hardly a blink of his dark eyes. Despite Lowry's lip service to interviewing rules, Kathy was in no doubt that his manner was intimidatory, and was intended to be so. He sat hunched forward across the table as if short of hearing, baring his teeth in what he might claim to be a smile. His crouching posture contrasted with Eddie's, sitting stiffly upright, head back on his thick neck, and Kathy wondered if Lowry might be physically envious of the other man, even while he seemed, with every gesture and word, to despise him utterly. Brock was sitting back, saying nothing, doing something with a pencil on a notepad as if the proceedings held no interest.

'You're a very, very stupid fellow, Eddie,' Lowry was saying. 'You could kill yourself taking stuff like that. You know that, don't you?'

'Sergeant,' the duty solicitor interrupted. 'Excuse me, but are you intending to lay charges in connection with the alleged possession of performance-enhancing drugs? Because if not, I don't see—'

'Do you mind!' Lowry screamed at her, furious. The violence in his voice and in his cold stare set the solicitor abruptly back. There was silence for a moment as Lowry seemed to struggle with his temper, before continuing in a more reasonable tone to Eddie. 'You do know that, don't you? Those are animal drugs, Eddie. What they give to horses.' He shook his head in amazement.

'Are they?' Kathy asked Leon. 'Did you get a look at them?'

He nodded. 'Yes. Stenbolol, the anabolic steroid, is a veterinary product, usually used for geldings in training. It's popular among body builders because it's available in tablet and paste form, rather than by injection like most animal anabolic steroids. Eddie could have got them from anywhere – they're common enough. He also had human testosterone tablets, and a cocktail of tranquillisers, too.'

'What sort of doses have you been taking, Eddie?' Lowry pressed him.

The solicitor frowned and sat forward to whisper in Eddie's ear.

'I'm asking, Eddie,' Lowry said in a menacing tone aimed at the lawyer, 'because I understand that taking heavy doses of this stuff can make you very tense and angry, is that right? Do you find that? Does it put you on a short fuse? Does it make you really mad when people muck you about? Does it make you want to sort them out with those great big bulging muscles of yours?

'And maybe your clever solicitor can understand now the relevance of my question to you, Eddie. Because if you'd been taking them before you got talking to Kerri, and if she mucked you about and wouldn't give you what you wanted, and if the steroids made you very, very angry with her, well, that might be something we should bear in mind, isn't it? You might not have been in full control of your faculties, see? You know all about that, don't you, Eddie, because you've used that excuse before. But the problem is, if you don't tell us about that now, if you keep silent, the court won't want to know about it if you try to bring it up later, when we've brought you to trial. Ask your brief, Eddie – go on, ask her. True or false, it'll be too late then.'

Lowry thumped the table with the flat of his hand and got to his feet and paced away as if he couldn't stand to look at Testor any more. Eddie stared after him, then turned slowly and looked at his solicitor.

Desai shook his head. 'I don't think Gavin's making any impression at all,' he murmured. 'I don't think Testor has a clue what he's talking about.'

The solicitor was frowning. She leant forward across the table to say something to Brock, who stooped to hear her point. While the two of them were taken up in this, Lowry, stretching his frame, sauntered round the table and suddenly ducked his head against Eddie Testor's ear, muttering something which the microphones didn't pick up. The body builder flinched abruptly, his eyes widened, and he shrank away from Lowry as if from a freezing draught. Lowry straightened, smiling grimly to himself, and strolled away.

'I wonder what he said,' Kathy murmured.

Desai shrugged. 'Fancy a coffee?'

'In a minute,' Kathy said. 'Brock's going to have a go.'

'Eddie,' Brock began, sounding as if he was only noticing him for the first time. 'Are you feeling all right? The lip, I mean. It looks sore. You sure?'

Eddie made no response.

'You like working at the pool, don't you?'

Eddie studied his fingers fixedly, waiting for the trap.

'I can understand that. It looks like a really nice place to work. I haven't been able to find the time to go down there yet, but I will, for a swim. How much will that cost me, for a swim?'

'Two fifty,' Testor whispered, 'three fifty at peak time.'

Brock nodded, as if this confirmed something that had been on his mind. 'I was reading about the pool in the brochures. An average length of fifty-three metres, width of eighteen and a half metres, and depth of one point six metres, that's what the brochure said, and I was trying to multiply the numbers together to work out how many litres it holds, at one thousand litres to the cubic metre.'

'One million five hundred and sixty-eight thousand eight hundred,' Eddie Testor said without hesitation.

Brock chuckled and nodded his head. 'That's absolutely right,' he said, and slid his notebook across the table to Testor. 'But it took me five minutes to work it out.' He grinned at the solicitor, who was looking very puzzled. 'No really, I'm impressed, Eddie.'

Testor ducked his head, clearly pleased with the compliment although reluctant to acknowledge it.

'Let's see,' Brock continued. 'If we assume the earth is a perfect sphere with a radius of six thousand three hundred and fifty kilometres, and the volume is pi times the radius cubed, what is the volume of the earth in cubic kilometres?'

Testor looked unhappy. 'Pi times . . . ?'

'Take a value for pi of three point one four one five nine,' Brock added.

'Oh.' Eddie's face brightened. 'Eight hundred and four billion three hundred and ninety-seven million, four hundred and fifty-three thousand four hundred and twenty-one point two five.'

Brock laughed out loud. 'That is simply amazing. I've heard of people who can do this, but you're the first I've ever met, Eddie. How do you do it?'

Testor gave a shy smile. 'I don't know.'

'Astonishing.' Brock looked at the solicitor. 'Isn't it?'

She gave a guarded smile, looking at Brock a little oddly.

'You really don't know how you do it?' Brock asked again.

'The answer just sort of comes into my head. I don't know how.'

'Well, you've got a very special kind of head there then, Eddie. Very special. Is that why you got that black eye? Has that got something to do with it?'

Testor looked unhappy, winced as he pulled a face.

'Your mouth hurts?'

He nodded.

'It was someone you knew, wasn't it, Eddie?'

Testor's face formed a deep scowl of denial.

'I can't do sums in my head like you, Eddie,' Brock said amiably, 'but I can see some things that are obvious. If it was a stranger who knocked you down in the street, like you said, your clothes would have been wet and dirty, but they weren't. There was blood on your tracksuit top from your mouth, but no dirt or rain. And things were upset in your flat, the chair knocked over, and the lamp. It seems obvious to me that you were knocked down in your flat, after you let the people in. So I assume you knew them. That's obvious, isn't it? Like two times two?'

Eddie wouldn't meet Brock's eyes. He stared down at his hands and made little flexing motions with his shoulders.

'Why did they hit you, Eddie? Was it to do with the way your mind works? Did they not like that?'

There was no reply.

After a moment, Brock took Kerri's photograph from the file and placed it in front of him. 'Tell me what goes through your mind when you look at her now, Eddie,' he said gently. 'Is it as simple as long multiplication? Or is it more difficult and complicated? Try to tell me.'

Eddie stared at the picture for a long while, then lifted his eyes to Brock's and said, sounding completely lucid, 'But I've never seen her before, sir. Never.'

Kathy and Leon went down to the canteen. The tables had been arranged in two continuous parallel rows, seats ranked down each side. Kathy wondered if the cleaners or catering staff who had set the furniture out this way thought that their customers liked to be lined up in ranks. She and Desai picked up their cups from the counter and sat down on opposite sides of a table.

'You seem a bit edgy,' Desai said, watching the way her eyes were following the uniformed men and women coming and going.

'Do I? Yes. I feel I should be doing something, but I'm not sure what.'

Part of the feeling, she knew, was coming from being here with Leon, behaving as if they were no more than professional colleagues rather than lovers. The functional indifference of the place seemed to mock their intimacy, and she wondered if she was being overly sensitive about it. Among the hundreds of officers who had served time here, others must have been in this situation, couples in unpublicised relationships. Did they feel out of place because of it? Did Leon? He gave no sign of it.

'I should have thought that things were looking promising,' he said. 'Testor is quite a weird character, isn't he? That stuff with the numbers. How did Brock get onto that?'

'There was something in his file, the psychologist's report. I didn't really pick it up at the time. That reminds me, I have to get back to Silvermeadow to look at another file. Are you going over there?'

Leon checked his watch. 'Brock asked me to collect Alex Nicholson for the briefing, and I need to call in at the lab first. Why don't you come with me?'

'No, I'll get a lift from someone else, don't worry.'

'Are you all right, Kathy?' he said suddenly, lowering his voice. 'Are *we* all right?'

She looked at his face, scanning the details of eyelids, mouth, earlobes, as if needing to memorise them again. 'Yes, yes. Sorry. I get preoccupied, you know how it is. When there are loose ends all over the place, and nothing makes much sense. You know.'

He nodded. 'Yes, I know. I'll catch up with you after the briefing, okay?'

'Mm.'

'This is an awful place, isn't it?' he said suddenly. 'I keep thinking that I want to grab hold of you, pretend we're somewhere else.'

She smiled. 'I know. I know exactly what you mean.'

9

Unit 184 was crowded for the team briefing that afternoon when Kathy arrived. She saw Dr Alex Nicholson standing talking to Brock in front of the plans of the centre, though she didn't recognise her at first because her long hair, previously jet black, was now an almost peroxide blonde. The psychologist had one hand in her hair, stretching, pulling at it absently while she thought about the point Brock was making. She was dressed in black jeans, trainers and a T-shirt with the message on the back PSYCHOLOGISTS DO IT IN YOUR HEAD. Kathy was struck again by how young she looked, more like a student than a teacher. Also how attractive. She'd get a solid turnout from her male students for her lectures, Kathy thought.

Brock called her over to introduce her.

'Yes, we know each other,' Kathy said, noticing the rather clever way the other woman had used the minimum of make-up to the maximum effect, especially around the eyes. 'We met in Orpington.'

'Hi.' Alex smiled back. 'The Angela Hannaford murder. I remember, of course. Leon said something about you working on this one.' She turned back to Brock with a question, and Kathy wandered over to her filing tray, half-filled with new material. She sifted quickly through it, stopping at a pouch sent out from central registry. She opened it and began to flick through the file inside.

She was halfway through it when the session was opened by Chief Superintendent Forbes, who wanted everyone to know how commendable their efforts had been so far, and how tantalisingly close to success he believed them to be. The monster who had killed Kerri Vlasich was in their hands, had been identified at the scene. One last push, he concluded, one last effort to find the extra strands of evidence that must still lie waiting out there to tie him to his brutal crime, and their hard work would be rewarded with public acclaim.

Though less lofty in his vision of their future rewards, and more circumspect in relation to Testor's guilt, Brock's report supported Forbes's general drift. Testor was an unusual man, not to be easily written off as a steroid junkie. He had suffered brain damage as a teenager, and his behaviour was unusual and difficult to predict. At one moment he would appear helplessly child-like, at another devious and calculating. He seemed extraordinarily passive and gentle, yet he had been capable in the past of blind and violent rage. They had been unable to find any sexual partners, of either gender, nor even evidence of sexual interest, yet his greatest hobby seemed to be his own body and its appearance. He could perform extraordinary mental feats, but also appeared to suffer confusion and genuine sporadic memory loss. And these characteristics were compounded by his eclectic drug habits. But the important thing to remember was that he *knew* he was odd, and had learned the hard way that his oddness got him into trouble. When pressure was put on him, as now, his instinctive reaction was to clam up, roll into a ball, and say nothing.

So he was not confident that they would get anything like a confession from him, and that meant they needed more eyewitnesses. They had one, a seven-year-old girl who, despite her age, was an extraordinarily confident witness, and who had, that morning, picked out Testor from a line-up without the least hesitation. But she was only seven. Others must have seen Testor and Kerri on that afternoon of the sixth, particularly during that crucial one-hour period from 5.30 to 6.30 p.m. when Testor had switched his meal break and couldn't account for his whereabouts. And then there was the matter of the beating that Testor had been given on the previous Sunday evening, apparently in his own flat, after he'd been allowed home after being questioned for the first time at Hornchurch Street.

As he said this, Kathy found herself wondering about the state of Gavin Lowry's knuckles. She glanced across at him, sitting on a table at the back of the room, looking as if he knew it all.

Eyewitnesses, then, Brock concluded, more eyewitnesses. Then he asked Leon Desai to bring them up to date on the forensic side. Leon got to his feet and spoke with his usual stylish composure.

'The lab has now identified the antigen antibodies in Kerri's hair, and confirmed a match with traces in the blood and some organs. It seems that during the final week of her life she took, or was given, ketamine hydrochloride. Ketamine, you probably know, is popularly known as "K", or "special K", and is taken as an intense hallucinogenic, but it can also cause paralysis and coma. It's used in various proprietary forms as a veterinary anaesthetic.'

'Hang on . . .' Gavin Lowry spoke up. 'Testor had animal steroids in his possession. Isn't that a bit of a coincidence?'

'Probably not,' Leon replied. 'It's true that Stenbolol, the anabolic steroid you found in Testor's room, is manufactured as a veterinary product, but it's widely available in gyms and among body-building types. We think the batch Testor had was manufactured in Holland and never legally imported into the UK. Similarly, ketamine hydrochloride is manufactured for veterinary use, but is bought and sold on the club scene as a rather risky alternative to Ecstasy. There's unlikely to be a link. Unfortunately the antigen tests can't narrow the ketamine down to a particular make or source. One indication that it was a veterinary product could be the way in which it was administered. Almost all veterinary ketamine makes are presented by injection, whereas the stuff they sell for kids is in pills. The pathologist didn't find any needle marks on Kerri's body, but they can be hard to spot. He said' – Leon hesitated, then went on – 'he said the best way to make sure would be to remove her skin. Apparently needle marks are more visible if you hold the skin up to the light.'

There was a general whisper of disgust at the thought of skinning the girl, but not, Kathy noticed, from Dr Nicholson, who observed their discomfort from beneath her fringe with a little smile of amusement.

'Well,' Brock said, 'maybe we should consider that. An injection might indicate whether or not it was self-administered, depending on where it was. Anything else, Leon?'

'Yes. The samples from the compactors. They've identified blood traces.'

There was a murmur of approval at this.

'But it's badly contaminated, and they can't say yet whether it's even human.'

A groan of disappointment.

'And it was from the orange compactor, not the blue one.'

There was silence as they tried to work out the implications of this, and the thought passed through Kathy's mind, how come forensic evidence so often seemed to be two-edged, clarifying and confusing at the same time?

Then it was Alex Nicholson's turn. She disarmed them immediately by saying that they knew far more about it than she did, and she had nothing brilliant to offer, but maybe it would be helpful if she sort of facilitated – she apologised for the word, which she hated, but they knew what she meant – a discussion, to get ideas out into the open. They might begin with Kerri's motivation. If she was really running away to see her father, why would she have been talking to Eddie Testor? Was it a chance meeting? Did she know him? Did she buy drugs from him? Could it be that she never had any intention of going to Germany, but instead wanted to frighten and punish her mother, and had used her friends to spread the false story unwittingly?

The group was slow to respond to this, but gradually one or two offered their ideas, which she wrote up on a white board, and a more general discussion began to build up. She was good at it, Kathy conceded, even with such a large and unfamiliar group, getting them to participate. Kathy herself said nothing for some time. She thought the focus on Kerri's character and motivation was leading nowhere, for the reason that they didn't really know enough; anything seemed possible. And so eventually she decided to lob a little hand grenade into the debate.

'What if this has nothing to do with Kerri and her father?' she asked. 'What if Kerri was no more than a chance victim? What if this has happened before at Silvermeadow?'

The room went very quiet.

Alex Nicholson was writing on the board at that moment, but she immediately swung round and fixed Kathy with bright eyes. 'Yes!' she said, as if she'd been waiting all the time for someone to suggest this. 'What about that?'

Lowry broke in, irritated. 'What if? What if? Come on, Kathy, we've killed this one. There's no evidence this has happened before.'

'But why shouldn't it?' Alex said. 'The method of disposing of the victim was perfect, or should have been. So perfect that it must have been very deliberate, surely. Not a lucky chance. So then, why couldn't it have happened before? Perhaps many times. Come on, Gavin' – Kathy thought it interesting that she already knew their names – 'let's just explore the idea for a minute. Because it changes everything, doesn't it?'

She let them think about it, then said, 'Kathy's right. Kerri becomes almost incidental, merely this month's target. The whole focus shifts. Instead of looking at character and motivation, we look instead at . . . ?' She left it hanging in the air, but they didn't get it. Nobody spoke, and eventually she answered her own question. 'Place! The setting becomes the central thing. Right? The place where it happens!' She turned to Brock, as if to check whether it was all right to go on, and he nodded with an indulgent little smile and she turned back to the group, and abruptly the tutorial was over and the lecture began.

'You see, one of the central concepts of the work that we've been doing at Liverpool is the idea that there is a pattern to the places that a serial offender chooses for his attacks. Kathy, of course, remembers this from the Hannaford case, where we used this. The pattern of where the victims are found can tell you things about the offender, most importantly where he himself is located in relation to the attack sites.

'But in this case we have the opposite: we have one single location, to which the victims and the attacker come. The place is the thing that draws them together. We can tell nothing about our offender from the distribution of sites, because there is only one site, but maybe we can tell a great deal about him from the character of the site, because this is a very unusual and distinctive place. We can imagine him being drawn here, coming here a lot, being very comfortable here, so that he keeps reusing the same location. So, you have to ask yourself, what is so special about this place for him?'

She took a breath and leant back against the table behind her, confident that she had their full attention.

'There's a phenomenon in shopping centres. You can see it if you watch people near the entrances, coming in. They march in, purposeful, heading straight for whatever it is they've come here for. They aim to buy it and get off home. But then something happens. Their eye is caught by the shop displays, and they begin to appear distracted. Their path becomes erratic. They slow down, and wander from one side of the mall to the other. The music is playing, and they stop and look at this thing and that. Maybe they take off their coat, because it's nice and warm in here. They have a kind of vacant look on their face now, and after a while they notice that they're tired, and that they're carrying shopping bags full of things they never thought of buying when they first arrived. So they sit down on one of the nice seats in the mall, next to a fountain, under a potted tree, and watch a fashion parade or listen to the local school band playing a selection of

Gershwin melodies, and they try to remember what the hell it was they came here for in the first place.'

Kathy noticed several smiles of recognition at this, and recalled how rapidly she'd been drawn into buying, almost without thought.

'This phenomenon is well known enough to have a name,' Alex continued. 'It's called the Gruen Transfer. The name comes from Victor Gruen, the architect who designed the first enclosed shopping mall, at Edina in Minneapolis in 1956. He had a vision, you see, that the modern shopping centre could be more than just a collection of shops, it could be a complete integrated environment, separate from the world outside, a perfect machine for consumption.

'Yes, a machine. The terms they use sound like they're talking about a machine. There are "magnet" stores that attract customers as if they were iron filings, and draw them past all the smaller shops, and sort of pump them around in "flows". If the distance between the magnets is too great, the flows are weakened and the efficiency of the machine is impaired. The aim is to get the maximum number of consumers past every single shop window. Dead-end malls, inaccessible upper floors, are a no-no. Everything has to pump and flow smoothly. In a well-organised centre there's a kind of ecological balance to it all – sorry, I'm mixing my metaphors. At the top of the food chain are the big magnet stores, or "anchors". They're top because they attract customers from miles around, so they can negotiate low rents with the developer, who's anxious to persuade them to come in. The small shops, which are dependent on the magnets to pull the customers past their doors, must pay higher rents, proportionately, to be able to take part in the process. And the developer is dependent on the small shops getting as big a turnover as possible, to pay the rents he needs to build and maintain the place.

'But, as Gruen realised, the underlying driving force is the psychology of the consumers, who are at the bottom of the food chain – the plankton that the higher forms of commercial life feed on. And to manipulate that psychology, almost any device is admissible, no matter how outlandish or weird it might at first appear. You can take your customers to the Polynesian islands, transport them to the Arabian Nights, you can raid history, literature, the movies, fairy-tales, anything at all that will distract them and keep them happily absorbed inside the machine. Whatever it takes, in fact, to sustain the Gruen Transfer.

'When you just had individual shops along a street, there wasn't a whole lot you could do to stimulate your customers' fantasies beyond sticking a Christmas tree in the window once a year. The cold reality of the street kept getting in the way. They really had to press their noses to the window and imagine awfully hard. But in an indoor mall, all that changes. The real world of the street is banished. The boundaries separating the consumer from the consumed are dissolved away. Fantasy and reality become interchangeable parts of the process of consumption. You can possess whatever you see.'

'Including the girl dressed up like Snow White who brings you your pancakes,' Brock said.

'Exactly, yes. That's really the point I was coming to. That it might be significant that Kerri actually worked here, and wore that uniform and a big happy smile, like she was an accessory, part of the whole fun process, like the wrapping paper and the music and the finger-licking food.

'He loves the mall, he eats the food, he wants the things he sees. He feels they're available, that they're really his, because that's the message of the mall. And he's become an insider, an expert in the culture of the mall. He knows how it works, he knows the security codes, he knows how they dispose of their garbage.'

Kathy didn't share in the general buzz of animated conversation that followed this presentation. She felt a chill in her stomach that came not so much from what Alex Nicholson had said as from the reverberations it set up with the file she had been reading just before the briefing started. It was the file on the lapsed prosecution of Dragan Vlasich.

One afternoon in the summer of 1992, the senior physical education teacher of an east London secondary school was looking out of the staff-room window at the children passing through the front gates and dispersing down the street. Parked near the gates was an ice-cream van. It was very distinctive, with an enormous illuminated fibreglass ice-cream cone mounted on the roof and the name MR KREEMEE emblazoned on the side. Mr Kreemee had been parked there regularly for the past several afternoons, catching the departing kids, and the teacher had noticed that one child in particular, a pretty, fair-haired girl called Helen Singleton from class 2E, had lingered by the hatch in the side of the van, talking to Mr Kreemee as he served the queue of her schoolmates. On this particular afternoon the teacher watched the queue dwindle until only Helen was left. Then he saw the side hatch on the van close, the girl walk to the rear of the van, the rear door open and her step inside. The door closed abruptly, and shortly afterwards the light inside the fibreglass cone went out. He quickly rounded up a couple of other young male teachers from the staff room, and they ran down to the street.

When they yanked open the rear door of the van they found Mr Kreemee inside on his hands and knees in front of Helen Singleton, who was seated on a stool. He claimed afterwards that he was offering her different combinations of toppings on her ice-cream cone and had dropped some on the floor, but the teachers didn't see it that way. They hauled Mr Kreemee out into the street and took him and the child back into the school, where Mr Kreemee, alias Dragan Vlasich, received some bruises and abrasions while waiting for the police to arrive. He was charged under section 20 of the Sexual Offences Act 1956, which states that it is an offence for a person acting without lawful authority or excuse to take an unmarried girl under the age of sixteen out of the possession of her parent or guardian against his or her will.

Vlasich claimed that it was all a terrible mistake, that when he was closing up to move to another location Helen had begged to see how the Kreemee ice-cream machine worked, that he had merely intended for her to look in through the back door, but that she had climbed in and the wind had blown the door shut behind her. Helen herself seemed confused, but didn't contradict his story. The teachers had intervened before any act of indecency had occurred, if that was what had been in Vlasich's mind. The Crown Prosecution Service hesitated, then abandoned the case. The charges were withdrawn for lack of evidence.

By the time Kathy finally managed to get Brock on his own to tell him about Verdi/Vlasich, twenty-four hours had elapsed since Harriet Rutter and Robbie Orr had first alerted her to him. Brock seemed startled by her information about his name change, as if it was something he might have half suspected and then dismissed. Then, as she told him about Vlasich's career as Mr Kreemee, he looked troubled.

'You could have let me know about this before, Kathy,' he said.

'I'm sorry. I tried to ring you last night on your mobile, but couldn't get through. Then this morning I was caught up in the hunt for Testor. I only got to look at the Vlasich file just before the briefing started.'

He nodded, frowning deeply. 'Yes, of course.'

'You don't like it,' Kathy said.

'It stinks, don't you think?'

'Yes. It gives me a bad feeling too.'

They were interrupted by Harry Jackson's discreet cough. 'Evening, folks. Phil said your team meeting was over and I might show my face. Ms Seager asked me to pass on all our congratulations on your result, and ask if there's anything we can be doing.'

'Thanks, Harry,' Brock said, preoccupied. 'We haven't actually got a result as yet, but we're hopeful. Did you know him?'

'Testor? Not in any professional capacity. I've spoken to him a few times, down the gym and the pool. Soon as I saw your photograph I recognised him. Bit of a queer 'un, eh?'

'You never had any inkling of trouble with him?'

'Can't say we did. But I hear he has a record, eh? Assault and criminal damage?'

'That's right. But he wasn't one of your rehabilitation projects, like Speedy?'

'No way. I hardly knew him.'

'What kind of checks do you do on your tenants?'

'I went through that with Gavin, chief. Credit checks and records of other leasings, that's basically it. We wouldn't run a criminal record check unless there was a bad smell coming from somewhere. And that has happened. Once or twice we got wind of a company with dodgy investors and decided to keep them out. But we certainly don't do checks on tenants' employees, if that's what you mean. That's down to them.'

'But you probably have a blacklist, don't you, Harry? I mean, apart from your daybooks and computer records, a careful ex-copper like you would likely have a blacklist of people who don't feel right for some reason, wouldn't you?'

Jackson smiled and tapped his nose. 'I couldn't admit that to you now, could I, chief? You've got to be careful these days, the way people are – litigious.'

Brock grunted, looking disappointed. 'Yes, yes of course. I understand.' He looked pointedly at his watch, then at Kathy, and said, 'Well . . .'

'But off the record,' Jackson cut in, 'between the two of us – sorry Kathy, three of us – if there was someone you were interested in, and if I knew him and had a feeling about him, well there'd be no harm in my passing on a view, informally like, would there now?'

'I should hope not, Harry.' Brock bent down to collect his papers from the table, as if no longer interested.

'Was there someone, someone else?' Jackson asked tentatively.

'Well' – Brock straightened with a sigh – 'feelings can be misleading, of course, as we all know, Harry. Going round this place I've had a few doubts about some of the characters we've met. But of course, they're in the business of selling, and people in that situation have to put on a bit of an act, don't they?'

'Someone in particular, chief?' Harry asked again.

'Well, take the chairman of the small traders group, what's his name, the ice-cream man . . .'

'Bruno? Bruno Verdi?'

'Yes, that's the one. He'd have to be a phoney, wouldn't he?'

Jackson looked stunned. 'Bruno? Well . . . I don't know about that, chief. A bit larger than life, maybe. But you shock me there, mentioning him in the same breath as a nutter like Testor, you really do.'

'So you've never had any reason to think of him as dodgy in any way?'

'Dodgy? No, quite the opposite. Bruno is a pillar of the community hereabouts. Very strong on law and order and keeping our guard up. He keeps a sharp eye on what goes on, and encourages his fellow traders to do the same. I rely on people like Bruno.'

'Live alone, does he?'

'No, he's married. Christ, if living alone was a crime I'd be up there on your suspect list.'

Brock smiled. 'Me too. No, I just wondered if he had someone to vouch for his movements.'

'Why? Has someone been putting the bad word on him?'

'I'm just naturally suspicious, Harry. We're checking again everyone whose code was used on the exit doors that evening of the sixth.'

'Ah, right. With you now, chief. Well, if I was asked to say who springs to mind when the word "dodgy" was mentioned, I'd be more inclined to think of the operator of a certain games arcade down in the Bazaar.'

'Winston Starkey,' Brock said. 'Yes, his code was used too. Anything specific, Harry?'

'I take it you checked his record.'

'Remarkably clean.'

'Hmm. The kids who go there are always causing trouble. I reckon he encourages them.'

'You keep a particular eye on Starkey, do you?'

'As you say, chief, we all have our little blacklists.'

It took a further hour before Brock and Kathy were able to leave the unit and go down to the food court to see Verdi. He welcomed them as if they were old friends, and it seemed to Kathy that he had been expecting them. She assumed Alison Vlasich must have spoken to him.

When Brock said they wanted a private word, he showed them into a storeroom at the back of the shop. There was a chair at a small table heaped with invoices, and Verdi brought two more aluminium chairs in from the café and closed the connecting door. They sat down, refusing his offer of a little refreshment.

'Have you tried my pistachio flavour?' he urged them. 'The peach? You must try, before you go.' Kathy pictured him on his hands and knees in the van with the little girl.

The room was lined with shelving containing boxes of disposable containers and spoons, paper napkins and detergent, as well as dried-food ingredients, and there was a pervasive smell of vanilla.

'We were surprised to learn that you are a close relative of the dead girl, Mr Verdi,' Brock began.

'Ah, yes. I am her uncle,' he said, smiling sadly. 'So tragic.'

'But you never mentioned this.'

Verdi shrugged, an exaggerated Latin shrug. 'I was so devastated that first evening, when I heard what had happened. I nearly fainted, you remember? And afterwards, well, it never came up.' He passed a hand in a smoothing gesture across his bushy moustache.

'It seems a strange thing to want to conceal.'

'No, no! I never tried to conceal it! It just never came up. I suppose I assumed that Alison might have mentioned it, if it was important. No?'

Brock shook his head. 'No. She didn't mention it either.'

'Oh, well . . . I suppose Stefan told you, then?'

Kathy thought, if Alison didn't warn him to expect us, who did?

'You've met your brother since he came over, have you? Only he seemed reluctant to come in here when he first arrived, and that seems odd, if his brother was working here. Has he been to see you?'

'Actually, no. My brother and I have had our differences in the past. We prefer not to meet.'

'What about your sister-in-law? How do you get on with her?'

'Alison? We're not close. We're not enemies, mind. Just distant.'

'You helped Kerri get her job here at Silvermeadow, I understand.'

'Yes, that's true. Alison mentioned that Kerri was looking for a bit of work, and I spoke to the people at Snow White's.'

'I suppose you drove her home after work, did you?'

Verdi gave an amused little smile. 'No, never. I live in the opposite direction, Chief Inspector. It was up to her to arrange her own transport. She was a very independent young lady.' More smoothing of the moustache.

'You got on well with her?'

'Well enough.'

'You were closer to her than to her mother, would you say?'

'No, I wouldn't say that. Look, that family has had its problems, with Alison and Stefan splitting up, and I didn't really want to get involved or take sides or anything. We don't have a lot of contact.'

He wasn't in the least perturbed by the questions, behind the defence of his moustache and his comic character. Brock said abruptly, 'Tell us about your change of name, Mr Verdi. How did that come about?'

'It was a matter of commitment, Chief Inspector.' He smiled complacently. 'That's really what it was.'

'Commitment?'

'If you want to excel in anything, you have to be prepared to give yourself one hundred and ten per cent to it. I wanted to be the leading Italian ice-cream man in Essex. So I became Bruno Verdi, the gelato maestro.'

'That seems a little extreme.'

'Is it? You want to be the best detective in Scotland Yard, eh? So you stop being Mr Brock, you become Chief Inspector Brock, which is something else entirely. Am I right?'

'What happened to Mr Kreemee?' Brock said quietly.

Verdi smiled to himself, his lids lowering briefly in reflection as if an anticipated moment had arrived. 'Mr Kreemee was just a stage, my apprenticeship if you like. Long hours for small change, at the mercy of the weather. But this' – he waved his hand round at their surroundings – 'this is where it was leading. This is what it was all about.'

'Helen Singleton, she was a stage too, was she? An apprenticeship?'

'Ah,' he shook his head sadly, 'now I wish you hadn't said that, Chief Inspector, I really do. That was an unfortunate misunderstanding that was cleared up at the time to the complete satisfaction of the police, but only after I had been exposed to a great deal of prejudice and abuse, and it isn't right that you should bring it up again now.'

'Where were you on the afternoon and evening of the sixth of December last, Mr Verdi?' Brock said.

'Good, at last. Now we can put all these insinuations to rest.' He smiled broadly. 'Every Monday and Tuesday afternoon I leave early, at around three p.m., and go home. My wife is very ill. She suffers from multiple sclerosis. On Monday afternoons I take her to the clinic in Basildon for her weekly physiotherapy treatment, which lasts from four till six. I am with her all the time. Then we pick up take-away Indian at the Koh-i-noor in Moor Street, and return home. On Tuesday, it's her hydrotherapy pool session.'

He reached across for a piece of paper on the table and presented it to Brock with a flourish. 'There. I've written down the names of the nurse and physiotherapist who saw me that Monday afternoon. It would be so strange if I wasn't there with my wife that they would definitely have noticed my absence. I used a credit card at the Indian restaurant, so I suppose you can get a time for that. All right?'

'Very comprehensive, Mr Verdi.'

'Yes. You see, if there was one time of the week when I simply couldn't abduct Kerri or anyone else, it would be Monday afternoon. No hard feelings, Chief Inspector – no, really, I mean that. I am a very strong supporter of the police, and I am glad that you have grilled me like this, because I know you will do the same with every other possible suspect.' He smiled broadly and wiped his moustache. 'Now, are you sure about that pistachio? It really is superb.'

They got to their feet and Verdi had his hand on the doorknob when Brock took the computer image of Eddie Testor out of his pocket and showed it to him. 'Do you know this man?'

Verdi shook his head. 'Sorry, no. Is he a suspect too?'

'Thanks for your help. We'll let you get back to your customers.'

They went back out into the food court, and walked in silence until they reached the top of the escalators, when Brock exclaimed, 'One hundred and ten per cent is right. One hundred and ten per cent phoney.' Then he added, 'The couple who put you onto him in the first place, Kathy, is it worth speaking to them again?'

'I get the feeling there's a bit of animosity there. They were probably just stirring up trouble.'

'Yes. All the same, I think I'll talk to them.' He looked at his watch.

'Unless we're getting somewhere with Testor, in which case it may not be necessary.'

But they weren't getting anywhere with Eddie Testor. Brock had given him to a team of three young detectives, two men and a woman, all of about his age, but the switch hadn't produced any results. Instead he had begun to complain of severe headaches and had given the name of his GP, who he said was familiar with his problem. The doctor had confirmed that he suffered periodically from severe migraines, identified the medication he should be given from among those found in his room, and said that he should be allowed to go to bed for twelve hours in a darkened room. Brock agreed that he be returned to his Aunty Jan.

Kathy tried the mobile phone number on the card that Mrs Rutter had given her, and was answered almost immediately by a whispered voice. 'Yes?'

'Oh, Mrs Rutter? It's DS Kolla. Can we talk?'

'Wait a moment, dear,' the voice whispered, and then, after a minute, she spoke again at normal volume but breathing audibly. 'I'm sorry, Sergeant. I'm at a concert. How can I help you?'

Kathy imagined her clambering over angry concertgoers at the Festival Hall. 'I'm sorry to disturb you, Mrs Rutter. Perhaps I should speak to you later. Where are you?'

'In the Plaza Mexico, dear, in the upper mall. We've been listening to a splendid performance by the school orchestra of St Vincent's. But we've had enough, I think, so your call was timely.' She immediately agreed to come to unit 184 with Robbie Orr.

'I think they live here,' Kathy said to Lowry, who'd just arrived back at the unit. She told him about Verdi.

'Oh yes?' he said. 'I might sit in on this. Okay?'

When Rutter and Orr arrived Phil showed them to the interview area. They seemed clearly gratified to be called upon again, announcing themselves in discreet and conspiratorial tones.

Brock shook their hands gravely. 'An archaeologist, Professor Orr. I always thought that must be a wonderful thing, ever since I heard Michael Ventris speak on the radio when I was a boy.'

'Ah Ventris!' Orr's eyes lit up. 'I remember that broadcast well. I met him, you know. Yes, yes. Extraordinary, quite extraordinary.' He saw the blank look on the others' faces and added, 'He deciphered Linear B, you see. Quite amazing. He had no right to do it. Well, it had baffled everyone else, and he was a total amateur, but he did it anyway. An architect, he was. Probably the only worthwhile thing any architect has done this century, I should say.'

Harriet Rutter gave one of the delighted chuckles that Kathy noticed she reserved for Orr's little quips.

'Did you ever work in Crete yourself?' Brock asked.

'Aye, indeed. Sir Arthur Evans was my inspiration, though I never met him, of course. I'm not quite that old. But I visited his house at Knossos not long after the end of the war. The commander of the German forces had used it as his residence, you know. Anyway, I stayed there and took part in the work for a couple of months. That was what I call real archaeology, with none of the modern methods they have these days: magnetometers and potentiometers and all their electronic gadgets, drenching the ground with their electro-magnetic rays . . . ha!' His face twisted in a wild sort of grin. 'When I began, with Thom, our favourite tool was the bayonet!'

'Tom?' Kathy queried politely.

'Aye. I was with Thom on North Uist, don't you know.'

The way he said this, it sounded like someone might say, I was with Scott in the Antarctic, or, I was with Armstrong on the moon.

'Really?' she said vaguely. She wanted to ask, Tom who?, but held her tongue.

'I can see by the look on your face that you've never heard of the great Alexander Thom, young woman,' he accused.

'I'm afraid—'

'One of the greatest archaeologists these islands have produced, no less. It was Alexander Thom who deciphered the meaning of the ancient stone circles and rings which exist across the face of this country. It was he who revealed the fact that, one thousand years before the earliest mathematicians of Ancient Greece, a civilisation flourished in these islands which made free use of Pythagorean triangles, and nurtured astronomers of such extraordinary accomplishment that they were familiar with the variations in the inclination of the moon's orbit three and a half thousand years before Tycho Brahe rediscovered them!'

'Is that right?'

'Aye, it *is* right! I spent the summers of fifty-seven and fifty-eight with Dr Thom, as he then was, surveying the great slabs of Sornach Coir Fhinn and Leacach an Tigh Chloiche. I was at his side as he strode the heather, driving his bayonet into the deep peat to find the fallen stones hidden beneath the surface. And I shared his tent at night, drinking his usque, as he refined his calculations of the true value of the megalithic yard.'

'The what?' Brock asked.

'The megalithic yard! It might surprise your young colleagues to learn that almost four thousand years ago, when they probably imagine these islands were populated by painted savages, there existed a common standard unit of measure, the megalithic yard, which was in use throughout the British Isles, from the English Channel to the Outer Hebrides, and was employed to set out the dimensions of all the stone circles throughout the land. Just think of that! Imagine how that standard length was maintained and propagated across a thousand miles of wild country without benefit of roads or writing. Eh? How did they communicate it? How did they agree upon it, to two decimal places?'

'Yes, I see,' Brock said. 'Quite a mystery.'

Actually it doesn't much surprise us, Kathy thought, for the good reason that none of us is that interested. She could see Lowry sitting unblinking, expressionless, almost as if he were asleep with his eyes open, while she had been thinking of the meal that Leon might have ready for her, and wishing that they could move on from the megalithic yard to more immediately pressing matters.

'It's a great mystery, indeed. A very great mystery,' Orr continued. 'But that is only one of many mysteries. For example, the skeletons of these people, the ones that we've discovered in their graves and burial mounds, are almost invariably young. It was practically a civilisation of teenagers, their life expectancy about thirty, that is all.' He glared balefully in the direction of the mall. 'Much the way our young people are heading today, one might think, from observing their goings-on in this place.'

'You keep an eye on them, then, the children here?' Brock said mildly, and Lowry immediately seemed to wake up and look carefully at Orr.

'How could one not, Chief Inspector? They swagger along the mall looking as if they've inherited the earth, instead of a self-indulgent fantasy of dope and baubles.'

'You're aware of children taking drugs here?'

'No, no, no. I don't mean that, exactly. I'm just referring to the emptiness of their lives.'

'But you keep your eyes open, all the same. It's that I wanted to speak to you about. Your comments to Sergeant Kolla here about

Bruno Verdi and the murdered girl, can you be more specific? Can you recall instances of him talking to her, for example? You'd assume they would talk, if they were related.'

'I . . . I'm not sure . . .' Orr looked suddenly uncomfortable, as if he'd been caught out telling tales he couldn't substantiate. Or perhaps, Kathy thought, it might be that he could remember the distant past a lot more clearly than yesterday.

'Well, that in itself was odd, you see!' Harriet Rutter broke in. 'When she referred to him as "Uncle Bruno" I thought, well, why don't they behave like family, instead of eyeing each other that way?'

'What way?'

'I don't know . . . warily, I suppose.'

'What exactly do you mean, that she was afraid of him?'

She frowned doubtfully. 'I couldn't really say that was it. It might have been, but I couldn't swear to it.'

'Or could it be that they had some sort of relationship that they didn't want to reveal to others watching, in public, like yourselves?'

'Ha!' Orr suddenly barked. 'Might be that!'

'Well, it might, I suppose. Oh dear . . . I don't want to slander the man. He may be a bully . . .'

'Is he?'

'Oh yes, in meetings. He loves to talk over people, and put them down. Especially women. That's one thing I'll say for Bo Seager – she knows how to put him in his place when he goes too far. But getting back to the poor girl, we did see them talking, do you remember, Robbie? Not too long ago. Perhaps three or four weeks ago, we were having our pancakes when he came over from his shop and tried to attract her attention. She pretended to ignore him, but he stood there, over by one of the palm trees, and stared at her until she went to him. They talked for a few minutes, and then she gave a toss of her head, and flounced off on her roller skates. Do you remember, Robbie?'

Orr looked unsure.

'Well, we did. I remember it quite clearly.'

Brock tried to prod their memories further, but there was little they could add, and after a while they left.

Lowry looked thoughtful. 'All right if I talk this over with Harry Jackson, chief?' he asked.

'I suppose so.' Brock nodded. 'We did ask him about Verdi and he seemed to regard him as a pillar of the community, but if you think you can get anything else out of him, go ahead.'

'You might find out if he warned Verdi that we were interested in him,' Kathy said. 'The way Verdi had everything ready for us it looked as if someone had tipped him off.'

'Harry wouldn't do that, Kathy,' Lowry said dismissively. 'What, you got your sights on Verdi as your serial killer, have you? On the strength of those two old farts' gossip?'

The way he said it, *your* serial killer, as if it was a personal foible, made Kathy flush. She saw Brock react too. 'Kathy's suggestion certainly got Alex Nicholson's attention,' he said quietly.

'Yeah, but . . .' Lowry shrugged, then shook his head as if he'd decided to keep his doubts to himself.

'Yes but what?' Kathy insisted.

'Well, if you ask me, it got the whole discussion off track. I mean she was more interested in that idea because that's what she does, isn't it? Study serial killers. Stands to reason she'd get fired up about it. But I don't reckon that helps us nail Testor, or whoever it was took Kerri.'

They broke up for the night in a mood of uneasy discontent, feeling that things should be going better than they were. Kathy phoned her flat, but the answering machine was on, then tried Leon's mobile. It rang for some time before he answered with a muffled hello, then a curse as he appeared to drop the instrument. Finally he got himself sorted out. There was a murmur of voices in the background.

'Ah, hi,' he said. 'I was about to ring you. How's it going? Are you home? You found my note?'

'No, I'm still at work. Where are you?'

'I got roped into going out for a meal with some people.'

Some people? 'Alex Nicholson?'

'Yes. Her and a few others. Some university people. I'd hoped you could have come with us.'

'Where to?'

He mentioned the name of a new restaurant in Chelsea that she'd read about and had thought of taking him when they next had something to celebrate.

'That's nice. Is it as good as they say?'

'Not bad. Very busy. It'd be better if you were here.'

'Well, enjoy yourself. See you later.'

She put down the phone a little too briskly, reflecting that she couldn't have afforded to eat there anyway, not after what she'd done to her credit card recently.

The others were calling it quits for the night, yawning, pulling their coats on, offering lifts, but Kathy didn't feel like going home and said she'd stay a bit longer. She was still there in front of the computer an hour later, working slowly through the missing persons index, when one of the centre security staff rapped on the mall door.

Kathy got up and opened it, letting the guard check her identification.

'You're the last one in the place,' he said. 'I'm locking up for the night. You staying long?'

'Maybe another half-hour? Is that okay?'

He nodded. 'Do you reckon you can find your way out with just the emergency lights? I could leave some of the main lights on, but then you'd have to switch them off.'

'No, that's fine,' she said. 'I have a torch, anyway. What about the carpark? Isn't there a dog patrol out there?'

'He won't be here till midnight, but I wouldn't wait till then. The dogs are very nasty. Silent, they are, until the last second, just before they bring you down.'

'How do you know that?'

'Cos they nearly got me one night.'

Kathy said good night and returned to her screen, continuing with her trawl of random correlations: missing girls of the same age as Kerri, same hair style, same occupation; perpetrators with surnames beginning with the letter V, of the same age as Verdi, same physical characteristics; references to ice-cream, to out-of-town shopping malls, to Snow White.

She checked her watch and was surprised to see it read 11.20 p.m. She switched off her screen, packed up her things and made for the door. As she turned off the lights in unit 184 and stepped out into the mall, she immediately understood the slight edge of concern in the security guard's voice about her finding her way out. It wasn't that she could get lost – she knew the layout of the place too well for that now. It was the overwhelming sense of being suddenly alone in a vast, empty darkness, a sense that triggered a momentary feeling of panic, a safety response hard-wired into the brain long ago: *Get back to the cave! Get back to the fire! Find friends!*

She stood absolutely motionless until the feeling passed, and as her eyes adjusted, the dark gradually became less impenetrable. Spots of moonlight, emerald green, speckled the pitchiness, further and further into the depths. It wasn't moonlight, of course, only the glow of emergency lights and exit signs, but their effect was magical all the same, creating pools and haloes of penumbra, so that the blankness slowly transmuted into a deep and mysterious forest landscape. And it was unnervingly beautiful, the tawdry daytime fantasy transformed and become real in the darkness.

Now the feeling of being quite alone in this strange place was intriguing, seductive. Kathy found that she couldn't just turn down the nearby side-exit corridor that would take her out into the carpark without exploring the moonlit forest a little further. And as she progressed along the mall the effect of being alone in a magical fairy wood was strengthened by glimpses of tiny lights from within the darkened stores on either side. She supposed that they were the winking lights of alarms and security cameras, the LCD displays of electronic digits, but the darkness made distance and perspective illusory, so that as they emerged from behind dark obstacles and vanished again into the shadows, it appeared to Kathy that she was seeing the lights of a distant village, or the gleam of rubies and emeralds in a shadowy cave, or the eyes of watchful creatures.

She reached the main square overlooking the rain-forested food court, and stopped there, absorbing the extraordinary sense of depth through the tree canopy, imagining herself hovering over a distant jungle canyon. For a moment the illusion was so powerful that she could almost see the shifting shadows of nocturnal beasts beneath the trees, hear the rustle of predators through foliage.

She suddenly stood rigid, ears straining. She *could* hear the rustle of movement.

She heard it again.

It seemed to come from behind her. She turned slowly, heart thumping, and saw the bamboo thicket not far away behind her right shoulder, the one that contained the crouching gorilla. There was no movement among the bamboo leaves now, no sound, the gorilla invisible in the shadows. She knew that the darkness that allowed her imagination to create a magic forest in the mall was equally capable of magnifying her terrors. But there *had* been a sound.

Then she jumped as something small and blurred burst out of the thicket. For a moment it seemed to hang in the air in front of her, fluttering madly, before rising up into the vault above and swooping away in the darkness. Of course, it was the small bird that had strayed into the mall and been unable, or unwilling, to leave. It had survived two or three days now, she thought. Probably there was plenty to eat and drink in here.

Kathy was aware of an odd effect. Her sight seemed less acute than before, her whole consciousness now focused on her hearing. And as she turned back towards the balcony overlooking the lower court she realised she could now hear another sound.

It was muffled, distant, difficult to decipher. She concentrated and thought she could make out some kind of music, but strange and ethereal, the rhythm broken into disjointed snatches. It seemed to be coming from the floor of the valley below. She found the top of the escalator and began walking down the motionless steps, straining to make out the sound.

Frustratingly, it was less clear down below than up above, and she circled the food court for several minutes, bumping into tables and chairs in the darkness, unable to trace its source. Then her wandering route took her towards the snake charmer and the entrance to the Bazaar, and the tinkling sounds became a little more distinct.

It was very dark down there, the faint light sources dying in the black depths of the Bazaar. The sound was certainly becoming clearer, beeping and pinging notes which came in a rush for a few seconds, then paused briefly before flying off in some new direction. It was like the pipes of some manic Pan playing in the midnight forest of a nightmare. And then she turned the corner and saw the flickering electronic flashes bouncing around the mouth of the games arcade, and she realised what it was. One of the machines had been left on.

She moved softly towards the steel security grille that had been drawn across the front of the games arcade when it had closed down for the night. The flashing lights were much brighter now, but all the same it took her a moment to make out the shadow that swayed backwards and forwards across them, and realise that someone was in there, playing the machine. He had his back to her, absorbed in the game, a slight figure against the bulk of the machine, silhouetted against the source of the flashing lights.

She put her face to the grille and was able to make out the baseball cap reversed on his head, long curls beneath, baggy trousers, the mobile phone clipped to his belt. His whole body was weaving and jigging as if he were dancing with his electric partner, whose staccato bleeping was becoming more and more excited.

By the flickering lights of the machine, she could barely make out the rest of the arcade space. He seemed to be quite alone, only this one game active. She wondered how on earth he had got there. Had he hidden somewhere in the place when Winston Starkey had closed

177

up for the night? Or did Starkey allow him to stay there, a homeless kid addicted to the machines – in exchange for what?

Whether he became distracted and made a mistake, or the game simply came to an end, the machine suddenly blared a triumphant fanfare of electronic trumpets and then fell silent, its lights calming to a steady post-coital glow.

He remained there for a moment, hands still on the controls, then he slowly raised his head and appeared to sniff the air.

He can smell me, Kathy thought, staying motionless as he began to turn towards her. She saw now that he was wearing knee and elbow pads, like a skateboarder.

'Wiff,' she said softly, not wanting to alarm him. 'Wiff . . .'

He swung round abruptly, staring at the corner where she was, but not seeing her in the darkness, his eyes still blinded by the flashing game. They were wide with fright. Before she could say anything else he gave a little yelp and spun away, plunging back into the shadows at the rear of the unit.

Kathy heard a scrape of metal, a scuffling and creaking, then silence. Like a little frightened animal, she thought, he must have scurried back to his hiding place. She tried to move the security grille, but it was firmly locked. Then she pulled out her torch and shone it into the far corners of the arcade, but could see no sign of him.

'Wiff,' she called gently. 'It's all right. I'm a friend.' She spoke towards the deepest shadows behind the furthest machines where she guessed he might be hiding. 'Please, come and talk to me. I won't hurt you.'

But there was no response, not a whisper of a breath nor the glimmer of a reflection from an eyeball.

Kathy looked at her watch and saw, again with surprise, how late it was, almost midnight. The dog patrol would be out in the carpark soon, and there was nothing she could do here. She switched off the torch and headed back the way she had come, hurrying now through the moonlit glades as if the silent dogs were on her trail.

She was in bed asleep when Leon returned in the small hours. He came in silently, and woke her with a kiss on her cheek. She struggled back to consciousness, smelling the cigarette smoke on his clothing and wine on his breath.

10

Kathy didn't sleep well, her mind troubled by dreams of dark forests and lost children. She rose early, made a pot of tea and left a mug beside Leon, but didn't wake him. He was still sleeping deeply when she left.

She was waiting for Winston Starkey as soon as the arcade owner opened up his premises. He looked as if he'd had a bad night too, and he hardly heard what she was saying as he rolled up the security grille. He made her repeat it, then stared at her with hostile suspicion.

'That's crap,' he said. 'I know the kid you mean, but he doesn't stay here, and if you get me into trouble telling people he does I'll sue you, see if I don't.'

Harry Jackson appeared, strolling round his domain on a first morning inspection, and joined them. He was startled by Kathy's story. 'You saw him in here? In the dark? At *midnight*?'

Starkey made an elaborate performance of insisting that they search the place. There wasn't the slightest trace of the boy. He and Jackson conferred while Kathy had another look behind the machines at the rear of the space, without result. By the time she left with Jackson she could almost believe that it had been a dream.

He led her out into the deserted food court and asked if they could have a word.

'Just to get this straight, Kathy. You were in here on your own, at midnight, were you? Did my people know? I didn't notice a note in their report.'

Kathy outlined her conversation with the security guard. She was aware of becoming defensive as Jackson probed.

'You know about the dog patrol, do you?'

'Yes, your man warned me. I left in time.'

'Hmm.' He said nothing for a moment, staring down at the toe of his polished shoe tapping silently on the patterned terrazzo.

'Is Starkey a suspect now, then?' he asked slowly.

'No.'

'But you were staking his place out at midnight. How about Verdi, is he a suspect?'

'Harry, I can't discuss—'

'You see, I thought you were reaching a conclusion on this case. I thought Eddie Testor was your prime suspect, no? In fact, I understand that Chief Superintendent Forbes is holding a press conference this morning to announce significant progress.'

'Gavin told you that?'

Jackson frowned at her. 'No, Kathy,' he said softly. 'The PR people at Hornchurch Street advised Bo's office last night. So what do you want me to tell my boss? That despite what Forbes is telling us, interrogation of our people is continuing indiscriminately all over Silvermeadow?'

Our people. It was the first time Kathy had heard anyone refer to Starkey as that.

The sense of unease still hung in the air of unit 184 when Kathy returned there. Chief Superintendent Forbes had arrived and was deep in conversation with Brock.

'I had assumed that we'd be able to announce that charges had been laid against Testor, Brock,' he said. 'Swift justice, that was going to be the gist of it, but now, well, what have we got?'

'Yes. Unfortunately the picture is still incomplete. The forensic side is particularly disappointing. Now you could say, given the hairless nature of our suspect, that the absence of any foreign hairs on or around the victim is a kind of positive, but it doesn't help much. One very young eyewitness placing the victim and the suspect in the same place in a public mall doesn't amount to enough either, especially since we assume from the evidence of the ketamine use that she could have been kept in a drugged state for a period before she was killed. But we've no idea where he might have done that. The clearest solution would be a confession, and so far that's not forthcoming. Testor is back at Hornchurch Street now, and I'll be going over there shortly, but I'm not optimistic.

'You heard about the attack on his house, did you? During the night, after the pubs had closed. Testor says he was woken by the noise of something clattering down the tiles above his bedroom. He says he thought he heard muffled voices out the front, but he didn't get up and have a look. It wasn't till the morning that he realised what had happened. Red paint was splattered all over the roof tiles and down the front of his aunt's house. There'd been a bit of rain during the night, which made it look worse, apparently. He said it looked as if blood was coming out through the bricks.'

'Hmm. Deplorable, of course, but understandable. People are angry, Brock.'

'Yes. All the more reason not to raise expectations prematurely. I'd suggest we concentrate on appealing for public assistance from the press. Unless something comes up soon to resolve things.'

Something did come up, almost immediately. The caller asked for Sergeant Kolla, and Kathy recognised the throaty voice of Kim Hislop from the Primavera Fitness Salon.

'Can I speak to you?' she asked, her voice low and anxious. 'I've got some information you should have, about Eddie Testor.'

'Fine. Shall I come to your office?'

'Yes, okay. Soon as you like.'

Kathy mentioned it to Brock on her way out, and he said, 'Fingers crossed. I'm on my way over to see Testor at Hornchurch Street now. Ring me if it's anything relevant.'

Kim Hislop was strung as tight as one of her male clients waiting for a total body wax. 'I'm sorry,' she said, 'but I thought I should let you know straight away. As soon as I realised. I think I've made a stupid mistake.'

'Really?' Kathy said. 'To do with Eddie?'

She nodded. 'Yes, to do with Eddie. I realised last night. It just came back to me. The sixth. He was booked in for his monthly on the following day, the seventh, but I had a cancellation for the sixth, and someone else wanted a booking on the seventh, so I asked Eddie to swap round, and he agreed. He was always very obliging. The thing was, I never entered it on the computer, only in the desk diary, so when you asked I never picked it up. I forgot.'

'So when did you see him, on the sixth?' Kathy asked, heart sinking.

'Five-thirty till six-thirty. I seem to remember he was a few minutes late arriving.'

'And this has just come back to you, Ms Hislop?'

'Yes.' She looked away. 'Sorry if it's confused things. You can see the desk diary if you like.' She passed it over to Kathy, pointing out the altered entries.

'I'd like to borrow this,' Kathy said.

Hislop looked unhappy. 'Do you have to?'

'It's evidence that could clear Eddie of a serious charge. I'll let you have it back this afternoon.'

There was a phone number written against the name of the woman who had been crossed out for the 5.30 appointment on the sixth. Kathy rang it when she got back to the unit. The woman answered and after checking her own diary confirmed that she had cancelled that appointment because of a clash with something else. The name written into Eddie's original time slot on the seventh was indecipherable, and had no phone number, and Kathy decided to let it go. She rang Hornchurch Street and asked for Brock. After several minutes Gavin Lowry answered.

'He and Forbes are on their way over here, Kathy. Anything I can do?'

'How's it going?' she asked.

'No change.'

'Has Testor come up with any story about what he was doing for the hour after five-thirty that afternoon?'

'No. We keep pressing him, and he just keeps repeating that he can't remember specifically, and he must have been working in the pool.'

'It looks as if he's got an alibi now.' She told him Hislop's story.

There was a long silence, then a slow, deliberate, 'Shit.'

'Yes.'

'Maybe you'd better get over here and tell Brock yourself. He'll probably want to see the book. So will Forbes. His press conference starts in an hour. His silver braid is all laid out for him.'

When they told Eddie the good news, he seemed no wiser than before. 'Oh, really?' he said blankly. 'Well, that must be it then.'

'That doesn't mean you didn't speak to Kerri,' Brock pressed him. 'We know you did. It just means you didn't speak to her for long on that occasion. You arranged to see her again later, is that it? You made a date for later?'

'Mr Brock,' Eddie said with the same patient tolerance, 'I told you already. Maybe I can't remember exactly what I was doing that afternoon, but I'm quite sure I never saw that girl before in my life.'

Since there were already press cameras and reporters arriving at the building they decided to wait until the press conference was over before releasing him.

Forbes began by introducing himself and then Stefan and Alison Vlasich, sitting on each side of him at the long table which faced the crowded room. The purpose of this press conference, he said, was to renew the appeal to the public for information concerning the whereabouts of Kerri Vlasich after she left school on the afternoon of the sixth of December. He briefly outlined the circumstances and underlined, reading from his prepared statement, the seriousness with which the police regarded such cases. This went on for a little too long, and he stumbled several times and paused for sips of water, his throat unaccountably dry. To Kathy he gave the impression of nervousness, despite the well-tailored uniform and air of command. She was aware of others in the room beginning to stir, restless.

He then asked Mrs Vlasich to say a few words, or rather, he referred to her as 'Mrs Kerri', and couldn't understand why she stared at him, wide-eyed, before she turned unsteadily to face the cameras. She winced as the lights focused on her, and made an agonising appeal, barely audible, for anyone who knew anything about her daughter's disappearance to come forward.

Everyone was relieved when she finished and Forbes turned to Stefan Vlasich, who delivered a couple of brief sentences in a low monotone.

Chief Superintendent Forbes then cautiously invited questions, and there was an immediate response from all sides of the room, everyone apparently trying to ask the same thing. Eventually one managed to speak for the rest. 'What about the man you arrested yesterday? We were expecting an announcement of charges being laid.'

Forbes cleared his throat. 'There seems to have been some misunderstanding. No one has been arrested. A man has been helping us with our enquiries, but no charges are being laid at this time.'

'But he's a prime suspect, isn't he?'

'Not necessarily, no. There's nothing I can add about that at this time.'

There was a hubbub of disappointment, then the crime reporter for the *Guardian*, a sharp young woman with a deceptively friendly smile, spoke up.

'Are you able to give us details yet of the cause of Kerri's death, or the circumstances?'

'We're not able to release that information yet, no.'

'Are you even certain she was murdered?'

Forbes hesitated. 'We're treating this as a murder inquiry.'

'That's not quite an answer, Chief Superintendent,' the reporter said with a smile. 'I understand this is being classified as an Area Major Investigation,' she went on, although it hadn't been announced, 'and we have Chief Inspector Brock here, and other officers from Serious Crime Branch.' She sounded puzzled. 'Isn't this level of response a bit unusual? Is there something you're not telling us?'

Forbes cleared his throat and launched into a laboured account of the seriousness with which crimes against children were regarded by the authorities.

'You think this sort of thing's getting out of control, do you?'

Forbes didn't like the use of that phrase, not at all. The police took all these cases very seriously, he explained, but independent analysis of crime statistics showed that the increase in reported assaults on children during the past five years was probably the result of increasing public sensitivity to the problem, rather than an actual increase in assaults per se.

'Well, not exactly, Chief Superintendent,' the *Guardian* reporter objected calmly, as if she'd known he'd say that. 'The figures for assaults by strangers tend to be obscured by the much larger number of assaults within the family, which tend to be more readily reported now. But if we extract the family assaults, it's clear that stranger assaults have been increasing at a fairly alarming rate, isn't it? Practically an epidemic.'

Forbes looked startled. It seemed as though he hadn't been told about the breakdown of the statistics. It occurred to Kathy that the reporter had been better briefed by somebody than he had.

Then he recovered. 'We can argue about statistics,' he glowered at the reporter, 'but meanwhile, Mrs Vlasich's daughter has been found dead in suspicious circumstances. Let's just concentrate on that, shall we? We'd like you to emphasize that we're particularly looking for witnesses who were in the Silvermeadow shopping centre and in the carpark outside from about five-fifteen p.m. onwards on the sixth, especially within an hour of that time.'

'Did Kerri have a medical condition, Mrs Vlasich?' someone called out.

'Who was her favourite pop group?'

The questions, innocuous and inane, flitted backwards and forwards for a while, and then the *Guardian* reporter put up her hand again. Forbes avoided noticing her for as long as he could, but eventually her voice cut in. 'Can you tell us when you last ran a major crime investigation, Chief Superintendent Forbes?'

The room went dead quiet. Forbes looked stunned.

'Only, there's been a suggestion that the force is so top-heavy with senior officers who haven't been actively involved in crime-fighting for years that they can't afford to put young officers, more in touch with the latest methods, in charge of important investigations like this. Is there any truth in that, would you say?'

Forbes stared at her for a long moment. Then he took a deep breath, drew himself up straight and said, 'If there are no more relevant questions, I believe Mr and Mrs Vlasich have had enough,' and he swept up his papers, rose to his feet, and escorted the couple out of the room.

When they were all safely back in the office next door, Lowry beamed at his chief. 'Well done, sir. You dealt with her really well.'

Forbes shook his head. He looked flushed, wiping a handkerchief across his brow. 'She seemed bloody well prepared. Hell's teeth, what a bitch!' Then he looked at Brock. 'Perhaps she's right. Perhaps this is all getting out of hand. We haven't even established that it was murder yet, and the cost! I had a look at the man-hour summaries last night, Brock. You should do the same.'

'Yes, I've seen them. Let's stick with it for a little longer, sir,' Brock murmured. 'Like you said, one more push.'

Kathy returned to the briefing room. The *Guardian* reporter was speaking to her photographer. She nodded to him and turned to leave. Kathy followed, out through the front doors and down the steps. She caught up with her on the pavement and introduced herself with a smile.

'Gavin Lowry said to say thanks,' Kathy said, 'and to let him know if you need anything else.'

The reporter stared at Kathy for a moment, face blank, then raised one eyebrow and gave her a little smile. 'You lot!' she said. 'You're worse than we are. I've been trying to get somebody to do that to my editor for months.'

She saw the smile disappear from Kathy's face.

'Come on,' the reporter said. 'You know these old bastards need shafting.'

★

Kathy found Eddie Testor down in the basement carpark with Lowry and a couple of officers, waiting.

'Is his solicitor going to take him?' she asked.

'No,' one of the men said. 'She had to go to court. We're organising a lift in a patrol car.'

'That's no good. They'll spot him straight away and tail you all the way.'

She looked at the cars parked around them and saw Lowry's, blocking a couple of others. 'What about it, Gavin?' she asked. 'We could take him in your car.'

'I've got better things to do,' he said, eyeing Testor sideways with distaste.

'If you're thinking of thanking the *Guardian* reporter, I already did it for you.'

'Eh?' He looked startled for a moment, then gave her a crooked smile and pulled his keys from his pocket. 'Take him yourself if you're that keen.'

'All right.' She held out her hand and he took the car key off the ring and gave it to her.

Testor looked bemused, but he followed her to the car and got in the back and lay down and let her cover him with Lowry's raincoat and newspapers. She closed the door firmly on him and nodded to his minders.

'Good luck,' one of them said.

There were reporters waiting in the road that accessed the rear of the building, expecting this, but instead of turning towards them, and so out onto the high street, Kathy turned left into the narrow service lane that ran behind the primary school, then out into the residential street beyond. After a couple of minutes she checked her mirror and said, 'All clear, Eddie. I'll stop and let you get in the front.'

She watched him out of the corner of her eye, slowly stretching the belt across his oversize chest and shoulders. When he finally succeeded she caught the look on his face as he surveyed the garbage in the car.

'Terrible, isn't it? It's not my car. Belongs to DS Lowry. What a slob.'

He didn't say anything.

'You two didn't hit it off, did you? What did he say to you, at the end of the interview yesterday? Nobody else heard.'

Silence.

'I'm not trying to trap you, Eddie. You could admit to every crime in the book in here and I wouldn't be able to use a word of it. It's only what you say in the station, properly witnessed, that counts. So you can relax.'

He said nothing at first and they drove on in silence, but then, as they got closer to his aunt's house he muttered, 'Thanks anyway.'

'What for?'

'You know, taking me away from there. I can't stand them cameras. The lights and noise they make, shouting at you all the time. I can't stand it.'

'Don't worry. People have a short memory. Keep out of sight and in a day or two they'll have forgotten all about you.'

But not yet, she realised, as she turned into the court in front of Aunty Jan's house. Distracted by the sight of the red paint, she didn't immediately appreciate the mood of the crowd milling around the front gate. Eddie's reaction was also slow, and they had spotted his distinctive pink skull long before he realised what was happening. Shouts went up and furious faces converged on the car, pressing against the windows as Eddie shrank from them. They closed around the rear of the car so that Kathy couldn't reverse back onto the street, and for a moment they were motionless, the people glaring through the glass. Then the car began to rock, fists began banging on the roof, and a terrible howling noise grew from the crowd.

There was another sound too, Kathy realised, of Eddie whimpering.

'Don't worry,' she said calmly, observing the distorted, almost animalistic expressions on the faces glaring in at them with a curious sense of detachment. There was no two-way radio in Lowry's car and she didn't think she had time to use her mobile phone. There was no sign of a uniform in the courtyard. She raised her wallet to the window by her side, showing her warrant card to the faces, but they didn't see, or didn't want to see.

'Oh hell . . .'

She put the car into first gear, held her hand on the horn, and let out the clutch gently. Slowly, painfully slowly, the car began to inch its way forward against the bodies pressing in on it, while she prayed that the lock would be sufficient to turn in one manoeuvre.

They became angrier, realising what she was doing, and some began chanting. Then the people at the back scattered and the car was abruptly hit a jarring crunch, and Kathy saw a metal dustbin rolling away from the rear wing. Some youths were picking it up to throw it again, and now a brick landed on the bonnet, shattering into pieces and scattering the people in front. More bricks came flying in as she accelerated, and just as she reached the street the dustbin struck again, collapsing the rear windscreen into the back seat.

'Shit, shit, shit!' Kathy fumed as she threw the car round the corner and hurtled away. She drove over a mile before she pulled in to the kerb. Eddie was crouched beside her, his arms covering his head, sobbing.

'It's all right now,' she said, aware of her heart thumping in her chest as she fumbled with the phone. 'What about your aunt?' she said, having almost to shout above his sobbing. 'Eddie! Stop this! Is your aunt in there?'

'I dunno,' he wailed.

She stared at him. This was the thug who'd battered a car to a heap with rage, and who may yet have tipped Kerri Vlasich into the compactor. She put her hand to her left ear to block out his noise and made her report into the phone. When she was finished she took a few deep breaths, trying to calm herself.

Eddie's head was shaking under the cover of his enormous arms. The sobbing had died away, and she heard a mumbled word. He sounded just like a terrified child.

'What did you say, Eddie? Put your arms down and tell me.'

He mumbled something she couldn't pick up.

'Put your arms down, Eddie. I can't hear what you're saying. There's no one around now. There's nothing to be afraid of.'

He slowly straightened himself, head drooping on unyielding pectorals, and whispered, 'He said that this time they'll put me away in a special prison, where the other men will use me like a girl.'

Kathy waited, watching his head rocking from side to side. Then he added, 'It's just not fair. All I did was give her the ticket.' And he burst into a flood of tears, unable to contain them any longer.

Among the debris on the floor were several packets of tissues. Kathy reached for one of them and slowly undid the wrapping and waited until the flow of tears died away.

'Here,' she said gently, handing the packet to him. He accepted it, and she said, 'You'd better tell me all about it, Eddie. There's no point going on like this.'

He sniffed and wiped and finally nodded. 'I was just doing a favour for Mr Verdi, that's all.'

'You know Mr Verdi, do you?'

'A bit,' he said cautiously. 'He works out at the gym. He . . . he's friendly to me.'

Kathy thought that the word 'friendly' didn't come out very easily. And she also remembered that Verdi had denied recognising Eddie's picture

'Go on.'

'Well, he wanted to do a favour for this girl he knew, only he didn't want nobody to know.'

'What sort of favour?'

'Her mum and dad had split up, and she wanted to go and see her dad in Germany, only her mum wouldn't let her go, which was really unfair, he said. So Mr Verdi agreed to help her, give her a ticket and some cash. He said he'd get into trouble if her mum found out, so he wanted me to give her the envelope one Monday evening, when he would be at the hospital with his wife, and nobody could say he had anything to do with it.'

'What exactly did you do?'

'She was going to come in to Silvermeadow on the bus that arrives at five twenty-five. I was to change my shift break around so I could meet her at five-thirty at the windows overlooking the pool, and give her the envelope. That was all. And that was what happened. This girl with the green frog bag, like Mr Verdi said, came in right on time, and I waved the envelope and she came over and said, "Hello Eddie, I'm Kerri. Is that for me?" and I gave it to her, just like Mr Verdi had said.'

'You hadn't met the girl before?'

'No.'

'And it was the girl in our photographs?'

He looked sheepish. 'I suppose.'

'Did you see what was in the envelope?'

'I didn't actually see. It was sealed up, but it was tickets and some money – Mr Verdi said.'

'Mr Verdi trusted you with money, Eddie? He wasn't afraid you might take it for yourself?'

'Oh no!' He looked shocked at the idea. 'I wouldn't do that to Mr Verdi.'

'You know him pretty well then?'

Eddie shrugged. 'He's an important man at Silvermeadow. He knows the people who run things.'

'I see. And what happened after you gave the girl the money?'

189

'She left. I don't know where . . . along the mall.'

'And you went to your waxing.'

Eddie shook his head sadly. 'No. I went and got a hamburger in the food court.'

'But Kim Hislop said—'

He looked very uncomfortable. 'I 'spect she was trying to help me. Maybe she got it mixed up. I don't know. I don't want to get her into no trouble.'

Kathy shook her head. 'Eddie, why the hell didn't you tell us this at the beginning? You've caused lots of people trouble by lying like that.'

'Sorry,' he whispered, squirming in his seat. 'I couldn't, see. Cos I'd promised Mr Verdi.'

'I understand. But now you must put things right, by telling Mr Brock everything. Okay? Mr Brock is a much more important man than Mr Verdi, believe me, and he can make a lot more trouble if you don't come clean.'

He nodded vigorously. 'Yeah, yeah. I want to do that. I couldn't keep it in no more.'

The press had gone from Hornchurch Street by the time they got back, and Kathy was able to drive in without difficulty. She took Eddie to an interview room to make his statement to Brock. When it was over they made some rapid phone calls, then sent a car to Silvermeadow to pick up the gelato king.

Verdi arrived with an air of benevolent mystification, Brock noted, an honest citizen trying be patient with the inexplicable ways of the police.

'Was it really necessary to bring me over here, Chief Inspector? I am quite short-handed today.'

'I'm afraid so.' Brock snapped down the switch of a recording machine and intoned the time and names of those present. 'We found a travel agent in Basildon who says you bought some tickets on the sixth of December. Tell us about them, will you?'

Verdi blinked, and Brock saw the signs of sudden panicked calculations. 'The sixth? Perhaps you would just remind me?'

'Why? Did you make more than one purchase of tickets around then?'

'Well, I don't think . . . I just don't recall.'

'One single ticket on the coach that stops at Silvermeadow en route from Victoria to Harwich, plus one single ticket for the night ferry from Harwich to Hamburg.'

'Ah!' His face creased in an exaggerated smile. 'Yes, of course, how stupid of me.'

Stupid indeed, thought Brock, and remarkably forgetful.

'Open tickets,' he said, 'valid during the following six months—'

Brock leant forward and spoke slowly, not trying to keep the anger from his voice. 'Don't insult my intelligence.'

Verdi drew back a little. 'Really, Chief Inspector! You're being very aggressive, if I may say. Maybe I should call my solicitor.'

'Maybe you should. Lying to police conducting a murder inquiry is an extremely serious matter.'

'Lying?'

Brock placed the computer image of Testor on the table. 'You never saw this man before. A lie. You had no idea what your niece was doing at Silvermeadow on the sixth. A lie.'

'This man?' He touched his moustache nervously as if it were a charm that might help.

'Eddie Testor.'

'That is Eddie Testor? No, I don't think . . . Well, maybe there is some similarity . . .'

Brock made an abrupt move of irritation.

'No, please.' Verdi took a scarlet handkerchief out of his pocket and wiped his face, which had gradually become almost as red. 'All right, look, I see you've been talking to Eddie, and if he's chosen to speak then I can feel free to tell you everything. I was keeping silent to protect him, you see. No, please, you're looking as if you don't believe it, but that's the truth of the matter.'

It occurred to Brock that it would be easy to underestimate this man, to write him off for his bluster and his lies as a fool. He guessed that Verdi had been playing this part, part clown and part bully, for most of his life, and might have become quite adept at using it to hide bigger, deeper lies beneath the phoney surface.

'The fact is, what can I say?' Verdi went on. 'I did try to help Kerri visit her father, my brother, over in Hamburg. Well, I felt it my duty, really. Alison was being very unreasonable in preventing it, and I could see it would end up destroying her relationship with Kerri, apart from causing heartache to the rest of my family – my brother and our elderly mother, who hasn't seen her grand-daughter in three years and isn't able to travel. Stefan, my brother, had been exchanging letters with Kerri for some months, using me as a post-box, and they had decided that they would get together for this Christmas, regardless of Alison. Anyway, I agreed to arrange Kerri's tickets, thinking she'd go over towards the middle of December. But on the Sunday night, the fifth, she came in to see me at the shop after she'd finished her shift and said her mother was driving her mad, and she was going to leave the following day, with or without my assistance. She said she would hitch-hike if I wouldn't help. I told her to calm down, and tried to persuade her to wait, but she was very stubborn. She wouldn't listen, so I phoned the family in Hamburg, and this travel agent I know, and made the arrangements.

'The following day I collected the tickets from Basildon, but I didn't want Kerri being seen anywhere near me or the shop on the day she was to disappear, or I was sure I'd be in trouble for helping her. On Mondays and Tuesdays I leave early from Silvermeadow, so Monday afternoon was a perfect time, and I arranged for Eddie to act as the go-between, to hand over the tickets.'

'Why Eddie?'

Verdi shrugged. 'He was just someone I knew who had no connection at all with Kerri or, as far as most people knew, with me. I just knew that he was a very willing lad, someone who could be trusted to run an errand.'

'Did you know he had a criminal record?'

Verdi frowned. 'The road-rage case, you mean? Yes, I knew about that. But I've never seen that side of him, and frankly I think he's got over all that. But of course, when Harry told me that Kerri had been murdered, that came straight into my mind.'

'Did you give him the black eye?'

Verdi lowered his head. 'When I got my thoughts together that Saturday night, after I heard what had happened to Kerri, my first thought was that Eddie had done something to her. There is something a bit weird about the boy, do you know what I mean? Sometimes he seems a bit simple or something. Maybe just too wrapped up inside his own head, I don't know. Anyway, that was the way my mind went.'

'Then why the hell didn't you say something to us?'

'I . . . I wasn't sure what to do. I was in the wrong, wasn't I? Helping Kerri and my brother to break the terms of the custody order, and helping the girl set off abroad all on her own. I felt responsible, and I wanted to see what Eddie had to say before I came to you. Only I couldn't find him that night, and the next day you were talking to him, and it wasn't till the evening that I went to his home and had it out with him.'

Brock stared at Bruno, a foot shorter than Eddie Testor and three or four stone lighter, and tried to imagine the little man beating him up.

'Who helped you?'

'Nobody. He'd taken something, I don't know what, and he was in a stupid mood. He played silly buggers at first, joking around, so I hit him a couple of times to make him listen and show him I was serious. He sobered up then, and told me that the police had spoken to him, trying to find out who had helped the girl run away, and he'd been really smart and made up some story for you about another man talking to her. While he was telling me this, I realised that he had absolutely no idea that anything bad had happened to Kerri. He believed she was safely in Germany, and that you'd been trying to trick him and he'd been covering for her and me. Once I was sure about that, I thought the best thing was for us to keep quiet. How could it help you to know what we'd planned? We had no idea what had really happened. So I told Eddie that making up stories about another man was really dumb, and if you spoke to him again he should just say he'd got confused, and deny he'd ever seen the girl.'

Brock sat back and scratched his jaw, considering Verdi. The man had tinted his eyebrows as well as his hair and moustache, he realised, and the effect at close quarters was to make his every expression seem exaggerated and false, like a stage actor captured in close-up on film, overacting.

'So your brother Stefan can confirm this story,' he said.

'Oh yes, certainly. You ask him.'

'And Alison Vlasich knew nothing?'

'Not a thing.'

'How much money was in the envelope?'

'Not a lot. Enough for emergencies. A couple of hundred quid.'

'Sterling?'

'Yes. Just a bundle of old notes I took from the till.'

'It was very trusting of you to leave all this to Eddie, and even tell him there was money in the envelope.'

'He's a good boy really.'

'Why did Ms Hislop at the fitness salon tell lies about his waxing session to give him an alibi?'

'Oh dear . . .' Verdi looked sheepishly contrite. 'I'm sorry. That was my doing. I hope she won't get into trouble over it. When there was all that talk on TV about a prime suspect and they showed that picture of Eddie, I thought I'd got him into real trouble, and I just wanted to do whatever I could to save him.'

'Short of actually coming forward and clearing him yourself with the truth. Truth seems to be a rather irrelevant concept to you, Mr Verdi. You're quite happy to pile lies on lies, and get any number of other people tangled up in the mess, if it'll help make us buy your story. How did you persuade her to do it?'

'Oh, you know, just a favour for an old friend.' He chuckled impishly. 'Please don't be angry with her. It's all my doing.'

Brock leant forward and said, 'We want to search your premises, Mr Verdi.'

'My shop? Well, yes, if you really think that's necessary. I hope you won't alarm the customers though.'

'Your shop, and your home.'

'Oh, my home? Oh no, I don't think I could allow that. My wife is an invalid, as I told you, and very easily distressed. It would be a dreadful intrusion. No, no.'

'Don't worry, we'll be very considerate of your wife's feelings. Where do you think you're going?'

Verdi had risen to his feet, chest thrust out as if about to deliver an operatic rendition. 'I am going to my sick wife's bedside, Chief Inspector! If you want to violate my house you'd better get yourself a search warrant.'

'Sit down, Mr Verdi. By lying to us in the way that you've just admitted you can be charged with obstructing the police. By persuading a third party to obstruct our enquiries you can also be charged with conspiracy and incitement. This is an arrestable offence. If I arrest you for that offence I may then enter and search any of your premises, without a warrant, for evidence relating to that or a connected offence, such as the abduction of Kerri Vlasich.'

Brock's explanation seemed to stun Verdi. Punctured, he slid slowly back down into his seat. 'Can you do that?' he asked faintly.

'Yes, yes I can, actually. And I will, unless you're prepared to accompany us to your home and invite us in to search it.'

Later, briefing Lowry, Kathy and the others, Brock said, 'You're looking for anything relating to Kerri: correspondence, photographs, personal articles, clothing and so on. And especially you're looking for ketamine. That's the key. Get Desai to brief you on what it may look like, bottles, pills, whatever. If you can find that, we're home and dry. Look everywhere, even under the invalid's mattress. No, *especially* under the invalid's mattress.'

Verdi's home was a small detached house, one of a row packed close together behind small front gardens – late Victorian, Brock guessed – with decorative brickwork around the doors and windows that produced a slightly fantastical effect, as if the builder had had a fairy-tale gingerbread house in mind. Mrs Verdi lived on the ground floor, her room at the front where she could sit propped up in bed or in a chair by the window, watching the traffic in the street. Brock guessed that with help from her husband she could also access a family room and kitchen at the rear, and a bathroom which had been specially built for her use.

When they had finished searching the family room, Verdi lifted his wife into her wheelchair and took her through so that they could search her bedroom. He did it with an air of wounded dignity, and surprising lack of effort, Brock thought, and he remembered that Verdi also was a regular at the gym. There was nothing but dust and old tissues under the invalid's mattress.

Upstairs was Verdi's territory, inaccessible to his wife, and mirroring the arrangement below, with his bedroom at the front and what he described as his 'den' at the rear. This room was locked, and he was obliged to hand Brock the key with a sullen look. It contained an exercise machine and some hand and bar weights, a TV/video player, and empty shelving covering one wall. When asked what the shelves were for, he said he was thinking of buying a set of encyclopaedias.

'Miniature ones,' Lowry muttered, measuring the spaces between the shelves. 'Eight inches? More like paperbacks. Or videos.'

As for ketamine, the only possibility seemed to be the medicine cupboard, full of Mrs Verdi's bottles and pills, from which samples were taken.

After less than two hours the search seemed to be exhausted and the team prepared to return to Silvermeadow. Verdi watched them packing up with a satisfied look on his face. When Brock thanked him for his co-operation, he said, 'Don't mention it, Chief Inspector,' barely keeping the sarcasm out of his voice. Then he added, 'That Rutter woman had something to do with this, didn't she?'

'I beg your pardon?' Brock replied.

'Mrs Harriet Rutter,' he repeated, spitting out the syllables of the name. 'She puts on airs and acts as if shopkeepers were her personal servants, and when someone like me stands up to her she gets to work with her poison tongue. I'm right, aren't I? She put in the word against me, eh? You won't say, but it's true. Her and that old fool that tags along behind her. Well, if you want some advice, you should take a long look at him. I've seen the way he tries to talk to the young girls. He gives them little presents, has he told you that? I've seen him do it, winking at them like a hairy old goat. You should check him out and that hut of his.'

'What hut is that?'

'The site huts down below the east end of the centre. He had the use of one of them as his workroom when they were doing their excavations. Didn't you know that? He's been at Silvermeadow longer than any of us. He'd know better than any of us how to make someone disappear from that place.'

When they were in the car, Brock said, 'Bruno Verdi has an amazing capacity for making me feel that he knows in advance when we're coming for him. All that fuss about getting entry to his home, and when we go there there's not a teacup out of place.'

'Those empty shelves . . .' Lowry said.

'Exactly. What about the huts he was talking about, Gavin? They've been searched, haven't they?'

Lowry didn't answer straight away. 'I . . . Yes, they must have been.'

'You don't sound very confident.'

'I was inside the building when we did the initial search, chief. Another team worked the carpark and external site areas. They'd have covered the site huts.'

'Get Harry Jackson to open them up for you when we get back. You and Kathy. Just to be on the safe side.'

I I

Harry Jackson appeared to be unusually unco-operative and out of sorts. He was barking at someone on the phone when they looked into his office, and slammed down the receiver angrily when he finished the call.

'Half my bloody staff are down with colds and flu. It's this bleedin' weather. And they're forecasting snow. Why are you interested in those flamin' huts?'

'Just checking, Harry,' Lowry told him soothingly. 'DCI Brock wants us to do it personally. Just give us the keys and we'll get out of your way.'

'Can't do that, Gavin. One of us'll have to accompany you. New policy from senior management. And I can't spare anyone.'

'New policy? You having us on?'

'Straight up. They're getting pissed off with you lot, I reckon. And I can't say as I blame them.'

'What's brought this on?'

'Your guvnor'll have to take it up with mine.' He glared angrily through the glass window into the general office beyond, then swore. 'Oh fuck it.' He looked at Kathy, who shrugged. 'Okay, I'll go with you. Is it raining?'

'Bucketing down.'

'Great!'

They walked the length of the service road to the far end of the basement, where a fire exit door gave access into a corridor which eventually discharged at the extreme east end of the building. They hesitated in the shelter of the doorway, bracing themselves before braving the rain cascading out of the louring sky. This area was remote from the mall entrances and no money had apparently been wasted on landscaping or on softening the functional shell of the building. The lower part of the wall alongside them was filled with steel louvres from which came a low mechanical murmur. An electric cable looped out through the louvres and stretched out to the first of two rusty orange steel containers of the kind used for bulk transport on ships and trains, which stood a dozen yards away across a mess of puddled clay. Wooden palettes had been laid on the ground to form a makeshift path to the doors of the containers.

'I'll let you two get wet,' Jackson said, handing the keys to Lowry.

'Who uses them?' Lowry asked.

'The far one was used by the builders, and is empty now, or should be. The archaeologists were given the use of the near one when they found some human remains here, early on in the construction.'

'Is it still in use?'

'The old geezer, Professor Orr, still has some gear in there, as far as I know. We don't have a use for it until they decide to build the next stage of the centre, and Bo lets him potter about. She reckons it's good PR to keep him and Mrs Rutter happy.'

'It's got electricity?' Kathy asked, pointing at the cable.

'Yeah. All modern conveniences. Some, anyway.'

Lowry ran out into the rain, jumping to avoid a broken piece of timber and coming down in a puddle, splashing the legs of his suit with yellow mud. As she watched him struggling to open the padlock on the steel door, the rain drenching him, Kathy felt a surge of sympathy. It hadn't been his week: a TV thrown at him, his car wrecked, now his suit.

'Is Gavin unlucky, would you say, Harry?' Kathy asked. It was a spontaneous remark, lightly meant, but she was surprised to see the look on Jackson's face, almost of alarm.

'What makes you say that?'

'Nothing really. He just seems to be having things go wrong for him.'

'Really? Gavin always had a reputation for being a lucky bastard.' And he glanced across with a look almost of sadness at the figure tugging in frustration at the padlocked door.

Lowry got the door open at last and went inside. Kathy took the other key and followed across the palettes, avoiding the puddle, and opened the door of the other container without difficulty. It was empty, as Harry had said. She locked up again and ran back to help Lowry.

'This is cosy,' she said, looking around at the table and chair, the filing cabinet and shelves of small cardboard boxes neatly labelled. It was much more comfortable than she'd expected, and even had a camp bed squeezed across the end of the room, and next to it a tall grey metal cupboard. A crudely wired distribution board was fixed to the wall above the table, and there were several electrical appliances: a desk light, two-bar fire and kettle. But cosy wasn't the right word, she decided. Actually, it made her think of a claustrophobic, windowless prison cell.

Lowry had hung his dripping raincoat on a hook by the door and was pulling on latex gloves. He was looking vaguely worried, Kathy thought, perhaps unsure how well his team of searchers had covered this in the first place. She also pulled on gloves and they began their search. On the table there were three small glass jars, one holding paper clips, another ball-point pens, and the third an assortment of coins. In the metal cupboard she found male clothing, old work clothes, a windcheater and a battered hat. A pair of wellington boots stood beneath them, thick woollen socks stuffed in the tops, and next to them an assortment of tools standing against the side, shovels and hand trowels.

Lowry was working through the filing cabinet, discovering a half bottle of whisky among the files of work schedules, reports and letters. When he reached the bottom drawer he stopped suddenly and said, 'Oh-oh.'

Kathy turned and saw him reach into the back of the drawer and pull out a black rectangle. He pulled the video out of the sleeve, examined it briefly and handed it to her. She read the title on the spine: *Teenage Sex Kittens*. 'Oh dear,' she said, and slipped it into an evidence bag. She felt disappointed but not especially surprised, like a nurse cleaning up after someone who might have been expected to behave better.

Lowry turned back and groped around some more, and after a moment sat back on his heels and offered her a second trophy, this time a coloured loop of elasticised ribbon, such as Kerri had used to hold her ponytail in place.

'I think that's all down here,' he said grimly.

'It's enough,' Kathy said.

They did a rapid search of the rest of the space without uncovering anything more, then put their coats on again and closed the place up.

Jackson was still standing by the open door, looking miserable. 'Finished?' he grumbled.

'We'll need to put a new lock on that one, Harry,' Lowry said. 'We'll be getting forensic down here.'

'How come? Find something?'

Kathy would have said nothing, but Lowry immediately showed him the two evidence bags, which Jackson peered at intently.

'Bloody hell,' he muttered. 'In there? I don't believe it. That old bastard.'

'Keep it to yourself, eh Harry?'

'Gavin!' Jackson said reproachfully. 'You don't have to tell me.'

The sky looked dark and threatening as Kathy pulled in at the kerb opposite the high street entrance to the estate. The rain had stopped, but few people seemed willing to come back out into the raw afternoon. A double-decker splashed up to a bus stop and a few bowed figures jumped off and hurried away. In the first courtyard the old man who had spoken to them after Lowry's near miss with the TV was outside his door, wheezing as he swept the paving. Kathy called good evening to him, and got back a suspicious glower.

Alison Vlasich was looking a little better. At least her expression was more lively, though she too had developed a cold, and this, coupled with tears and loss of sleep, had turned her pale skin raw pink beneath her eyes and nose.

'I'd really rather go back to work,' she said, 'only the doctor said give it a week. I don't know. What do you think?'

'Why don't you give her a ring and say you feel ready. You're looking more yourself.'

'Yes. I've been getting out a bit, to the shops and that.'

She led Kathy into the sitting room and they sat down. There were perhaps a dozen cards of condolence standing on the shelf beside the TV, including one large one with many signatures inside it.

'From Kerri's class,' Alison said, following Kathy's eyes. There was also a large bunch of red roses in a vase on the table.

'Has Bruno been in touch today?'

'Not today, no. Why?'

'He's admitted to us that he'd been planning with Kerri to help her go to her father for Christmas.'

'Oh.'

Nothing much seemed to register on Alison Vlasich's face, neither surprise nor anger.

'You don't look surprised, Alison.'

'No,' she whispered. 'I suppose I'm not.'

'You suspected this?'

'Not so that I could put it into words . . . but now you say it, yes, I think I knew, really.'

'Aren't you angry?'

She shook her head slowly, avoiding Kathy's eyes. 'No. He was trying to do the right thing, for Kerri, and for me.'

'For you?'

'He was worried about the way Kerri was behaving, the way she was talking to me. He felt it might be better for both of us if we had a break for a while, and if Kerri got away from some of the friends she was in with.'

'What, Naomi and Lisa?'

'No, the other ones, wild kids. He thought, if Kerri got away for a while it might change her attitude.'

There was something in this that Kathy felt she was missing. Something about the air of guilt with which Alison Vlasich told it, and the careful and protective way she and her brother-in-law gave out each piece of information about each other. And suddenly Kathy wondered if it was possible that there was something more to the relationship between them. Was this what had made Kerri so rebellious and difficult, and led her uncle, and perhaps in the end her mother, to want to let her go?

'So you think Mr Verdi was really trying to help?' Kathy asked, and saw Alison glance at the bunch of roses, then away quickly, with a touch of a smile in her tired eyes. 'Oh yes. He was just trying to do the right thing, as an uncle.'

'He seems very devoted to his wife.'

The smile vanished. 'Yes, very.'

Kathy said, 'There are one or two loose ends we're trying to tie up, Alison.' She took the plastic bag with the hair ribbon from her bag and handed it to the other woman. 'Do you recognise this at all?'

Little creases of worry formed around her eyes as Alison Vlasich took it and examined it carefully. 'It's the type that Kerri wore.'

'Could it have belonged to her?'

'I don't think it could be hers, no. It's blue, you see, and Kerri liked to wear red, and green especially, because she had green eyes.' This memory had a sudden paralysing effect. She sat, immobile, as she tried to come to terms with it, and eventually Kathy reached forward and gently took the bag from her fingers.

'I'm sorry, Alison,' she said. 'Would you like me to make a cup of tea or something?'

'Oh . . . I didn't think.' She stood up abruptly. 'I'll do it.'

They went together into the little kitchen, where Alison put on the kettle.

'Do you remember Kerri ever mentioning a man called Orr? Or the Professor, something like that? An elderly man who's a bit of a regular at Silvermeadow.'

'No, never.'

'What about a younger man called Testor, Eddie Testor, who works in the leisure centre?'

'Sorry, no. Are they suspects?'

'They're just part of a long list of names we're trying to sort out, Alison. It doesn't matter. Would you mind if I had another look in Kerri's bedroom?'

Alison shrugged and turned away, setting out teacups on a flower-patterned plastic tray.

Kathy went through to the girl's room, unchanged since their first visit. Kerri herself was beginning to become a cipher in all this, she thought, the victim, an increasingly remote figure, and the room, with its commonplace postcards and posters and small possessions, was a sobering reminder that she had been real, and ordinary. There was the table at which she would have sat, daydreaming over unopened homework books perhaps, and written letters to her father. On the table was a small hand-painted box, containing mementoes, trinkets and foreign coins. She opened the box and tipped the contents out onto the desktop. There were Italian lire, Belgian and French francs, Spanish pesetas, German pfennigs. There was one coin unlike the rest, very old, black and misshapen, its faces so worn smooth that it was impossible to make out any lettering. She lifted it up to the light as Alison came in to the room.

Kathy handed it to her. 'Any idea what this is?'

'No. Is it important?'

'Probably not. Can I hang onto it for a day or two?'

'You can have it as far as I'm concerned.'

They returned to the sitting room and sipped at their tea in silence for a while. Then Kathy said, 'You have friends at work, Alison?'

'Yes, well, work–mates, you know. I like the hospital. There's always lots of things happening, lots of people around. You can't feel too sorry for yourself there.'

'PC Sangster mentioned to me that when this all started, you told her a story about an old woman in the hospital who thought she'd lost her daughter at Silvermeadow, do you remember?'

'Yes. I feel embarrassed about that now. I think I got it mixed up. She explained that you hear lots of funny stories like that, that mean nothing.'

'Yes, but all the same, we could check it again, just to be sure. Can you remember who the nurse was who heard her talking about it?'

'No. It was one of those friend–of–a–friend stories.'

'Could you ask around for me, do you think?'

She looked doubtful. 'I could try, I suppose.'

Kathy could see that the idea of raising such a thing with the people at work troubled her, and said, 'Just a name. Someone I could follow it up with.'

Robbie Orr was mortally outraged by Brock's suggestion that the pornographic video tape belonged to him. They had found him and Harriet Rutter at Silvermeadow in Plaza Mexico again, this time watching an unveiling of next year's new Ford among the haciendas and cacti, and she had insisted on accompanying him to Hornchurch Street. They had sat her in a waiting area, no more than a row of seats in the corridor near a temperamental coffee machine, looking out of place and out of sorts, while Orr was taken to an interview room.

'How dare you insinuate, sir,' he bellowed, eyes blazing, 'that I am the owner of such trash!'

'It's not a criminal offence,' Brock said calmly, thinking that Orr's outrage seemed rather excessive, unless he understood the context of the find, and the construction that might be put upon it. 'It's just that we'd like to establish whose it is. It was found in the site hut, in your filing cabinet, among your reports and papers.'

'Nonsense!' Orr roared. 'Impossible!'

'It's true.'

'Well, someone else has put it there.'

'Who?'

'One of your people perhaps! I've read about this – police fabricating evidence when they run out of ideas. Well, let me assure you that you've taken on the wrong man this time, sir. I have a reputation for probity, you will find, and friends to support it. Why, the chancellor of my old university is a friend of the Home Secretary—'

'Let's not get carried away, Professor,' Brock murmured. 'The video was found in your filing cabinet by two of my officers. Actually we're less interested in it than in what was found with it.' He showed Orr the hair band.

Orr peered at it for a moment. 'You don't mean to say that this belonged to the lassie?' His fury seemed to evaporate as he said it.

Brock raised an eyebrow but didn't reply. If Orr knew the answer to that then he would mostly likely stick to a pose of outraged innocence. Brock waited, eyes fixed on his face.

'But that is . . . monstrous . . .' Orr said, with rather less confidence. 'In my filing cabinet? All I keep in there, apart from the papers, is a wee bottle of whisky.'

'Yes, we found that too.'

'You're serious about this?'

'Very.'

'I don't know what to say.' Orr's indignation had gone. 'Well, for a start, you can take my fingerprints. You'll find they won't match anything on those things.'

'That would be most helpful. We'll do it now, if you don't mind. One of my officers will fix it up.'

As he got to his feet, Brock sensed the man's mood change again. From outrage to shock, he now moved on to prickly martyrdom. A thought occurred to him.

'In any case,' he said scathingly, 'why in blazes would I keep a video in the site hut when there's no machine there to view it on, eh? It makes no sense.'

'That's a good point. Who else has a key to the hut, do you know?'

'The security people, of course, and I was given one. But I had others cut when we were in the thick of our digging. Time was short, we worked round the clock, and I gave keys to some of the other people in the team. I never got them all back.'

'Do any of them have any connection with Silvermeadow now?'

'Not to my knowledge.'

'So you have no theories about how these things could have got in there?'

Orr sat gauntly upright, stiff with bruised dignity. 'I don't care to speculate, sir. That seems to be your job.'

Brock sat with Lowry and Kathy in an adjoining room while Orr's prints were being taken. 'Let him stew on it for a few minutes, then we'll go through it again. What bothers me, Gavin, is that we can't be sure that drawer was searched the first time.'

He saw the discomfort return to Lowry's face. When he had questioned the two officers who had searched that part of the site, one had claimed that they'd searched the drawer and seen nothing, the other that they'd never opened it.

'What else might we have missed?'

Lowry clenched his jaw. 'I told them to work fast, chief, and it was a huge complex to cover with the men we had. We got round the lot in half a day ... Yeah, none of us could swear we didn't miss something. It would take a week to do it properly. Not only that, the plans we were using were very simplified. They didn't show all the store cupboards and plant rooms and stuff like that. We just had to use our judgement what we opened up and searched.'

Brock felt a twinge of unease. It wasn't Lowry's fault. He'd done exactly as Brock had instructed him. 'Fair enough. But we may just have to do it again.'

He heard Lowry mutter under his breath, 'Christ.'

'What's the problem, Gavin?'

'Two problems, chief. Manpower – the chief super'll do his nut. And the centre management. They're becoming difficult. I think they want us out of there. Harry said he'd got new instructions not to give us access unaccompanied.'

'I think I may be responsible for that,' Kathy said. She also was looking uncomfortable, and told them about her late encounter in the games arcade the previous night, and Jackson's reaction that morning.

'You're telling me that a boy was in there, playing arcade games at midnight? When the place had been locked up and secured?' Brock's feeling of losing control was growing by the minute. 'Good grief, Kathy!'

'I know. But I've no idea how. I searched the place myself this morning with Jackson and Starkey. There was no sign of anywhere he could have been hiding overnight, and no way he could have got out without triggering the alarms. They ... well, I don't think they believed me. They said I must have got confused by the flickering lights from the machines in the darkness. I wish they were right.'

Brock thought, working out the implications. Finally he said, 'All the more reason to make another search, then.' He thumbed through a notebook for a number, lifted the phone and dialled.

'Harry, how are you?'

'Not too bad, chief. What can I do for you?' The voice was cautious.

'Those plans you gave us of Silvermeadow, they've been giving us a bit of trouble.'

'How come?'

'They don't show much detail. Plant rooms, store cupboards . . . We're just beginning to realise what we missed.'

Brock let that sink in. The line was silent, then he continued, 'You must have more accurate plans somewhere, don't you?'

'The property manager,' Jackson said slowly, 'holds the technical plans.' He stressed 'technical' as if it were something dangerous and obscure. 'But I wouldn't imagine you'd need—'

'I'm afraid we do. It's beginning to look as if we're going to have to search the damn place again.'

'I don't think management will buy that, chief.'

'I'm not that keen on it myself, Harry.' Brock's voice hardened suddenly. 'It's a mistake that's going to make us *all* very unpopular. I'd better speak to Ms Seager.'

'Hang on, chief. How urgent is this?'

'It's urgent. I want some action tonight.'

'Tell you what. Leave it with me for half an hour. Let me see what I can do. Let me get back to you.'

The phone rang again as soon as Brock replaced it. Bren was on the line, sounding fired up.

'I think we've got something on North, Brock. Can we talk?'

'I could do with some good news. Where are you?'

Bren was in the building. They arranged to meet and Brock rang off.

'Gavin, something's come up on another case Kathy and I are working on. Would you look after Orr? I doubt if you'll get much out of him, but try anyway.' He noticed a set look about the mouth as Lowry jumped to his feet, as if he was determined to redeem himself. 'Don't be too rough on him,' Brock added, but Lowry was already through the door.

Bren looked rejuvenated, Brock thought, his big, deceptively gentle-looking countenance alight with good spirits. Burrowing away quietly in the undergrowth with a small team of his own, he had emerged into the light with something tasty, clearly.

'One of the lines we've been taking is that he came here from Canada,' he said, his soft West Country burr more pronounced than usual. 'We've been checking arrivals, money transfers, that sort of thing. You wouldn't believe the number of Canadians who have come over for Christmas. Then we thought he might have got himself a motor to get out to Silvermeadow, so we've been checking car hire places too. Yesterday we called in at a small independent rental outfit at Redbridge. Two weeks ago they hired a blue Golf to a man who offered a Canadian passport and driver's licence as identification. Name of Keith Nolan. He was on our list of tourist visitors, arrived at Heathrow unaccompanied in mid-November. We also had him down as cashing several American Express travellers' cheques issued in Montreal, at a bank in Barking on the thirtieth of November.'

Brock thought. Redbridge, Barking, both on this side of London, both within a dozen miles of Silvermeadow. And there was more coming, he could see from Bren's manner, building up to the big one. His method was reassuringly sane and straightforward, searching the bureaucratic web of authorisations, accounts, documents in which everyone who travelled or hired or got sick or bought something became inevitably entangled. It made the Vlasich investigation at Silvermeadow seem uncomfortably messy by comparison.

'We've been passing the more promising ones back to the Canadian police for checking,' Bren continued. 'We just got word on Nolan. He was born in the same year as North, but he died ten years ago in a road accident in Quebec.'

'Great,' Brock murmured. 'I don't suppose the car rental place took a photocopy of his identification?'

Bren grinned, and handed Brock a sheet of paper, a photocopy of two pages from a passport, including the photograph of Nolan. 'What do you reckon?'

'Yes,' Brock said simply. 'We can see what Pauline Lewins thinks, but yes, I think that's him.'

'So do I.'

'We have a name, a car, a photo. What else do we need?'

'More legs and a bit of time. We're working on accommodation now, hotels, b and bs, rented accommodation . . .'

'How long was the Golf hired for?'

'Four weeks. To be returned on the twenty-eighth of December.'

'He may have more than one alias.'

'Sure.'

Brock saw Bren hesitate, glance at Kathy, then back to him.

'I was wondering if you might want to get more involved now, chief.'

Of course he did. The thought of Nolan was tantalising, irresistible.

'You've done well, Bren. Give me twenty-four hours to finish off a few things with Kathy at Silvermeadow, then I'm all yours.' He didn't really mean *finish*, for he had no hope of that. But he would need a little time to extricate himself and make sure that Kathy was put in charge of the Vlasich investigation.

Harry Jackson phoned shortly after this, sounding more confident than the last time they'd spoken. He'd arranged a meeting for Brock with Bo Seager in an hour, at 6.30 p.m., to sort out 'ongoing protocol', as he put it. He had also arranged for the property manager, Allen Cook, to be in his office, just along the corridor from the centre manager's, around that time to brief Brock on available plans.

They picked up Gavin Lowry on their way down to the car. He seemed tense after questioning Orr, from which, he said, he had discovered nothing of interest. With some probing from Brock as they drove out to the motorway he admitted that the old man had irritated him a good deal. 'Pompous old fart!' he said in a sudden burst of anger. 'Knows everything, and all of it completely pointless. He reminds me of our old history teacher at school. So fucking smart!' Then he added in an undertone, 'We sorted him.'

'How?' Brock asked mildly.

'Oh, one of the boys said he'd tried to interfere with him.'

'Had he?'

'No. They suspended him anyway, and he had a nervous breakdown.'

Brock noticed Kathy glance sharply up at Lowry's reflection in the rear-view mirror, then snap her eyes back to the road.

'I hope you didn't try the same on Orr, Gavin,' Brock said.

'What, plant that tape in his filing cabinet?' Lowry laughed. 'No, but after listening to him droning on for half an hour I was capable of it, believe me. Who the hell is Harding?'

'Should I know?'

'Exactly! He says, "I was with Harding in Jordan", like you should know what the hell he's talking about.'

'You weren't too rough on him, were you, Gavin?'

'Not nearly rough enough, chief,' Lowry growled back. 'Not nearly.'

They arrived early for the meeting with Bo Seager, and found the office of the property manager, Allen Cook. He was a brisk, wiry man, with the certificate of an engineering degree framed on the wall behind his desk. He eyed Brock with interest as he listened to what he wanted, one technician to another. When Brock showed him the plans that Harry had supplied he shook his head dismissively.

'Very crude. Detailed building plans are all on the computer there, and you can have a print-out at any scale of detail or layer of system you want, from structural grids to electrical or plumbing layouts. I imagine you'll want the spatial plans, with partitions, doors, room layouts and so on.'

'Yes, that sounds like it.'

'There's a slight problem though. These plans are essentially the original construction set, which we've modified and updated from time to time to include work done by tenants. You have to understand that up to half of the value of construction in a shopping centre like this is fitting-out work done by the individual tenants' contractors. They come into the basic shell that the owner provides, and they put in their own ceilings, partitions, services, fittings, finishes. They have to get this work approved by the owner, and they lodge copies of their plans with us to put on to our master. But they don't all work on AutoCAD like us, or a compatible software system. Some don't do their plans on a computer at all, and they give us paper sets.'

He went over to a plan chest of wide, shallow steel drawers and pulled one of them open and drew out a construction drawing from the top of the pile inside. He laid it on the table, spreading it with his palm to flatten its creases.

'This is the contractor's fitting-out drawing for a shoe shop in unit seventy-three, a medium standard unit. They put in a toilet and small staff room at the back there, and an office here, this curving wall between men's and women's shoes and this wavy ceiling, shelving, racks, a store front that folds away, plus the services – lighting, air-conditioning ducting, smoke detectors, sprinklers, plumbing – all tapping into the main lines we bring to the rear of the unit. The problem is that someone at this end then has to put this manually into our master plan – it would be difficult to scan a plan like this directly in. This has not been done consistently. I've been here nine months now, and I've hardly begun to get to grips with the backlog of plans that haven't been entered onto the master set. Harry Jackson has a lad who's a bit of a computer whiz, and I pay him to work on it from time to time, but he can't keep up.

'Also, as you can see' – he pointed to pencilled notes and alterations on the original print drawing – 'changes get made during the course of construction. In this case they had to change their toilet layout when they discovered where we'd put the connection point for their drainage, and that altered the layout of all the surrounding walls, just slightly. I couldn't guarantee that what's down there now is exactly like this, either. I know they also changed the alignment of the curved wall, because there was a grid of sprinkler heads already in the ceiling, and the wall would have interfered with them.

'Now if we compare this sheet to the master plan on the computer . . .' He went over to the machine on the next table and worked at the coloured plan on its screen until he found and enlarged the area around unit 73. 'Very different, you see? Our master hasn't been updated yet. You get the picture.'

Brock was feeling the way he often did when people demonstrated computers to him. Irritated and depressed. He could sympathise now with Jackson's warning description of Cook's plans as 'technical'. And he could understand why he'd stuck to his 'crude' plans.

'Frustrating, I know,' the engineer said. He went over to a rack standing in a corner of the room, and slid from it a set of plans clipped together on a wooden handle, and laid these down on the table. 'This is probably the sort of thing you want. One to five hundred scale plans of the spatial layouts of each level, with the landlord's structure in black lines and tenants' additions, as far as we've recorded them, in red. I can give it to you at an enlarged scale if you want, one to two hundred say, but that would cover several sheets for each level.'

Brock stared at the plans, rubbing his hand through his beard, his feeling of irritation becoming rapidly compounded by a sense of unease. 'So inside their own shops, tenants could have built rooms, cupboards, cavities that don't appear on these plans at all, and that you don't know about?'

Cook nodded. 'Certainly. We *should* have a record of it some-where, but I couldn't guarantee it. You know, they get a builder in for a job they've agreed with us, and then they say to him, "While you're here, give us a price for putting up an extra couple of walls over there." It happens. And it's always a last-minute rush, and they know if they apply to us for approval it'll slow them down . . . You understand.'

'And what would be the best way for us to check this?'

Cook considered. 'The best way would be to hire a team of surveyors to come in and make a survey, take spot room dimensions using laser equipment, check variations. I'd love it if you did. We could use an accurate set of plans.'

'How long would that take?'

'This is a big place. At least a month to do it thoroughly, I should think. And it would cost.'

'We don't have a month.'

'What exactly are you looking for?'

'We think that the murdered girl may have been held somewhere before the killer put her body into the compactor. We did a close search of the areas immediately in the vicinity of the machine, and a broader search of the whole complex, but we didn't find this place, if it exists. That's what we're looking for, Mr Cook. What would you advise? Say you had twenty-four hours, not a month. What would you do?'

The engineer considered that for a while. 'You have to try to *think* like the murderer, don't you? That's what you do all the time, I suppose.' He seemed amused by that thought. 'Well, I think you'd have a problem getting up to much in the larger units. There would be people coming and going all the time, asking questions, noticing anything odd. In the small units on the other hand – I mean the very small units, with just one or two staff at quiet times . . . Was it a quiet time when she disappeared?'

'Fairly quiet.'

'Right . . . Yes, you might be able to get away with it. Say you're the sole owner of a small business. A small card shop, for instance, or coffee shop—'

'Or a games arcade or gelato shop,' Brock suggested.

'That sort of thing. You could have a quiet spot of building work done as part of a larger alteration, then change your employees, and after a while there wouldn't be anyone but you would know.'

'Trouble is, we've had a reasonably close look at most of the likely candidates. But we can do it again.'

'Yes. But I was going to say that the quietest and most undisturbed places of all, if you had access . . .' Cook pondered.

'Yes?'

'Well, they're not even on the plans you had. Look, I'll show you.'

They looked over his shoulder as he adjusted the image on his computer screen again.

'Those plans you had are the type we give visitors, members of the public. They don't need to know about these, for instance.' He pointed to an array of rooms on the screen. 'Those are plant and service rooms, electricity sub-stations and the like.'

'We checked out a number of plant rooms along the service road,' Lowry said.

'Yes, but there's plenty more. Like those, on the lowest level, around the main plenum.' He indicated a long narrow chamber which zig-zagged across the width of the screen. 'It runs the length of the basement beneath the loading platform.'

Brock turned to Lowry, who shrugged and shook his head.

'Go on,' Brock said. 'What's a plenum?'

'It's the final big duct used for gathering all the exhaust air from the centre – its lung, you might say. The whole building breathes tempered air, see, which percolates through every part and finally ends up in the plenum. It starts at roof level, where outdoor air is treated in the rooftop plant rooms, washed, scrubbed, dried, cooled or heated to twenty-two degrees C, then pumped into the upper malls. From there it gets drawn in to the shop units by extract ducts at their rear, in the ceilings of the rear service corridors, then down in a series of big drop ducts to the lowest level where it discharges along with the exhaust air from the service road and basement areas into the plenum chamber. From there it's pulled by big fans through heat exchangers to recover waste heat, then discharged to open air again at the end of the building.'

'Can you get into these ducts?'

'Into the plenum, yes. There's access for maintenance, and to the plant rooms that support it. But not for general use. Between maintenance inspections you could wander around down there for months without being disturbed, provided there wasn't a plant failure or a rat plague or something.'

'Good grief,' Brock said. 'Why the hell didn't we know about this before?'

'Well, probably because there's a very good reason why your murderer wouldn't be down there.'

'Really?'

'Yes, you see, the access is through the security centre. That would make it a bit tricky for him, wouldn't it?'

They thanked Cook and crossed the corridor to the entrance to the management offices.

Brock found Bo Seager tense and preoccupied, with Nathan Tindall ominously silent on the opposite side of the room. Both seemed subdued by the presence of a solicitor representing the company which owned Silvermeadow.

Bo began by saying that Harry Jackson had not made it clear what Brock wanted a meeting for, and then asked peremptorily what they'd been doing in Allen Cook's office. Brock's answer, that they'd been checking the building plans to see if there could be areas they'd missed on their earlier search, didn't seem to reassure her. From her comments he gathered that the initial euphoria over the turnover figures arising from the publicity had worn off, and this was confirmed by the solicitor, who quickly established himself as the spokesman for the management group. Their board, he explained, was now deeply disturbed that the company name should be associated with this sort of notoriety, which was absolutely contrary to the image and values they had all worked so hard to project. The board demanded a speedy resolution.

'I understand you have been interviewing various of our tenants,' he said. 'May I ask whether you intend to make any arrests, or lay any charges?'

'Not at present.'

'From my reading of the situation, we have bent over backwards to facilitate your demands for access to Silvermeadow to assist your investigations, Chief Inspector. But enough is enough. This is private property you're camping in.' He smiled thinly. 'You don't need me to remind you that if you'd applied for a warrant to enter this centre it would have entitled you to one visit only. This open-ended, interminable access is simply unacceptable. It is disrupting my client's operations and creating a highly negative climate at a critical point in the trading year.' He cleared his throat and looked over at Bo Seager.

'Four kids tried to mug Santa this morning,' she said in a sombre tone.

'*Santa*, did you say?' Lowry asked, looking startled.

'Yes. Santa was in his grotto next to the magic roundabout on the upper mall, with a line of toddlers and their mums queuing up to see him, and the four of them marched up and started laying into him.'

'What, to rob him?'

'No, no, just for the pleasure of it. Fortunately control spotted them on the cameras coming in the west entrance, and radioed the mall security. They caught up with the little bastards just as they were getting really stuck into poor old Santa.' She turned to Brock with a concerned frown. 'He's seventy-two, Chief Inspector.' Brock noted the formal title. No more David, at least not in front of the suits. 'He's been doing it for twenty years. We inherited him from a department store that closed down in Dagenham. The thing was, when Harry asked these little creeps what they thought they were doing, the ringleader said, cheeky as anything, "Well, this is murder-mall, yeah?" Like it's open season, or something.'

'The point is, Chief Inspector,' Nathan Tindall broke in angrily, 'this can't go on. We're going to have to ask you to vacate unit one-eight-four.'

Brock turned to see what Bo had to say, but she remained silent.

'And any further incursions will have to be supported by a warrant,' the solicitor added, 'which we shall oppose, bearing in mind there's no conclusive evidence we're aware of that a crime has been committed on this property, or that any further evidence relating to the disappearance of Kerri Vlasich is to be found here.'

Brock studied his fingernails, letting them wait for his inevitable objections, then said abruptly, 'I agree. I was coming to the view myself that a visible police presence here was becoming counter-productive. I suggest that we make a press statement to the effect that the investigation here is being wound down and moving elsewhere.'

He was aware of Lowry looking at him, startled, while Bo Seager appeared intensely relieved.

'Well,' the solicitor smiled, 'good, good.'

'From our discussion with Mr Cook,' Brock went on, smiling back, 'we are just a little concerned that we may have missed one or two areas in our original search that may prevent us from making a conclusive final report. The coroner hates loose ends, you understand. That's my only concern.'

The solicitor frowned. 'How long, exactly, are these loose ends?'

'Mr Cook has estimated that it might take a month to be a hundred per cent sure we haven't missed anything.'

This produced a spluttered protest.

Brock let it run for a moment, then lifted his eye to see Bo Seager's reaction. She was considering him closely. She shook her head and said, 'No.'

'The problem is that some of your tenants seem to have been building rabbit warrens inside their tenancies, without getting approvals. I have to say that the fire brigade might be concerned at some of the things we've seen. Without a definitive plan—'

'How long?' Bo said.

'We might be able to do enough to satisfy the coroner in, say, twenty-four hours. But we'd need complete access.'

Bo looked at him coolly for a moment, then turned to the solicitor and murmured something about peanuts. He shook his head sharply, and Bo looked back at Brock without a trace of expression on her face.

'Tell you what,' she said, 'let me consult with my colleagues here and get back to you. We may have to get approval from above. Will tomorrow morning be okay?'

'Tonight, Bo. There are some areas we want to check tonight.'

'Leave it with me.'

12

Kathy thought she understood Brock's mood well enough as they waited. He was annoyed with Lowry, but most of all with himself, for the way in which the initial search of the huge building had been conducted. It was difficult now to know what would be worse: finding nothing after yet more wasted effort, or turning up something that should have been discovered five days before. She watched him stomping among the teams as they assembled and studied the copies Allen Cook had provided of the most current plans. They fell silent as he joined each in turn, hands in pockets, face dark, making them feel edgy.

While they waited they were joined by a dog handler and also by a small SOCO team accompanied by Leon Desai. Kathy felt an odd sense of embarrassment at waiting in the crowded room with him, as if somehow their private life, as well as Silvermeadow's, was under scrutiny. She was aware of him trying to catch her eye, and of herself finding ways to avoid it.

Bo Seager's call finally came, and they filed out. Lowry was to take most of them down to check the smaller units in the food court and Bazaar areas, while the remainder, including the handler and his dog, took the stair down to the service road and along to the security centre, where Cook was waiting for them with a box of hard hats. The two security staff on duty watched them with vague curiosity as they tried out the hats, and some put on overalls and boots, before following Cook through to the back of the centre and down a corridor which brought them to a locked door marked AUTHORISED ENTRY ONLY. He unlocked it, hit a light switch and led them down a sloping ramp.

Kathy found it hard to say what made the place seem suddenly so different. The harsh bulkhead lights, the bare concrete tunnel descending into darkness, the silence disturbed only by their footsteps and the distant murmur of machinery, all made it feel as divorced from the bustle of the service road as that had seemed from the life of the mall. It really did feel like descending into an ancient tomb or catacomb.

They reached a space at the bottom of the ramp, a kind of chamber whose walls contained a number of doors. Cook used his key to open them, and people moved off into the plant rooms that lay beyond. Kathy, Brock, Leon, the dog handler and two SOCO men remained. Cook took them to the last opening, a low double doorway of louvred panels, and said, 'No lights beyond here, folks. Watch your heads. We're going into the lungs of the beast.'

Kathy stooped and followed Leon through the opening and into the pool of light formed by Cook's flashlight as he helped them through. As he straightened, Leon, the tallest one among them, hit his hard hat against the low concrete roof with a clunk.

'Watch yourself,' Cook warned, and Kathy grinned at Leon, her earlier reserve gone. He smiled ruefully back.

Their torches showed them to be inside a concrete tube, wide enough for half a dozen people to walk abreast, and extending as far into the distance as their torch beams could reach, the grey concrete walls and ceiling punctuated by grilles for incoming ducts. The murmur of hidden machinery was louder now, and as they moved on they felt a steady gentle breeze of warm air being drawn past them towards the main extract fans at the far end of the duct.

Kathy, thinking again of Wiff's disappearing act, said, 'From what you said, this duct connects into every shop in the centre. It's like an underground mall system. Couldn't intruders use it?' To her ear her voice sounded hollow, echoing in the air inside the tube with its acidic concrete taste.

Cook answered, 'Yes and no. The air exhaust system, as I said, links all the spaces of the building from the rear of the shops through to the plenum. It's low pressure so the ducts are quite large, and they penetrate all the fire divisions of the centre, so that potentially they could completely bypass the fire safety system which divides the centre into manageable compartments. A fire starting in one part of the centre could pass through the ductwork and send the whole place up in no time. So to avoid that possibility, the ducts are fitted with intumescent grilles every time they penetrate a fire division wall or floor.'

He pointed to the succession of grilles filling the holes along the ceiling of the tunnel.

'An intumescent grille is like a sort of open honeycomb, coated with a material which intumesces – that is, foams up – when it gets hot. So, as soon as the hot smoke and gases from a fire pass into the ducts, the grilles foam up and seal themselves and the fire is contained. By the same token, the grilles would prevent a mouse, let alone a person, making their way through the ducts.'

They came to a corner where the plenum took a swing to the left. As they rounded the bend and the torch beams swayed across the dark space ahead, the engineer gave a muffled exclamation. Kathy followed the direction of his beam, and saw the black voids in the ceiling where a succession of grilles had been removed and stacked against the wall. Halfway down this length of tunnel, about fifty yards away, a stepladder was set up beneath one of these openings. As they walked towards it Kathy heard the faint muffled sound of each shop in turn coming through the holes in the ceiling: pop music, voices, mechanical humming. At the stepladder she caught the distinct pings and raucous electronic fanfares of the games arcade overhead.

The engineer went up the ladder, hauling himself up into the hole and disappearing for several minutes. When he returned he looked shaken.

'I wouldn't have believed it possible,' he said. 'Someone's cleared a way right up into the unit.'

'Could they get in and out?' Kathy asked.

'A small person, yes. Through the grilles. You can lift them out if you know how to do it.'

Another twenty yards and the plenum changed direction again, reflecting a crank in the plan of the mall above. Nearby was a short branch tunnel off to the right, and Kathy turned that way to check it.

She would have missed Wiff's den, tucked away to one side at the end, if the dog, which had followed her, hadn't started barking excitedly. Wiff had transformed a corner of the duct into a teenager's bedroom. Everything was there: a sleeping bag, clothes, posters, small pieces of furniture, a battery-powered light, junk food and drink containers all over the place. Most of the stuff looked new, many items still with security tags and price labels. From the variety of labels, he had looted many different stores in the centre to build his nest.

Next to the sleeping bag was one of the Manchester United books she had seen him studying in the bookshop in the mall the previous Sunday morning.

'Brock, here!' she called.

As he joined her, followed by the others, she was suddenly aware of a rhythmic sound. She swung her flashlight towards its source and saw a clock with a happy Mickey Mouse face and a comforting tick.

'All right, hands in pockets if you please, Mr Cook,' Brock said.

The engineer stared at him blankly.

'Don't touch anything. It would be best if you would retrace your steps, and leave us to carry on the search down here.'

The man nodded and withdrew, his light beam and silhouette disappearing down the tunnel, while the handler and his dog moved on to continue their search in the other direction. Brock and Kathy stood against the duct wall as Leon and the SOCO team moved in.

'This belongs to the boy I told you about,' Kathy said. 'In the games arcade. Wiff Smith. I'm sure of it.'

'How long's he been living down here, I wonder?'

'Winston Starkey should know how long he's been coming here. And Speedy and the other camera operators, you'd think they would have spotted him.'

'Like a mouse, down here in the dark.' Brock shook his head sadly. 'Hard to believe, isn't it?'

'Brock, look at this.' Leon was kneeling, his torch beam on something lying in a fold of the sleeping bag. He carefully pushed the cloth back to reveal the small glass bottle.

'Can you read it?'

The printing on the label was tiny, and Leon had to crouch low to make it out. Finally he read, 'Ketapet, ketamine hydrochloride, one hundred milligrams per millilitre, twenty-millilitre multidose vial. There's a syringe here, too. Empty, but used, I'd say.'

'Like Kerri,' Brock said. 'Just like Kerri. A mouse that's taken a poison bait.'

He and Kathy watched silently as the others worked methodically across the area, taking photographs, recording items. One of the SOCOs looked up from examining an old blanket against the far wall. 'What colour is the kid's hair, Kathy?'

'Black. Bit greasy-looking. Probably doesn't bathe much.'

'I've got blonde over here. Several strands, about six inches long.'

★

Kathy stared at the graffiti'd holly wreath with its YULETIDE GREETINGS silver message, listening to the door chimes dying inside the house. When Mrs Tait opened the front door a waft of fried liver and onions billowed out into the cold night. She told Kathy that Naomi was at her friend Lisa's flat, and Kathy thanked her and continued along the deck.

As she was crossing the bridge connecting the deck to Jonquil Court, she became aware of some kind of argument ahead, a woman's voice, angry and high-pitched, interspersed with laughter. When she reached the corner of the court she saw the woman, elderly, her shoulders stooped over a walking frame, head thrust forward belligerently towards a group of children dancing in front of her. In the stark glare of the deck lights, heavy bulkhead fittings protected by wire cages, her face and neck reminded Kathy of the leathery head of an old tortoise, a pet she'd had as a child. The woman was screaming, 'Bugger off! I'm a copper in disguise! Bugger off or I'll arrest you!' This was causing a good deal of merriment among the kids, who were finding new ways to goad her to more and more ludicrous claims. 'I thought you was a paratrooper, granny!' one of them yelled, poking her in the ribs with a stick.

'Hey, stop that!' Kathy called, striding up to them.

For a moment they were undecided, then they saw the look on her face and began to scatter, calling back abuse at the old woman as they ran.

'You all right?' Kathy said to her. 'Where's your home, dear?'

But the old woman knew that danger lurked everywhere. 'Keep away from me!' she screamed at Kathy. 'Keep away or I'll arrest you! I'm a bleedin' copper I am!'

'Okay, okay,' Kathy said calmly. As she carried on towards Lisa's front door, she added, 'Just get yourself home. It's the safest place to be,' and immediately doubted the wisdom of her advice.

Lisa answered her knock with a timid and somewhat reluctant invitation to come in. She was alone in the flat with Naomi, and when Kathy asked when her mother would be home, Lisa seemed uncertain. On the dining-room table was a stack of half-opened sweets of various kinds: Yorkie and Bounty bars, tubes of Rollos and Smarties. Child comforters, Kathy thought, and they did look very young the pair of them, dark eyes in pale faces examining her cautiously as they all sat down.

'I wondered what you girls could tell me about a boy who hangs out in the mall. His name's Wiff, Wiff Smith. You know who I mean?'

They both nodded mutely.

'Well? What's his story?'

They shrugged vaguely. Naomi said, 'Dunno really.'

'Where does he come from, any idea?'

They looked at the floor, heads shaking.

'Does he go to your school? No? Does he have any relatives? Brothers or sisters? Any special friends? What about Winston Starkey, in the games arcade? No?' Kathy sat back, watching them. 'You're not being much help, girls. Please think, will you? Anything at all.'

Silence.

'We're worried that something may have happened to him, like Kerri,' she said, and that brought their heads up, eyes widening. 'We've found where he lived.'

'Where?' Naomi whispered. 'Where was that?'

'Under the mall at Silvermeadow, in the basement. It seems he had a sort of den hidden down there. Did you know about that?'

They did; she saw it in their eyes shifting away.

'He told us . . . he said he lived there, under the centre. We didn't believe him. Not at first.'

'But later?'

Naomi nodded. 'He said he knew things, saw things.'

Kathy leant forward. 'What things?'

But her interest seemed to frighten them. They looked away, at the Yorkie bars and the blank TV screen in the corner of the room.

Then Naomi asked another question: 'Why do you think something's happened to him?'

'We're not certain, but we think he's been given a drug.'

'Which one?'

The question, asked very rapidly, brought Kathy up short.

'It's called ketamine. People also call it K, or Special K. Have you heard of it?'

But even as she asked, Kathy saw that they had, for Lisa had burst into tears, and Naomi looked stunned.

'Come on now,' Kathy said, a firmer note in her voice. 'Tell me. Tell me what you know. It's important.'

'Kerri . . .' Naomi began hesitantly. 'She was trying K.'

'Yes?'

Naomi nodded reluctantly.

221

'Where did she get it from?'

'We didn't know. Someone was selling her stuff.'

'You have no idea who?'

Naomi hesitated and looked sideways at Lisa, who was absorbed in her hankie. 'No, but . . . I think . . .'

'Yes?' Kathy had to work to control her frustration and sound calm.

'Wiff was his legs.'

'His legs?'

'That's what she called him, his legs. Wiff did the running around for him.'

Kathy had a sudden vivid image of Winston Starkey in the role of Fagin, sending out his army of little waifs to sell his drugs. 'You must have had some idea though, who he was working for? Come on, Naomi. Was it Starkey? The man who runs the arcade?'

The girl shook her head and stooped, struggling with some immense difficulty.

'He sees everything. He knows everything . . .' she whispered. 'That's what Wiff said. He watches us. He'll hurt us if we tell on him. Wiff warned Kerri, he told her not to tell anyone or the man would kill her. Wiff was scared of him too. Everyone is.'

'Naomi,' Kathy said intently, 'Kerri is dead, and now Wiff is missing. You must help us to stop this man before it's too late. What else did Wiff tell you?'

'Wiff said he has protection. I think it may be one of those men,' she whispered. 'You know, in the black uniforms. Security. Someone in security. He knew Wiff was there, in the basement, but he let him stay.'

'Security?' Kathy froze. The guardians of the entrance to the plenum.

'Yes.'

'You've no idea who?'

The girl shook her head. Lisa looked from Naomi to Kathy and renewed her weeping.

Kathy took out her notebook and waited. Harry Jackson sat at the desk in his office in the security centre, head bowed. She had expected denial and protest at the integrity of his staff being questioned, but instead he had turned away and lowered his head as if some private nightmare was turning into reality. Brock stood in front of him in the centre of the room, hands deep in the pockets of his overcoat.

'Couple of days ago,' Jackson began heavily, 'I'd have said no, no way. Then Bruno came to me. He'd overheard a couple of kids talking in his shop. They were discussing getting hold of some stuff for the weekend. They wanted Ecstasy, to take to some big gig that was on. At first he thought they were talking about amphetamines, because he heard the word "speed", but then he realised they were talking about where they were planning to get it from. From a big supplier called Speedy. I told Bruno he'd got it wrong. It couldn't be our Speedy. Hell,' – he gave a flat laugh – 'he can't even walk. How could he be in business?'

'How does he get around?' Brock asked.

'He's got a van, specially modified, paid for from his compensation from his accident. He can get in and out and drive it himself. And he's got a bungalow, no steps, where he looks after himself. His de facto left him with their little boy when he had the smash. But how could he run a business? He never even went out into the malls where the kids were.'

'It seems he had help,' Brock said. 'The boy, Wiff, was his legs. Maybe there were others.'

'While he watched them at work on his screens,' Kathy added.

'Christ.' Jackson shook his head, rubbing his face in disbelief.

'Where is he now, Harry?'

'He left hours ago. I came down here after I spoke to you on the phone this afternoon, and he was on duty then. I got talking to him about which parts of the building you lot had searched last weekend. He wanted to know why I asked, and I said you were thinking of doing a new search, into places you'd missed last time.'

'He seemed interested, did he?'

'Yeah, very.'

'Then what?'

'I went back upstairs, then returned down here about five p.m. Speedy had gone – home they said. Finished his shift early. I was a bit pissed off, because half our people are down with flu, and I'd wanted him to work late.'

'Was he alone down here when you spoke to him about the new search?'

'Yeah. The next lot weren't due on for half an hour. Want me to try him on the phone? I can say I'm checking tomorrow's roster.'

'Yes, why don't you do that.'

Jackson checked the number on a list pinned over his phone, then dialled. He listened for a while to the number ringing, then hung up. 'Not even an answering machine.'

'Do you have the number of his vehicle? What about relatives? Friends? Next of kin?'

Jackson got up and went over to a filing cabinet and began to thumb through a file.

Kathy said, 'How about I get over to his home and start asking the neighbours?'

Brock nodded. 'Take Lowry if he's around.'

She ran up the service stairs and along the corridor to unit 184, but he wasn't there. In fact no one was there except the immovable Phil, bent over his schedules. She told him where she was going and went on out to her car.

Kathy turned into the street and slowed the car down to walking pace. All the houses were bungalows, set back behind hedges and ornamental trees. She picked out a number and worked out which one must be Speedy's. It was in darkness, no lights showing at any of the windows. With barely a sound she crept the car to the kerb outside the house next door, and switched everything off. Almost immediately she noticed the corner of the curtains in a lighted window of the neighbours' house inch open, and a suspicious face spy out at her.

So much for the inconspicuous arrival, she thought.

She got out of the car, pulled her coat tight around her against the wind, and walked to the gate of the neighbours' house and up the front path. The curtain flicked down. Her finger had barely touched the button of the doorbell when the door came open on a chain.

'Yes?'

Kathy saw nothing, then dropped her eyes two feet and saw an elf-like face. She showed her warrant card.

'Oooh! It's the police, Walter!' the little woman called over her shoulder. 'I think.' She turned back to Kathy and squinted at her fiercely. 'How do I know you're not a fraud?'

'I'll give you a telephone number to ring, if you like. The Metropolitan Police at Scotland Yard.'

'Oooh! Scotland Yard! What do you want?'

'Can I come in?'

'Tell me what you want to talk about first.'

'Your neighbour, Mr Reynolds.'

The door opened in a flash.

'What has he done? You know he was a biker once? A Hell's Angel.' She said the name with hushed relish.

Kathy stepped into a hallway heavy with the smell of fried fish, and was led by the little woman into the front room from which she had been observed. An equally tiny man was in there, working intently with a pile of matchsticks, from which he was constructing a huge model of a sailing ship.

'Good evening,' he said without interest, and without looking up from his task.

It occurred to Kathy that it was almost big enough for the pair of them to climb on board the ship when it was finished, and sail away.

'I just wondered if you've noticed any movement from next door this evening,' Kathy asked.

'Movement?' the woman said, eyes gleaming, as she switched off a small TV set in the corner. 'Drug dealing, do you mean?'

'Why do you say that?'

'Oh, it's what you read in the papers, isn't it? Everybody does it these days.'

'Have you noticed anything?'

'Well, we did see Speedy coming home in his van. When was that, Walter? About five, or six?'

Walter grunted noncommittally. He was preoccupied, checking his matchstick construction against drawings and photographs spread out on the table.

'After that I went into the kitchen to cook dinner. But Walter saw someone else arrive, didn't you?'

'Did I?'

'Yes, you know you did. You said, Speedy's got visitors.'

Walter didn't seem inclined to make the effort to confirm or deny this, and Kathy had to ask him to please think back. He put down his minute tools with a sigh of resignation.

'I heard a car engine, but I don't know if it was Speedy's or someone else's. I looked out the side window' – he nodded at a small window whose curtain was drawn back – 'and I thought I saw someone out there.'

'With a box,' his wife prompted him.

'How large a box?'

'A big one,' the wife jumped in. 'Walter said, "looks like they're getting rid of a body".'

When she saw the look on Kathy's face, the woman sucked in her breath. 'Oh, you don't really think . . . ?'

'It may just have been Speedy,' Walter said. 'You can't see very clearly. Look for yourself.'

'Yes, but his kitchen light was on then,' his wife objected. 'And you said—'

'I know what I said.' Walter sighed. 'But I couldn't really be sure.'

'But Speedy would have been in his chair, Walter.'

Walter shrugged.

'Do you remember when the house lights went off next door?'

'I think that must have been while we were having our dinner. I don't remember them being on when we came back in here.'

Unable to get anything more concrete, Kathy gave the woman a card, which she accepted with a very satisfied expression, as if this was a trophy that could come in very handy.

The east wind sighed and blustered as Kathy walked back out to the street, pushing the buttons on her mobile. Brock answered. 'The house is in darkness,' she said. 'His neighbours think the lights went off sometime before eight p.m. But his van's still in the drive.'

'We're on our way,' he replied.

She walked along the street looking for any other observant neighbours, but the suburban bungalows were all buttoned up tight against the winter night, and she turned back to Speedy's house and walked down the front path. She knew she was being observed by at least one pair of beady eyes from next door, and took comfort from the fact that the little woman probably had the phone in her hand, two nines already dialled.

She hesitated at the front door when a phone close by inside suddenly started ringing. She waited, but nobody made a move to answer it, no lights came on. The phone stopped ringing and she tried the doorbell, but got no response. She pushed on the door, but it was firmly locked.

She moved round the side of the house, down the drive where Speedy's van was parked. It was impossible to see inside its tinted rear windows to make out if it contained a box. She was still visible from the neighbours' window, but as she approached the gate leading into the back garden she came to thick evergreen bushes that blocked their line of sight. The gate clicked behind her. The windows were curtained, all in darkness.

A ramp had been formed up to the back door so that there was no step for a wheelchair to negotiate. She tried the door handle and it turned: the back door swung open and a billow of warm musty air spilled over her.

'Hello?' she called into the darkness. 'Speedy? Anybody home?' There was total silence for a moment, then a soft thump from somewhere inside the house.

She took a deep breath and stepped into the dark kitchen, making out unusually low worktops. The dark void of the doorway on the far side was broad, the proportions of everything subtly different from what she was used to. She walked carefully towards the doorway, ears straining, trying to acclimatise her eyes to the interior darkness, unable to see the light switch. There was a hall beyond, another wide doorway facing her, leading into the other back room.

She made out that this door was closed, and she put out a hand and found the handle and very gently began to ease it open. A flickering green light came through the opening, and a smell, rancid and unpleasant. Then suddenly, low down and fast, a dark shape leapt through the gap towards her. Kathy jumped back with a cry, then saw a cat disappear through the kitchen door. She swore softly and put a hand to the light switch now visible at her shoulder, and blinked as light flooded the hallway. Then she pushed open the door and looked into the room. There was enough light coming from the hall and from the digital displays on a rack of electronic machines for her to see the outline of Reynolds's wheelchair. Her eyes were drawn to the void above the back of the chair where his head and shoulders should have been.

The smell was overwhelming now in the hot room. Vomit. She reached to the wall beside the door and fumbled with the switch, then saw the limp forearm on the floor beyond the wheelchair, the syringe nearby. Behind her she heard voices, then Brock calling her name.

They found Wiff in a bedroom at the front of the house, lying curled, fully dressed, on the bedding. He was clutching a brand-new pair of roller blades to his chest, and the headphones of a Walkman were in his ears. There was an angelic smile on his face, a dribble of foam at the corner of his mouth. There was no pulse in his skinny little throat, and his hand was cold.

★

Leon sniffed as he got in and closed the door of the car. Kathy said, 'Sorry. I think I've still got some of the mess on my shoe. I tried to clean it, but I can't seem to get rid of the smell.'

'You sound tired,' he said.

'Yes. It's just hitting me. It's been a long day.' What she really wanted was to put her arms round him and close her eyes for a few minutes, but what with the ambulance and the patrol cars and the SOCO vans and the neighbours, there wasn't much hope of that.

'How's it looking?' she asked.

'Dead around three hours, he thinks. Probably of asphyxia. Choked on his own vomit after he fell to the floor.'

'The bottle on the floor beside him, was it ketamine again?'

'That's what the label says. He's got a fair old chemist's shop in there: grass, amphetamines, a variety of other pills, and Ketapet. There was a pack for two dozen bottles in the fridge, with two unopened and one half-used as if he'd been experimenting with doses.'

'Could somebody have killed him?'

'It's possible, but there's no indication of anyone else having been there.'

'No visitor, like the neighbour said?'

Leon shrugged. 'No visitor, no box. How reliable are they?'

'They're not really sure what they saw.'

'I think the view is developing that he gave Wiff a shot back in the plenum to calm him, then brought him back here and gave him some more, then took some himself and OD'd. There were wheelchair tracks in the dust of the duct floor leading to Wiff's den, though we can't say how old.'

'Is there anything else to connect him to Kerri?'

'Yes. We've found the green frog bag, in one of the bedrooms, in a cupboard.'

'Oh,' Kathy said, voice flat, and turned away. It all seemed somehow both inevitable and wrong at the same time.

'We're concentrating on that room at present, looking for hair and fabric samples. We'll take his van away to check it.'

'What was that equipment in the room he was in?'

'Video editing and copying machines. There are quite a number of tapes. I don't know what of.'

'Maybe of us.'

'Maybe. I don't care.'

She was still thinking about Kerri's green bag in Speedy's cupboard and didn't pick it up right away – the slight edge in his voice, as if he'd been thinking about this and come to some decision.

'Don't you?' she asked.

'Why should we care? What kind of job is it if you have to care about that?'

'It isn't that. It's just that it's private, between us. Nothing to do with anyone else.'

'Yes, but if it isn't private any more, does it matter?'

'. . . I'm not sure.'

He gave a short laugh. 'No, you're not, are you? Christ, Kathy, it happens all the time. Boy meets girl. Who cares?'

Kathy blinked with surprise. This conversation had gone off the rails somewhere and she wasn't sure how. 'No, you're right. It doesn't matter. You sound angry. You don't think I'm ashamed of us, do you?'

He sighed and looked away. 'No, I'm not angry. I understand. I understand exactly, because I'm much the same. You want two lives, a public life and a private life, with no connection whatever between the two. And that's impossible, especially while we're working together like this. If it isn't Speedy's tapes it'll be something else. Hell, these guys are supposed to be detectives. I'm astonished they haven't spotted the difference in us already.'

'Have I changed?'

He looked at her, face softening. 'Yes,' he said quietly.

Then he turned way again as another patrol car drew up fast to the kerb, lights flashing, and Chief Superintendent Forbes got out.

Leon reached for the door handle. 'I'd better go. We'll talk about this another time, when we're not so tired.'

She watched him walk back to the house, and said to herself, bewildered, 'Talk about what?'

13

It was late in the small hours by the time they returned, separately, to Kathy's flat and fell exhausted into bed, and by morning Kathy had forgotten the conversation in the car. The wind had dropped, and from the bedroom window the city was bathed in a silvery light from low luminescent cloud. The sense of stillness matched Kathy's mood. She had slept deeply and felt detached from the events of the previous day, as if they had unfolded too rapidly and needed time and distance to absorb.

She made a pot of tea and took it back to bed, and they made love. They were good at it now, with a developed understanding of each other, and when it was over she felt completely at peace.

'We should get away this weekend,' Leon said. 'Get some time together after all the hours we've put in this week.'

'Mmm. That sounds good. Do you think we can? Will we wind things up today?'

'Depends on the preliminary PM results, I suppose. But I reckon there'll be a lull, if not an end to it.'

'Nice word,' she murmured, curling into the crook of his arm. 'Lull . . . lull . . . lull.'

By midday the evacuation of unit 184 was well in hand. Phil had finally been dislodged from his post at the door, and men with hand trolleys were moving boxes of computers and files out into the rear access corridor to the service lift, and down to a truck in the basement. Gavin Lowry came over to speak to Kathy.

'Nice meeting you,' he said. 'Hope we get to work together again, next time I need a new car.'

'Yes. Sorry about that, Gavin. And I'm sorry I won't be able to see how your campaign against the grey crust works out.'

'Read about it in *The Job*.' He grinned.

'Maybe Forbes can go for Harry Jackson's job. I hear he's resigning.'

'He offered his resignation, but Bo Seager wouldn't accept it. Reckoned he wasn't culpable.'

'Do you think that's right? You'd have thought he should have picked up a few warning signals about Speedy. He was his appointment, wasn't he? Knew him from the old days before his accident?'

'Yes. I guess Harry's fault, if he has one, is that he tends to be too loyal towards his team.'

Kathy smiled at him. 'That's not a mistake you intend to make, eh Gavin?'

He looked hurt. 'This from the woman who trashes my car.'

They shook hands and Lowry left to accompany the truck back to Hornchurch Street. Kathy went through to the rear office, where Brock was sorting through papers, pushing most of them through the slot of a locked bin for shredding.

'Well, Kathy.' He stretched and straightened his back, and walked over to the door to check on progress with clearing the place. 'I asked for twenty-four hours, but I honestly didn't think we'd crack it in the time.'

He seemed relieved but hardly elated, she thought. 'You're sure we have?'

He glanced at her. 'Certainly looks that way. Lowry and the others didn't come up with anything suspicious in the shop units, and they did a pretty solid job this time. Bo Seager's just been on to me about a deputation from the small traders led by our friend Bruno Verdi complaining about how thorough we were. Everyone seems very relieved to have us leave Silvermeadow. Our SIO especially. Can't wait to have us off his patch. We'll let his people wrap it all up.'

'While we concentrate on North.'

'Exactly. We've got plenty of leads on Keith Nolan to follow up. However, I was talking to Bren this morning . . .' He turned back from the door and came and sat on a box next to the chair Kathy had taken, lowering his voice as he went on. 'An idea occurred to me. I thought it might be worth us making one last little effort here tomorrow, unofficially.'

'Saturday?'

'Yes. It was last Saturday that North, if it really was him, was spotted. If he has some particular interest in the place, he might make a repeat visit. I've asked Bren and a few of the lads to spend the day with me here, on the off-chance.'

'You'll be lucky to spot him in the Saturday crowd. It's the last Saturday before Christmas.'

'So they tell me. We'll be in a couple of emergency road assistance vans, parked at the two main entrances onto the site, watching car drivers as they come in and out. Another lad'll watch the bus station and taxi rank.'

'And there's the WPC in the shop,' Kathy said, thinking.

'No. Forbes has pulled her out.'

Kathy felt him looking keenly at her.

'I did wonder if you would be interested in a new career for a day.'

She had seen it coming, and had already begun to resign herself to it. The weekend with Leon would have to wait.

'It's a long shot, Kathy, no doubt of that.'

She nodded. 'What about putting somebody in the control room to watch for him on the screens?'

'Yes, Jackson would probably be delighted, what with half his staff ill. But I'd rather not tell him what's going on. His own security isn't looking too good at the moment. Let's keep this to ourselves.'

As she was leaving, Kathy met Sharon in the mall. She was giving directions to an elderly couple, confused and lost, and when she caught sight of Kathy she waved to her to wait. When she'd finished with the shoppers she came over and said, 'I hear you're going.'

'Yes. Looks like we're all finished here, Sharon. You're back on patrol, I see.'

'We're very short-handed at the moment.' She looked uneasily at Kathy. 'You're quite satisfied, then? About Speedy? That he killed those poor kids?'

'It looks that way.'

'Oh . . .' Sharon lowered her eyes.

'Yes, it's a bit of a shock, isn't it?'

'I'd never have believed it, to be honest.'

'What, because of the wheelchair?'

'Oh no, I think he *could* have done it, physically I mean. I've seen him down the gym. He was very strong in his shoulders and arms. No, I just wouldn't have believed he would. And especially not Wiff.'

'Did you know the boy?'

'Yeah. Speedy had him down the security centre once, showing him the computers and stuff. He was really fond of him, I thought. You know, protective. He felt sorry for him, homeless and that.'

'Did the other security people know about Wiff?'

'Probably not. Speedy didn't want Harry to know. Didn't think he'd approve.' She stared down at her toecaps, polished shiny black, immaculate like the rest of her uniform, the way Harry would like it.

'Something bothering you, Sharon?'

'Yeah . . . It may sound stupid, but it isn't possible somebody else could have killed Speedy, is it, and made it look like Speedy did it?'

'What makes you say that?'

She shrugged, uncomfortable. 'I suppose I just can't believe it really.'

'That's often the way. People can't believe that the nice man they worked with for years could really be a killer.'

'Yeah, only . . . Speedy had this way of annoying people. He'd do things to get under their skin.'

'Yes,' Kathy agreed.

'I think he did it because he couldn't stand them feeling sorry for him, so he'd do something to piss them off. I said to him once that he should be careful or someone would belt him one, wheelchair or not. And he said he didn't worry, cos he knew too much.'

'What did he mean by that?'

'I don't know, and he wouldn't tell me. He just said he saw more of what went on stuck in front of his screens than the rest of us did on our two legs. Well, I wondered if he'd pissed someone off good and proper this time. Someone who didn't care what he knew.'

'Or cared too much. Nothing else? What about his drugs? You must have known about them.'

Sharon looked unconvincingly defiant. 'What drugs?'

'Come on. His place was full of stuff.'

'Was it? I don't know . . . sometimes he did seem out of it. I thought he was on medication.'

'He was dealing, Sharon. That's what we're told.'

'I didn't know that, honest. How could he have done, in his chair?'

'Wiff was his legs, ran his errands.'

'Oh.' She looked genuinely shocked. 'I didn't know that.'

'But you had a pretty good idea he was taking something.'

She nodded.

'Then surely Harry must have realised too, eh?'

'Yes, maybe. I saw Harry getting stuck into him once, and I thought it might have been about that. Speedy was really doped up at the time.'

'Well, we don't have anything to say we're wrong at the moment, Sharon. But if you think of anything, give me a ring, will you?' Kathy wrote her mobile number on the back of a card and handed it to her. They shook hands and said goodbye.

Leon was already there when Kathy got home. He was sitting at the table by the window with a mug of tea, absorbed in a road atlas. Rain was beating against the dark window, making the distant streetlights glimmer liquidly.

'Hi,' he said. 'Tea's fresh. Come and sit down.' He fetched her a mug.

'What are you doing?'

'Looking for places to spend a lull in. There's Lulham in Herefordshire, and Lullington in Derbyshire, and another one in Somerset. Or how about Lulsgate Bottom? Sounds good, eh? My money's on Dorset; we can get four lulls in one hit, all within walking distance: East Lulworth, Lulworth Castle, West Lulworth and Lulworth Cove. That's an irresistible concentration of lulls. What do you reckon?'

Kathy smiled. For a brief moment, before he lifted his head, he reminded her of an earnest schoolboy doing his homework assignment. Then he looked up at her with his intense dark eyes and her stomach tightened. 'I'm sorry. I can't go. Brock wants us to work tomorrow.' She put her arm round his shoulder. 'And it's going to be a total waste of time. But I have to go.'

'Oh. Too bad. Another time.'

She suppressed an impulse to say, no, we'll go, there won't be another time, not like this. But instead she nodded. 'Yes.'

'Next week,' he said. 'I thought of going up to Liverpool for a day or two. We could go together.'

'Liverpool?'

'Yes. I want to have a look around.'

'Why?' She felt a small chill inside her.

'I'm thinking of applying to go there.'

'A transfer? Why?'

'No, no. I'm thinking of doing a masters. Investigative psychology. I'd ask for leave for twelve months.'

Kathy sat down facing him across the table and stared at him, saying nothing.

'I'm stuck, Kathy,' he went on patiently. 'To move up I need some more qualifications. The Liverpool M.Sc. is exactly what I need. I'll show you the brochures.' He made as if to get up, but then, seeing the look on Kathy's face, didn't move. 'What?'

'That's where Alex Nicholson teaches, isn't it? Did she tell you about it?'

'Yes, that's right, while we were having dinner the other night. I was explaining the problem I have, and—'

'What problem? You never told me you had a problem, Leon.'

He leant forward, mildly exasperated. 'But you *know* how it is. I can't go beyond sergeant as laboratory liaison.'

'We didn't discuss this. You've only been here a few days, and you've already decided to move on.'

'It's not like that!' he protested. 'Look, Kathy, you should be thinking about this for yourself, too.'

'What?'

'You haven't got a degree.'

She flushed. 'I know that.'

'Well, you should get one! Hasn't Brock ever told you?'

'No!'

'Well, he bloody well ought to have done. He's a negligent supervisor.' He sat back and folded his arms in a pose that Kathy found quite astonishingly, insufferably smug. The anger flared inside her.

'Fuck you, Leon,' she said. 'He's ten times the copper you'll ever be.'

'But he's near his used-by date, Kathy,' he replied coolly. 'Things are different now, you know that. Look' – he held up his hands in truce – 'this is stupid. I'm not going to fight about this. You know I'm right. I just didn't . . . find the right way to put it.'

'Damn right,' she muttered fiercely. 'And I haven't got time to get a degree. If I was going to get one I should have done it years ago. It's too late now. I can't stop what I'm doing just to get a paper qualification.'

'Wrong,' he said, more gently. 'You must make time. Do it part-time. I'll help you.'

'Oh sure. From Liverpool.'

'That's just for a year, for God's sake. And it's only a couple of hours away.'

She relented eventually, and they made it up and prepared a meal together and generally agreed to be sensible and adult. It would have been all right if she hadn't known as soon as she saw Alex Nicholson that she was going to be trouble, and if they hadn't both initially told themselves, as a kind of insurance, that this was never going to work out anyway.

14

The following morning Kathy put on what she hoped would pass for shop assistant's clothes: a white blouse and navy cardigan and skirt. She pulled and clipped back her hair to try to avoid cursory identification by Harry Jackson's staff, and drove to Silvermeadow where she duly reported for duty at Cuddles, the soft-toy shop. The manager gave her a quick introduction to handling cash and credit-card transactions, then had her memorise the shop's mission statement ('We aim to bring joy to young and old through the medium of soft cuddly toys'), before placing her at a checkpoint in the middle of the shop, with a clear view of the large badger in the open shopfront facing the mall.

At ten a.m., when the centre opened its doors, she had a call on her mobile from Brock to say that the two vans were in position at the site entrances, ready for the day. She was armed with an extendable baton and a pair of handcuffs in the pocket of her skirt.

By lunchtime she felt she had pretty well exhausted whatever interest was to be derived from selling soft toys, and was glad of a break. She sat in a small staff room at the back of the shop, keeping an eye on the customers through the half-open door while she ate a sandwich, before returning reluctantly for the afternoon shift. Shortly afterwards she was in the middle of an electronic funds transfer transaction for a heavily built, extensively tattooed truck driver clutching a five-foot orange giraffe, when she caught a fleeting glimpse of a man standing at the edge of the swirling mall crowd, staring at the badger. She looked hard, trying to make him out, and immediately he turned away and disappeared into the mass of people.

While the truck driver and the rest of the queue looked on in surprise, Kathy abandoned her till and hurried towards the front of the shop. She was almost at the mall when she was stopped by a penetrating female voice. 'Sergeant! Sergeant Kolla! What on earth are you doing, serving in here? Is this a part-time job?'

Harriet Rutter emerged from behind a column, blocking Kathy's way, and she had to weave past her to get out into the mall. She could see no sign of anyone looking like North's pictures. She turned back, told Mrs Rutter to keep this to herself, and rejoined her queue.

At six, tired and exasperated at the waste of the day, Kathy phoned Brock to say she was leaving. He thanked her, apologised, and mentioned that an Armacorp security truck had driven down into the service road twenty minutes before, and she might like to check it on her way out. She took the first exit corridor she came to on the mall, used her code to pass through the fire door, and descended the concrete stair into the basement and out onto the loading platform.

Fifty yards to the left a couple of men in overalls were unloading a truck reversed against the dock. The Armacorp van was parked about the same distance in the opposite direction and on the other side of the service road, engine running, warning lights flashing. She walked in that direction and made out the driver behind the green armoured glass of the front compartment, waiting, and then saw him looking into his side mirror as two other guards, wearing uniforms and visored helmets and laden with bags, emerged from the doorway of a service stairway. They dropped the bags into a hopper in the side of the truck, one of the men spoke a couple of words into the radio clipped to his tunic, and they strode on to the next service stair, the van following slowly after them.

Kathy lifted her phone and reported to Brock again. 'I'd say they're nearly finished. Looks like they're on the final stair.'

She walked on along the loading platform towards the exit ramp, past the security truck, giving the driver a wave as she went by. It was a shock, after the continuous sunlight of the mall, to realise that it was dark outside, the day over. Somewhere out there across the bleak, wet carparks, Brock and Bren and their teams would be huddled inside their cramped vehicles waiting for a decent excuse to go home.

She reached her car eventually, after forgetting where she'd left it. There seemed to be an incredible number of vehicles on the site, and as many coming in as leaving.

Her phone rang as she started the engine.

'Kathy? Brock again. What's happened to the security truck?'

'I don't know. Hasn't it left yet?'

'We haven't seen it.'

She drove back to the mouth of the service road and parked on the roadside, running back down into the basement. The truck was still where she'd last seen it, lights still flashing, driver still sitting behind his bullet-proof windscreen drumming his fingers. She went up to his side window and showed her warrant card.

His voice squawked through a loudspeaker. 'What's the problem?'

She spoke into the microphone. 'You okay?'

'Yes. My crew's been delayed upstairs. One of the big stores wasn't ready for them. Rushed off their feet they are.'

The driver was nervous, she could see.

'Big takings today?'

'Biggest day of the year this is. Bigger than the sales. We picked up almost ten million this time last year. Reckon this year it'll be more.' He went on drumming his fingers, then said something into his radio, waited, shook his head. 'They're not picking me up. Reception's bad down here.'

'Want me to go up and check?'

'Yeah, that'd be good. Thanks. I can't step out of here. They're on the upper level. Two blokes in uniform. Tell them to get their fingers out. Base is getting stroppy.'

Kathy went through the door the men had used, wondering what to say if she met some of Harry's security people, but the stairway was empty all the way up to the top floor, making the bustle of the crowded mall seem all the more chaotic when she reached it. It took her ten minutes to check the main stores within range of the service stair. All confirmed that they'd handed over their day's takings to the two Armacorp security guards at least twenty minutes before. With a growing sense of unease she ran back down the stair to confirm that the security truck was still there, still waiting for them, then she rang Brock.

Afterwards, recalling what happened next, Brock had a sense of events unfolding with a desperate slowness, as if, no matter how hard they tried to speed them up, they could only unravel at a predetermined pace. Having called for assistance, Brock had his team close the exits and check every shopper — exhausted, frustrated, quarrelsome and broke — as they tried to leave by car or bus. Meanwhile the rain descended more heavily, the wind picking up viciously.

The stream of traffic arriving at the upper site entrance closest to the motorway became blocked by some exiting vehicles trying to detour around the police checkpoint, and the resulting queues of incoming cars developed so rapidly that they had tailed back down the exit ramps and onto the M25 before anyone could control them. A number of tailgate smashes in the ensuing chaos ensured that the London orbital motorway was soon brought to a complete halt in the southbound direction, which didn't help the armed robbery squad and Armacorp support vehicles attempting to reach the site from the north. Police and TV helicopters circling overhead completed the atmosphere of catastrophe.

In Silvermeadow itself, while police searched the retail floors for any sign of the two missing guards, Brock conducted a stilted interrogation of the Armacorp driver, who still refused to leave his locked cabin without instructions from base, and who stared out at the figures surrounding his truck like a worried goldfish in a green glass tank. This was only the third time he'd been out with the two other crew, he said, and though he didn't know them well, he found it hard to come to terms with the idea of them making off with the final load of cash.

'How much?' Brock asked, and got the tinny reply, 'A million? Maybe two.'

Each of the half-dozen staircases would have yielded something like that from the blocks of shops they served, apparently, four or five times their normal Saturday takings. Despite the amounts involved, the collection arrangements here, in enclosed and secure service areas, were considered relatively low-risk, and the difficulties that conventional bandits would experience in making a getaway added to the sense of security. The possibility of two guards laden with cash bags conspiring to walk off into the blue didn't seem to have been taken all that seriously.

'How do you know it's only the last load they took?' Brock asked.

'Because I saw them deposit the previous loads in the cash hopper.' He pointed over his shoulder, and Brock bent to examine the steel door built into the side of the truck.

He straightened again and spoke at the microphone. 'You saw the actual cash?'

'No, no. The bags.'

'Maybe we should check what's in them, eh?'

'Can't.'

The whole essence of the security system was that no one, neither driver nor crew, could open the secure box built into the vehicle's body. Once the cash bags were in there through the hopper, only base could access them again.

It was almost half an hour before the Armacorp base vehicle, escorted by a police patrol car, managed to weave its way through the road chaos and scream, lights flashing and horn blaring, down the service road ramp. Four men got out, three very bulky and menacing, and one diminutive, wearing rimless glasses and a leather coat and looking like a Hollywood version of a Gestapo officer, Brock thought. The driver of the security truck at last consented to open his door and step down, saluting the new arrivals with pointed dignity. They conferred briefly with Brock, then the small man, screened by his minders, entered the rear of the vehicle like a sinister midwife to release the treasures from its belly. These comprised forty-three cash bags, some containing coin, some bulked out with crumpled paper and cardboard, all devoid of banknotes.

Not long after this detectives radioed Brock to report that they had encountered a locked cleaners' store, located just off the first of the service stairs which had been used by the security guards, and the door latch wouldn't budge, apparently jammed shut with superglue.

When he joined them Brock recognised the smell that hung in the air of the corridor outside, a smell familiar from the firing range.

'Hercules powder,' one of the two detectives, a gun freak, said to him, sniffing the air like a connoisseur.

'Sure,' the other said sceptically, lifting the ram to swing at the door.

'No, straight up. Bullseye, I reckon. Yer Vectan and yer GM3 are sweeter, like. Know what I mean?'

'Bullshit,' the other grunted.

'Get on with it,' Brock said, and the man nodded and swung the ram against the lock. It burst open on the second swing, revealing the foot of the first of the two bodies on the floor inside.

From their positions in the cramped space, it appeared as if the two men had been forced to crouch on their knees among the buckets and bottles. Their black tunics, with the Armacorp flashes and radios, had gone, as had their helmets. They had knelt with their backs to the door, and a bullet had been put into each head at point-blank range.

Brock called a hurried briefing in unit 184. Bren Gurney and several others from Serious Crime were there, as well as two senior officers from the Robbery Squad, the leather-coated man from Armacorp, and Gavin Lowry and others from the local division. Chief Superintendent Forbes put in a brief appearance just as they were getting under way, feeling obliged to register a formal protest at Brock's lack of consultation with his officers, and to suggest that the outcome might have been very different with local backup. No one was very interested in this.

'Needless to say,' he said stiffly, 'we shall provide all the support we can. But we will expect to be kept informed in return. I propose that DS Lowry act as liaison, since you've already worked with him. You agree, Brock?'

Brock nodded.

'Good. At least,' Forbes added, with a prim little smile, '*our* Silvermeadow case is satisfactorily resolved.'

As Forbes left, Brock overheard the senior Robbery Squad man say to Bren beside him, 'What's his problem? What case is that?'

'A murder. Teenage girl abducted from here a couple of weeks ago. We were assisting each other in our respective inquiries.'

'Oh yes? No connection with North?'

'No,' Bren said decisively. 'No connection at all.'

Brock found Bren's confident answer vaguely troubling. It stirred a question that had been lurking in the back of his mind for some time.

Lowry, meanwhile, moved over to sit beside Kathy, giving her an amused little smile as she met his eye.

'But of a sly one, aren't you, Kathy?' he said. 'Letting me think you were all finished up at Silvermeadow.'

'When we last spoke I thought we were. Anyway, this wasn't your case.'

'It is now, by the looks of things. It seems you lot need a bit of help.' He grinned. 'So you and Brock and Bren and half of SO1 were actually *here*, were you, when this happened? One of these geezers told me you'd been here all day looking for this North character, waiting for something to happen, only when it did, you didn't notice it. I told him he must have got his facts wrong, eh? I said, come *on*, this is the famous DCI Brock's team!'

He was enjoying himself, fairly bubbling with it.

Kathy muttered, 'Sod off, Gavin,' through clenched teeth.

'Tell you what,' he chuckled. 'Makes me feel a lot better about my car.'

Then a new thought seemed to strike him. 'You were probably never interested in the Vlasich murder at all, were you? You just used it as a cover to be here, on the lookout for North. Did Harry Jackson know? No? Where is Harry now, anyway?'

That was a question that had occurred to Kathy too. If the security staff were so short-handed, where the hell was Harry Jackson?

Brock interrupted, calling the group to order with a rapid summary of how they now believed the robbery had been carried out. Two men, it was thought, had hidden in the cleaners' store cupboard beside the first staircase and waited for the security guard crew, whom they had ambushed and murdered. They had then followed the expected pattern of collections from the shop units, removing the contents of the cash bags before depositing them in the security truck hopper. As each zone served by a stairway was cleared, it appeared that a common pass code, one allocated to emergency services, had been entered into the security lock on the doorway connecting that service stair with the mall. In other words it looked as if the money had been transferred to one or more accomplices waiting in the malls.

'Perfect cover,' Brock announced. 'The place was packed with people with bulging shopping bags. They could walk out without the least suspicion. Even if something had happened down in the service road to arouse suspicion and cut the operation short, the people in the mall could stroll away without suspicion. They might have been women for all we know, frazzled shoppers with bags and pushchairs and kids hanging from their elbows – maybe the little girl North was seen with a week ago. And when the two gunmen got to the final stairway without a problem, they simply took off their jackets and helmets and joined the crowd and walked away too.'

'How come the driver in the security truck didn't twig what was going on, chief?' someone objected.

'We'll be looking a lot more carefully into that,' Brock said, 'but so far his story seems plausible. The two men he saw going from stair to stair were the same build as his crew, and were wearing their clothes and radios. While they were out of sight they followed procedure exactly, reporting in every two minutes until the very end. Radio reception wasn't perfect, but the voice that made the reports was like the one the driver expected to hear: east London, working class, a bit breathless from the stairs.' Brock nodded to the man in the leather coat at his side. 'Mr Brown's initial assessment is that he's probably telling the truth. But it's likely they had some inside help at Armacorp, and we'll work on that assumption.'

'And at Silvermeadow?' someone else asked.

'Yes.'

One of the Robbery Squad officers put up his hand.

'You're certain it's our friend, Brock?'

'I think we can be pretty sure of that.'

'So he'll be aiming to leave the country again?'

Brock frowned. 'I think that may depend on the little girl he was seen with last weekend.'

'How do you mean?'

'If she was part of a new family he brought into the country with him, it wouldn't make sense to bring them in just to do a job, would it? Maybe he intends to settle down with them here. Maybe he thinks enough time has passed for us to have forgotten about him.'

They considered this doubtfully. 'Risky. Where was he hiding, do we know? Argentina, wasn't it? Good cover, a family of tourists from Argentina.'

'We believe he had moved on to Canada. We had a report of him there over a year ago, and we suspect he may have entered the UK at the end of November under a Canadian passport in the name of Keith Nolan.'

The officer drew a sheaf of files and loose papers from his briefcase. 'We grabbed what we could on our way out, but it sounds as if you've got more current info on our friend.'

Bren brought the newcomers up to date on what they'd discovered of Nolan's movements, as well as the current whereabouts of North's relatives and known associates. From this they began to compile a priority list of raids to be co-ordinated for that night.

When Brock asked for further comment, Kathy, with some reluctance, spoke up. 'I think I might have seen him this afternoon, about two p.m., outside Cuddles on the upper mall. It was only for a second, and I couldn't be sure, so I didn't report it. But I'd like to check the centre's camera tapes.'

Brock gave her a wry smile. 'Yes, I was coming to that. You'll need quite a bit of help. We have to analyse every tape that was running in this place this afternoon. We know the timing of what we're looking for, but that's about all. We're looking for men with black trousers, men of the right build, men who look like our most recent shots of

North, little girls like the one he was with last weekend, and anyone on Bren's list. It's going to take a big team, and lots of machines. Can you help us, Gavin?'

An hour later Kathy and half a dozen other officers were seated in front of VDUs in a room at Hornchurch Street, starting to go through the first batch of tapes from Silvermeadow. It was going to be a long night, she guessed, for all of them. Once search warrants were issued the raids would begin, the questioning of known associates, the gathering of evidence. She had told Leon she'd be home by eight at the latest, and they had planned to go out for a meal. She'd tried his mobile number a couple of times, but the line was busy. For all she knew he might have been called in to the hunt too, looking for forensic clues at Silvermeadow.

The video watchers had plans of the shopping centre marked with the camera zones, and Kathy began with a tape for zone 16, in which Cuddles was located, and covering the early afternoon period. The screen began sequencing through four views of the mall, each held for a few seconds in turn. She identified the view that corresponded with the area outside the soft toy store, and fast forwarded to the time at which she had seen the figure in the mall.

But he wasn't there. She found the right time, for in one of the short sequences she saw herself emerge from the shop, and Mrs Rutter waving an arm at her, but by then the man she was after had disappeared off the bottom of the frame, while in the previous clip, ten seconds before, he was still invisible in the crowd.

As she searched through that and the other tapes, trying to find any signs of North before and after her sighting, and getting annoyed with herself for the slow and inefficient way she was working the machine, and frustrated by the mechanical way in which the cameras cut in and out of scenes regardless of their possible importance, she realised how much easier this would have been with somebody like Speedy at the controls. Without his inquisitive eye to guide it, the whole system was clumsy and arbitrary, as likely to miss a crucial event as capture it. How fortunate for North and his accomplices then that Speedy hadn't been around. And who knows but that Speedy's cunning, prying eye might even have recognised someone among them, and zoomed in and followed the suspect, maybe right out to their car, and caught their registration number, and the faces of the others . . .

But he hadn't, and without that guiding hand the tapes were

frustratingly unhelpful, the external ones completely useless, with only distance shots of acres of rain-battered cars, dazzling headlight flashes, and tiny black figures scurrying through the darkness.

The removal of Speedy had been very lucky for the robbers in another way too, of course, for it had closed the Vlasich murder case and with it unit 184 and the police presence at Silvermeadow. North would presumably have seen the press reports of Speedy's death on Friday, but would he have realised its implications for his operation?

Kathy returned to scanning the tapes, but without much enthusiasm. She found it hard to concentrate in the way that was necessary, as the others were doing, systematically freezing frames and identifying figures to be later enlarged and enhanced and printed out for identification. After a while her mind returned to Speedy.

Because they had only been aware of the first crime, Kerri's murder, when Speedy died, they had never really doubted the connection between those two events. But suppose Speedy had been removed in order to clear the way for the second crime, the robbery? Perhaps he had even seen something on his screens to warn him of what was coming, as Sharon had hinted, and had had to be disposed of, and in a way that would make the police assume a connection to Kerri's murder, rather than forewarn them of the robbery.

This was fanciful, she told herself, and she was getting tired. There had been ample forensic and other evidence to link Speedy to Kerri's murder, from her backpack to the ketamine and hair samples – although Leon had seemed concerned at the absence of Kerri's fingerprints at either Wiff's den or Speedy's house.

Kathy tried his mobile again. It was switched off. Her phone at home was on the answering machine. She sighed and returned to her task.

In another office, Brock was sitting down with Bo Seager. Like Harry Jackson, she too had been away from Silvermeadow when the robbery had happened, and had phoned Brock soon after learning of the details, insisting that she come to Hornchurch Street rather than meet at the shopping centre. She was tense, agitated even, and asked if she could smoke a cigarette. When it was alight she continued fiddling with the gold lighter while she asked Brock to describe to her exactly what had happened.

At the end of it she said flatly, 'This is terrible.'

Brock said nothing, watching as she slapped the lighter down on the cigarette packet on the table, then tapped the filter tip of her cigarette up and down on the lighter, her eyes fixed on it without seeing, eyelids blinking rapidly.

'Now we have five dead,' she said. 'They're really going to have my ass.'

'They?'

'The board.' She took in the questioning look on his face. 'Oh yes. This will be my fault. Nathan Tindall is desperate to have my job. He feeds poison to all the other money men on the board.'

'It's hard to see how they could blame you for any of this.'

'I get the blame for everything that happens inside those eighty acres, David. That's my job.'

She took a deep lungful and then exhaled, speaking through the smoke. 'They had inside help, did they?'

'We don't know yet.'

'But you think?'

'I'd rather not say at the moment.'

She nodded, as if he'd confirmed it. 'Of course they did. And I guess it could be me, right?'

'Could it?'

'Why not? We'd all think about it for a million or two. I got Harry Jackson out of the way, didn't I?'

'Did you?'

'Yeah. I sent him to a security conference that's on in London at the moment. We agreed months ago that he should go. Really bad timing, so close to Christmas.'

'Where was this?'

'At the Barbican. Ironic, isn't it? He missed his own case study.'

'Is there any other reason I should suspect you, Bo?' Brock asked, smiling.

'Actually there is.' She took another deep draw on her cigarette. 'You see, I've seen this done before.'

The smile vanished from Brock's face and he leant forward. 'Go on.'

'In Canada. About two years ago I spent a month in Toronto, as part of a centre management course. I was mainly based downtown, in the Eaton Centre, but while I was there there was a big hold-up at one of the suburban shopping malls, at Yorktown. Most of the big out-of-town North American centres don't have the service tunnel

247

arrangement we have at Silvermeadow because it's relatively expensive to build and maintain, but Yorktown was like us, too big for its site, so they put the service bays underneath to save space. One day some bandits got into the service areas and hid out until a security truck arrived and gathered up the cash from all the stores. On the final pick-up they jumped the guards, took their uniforms and calmly climbed into the truck, and the driver drove off with them inside. They hijacked him once they were out in clear country. But they made a mistake.'

'What was that?'

'They tied up the guards and locked them in a storeroom, but one of them managed to make enough noise to attract help. The cops caught up with the truck before the gang could clean it out, and they nailed them all. This lot didn't make that mistake.'

'No, they made very sure that couldn't happen. Interesting. And the Canadian gang had inside help?'

'The security man at the service road entrance checkpoint. He'd got bored with his job, and had passed the time working out how it could be done. He mentioned it to his brother-in-law, who knew some bad people. But for a time it looked as if someone in the centre management office had been involved, maybe even the centre manager himself. The police gave him a tough going over, and afterwards the centre owners got rid of him anyway, just in case.'

'I see.' Brock rubbed a hand through his beard thoughtfully. The connection with Toronto corresponded chillingly well with what they suspected of North's movements. It sounded as if he hadn't been idle while he'd been away.

'If our case did follow your Canadian model, who would you nominate as the insider?' he asked. 'Assuming it isn't you.'

She shrugged. 'Speedy? Who else?'

'Yes. Well, with or without your help, that place of yours seems to have become a magnet for killers, Bo.'

'Yeah.' She stubbed the cigarette out angrily. 'It's a nightmare, Brock. A dream that's turned sick. I'll tell you that for nothing.'

It was after midnight when Kathy got home. There were the remains of a take-away Chinese meal on the table, an empty bottle of Chilean red beside it, and Leon asleep on the sofa. He opened his eyes and watched her for a moment as she stood at the table scavenging the remains of the beanshoots and noodles.

'Hi.'

'Hi.' She shot him a smile as she lifted the fork to her mouth. 'Sorry about the meal,' she mumbled, mouth full.

'Haven't you eaten?'

'Not much. You know how it is.'

'Serious, is it?' He yawned and slid a hand across his hair.

'Ten million quid. Two dead.'

He nodded. 'That's what they said on the news.'

'Then you know about as much as me,' she said, and turned back to scrape at the foil container.

'And tomorrow?' he asked.

She shrugged, came over and slumped down beside him. 'I'll have to go back. I'm really sorry.'

'That's okay. I understand.' He stroked her brow.

'Tuesday evening. I'll go with you to Liverpool.'

His fingers hesitated in their caress through her hair. 'You sure? Can they spare you?'

'Oh yes. This is a manhunt now. I'll check with Brock, but I'm sure it'll be okay.'

'I could leave it till after Christmas.'

'No, I want to get away with you. Really, I'm interested. I'm sorry I reacted the wrong way before.' It occurred to her that she seemed to be saying sorry a lot. 'What did you do tonight?' she asked.

'Not much. Bit of TV.' He sounded bored and glum.

'What about tomorrow?'

'No idea. Do you think Brock will need me on your case?'

'He hasn't contacted you?'

'No.' He looked rather forlorn.

'I think the Robbery Squad have their own lab liaison.'

'Oh, well. I can wash my hair,' he said with a sigh. 'And watch your new microwave. And polish your new TV.'

'Sorry.'

'Don't be. But maybe we should think about moving closer to that place. The way things are happening to them, they need you there permanently.'

'I could fix you up with a job at Cuddles.'

'Thanks. Golliwogs section, I suppose.'

Kathy laughed. 'The lab hasn't come up with anything new on Speedy and Wiff, has it?'

'Not as far as I know.' He yawned again, filling his lungs noisily.

'They're handing it all over to division now. Why would the kid own an antique coin, do you think?'

'Wiff?'

'Yes, among his stuff. Seemed odd.'

'What did it look like?'

'Nothing much. Small, black and worn smooth.'

'That reminds me of something.'

'My cock, do you mean?'

Kathy laughed and slid her hand up his thigh. 'Yes, of course,' she said. 'That's it. I think of little else.'

'Liar,' he said.

15

The next morning Essex was shrouded in fog. It muffled the sound of traffic on the motorway and forced it to slow to a crawl in the denser pockets, where the light of the hidden sun barely penetrated.

When she finally reached the Silvermeadow junction Kathy stopped at the top of the exit ramp and gazed out over the site. The grey building was a ghostly presence in the mist, like an alien craft freshly landed in the fold of the slope and surrounded by a scattering of cars, capsules attendant on the mother ship. In contrast to the deathly gloom of the morning, it was clearly alive, for light glimmered from its spine along the route of the mall arcade, and Kathy could almost swear that she could make out the faint tinkle of jingle bells, even at that distance. A few dark huddled figures were scurrying between the cars and the centre, parasites trapped in a world of machines.

She thought of her imaginings of the previous evening, that Kerri's murder and North's robbery, and all the accompanying deaths and mayhem, might be part of one conspiracy, not two, and immediately felt the improbability of the idea, as if the daylight, even daylight as dim as this, cast things in a more realistic light. Crime happened like everything else, not at evenly spaced intervals but in clusters and bunches. Feast or famine. Nothing for a time, then all at once. So Silvermeadow was catching up with its normal crime load after a quiet interval. The fact that both series of crimes had happened here was simply coincidence.

Everyone else seemed to believe this. Not that it was discussed, but when she walked down through the service road and spoke to a SOCO crew combing the basement for further evidence without much hope or enthusiasm, and again when she went upstairs to the temporarily reoccupied unit 184 and talked to the few people there, Kathy had the clear impression that everyone took it for granted that Silvermeadow was no longer relevant, that the real centre of the action had moved elsewhere. Like stage hands cleaning up on the morning after a big show, they saw themselves as far removed from the real actors, who were now waking, no doubt, to champagne breakfasts in some remote first-class hotel, or on a jumbo jet high above some distant ocean. Silvermeadow, they seemed to feel, had been the innocent setting for the robbers' latest gig, just as it had unfortunately accommodated Kerri's killer.

She walked along the deserted upper mall and came once again to the balcony overlooking the food court and rain forest, giving a nod to the gorilla who still crouched in his bamboo grove. But Silvermeadow wasn't innocent. After spending a week here, nothing about the place felt coincidental or innocent. From start to finish the centre was calculated and manipulative, dressed up to deceive. If it had been a suspect rather than a place, she would have said its manner was guilty as hell.

As if the beast could sense her thoughts, the escalators in front of her gave a sudden growl, then lurched into motion, and simultan-eously from the trees below came the twitter of electronic parrots. Two disparate events, Kathy thought, still caught up in her doubts. What links the parrots and the escalators? The place, the time, and the hidden hand that presses the switch. And if you wanted to find that hand, it wouldn't matter which event you investigated, because both would lead back to the same place.

From one of the food units down below came a rattle of a security grille being raised. It came from Bruno's Gelati, and as she watched she saw the owner step out and gaze around at his patch of the food court. He was wearing a black waistcoat over his white shirt today, and was looking very sleek and pleased with himself, his hair and moustache gleaming with oil in the bright Mediterranean glow of the lights. He moved among the tables making small fastidious adjust-ments, straightening a chair here, wiping a surface there. As Kathy watched him she recalled the story of the little girl he had enticed into his ice-cream van. *Mr Kreemee*. The thought made her feel slightly sick, but then, she reminded herself, the story had no significance for their case. Just another coincidence, that he should be here, that it should be his niece who had been taken. The world was full of coincidences, and the fact that a violent robbery had followed hard on the heels of a murder was just one more. She turned away from the rail and walked away.

By Monday Brock felt as if he had covered most of the British Isles. He had started on Sunday by going down to Southampton to check a possible sighting on a Channel ferry, and once on the move he had found himself unable to stop, with urgent calls coming in from all over the country, demanding his attention. From Southampton he was driven up to Lincolnshire to inspect a private airfield from which unauthorised flights had been reported, then over to Holyhead to question sailors on the Irish boat. He had then attended a raid on a rented farmhouse in Cumbria and been flown out on a helicopter to a Liberian tanker making odd manoeuvres in the middle of the North Sea. When he finally returned to London he was feeling numb from frantic but useless movement. Bren and the others had been no less active and no more productive in the south-east, and when Brock called his team together at Queen Anne's Gate on the Monday evening there was a clear conviction among them that the trail had gone cold.

They gathered – Bren, Brock, Kathy and three others – in The Bride of Denmark, a very small pub improbably assembled in the basement of their annex offices by a former owner of the building, from the fragments of Victorian London pubs demolished by the Blitz or redevelopment projects. It had been a labour of great love and eccentricity, and Brock felt a personal obligation to protect it from the threats of the Met's Property Services Department, which regarded the presence of a pub inside a police headquarters building as dangerously frivolous. Over the years he had armed himself with a number of important-sounding opinions from heritage bodies, and staff turnover at PSD had ensured a level of amnesia about departmental squabbles that weren't likely to enhance anyone's career prospects. The main snug could barely hold the six of them, the pew seats and the tiny bar behind which Brock sat nursing a large glass of whisky staring at a large stuffed salmon facing him from a glass case on the opposite wall. He perfectly understood its attitude of grim preoccupation. As they talked, the lack of options now available became painfully apparent.

'It stands to reason,' Bren murmured. 'North wouldn't have set up a smooth snatch like that without having an equally slick getaway lined up. I'll bet they dispersed and were on a boat or in the air before we'd even twigged what had happened.'

As baffling as the escape route was the silence that had surrounded the whole operation. The police had rounded up and questioned all North's known associates and relatives without the least hint of a contact, and usually well-informed snouts and sources seemed as surprised by the coup as everyone else. Bren took this especially to heart. 'I had a week,' he said. 'We knew for a week that he was around, and apart from the Nolan lead I didn't get one whisper of where he was or what he was up to.' Keith Nolan, if he existed, had still not been traced, nor had his papers been used to leave the country.

Forensic examination of the 9mm bullets used to kill the two guards, and of the bags which the robbers had handled, had also yielded nothing. Now the only hope seemed to lie with the dozens of security video tapes recovered from Silvermeadow that Saturday from individual stores as well as the centre's main system. Teams were still sifting through this material, building up a portrait gallery of thousands of people who were in the centre in the minutes during and immediately after the robbery.

Brock drained his glass. 'So we do it the hard way. It usually comes down to that anyway. While we wait to see what the tapes tell us, we'd better go back to the beginning. North had information from the inside. Someone at Armacorp or at Silvermeadow, probably both. Let's focus on that.'

'He might have worked it out for himself,' Bren objected. 'The Saturday evening pick-up followed a pretty dependable routine.'

'What about Speedy Reynolds? Couldn't he have been the contact?' Kathy suggested. A couple of heads shook in disagreement. 'I know we've been through this before, but it is bloody odd that one of their security people should die in suspicious circumstances just two days before a major robbery.'

'Not if he'd been involved in a second serious crime that had occurred a week before, which he had,' Bren said with weary emphasis. 'The evidence ties him firmly to Kerri's murder, not North's hold-up, Kathy. Let's not make things any more complicated than they have to be.'

Brock valued Bren's tendency to keep things simple and focused, though he found Kathy's willingness to complicate them much more interesting. However, there was another reason why he should back Bren's approach, at least for the time being.

'He's also not in a position to help us, Kathy,' Brock said quietly. 'Like the two Armacorp guards who were murdered, one or both of whom could also have been North's inside source. So we should probably concentrate on the more hopeful assumption that his contact, if there was one, is still alive.'

'If he is then he's still in place,' one of the others said. 'We haven't been able to identify anyone from either Armacorp or Silvermeadow who's gone missing over the last few days.'

'Right,' Brock said, and began to divide up the tasks, most of them already covered during the previous days and which now would have to be done again.

At the end of it he looked thoughtfully at Kathy. 'Not convinced?' he said.

She shrugged. 'I don't . . .' she began, then stopped. 'Doesn't matter.'

'Tell you what,' Brock said, guessing that she'd not want to voice her doubts until she had something concrete to offer, but trusting her instincts, 'why don't you have another look at Speedy's movements, just to be sure. And while you're at it, you can go over the work schedules of all the centre security staff for the last few weeks again, see if you can spot anything that the rest of us missed.'

Kathy nodded. 'Yes. Right.'

'We've run out of ideas,' Kathy said, pushing the piece of veal around with her fork. They had decided to take a late meal at their local Italian, La Casa Romana, after it had become clear that Leon was mildly pissed off at spending another night kicking his heels in the flat on his own.

'If you don't want that I'll eat it,' he said.

She passed it over. 'How was your day then?'

'Boring. Checking statements of evidence. Again.'

'Oh.'

'Brock can't be too popular at the moment, can he? Letting North commit murder and armed robbery right under his nose.'

Kathy thought he sounded rather sanctimonious as he said this. 'Under *my* nose actually.'

Leon shrugged, chewing. 'His operation. So why have you run out of ideas?'

Kathy found this question rather irritating too, almost as if he were trying to rile her. In fact, she decided, he *was* trying to rile her. 'Maybe because we've had no bloody help from forensics,' she told him tartly.

He didn't look up from his plate. 'There wasn't much to go on from what I heard. Two nine-millimetre bullets? Not even the cases.'

'I don't mean that. I mean before.'

'Before?' He looked at her now, puzzled.

'Yes. I mean, you couldn't be sure that Kerri Vlasich had ever been in Speedy Reynolds' house, or that someone else hadn't been there and removed something, or that he'd really killed Wiff, or . . . or any damned thing.'

She was tired, she knew, and the wine had relaxed her caution with him, her care to do the right thing, which sometimes was an effort. But it was more than that. She wanted to get angry, she realised. She wanted to blow away the fog that had been gathering in her head around this bloody case.

'And what has that got to do with Upper North?' he said coolly. It was a classic Desai defence, she thought. When attacked, go for the logical jugular, not the emotional underbelly.

'I don't know, do I? Because the forensic stuff is all so inconclusive.'

'Kathy . . .' He laid down his knife and fork with deliberate patience. 'No one has suggested any connection whatsoever between Kerri Vlasich's death and the robbery of the security truck, have they? Or have I missed something?'

'You mean apart from the coincidence of time and place?'

'That was circumstance, not coincidence. If you have a huge shopping centre with stacks of people and money passing through it, you're going to get crimes happening there. That's life, not a conspiracy. If the two things had happened in Brentwood high street, you wouldn't have given it a second thought, even though it's probably got a lot less shops and visitors than Silvermeadow mall.'

There was some justice in that, but Kathy didn't want to hear it. She changed tack and went for the underbelly. 'That's just blinkered thinking,' she said, slightly surprised to hear how passionate she sounded, when she really wasn't sure just what she thought. 'You want to put everything in neat and tidy compartments, right? You want to separate things and put ribbons around them' – she was about to say 'like degrees after your name', but stopped herself – 'but life isn't like that, Leon. Life is all mixed up, for God's sake.'

He stared at her for a moment in surprise. She had spoken too loudly, she realised, and people at neighbouring tables were eyeing her.

'I think maybe *you're* a bit mixed up, Kathy,' he said eventually, quite softly.

'That's condescending crap!' she snapped back, and turned away from him. She felt herself trembling, and the thought came into her head, *What the hell am I doing?* She realised that John, the proprietor, was gazing at her from behind the bar, a slightly puzzled look on his face. He caught her eye and came over to them.

'All done here?' he said. 'Like to see the dessert menu? Coffees?'

They both said no, giving him flat smiles, and without looking at each other.

'I should tell you that we won't be open tomorrow night, just in case you were thinking of coming in.'

'Something on?' Leon said.

'Gran's ninetieth. We're having a family get-together. Five generations.'

'Five?'

'Yeah. Gran's ninety, Mum's sixty-six, I'm forty-one, Gina's twenty-one, and her baby's almost two.'

'Wonderful,' Leon said, without enthusiasm. 'Give Gran our best.'

'Yeah, I will. So we're closing the restaurant to have the party in here. But we're having open house for our regulars between six and seven to drink the health of the old lady, if you can join us.'

'Thanks, John,' Leon said. 'We'd like to do that, but we're going up north tomorrow evening. At least,' he added coolly, 'I am.'

Later, when they got home, Kathy grabbed him and kissed him and they told each other they were being silly and needed to have a good swim, or a good fuck. Though even while they were doing that, Kathy couldn't help thinking: What do you mean, *you* are?

Afterwards, curled against him, Kathy asked him drowsily what he'd meant.

'Nothing,' he said. 'Are you still on?'

'Of course.'

'Good. I've booked a room at the Adelphi. For two nights.'

'Two?'

'Yes. I thought we could come back on Thursday evening, give us

257

more time. The train leaves tomorrow at eight p.m. What do you think?'

'Perfect,' she said sleepily.

'You'll get away from work in time?'

'Of course. I do have a life . . .'

16

Kathy woke in sober mood, and sensed the same in Leon. They washed, dressed and breakfasted with care not to give offence. But there was another mood beneath the caution, which Kathy felt and kept to herself, one of private determination.

She stopped first at the incident room in Hornchurch Street to pick up some materials. There was one message for her there, several days old, marked 'not urgent' and therefore put aside in the panic over the hold-up. Alison Vlasich had rung. Kathy hesitated, reluctant to be distracted from what she'd planned to do that morning, then dialled the number and arranged to call into the Herbert Morrison estate right away.

Prepared by her phone call, Alison Vlasich answered the door immediately when Kathy arrived, her face fresh with make-up.

'I wasn't sure if I'd catch you in when I phoned,' Kathy said. 'I thought you might be back at work.'

'Yes, I am. I started back yesterday, but I'm not on till eleven.'

'That's good, that you're back. And are you getting out a bit, with friends?' Kathy looked round the living room for any signs of a male admirer, but all she could see was the striking neatness of it all, as if Alison lived here like a ghost, without disturbing anything.

'Now and again. Sit down.'

'Thanks. What can I do for you?'

'It was about that story at the hospital, about the old woman with the missing daughter, that you asked me to check.'

'Ah, yes. Did you find out any more about that?'

'I did speak to the cook, but she couldn't remember who she'd heard it from. She thought it might have been one of the nurses from Sister McLeod's ward, but she wasn't sure . . .' Her voice tailed off.

'I'm sorry. It's not much help is it? I could have told you over the phone.'

Kathy guessed that Alison needed to feel she was doing something to help, and she said, 'No, that's fine. That's useful. I can speak to Sister McLeod if I need to follow it up.'

'Do you think you will?'

'Maybe not at this stage. It doesn't look a very promising line of enquiry after all.'

'Oh.' Alison nodded sadly. 'I'm glad really. I wouldn't like to think that there've been others. But you're still working on the case?'

'Still trying to tie up loose ends,' Kathy said, and, more to sound convincing than anything more positive, she took from her shoulder bag an A4 envelope she'd picked up at Hornchurch Street. She slid out the photographs onto the coffee table, stills blown up from the security camera shots of North a week before together with file pictures of some of his old associates. 'I don't suppose you've ever seen this man before?'

She imagined what Leon would think of the question: a stab in the dark. And of course Alison hadn't seen him before. And yet Kathy, watching her shake her head blankly, felt a small pang of irrational annoyance at fate, such as you feel when your lottery ticket doesn't make you rich, even though you know the odds are fourteen million to one.

'Sorry. Was it important?'

'No, not in the least.' Kathy gathered up the pictures and glanced at her watch. 'I'd better get going.'

'Me too. I'll need to go for my bus.'

'It's West Essex General, isn't it, where you work?' Kathy said. 'I'll drop you off if you like. It's not out of my way.'

On the road they talked about neutral things: the hospital and the problems and advantages of working for big organisations. Then, as Kathy turned into the carpark, Alison pointed to a side wing and said that that was where Sister McLeod's ward was.

'I suppose . . . I could show you how to get there if you wanted.'

It was as if they both felt compelled to follow through with this, though neither was enthusiastic.

'Oh, yes,' Kathy said. 'Yes, I suppose you could.'

Kathy studied the illuminated information map in the foyer of the hospital, trying to work out the way to geriatrics, but without success. The plan looked like a wiring diagram or printed circuit, with a maze of corridors and departments. Even with a route map she doubted if she could follow the way. Fortunately, when she asked at the enquiries desk, she discovered that the administration of West Essex General had solved this problem. The main circulation routes had recently been 'themed', the woman explained, to make it easy to find your way around, the themes being modelled on popular TV series. Thus you might follow the Coronation Street route to obstetrics and gynaecology, or Dr Who to orthopaedics. As she followed Emmerdale to geriatrics, Kathy began to feel that the make-believe world of the mall was leaching out into the world at large, and wondered if the nurses would be dressed like milkmaids. Thankfully they were not.

Sister McLeod was a big, black, irrepressibly cheerful woman whose principal therapeutic quality lay in her ability to dispel introspection and self-pity among the old wrecks in her care. Kathy followed her down the ward to her little office, her banter leaving a trail of wry chuckles and wincing smiles in their wake.

'Alison Vlasich?' She pondered as they sat down. 'Is she a redhead?'

'No,' Kathy said. 'Light brown hair, shoulder length. Thin, pale complexion.'

'Anaemic-looking? Looks like she needs a good steak and a Guinness?'

'Yes, I'd say she does.'

'I think I can place her. In the kitchens, behind the counter. So it was her daughter they found? Poor woman, that's terrible.'

'She happened to mention to us that she'd heard stories here of another girl disappearing at Silvermeadow.'

'Here? Really?'

'Yes. Apparently one of the nurses on this ward told one of the cooks about a patient here, an old woman, who was saying she'd lost her daughter out there.'

Sister McLeod frowned. 'I don't remember that one. How long ago would that have been?'

'We're not sure. Maybe last spring or summer.'

The nurse shook her head doubtfully, took down a book from a shelf behind the desk and began thumbing through its pages. It seemed to be a daily record, each page a day. She worked her way slowly through the days, pausing from time to time over a name.

'I had a fortnight in Marbella second half of August,' she said. 'You been there?'

Kathy shook her head.

'Nice. Hot though.' She turned back a page and frowned, stroking a name with her finger tip. 'Velma. She had a photo of a daughter . . . about all she did have.'

'Velma?'

'That's what it sounded like, but no one knew her name for sure. Admitted here on the twelfth of August. Gave us a bit of a scare at first. Thought she might be a TB case.' Sister McLeod turned the pages. 'Yes, here. She died during the night of the twenty-eighth of August, while I was away. Pneumonia.'

'And you think she might be the one?'

'I don't know, but I remember she did go on about the girl in the photo. She was in a bad way when she came in. Been living rough. She didn't seem to speak much English and she had no identification.'

'How old was she?'

'Hard to say. Her skin was weather-beaten and leathery and she looked seventy-plus. But the post-mortem reckoned she was still ovulating, or would have been if she hadn't been in such a state. I remember we talked about it the day I came back.'

'Who do you think might have been the nurse who spoke to the cook?'

'Well, could be several . . .' She looked through the book again and read out a few names, some of whom had moved on to other wards or hospitals, and others who were still at WEG. Finally she said, 'Jenny Powell perhaps. She's still here. You could try her.'

'She was on the ward at the time the woman was here?'

'Yes, and she likes mysteries.' She grinned at Kathy. 'Especially tragic ones.'

Nurse Powell wasn't due on until the afternoon shift, but Sister McLeod phoned the nurses' home, and after some delay Jenny Powell came to the phone, exchanged some weary curses with the other nurse and spoke to Kathy. She remembered Velma well, she said, the old, mad lady who had kept the ward awake at night speaking in tongues, none of them English. Her fretting, feverish appeals had been to God rather than the health service, for she invariably clutched a crucifix in one hand and a small framed photograph of a girl in the other. The girl was black-haired, dark-eyed like her, and in her lucid moments she had told anyone who would listen that she was 'daughter, daughter'. In Velma's coat pocket they had found a grubby folded sheet of paper on which someone had printed a message with a marker pen.

'It said something like "have you seen my daughter"? or "help me find my daughter", something like that.'

'I see,' Kathy said. 'And what was the connection with Silvermeadow?'

'That's where they brought her from. She collapsed in the mall there, and they called an ambulance.'

Nurse Powell added that the hospital administration had notified the police and the social services about Velma and her message, in the hope of tracing her identity and family, but as far as she knew nothing had come of it.

There was a quick way to get from geriatrics to administration, apparently, but only regulars were advised to try it. Kathy took the safer route back to reception by way of Emmerdale and then followed The Benny Hill Show out to the offices of the hospital administration. After a couple of false starts she was taken through a vast open-plan office to the work station of the records manager (stakeholder services), a middle-aged woman who was focused on devouring a large cream bun. After wiping her mouth and fingers she shook Kathy's hand and offered her a chair while she searched her computer for 'Velma'. It didn't take long, and when the file came up on the screen it was clear that the computer knew no more about the woman who had died on the twenty-eighth of August than Sister McLeod and Nurse Powell – no name, birth date, nationality or next of kin. It had allocated her a patient number, with a cross-reference to another number with an 'R' prefix.

'R for repository,' the woman explained. 'Her belongings were sent to repository.'

'Are they still there?'

'Should be. We keep unclaimed property for twelve months, then dispose of it. It doesn't look as if it's been claimed, if there's still an R number on file.'

'Can I have a look?'

'You can look, but if you want to remove it you'll probably have to apply to the coroner's office.'

The woman guided Kathy back to the lift lobby and told her how to get to the enquiry counter of the repository in the basement, where she filled in a request form and was presented with a large brown cardboard box with reinforced corners, with the R number printed on its label. Inside were Velma's few pathetic remains. The largest item was her black coat, threadbare and grubby. Holding it up by the shoulders Kathy could see how small she must have been, the shoulders as narrow as a child's. There was a label at the collar, but the maker's name, KORDA, meant nothing to Kathy, and there was no care label or other clue as to its origins.

There was one plastic bag containing articles of ill-matched clothing which looked as if they had come from a charity or second-hand shop, and another smaller one with personal possessions. Inside was the crucifix and framed photograph of the girl, as well as a small plain wedding ring, a purse with a few coins, and a small bag of cough sweets. There was no printed message.

'I'd like to borrow the photograph,' she told the man behind the counter. 'To check with our missing persons files.'

'Yeah, don't see why not. You'll have to sign for it.'

She did so, and managed to find an exit to a staff carpark, from which she made her way out to the street, and eventually back to the visitors' carpark in which she'd left her car.

She drove out to the suburb in which Speedy lived, and this time the hope of a lottery win seemed more likely, even inevitable. If there was a connection between Kerri Vlasich's murder and the robbery, then Speedy, dying so neatly in between the two events, was surely it.

Kathy began with the old couple next door to Speedy's house. They examined the photographs of North and his old associates with greedy interest and a running commentary: 'Ooh, look at this one! He's evil, isn't he? Wouldn't want to meet him on a dark night . . .'

Only they couldn't recall seeing any of them before.

Kathy tried the whole street with no more success, and finally returned to her car, defeated. The only mildly relevant information she'd gathered had been the suggestion from a woman across the street from Speedy that he was sometimes visited by someone in an Audi, or an Opel. Kathy took out her notebook to check which it was, and opened it at the notes of her meeting with Sister McLeod.

As she scanned the pages, the date twelfth of August, when Velma had been admitted, suddenly struck her. She flicked back to earlier notes, but couldn't find what she was looking for, and finally started up the car and returned to Hornchurch Street, where she began searching through the boxes of material that had been brought back from unit 184 at Silvermeadow. Eventually she found her photocopies of Harry Jackson's daybooks, and thumbed through to the entry she was after.

★

When she reached Silvermeadow a watery winter sun was gleaming on the cars which half-filled the carpark. A van with a TV current affairs programme logo was parked at the foot of the service road ramp, and Kathy saw the solid figure of Harry Jackson further along the unloading platform with a knot of technicians, pointing out the stairway and storeroom where the two guards had been found.

She walked over to the security centre and found Sharon on duty at the control window.

'Hi,' she said. 'Can I come in?'

'Course.'

Kathy stepped inside. 'Harry giving guided tours is he?' she said.

'Trying to calm them down. Some hope! They want all the nasty details. You were here last Saturday, weren't you, Kathy? Maybe you should speak to them.'

'No thanks.'

'I'm really glad I wasn't here. It makes me feel sick to think about it, them shooting those two guards like that, in cold blood, like an execution. It could have been me, or any of us.'

'Yes, well, you lot were a bit thin on the ground that day. That's what I wanted to talk to you about. I'm doing a follow-up, rechecking where everyone was on Saturday afternoon.'

'I thought you'd got all that information.'

'Yes, well,' Kathy shrugged, 'just making absolutely sure, you know.'

'Sounds as if you're stuck.'

Kathy smiled and opened her clipboard with the schedule compiled from the statements which had been previously taken from the security staff. 'They showed you photographs, didn't they, Sharon?'

'Yes.'

'Just take another look, to be sure.'

Kathy opened the envelope and laid out the pictures once more. Sharon shook her head firmly.

'All right. So where were you on Saturday?'

'With my fiancé, doing Christmas shopping.'

'Here?'

'No, I have enough of this place in working hours. We went into Brentwood. We were there all afternoon. It was bedlam.'

'Right.' Kathy checked off the entry in the schedule, then looked out of the window and pointed at the group further down the service road. 'And Harry was in central London, at a conference . . .'

Sharon gave a vague smile but didn't say anything.

'Did he have a good time?'

Sharon shrugged and looked away. 'S'pose. Better ask him.'

'Didn't you talk about it?'

'We mostly talked about the robbery.'

'Yes . . .' Kathy looked closely at the other woman, wondering why she was sounding so evasive. 'But . . .'

'But?' Sharon turned and stared blandly at her in an unconvincing demonstration of frankness.

'But you also talked about Harry's conference, right?'

'Oh . . . yes.'

'Well?'

Sharon blushed suddenly and turned away. 'You'd better ask him.'

'I'm asking you, Sharon,' Kathy insisted. 'Come on. What's the problem?'

'What do you mean, problem?'

'I'll tell you what I think: I think you don't like telling fibs to coppers.'

Sharon's blush deepened sharply. 'You'll lose me my job,' she muttered. 'That's what's the problem.' She looked out of the control window towards her boss and the TV crew.

'I can be discreet, you know. What's he done?'

Sharon sighed. 'Oh, it's nothing really, but I don't want to sneak on him. We bumped into him when we were shopping that afternoon, about two.'

'At Brentwood?'

'Yeah. He said he'd got bored with the conference and come back early. But he made me promise not to let on to Bo or anyone else. Wouldn't look good.'

'I see. He was on his own, was he?'

'I think he was looking for someone. That's what it looked like, when I spotted him. He seemed embarrassed to meet us – because of the conference, I suppose.'

'And you didn't mention this before, when you were interviewed?'

'I wasn't asked, was I? Anyway, it's not important, is it?'

'No, no. You're right. I think we should do as he asked and just keep it to ourselves, don't you?'

'Thanks.' Sharon grinned with relief. 'I mean, it's not as if it's the first time.'

'Really?'

'Yeah. He slips off for an hour or two sometimes and gets us to cover for him. Speedy used to reckon he had a secret girlfriend.'

'What, Harry?'

'Well, he's not that old . . .' Sharon blushed again. 'I mean, he's in pretty good nick. Considering.'

They both laughed and Kathy sat down beside her and they went through the list of all the security staff, checking off from the work schedules where they would have been on the Saturday.

When they were finished Kathy glanced out of the window again. Harry Jackson and his visitors had moved further on down the service road.

'Okay, now I'd like to ask *you* to be discreet, Sharon.'

'Oh yes?'

'I still have one or two loose ends from the Kerri Vlasich case that I should have tied up days ago, and I don't want Gavin Lowry and the others knowing I forgot. I don't think it's important, see, but I have to put in a report. Maybe you could help me.'

'Yeah, if I can.'

'Okay, well, there was an entry in your daybooks for last August I needed to check.'

'I'll get it,' Sharon offered, but Kathy took the photocopy of the missing page from her bag and showed it to her.

'This is the one. Were you around on that week, do you remember?'

Sharon studied the entries. 'That's my handwriting and initials. The two cars broken into on the Wednesday. I remember now. It was hot. People were leaving their car windows cracked open.'

'Right. What about the entry on Thursday, the confused woman?'

Sharon frowned, thinking. 'Yes, I remember. We'd had problems with her before. She was mental, I reckon. Nobody could understand what she was saying. She passed out in the mall, and we called an ambulance.'

'How big was she?'

'Oh, tiny. Fierce dark eyes. She had a bad cough, too. Spitting and coughing over everybody. Yuck.'

'Black coat?'

'Ye-es. I think she did.'

'Did she have a sign?'

'A sign?'

'Yes. A message on a piece of paper?'

Sharon shook her head. 'Don't remember that. Mind you, she tried to hide or run whenever anyone in uniform appeared. Oh yes, I remember! She was begging, that was it. Stopping people in the mall and pestering them. Speedy caught her on tape.'

'Did you get a name?'

'No idea, sorry.'

'You say there'd been trouble with her before, but I didn't notice any other daybook entries.'

'Well, sometimes Harry would say not to bother putting trivial things in the book. Why? What's the interest?'

'She had a daughter we were trying to track down. This is her picture.' Kathy took the photograph from her bag.

'Oh, I think I know her . . .' Sharon squinted at the portrait. 'She looked a bit older than this. Hang on a tick.' She got up, brought over a couple of the daybooks and began to turn the pages. 'Somewhere . . .' It took her a few minutes, but eventually she found the entry, almost illegible, in late May.

'That's Carl's writing. He's hopeless.'

'What does it say?' Kathy asked, peering at the scrawl.

'"Cash theft at supermarket, f. employee, police called." Carl and I both went. One of the girls who restocks the shelves was caught taking money from the handbags of other women who work there. This was her.' Sharon nodded at the photograph. 'She was thin as a rake, and refused to say a word. The store insisted on making a formal complaint so they could get rid of her, but in the end it was them who got into trouble.'

'How come?'

'They said the girl was called something ordinary, like Mary Smith or something, but they couldn't provide proof of identity, or age, and when they checked her social security number it was wrong. Social services and the tax people got onto it. Someone said the girl was on the run, or an illegal immigrant.'

Kathy thought, Wiff Smiff and Mary Smith. 'What happened to her?'

'Dunno. We saw her in here a couple of times afterwards, I remember, and kept an eye out for trouble. Then she stopped coming, I suppose.'

'Like Norma Jean,' Kathy said.

'Norma Jean?'

'Oh, she was another trouble-maker in the daybooks, Sharon. Before your time. You've never heard the others talk about her?'

'No, can't say I have. Have you asked Harry?'

'It doesn't matter. It's all history now. I just had to cover any possible similar incidents in my report. You don't know of any, do you? Girls reported missing?'

'You don't think Speedy—'

'No, no. The case is closed. And as I say, I'd be grateful if you didn't mention to anyone that I was in here tying up these loose ends. I should have done it before.'

Kathy left, avoiding Harry Jackson and the TV people.

At Hornchurch Street she found Bren and Gavin Lowry together in the incident room, checking through interview statements. They looked up as she came in, and Bren said, 'Something going on, Kathy? You look pleased with yourself.'

'Not sure,' she replied. 'Have we got Harry Jackson's statement about last Saturday here?'

'Yeah,' Lowry pointed at a pile of paper. 'Silvermeadow staff statements. Why? What's up?'

'Tell you in a moment.' Kathy pulled off her coat and sat down at the table, searching through the papers until she found what she wanted. The two men waited in silence while she read, nodding as she scanned the single page.

'Right,' she said, handing it across to Bren. 'Harry Jackson says that he was at the conference at the Barbican all day Saturday until five p.m., and then caught a train out to Upminster where he'd left his car. He then drove home, arriving there about six-thirty.'

'Well?'

'I have a witness who saw him in Brentwood high street at about two o'clock. They say he looked as if he was waiting for someone he'd arranged to meet.'

Bren said, 'Interesting,' but Lowry looked incredulous, shaking his head. 'No, no,' he said. 'Not Harry. They've mistaken him for someone else. Who is it anyway?'

'Someone who works with him every day, Gavin. Sharon, one of his security staff. And she and her boyfriend talked to Harry in Brentwood, and he was embarrassed and told them to keep it quiet that he was there instead of at the conference.'

Bren was on his feet. 'I'll get Brock.'

269

Kathy and Lowry remained sitting at the table in silence for a while, then Lowry, scowling, shook his head and said softly, 'No. Not Harry.'

Lowry sat with his hands locked together on top of his crisp haircut. Brock took delivery of more coffee and a plate of sandwiches and closed the door again, catching a glimpse of the faces in the outer office, peering over to see what was going on.

'You must know him as well as anyone,' he said, putting the plate on the table between them.

'He was my DI for four years at West Ham when I was getting started. He looked after me. More than that, he was a mate. And I think you're wrong about this,' Lowry added, eyeing the file that lay closed in front of Brock's place. 'There'll be an explanation. Ask him.'

'I shall, but not yet. You'd describe your DI as a mate, would you?'

'I was newly married at the time, and Connie, my wife, got to be friends with Harry's wife, so we got to know each other socially.'

There was something, the hint almost of a sneer, Brock thought, as if Lowry didn't approve of Harry's wife.

'He and I played snooker, though he was out of my league. We just hit it off. Yeah, he was a mate. Still is.'

'Did you remain friends after you moved to Dagenham?' Brock asked, helping himself to a sandwich.

'At first, then they got divorced. You know how it is. We were friends with them both, felt awkward about them splitting up and ended up losing touch with both of them. We met up again with Harry by accident, when he left the force and went to work at Silvermeadow. Connie went out there soon after it opened. Couldn't keep away, could she?'

There it was again. Perhaps it was his own wife he despised, not Harry's, and he had fallen into that little habit, the tiny curl of the lip, the put-down remark, whenever he mentioned her.

'There's worse things than shopping, I suppose,' Brock said absently.

'Depends what she spends!' The response came back too fast. 'Anyway, Harry came up to her in the mall. Said he'd recognised her on the security camera. Since then we've been out together a few times, and we keep in touch through work as well. I've become a sort of informal liaison with Silvermeadow.'

'Have a sandwich.' Brock pushed the plate across, but Lowry shook his head. 'He didn't remarry? What about a girlfriend?'

'No. He's past that.'

Brock smiled. 'We're never past that, Gavin.' He watched Lowry's face relax a little.

'Well, he's never let on to us.'

'Expensive tastes? The horses?'

'Nah, not Harry, chief. He's steady, steady as a rock.'

'Has he been pumping you while we've been working on the Vlasich case?'

Lowry looked uncomfortable. 'No more than you'd expect. It's his patch. Of course he'd want me to keep him informed of what we were doing.'

'Naturally. But nothing you recall that seems significant, now, thinking back?'

Lowry shook his head, then said tightly, 'If he's been up to something, I'd like to be the one to nail him, chief.'

'I don't think that would be a very good idea.'

'Why not?' Lowry demanded.

'Because the most important thing now is finding North. If Harry is mixed up with him in some way, we're not going to get any closer by letting him know we're onto him. I'm actually thinking, Gavin, that we might have to send you on a course somewhere far away. Or you might take Connie away on a surprise holiday until this is over.'

'What?'

'He's an ex-copper, and he knows you well. You're going to bump into him, and he'll see it written all over your face. He'll know, and our best chance of tracking down North will be gone.'

Lowry looked devastated. 'Don't you think he might be suspicious if I suddenly disappear in the middle of the investigation?'

Brock shrugged and took another sandwich. He was interested to see how far Lowry would press this point.

'Look, chief,' Lowry protested. 'I'm the one who knows him! If he knows where North is, I've got the best chance of finding out.'

'And how would you do that, Gavin?'

Lowry thought for a moment. 'Maybe . . . maybe there's some link between North and Harry that I could spot. Someone they both know, or a place. I don't know. I could talk to Bren, go through everything he's gathered on North.'

Brock considered this. 'Maybe. But I don't want you running any risk of meeting Harry. You stay here. Don't go near Silvermeadow, okay?'

Lowry nodded.

'You might think about places he may have mentioned to you in the past. A property somewhere? A caravan maybe, a place he used to rent?'

'I'll try.'

'What about Connie? Could he have mentioned something to her?'

'Possible, I suppose.'

'Speak to her. Get her to think back. Then keep your head down. Warn Connie to tell him you're out if he rings. If you have to speak to him on the phone I want to be beside you with a recorder going.'

After Lowry left, Brock opened the file and pondered. He felt reasonably sure that the help Lowry had given Jackson arose out of nothing more than innocent loyalty to an old friend. But if it was more than that he would certainly alert Jackson now. What would happen then? How steady was Harry's nerve these days?

He scanned the page in front of him until he came to the note about Ilford. Two years before he retired from the force, DI Harry Jackson had been transferred to Ilford. He had been there when North and his gang had robbed the local Midland Bank, knocked out Pauline Lewins's front teeth, and shot Fairbairn the branch manager dead. That was surely why Brock had recognised Jackson on their first meeting, for although Jackson hadn't been directly involved in the hunt for North, there had been considerable contact between Brock and his team and local officers in the days after the robbery.

So what? North had committed armed hold-ups in a dozen different police divisions before he fled the country, and hundreds of officers would have had direct experience of his handiwork. All the same, Brock would have been happier if Lowry had mentioned Jackson being in Ilford, although he may not have known. But surely Jackson would have remembered why Brock recognised him?

The unmarked car had slowed as Harry Jackson's Opel showed its brake lights a hundred yards up ahead and pulled over to the kerb. As they cruised past, the two men had seen Jackson behind the wheel, a mobile phone to his ear. They stopped just short of the next corner and waited, distracted for a moment by the karaoke din coming from the crowd in the Red Lion, audible even through car windows closed tight against the cold wind.

'How long did he talk?' Brock asked.

'Not long, sir. No more than a minute.'

He recognised the ponderous, formal manner of the two men as their defensive reaction to the mortification they must be feeling.

In the mirror the driver had seen Jackson's indicator, and then the Opel moving forward again. He'd let it go well past before he pulled out after it. A second time it had stopped, and again they'd overtaken it. But this time it had made a rapid U-turn and disappeared fast back the way they had come.

'I pulled over,' the driver reported, 'and waited till Jackson's tail lights had rounded the bend in the road, then swung round after him. When we reached the bend, the road ahead was empty. I put my foot down until we were stopped by the next set of lights. Then I saw him in the mirror, sitting on my tail.'

'He'd spotted you?'

The driver gave a stiff nod, as if the gesture hurt. Brock knew that it wasn't necessary for him to labour the point. These two were from TO14, specialists in covert surveillance.

'When the lights changed I drove slowly back the way we'd come, to his flat. He followed on my tail all the way.'

Harry had had a little game with them, Brock thought. Why would he do that?

'Sorry, sir,' the driver said, through clenched teeth. 'I'd swear he changed his pattern after the phone call, as if he'd changed his mind about what he was going to do. It's possible he spotted us then, because the traffic was thin.'

Brock sensed the 'but', unspoken because the man didn't want to sound as if he was making excuses.

'I need an honest assessment,' he said. 'I'm not interested in anything else. You were there, I wasn't.'

The other man spoke up. 'He was tipped off, chief. That's my honest opinion. Whoever phoned him told him he had a tail.'

Brock nodded. There wasn't much point in being coy with Harry Jackson any more.

He seemed in cheerful mood as he was shown into the interview room, his face fresh and pink as if he'd just had a run or a good laugh.

'Evening, Mr Brock,' he said, taking the offered chair. 'Your lads were very silent on the way in. I was trying to tell them they didn't need to pick me up. You should have given me a bell and I'd have come straight over. Is it about my little game with your boys in the Astra? Couldn't resist it.'

'Has he been cautioned?' Brock asked. Bren shook his head.

'Cautioned?' Jackson said, shocked, and Brock began to intone the formal words, ignoring his protest.

'That's well out of order, chief,' Harry said. 'Okay, I had some fun, but it's me you're talking to, Harry Jackson, twenty-one years in the force.'

'Who rang you in the car this evening?' Brock said sharply. 'Who warned you about the tail?'

Harry smiled. 'Don't know what you mean there, chief. I spotted the Astra myself, no bother.'

'Who was on the phone?'

'Some call centre, doing a survey on voters' attitudes. I told them to get stuffed.'

'Where were you on the afternoon of Saturday last, the eighteenth of December?' Brock said abruptly, and watched Harry's face go pale.

'Oh.'

They waited in silence as he looked from one to the other.

'Caught me out, have you, chief?'

Brock said nothing.

Harry bowed his head, groaned softly and said, 'Well, that's it, isn't it? That's me finished.'

'I want a statement,' Brock said. 'Last Saturday afternoon.'

'Yeah, yeah.' Jackson sighed, turned towards the tape machine and began to speak slowly, eyes lowered. 'I left the conference in central London at about twelve-thirty, and caught the tube out to Upminster, where I'd left my car. I drove over to Brentwood and parked in the town centre. I got a sandwich at a pub, then went to Boots, where I stood outside on the pavement and waited.'

'What time was that?' Brock said.

'I got to Boots at five to two. I'd arranged to meet someone there at two. They were late. At about a quarter past, I was seen there by Sharon, who works for me at Silvermeadow, and her male companion, don't know his name. My rendezvous arrived soon after they left, around twenty past two.'

He stopped and seemed disinclined to go on.

'Come on, Harry,' Brock said wearily. 'Get it over with.'

'Yeah ... We walked to my car—'

'We?'

A scowl came over Jackson's face. 'No names, Mr Brock. I won't tell you that.'

Brock looked at him, thinking that he was to be pitied. 'Go on then.'

'We walked to my car, and I drove us home to my place in Dagenham, where we stayed for the rest of the afternoon.'

'Eh?' Brock said, as if he'd misheard. 'Doing what, for God's sake?'

Jackson flushed, glared at Brock, then said. 'What do you think? We went to bed.'

'You what?' Brock said. He tried to get his mind around the idea of Harry Jackson and Upper North in bed together.

'You heard,' Jackson said truculently. 'I took her back to pick up her car at Brentwood at about six, maybe a bit later.'

'Her?'

'Yes, *her*. Jesus, what do you think I'm saying? *Her*, my girlfriend. Who do you think?'

'Whose name you can't reveal for fear of compromising her reputation.' Brock shook his head sadly. He felt genuinely upset that a man with Jackson's experience could offer him such a pathetic cliché. 'Gavin Lowry told me you were too old to have a girlfriend, Harry.' Jackson looked at him with a startled expression. 'I disagreed with him, but maybe I was wrong. If you think anyone's going to swallow that old line you must be well past it.'

At that moment there was a tap at the door and Kathy looked in. 'Sorry to interrupt, sir. There's something I need to check with you.'

Brock got to his feet. 'Don't say a thing until I get back, Harry. I wouldn't want to miss a word of this.'

Outside the room, Kathy said, 'We've traced the number that rang Jackson's mobile at twenty to eight this evening, Brock. This is the number, and the name and address of the subscriber.' She gave him a slip of paper.

He read it and felt that chill that comes when some unavoidable truth finally has to be confronted. It was Gavin Lowry's name and address.

'You're not surprised?' she asked.

'It was one of the possibilities,' he said, though he had never really believed it. He had given Lowry the opportunity to betray them, confident that he would not. He had been wrong.

'I got them to double-check. There's no mistake.'

'The bloody fool.'

'Yes.'

He felt Kathy's silence as he came to a decision. 'Get him in here.'

He could see Lowry was puzzled that they should meet in an interview room, and that Kathy should be loading the recorder with a fresh tape. He looked tired and there was a smell of whisky on his breath.

'I was just about to hit the sack, chief,' he said, yawning broadly. 'Something up?'

'Yes,' Brock said grimly, and began to recite the caution while Lowry stared first at him, then at Kathy, stunned.

'Where were you at twenty to eight this evening, Gavin?'

'What?' He blinked stupidly like a man trying to force himself awake from a dream.

'Seven-forty. Think.'

'Sir, I don't understand—'

'Just answer.'

Lowry gaped for a moment, then said, 'At home.'

'You're quite sure about that?'

'Yes. Why?'

'Did you make a phone call at that time?'

'No . . . no I didn't. What is this, chief?'

'I'm going to repeat that question just once. Think before you answer. Did you make a phone call this evening at seven-forty?'

Lowry flushed. 'I just said no.'

'Someone rang Harry Jackson on his mobile at that time and tipped him off that he was being tailed. Why did you do that, Gavin?'

'Me! Don't be daft, chief! I wouldn't have done that, would I? Did he say I did?'

Brock handed Lowry the sheet of paper Kathy had given him.

'What's this?'

'Mercury's record of the call. That is your home number isn't it?'

Lowry stared at it, eyes wide, then shook his head. 'I don't know what this is, Brock. Have I been set up?' He looked in turn at Brock and Kathy. 'Look, look, look . . . when I got home this evening, Connie had the meal ready. We ate, then I talked to her about Harry, just like we agreed. We discussed it. She was upset and couldn't believe he was bent and I had to go over it several times. Around seven-thirty she took the boys up to bed. She'd planned to go out to the pictures with a girlfriend from work, but she said she didn't feel like it any more, after what I'd told her about Harry, so she had a bath instead.'

'After she phoned her friend?' Kathy said quietly.

'Her friend?'

'To tell her that she wasn't going to the pictures.'

'Oh, yeah . . .' Lowry's mouth hung open, and he looked as if someone had smacked him on the head quite hard. 'You're joking. She wouldn't have . . .' Brock recognised the note of contempt again. 'The stupid bitch. I told her. I explained! The stupid, stupid bitch!'

'You're suggesting what, exactly?'

He shook his head in exasperation. 'She was upset that you suspected Harry. She was sorry for him. Connie must have rung him up and tipped him off.'

Jackson looked up as Brock and Kathy came back into the room. He was looking wearier now, tie loosened, shirtsleeves rolled up in the over-heated room.

Brock placed the record of the Mercury call in front of him. 'The number that rang you at seven-forty this evening.'

'Oh Christ.' Jackson lowered his head abruptly, shoulders sagged. 'He knows, does he, Gavin?'

'Know what? Come on, Harry. I need it for the record. All of it.'

Jackson closed his eyes and took a deep breath before replying as if delivering a formal report. 'The woman who spent the afternoon of last Saturday with me was Connie Lowry, DS Lowry's wife. We've been seeing each other now for over two years.'

'You're lovers?'

'Yeah.'

All the fight seemed to have gone out of Harry. He slumped forward on his elbows. Brock thought, Gavin knows she made the call, but the idea that the two of them – his stupid wife and his friend who was past it – might be having an affair had never entered his head.

'Tell the truth, it feels good to say it out loud. Get it out in the open. Two years of bliss and quiet desperation . . . Christ, she and Gavin only went out for six months before they got married, and we've been lurking in the bleedin' shadows for four times as long.' He looked at Brock, wanting to explain. 'It's a rotten thing to do to a mate, but we never planned for it to happen. Gavin took her for granted, usual thing, just assumed he could live his life the way he

277

wanted and she'd cope. He didn't even notice she was miserable, needed help. She started coming to the mall, regular, and we'd have a coffee, and talk. After a while, well . . . I was the one who was there for her.'

Brock looked down at his blank note pad, trying to suppress a momentary vivid picture of Suzanne. He had no doubt at all that Harry was telling the truth.

'I didn't think it could happen at my time of life, Mr Brock, but it did. It crept up on me. One day I was pouring out a cup of tea, and I realised that I was thinking about her all the bleedin' time. Couldn't help myself. Like some pathetic teenager. But that doesn't stop you feeling guilty. Yeah, I'm glad it's out in the open now.'

'What did you mean earlier, when you said that now you were finished?'

'My job, at Silvermeadow. I'm already under a cloud with everything that's been happening, and this'll be the final straw, I reckon. They'll have my guts, mine and Bo Seager's.'

'Why her?'

'Politics, chief. Nathan Tindall wants her job, and now's the time for him to make his move.'

Connie Lowry guessed why they'd come as soon as she saw them standing there on her doorstep. Brock could see it written all over her face. She was in her dressing gown, for it was after midnight, but she didn't look as if she'd been asleep.

'Yes?' she said cautiously.

He introduced himself and Kathy, and she led them into the front living room of a neat, well-cared-for home, made comfortably untidy by the wooden train set the little boys had been playing with earlier, while she and Gavin had been discussing Harry Jackson.

'I wondered . . . when you called Gavin in,' she said. 'You've come about Harry, haven't you?'

Brock nodded, and she did the same, a mutual understanding.

'You know then, about him and me.'

'He told us you've had a relationship for a couple of years.'

She coloured slightly. 'Yes . . . well, it's a relief, really, to have it out in the open at last.' She didn't sound entirely convinced about that. 'Does Gavin know?'

'Yes.'

'Good. I don't want to see him. Will you tell him that? Tell him I don't want him to come back here tonight.'

'Why don't you tell him yourself, Connie?' Brock said quietly. 'He's at Hornchurch Street station. Why not give him a ring?'

'No. I don't want to talk to him. I couldn't. Not yet.'

Brock shrugged. 'Can you tell us where you were last Saturday afternoon, Connie?'

'With Harry. We met outside Boots in Brentwood shortly after two, and went back to his house. We try to see each other at least twice a week.'

'What about your boys?'

She blushed, but her voice remained firm. 'A friend of mine looks after them. She knows about Harry and me.'

'How long did you stay with him?'

She thought. 'Till after six. We listened to the end of the six o'clock news on the car radio when Harry drove me back to Brentwood. Gavin wasn't due home till nine that night.' She looked at them defiantly. 'You have to live like that, when it's a secret. But not any more.'

On the road back, Brock said, 'Oh well, another false trail.'

'Yes,' Kathy said. 'Sorry.'

'Not at all. It looked very promising.'

'Poor Gavin. He must think I'm bringing down some kind of curse on him. First his car and now his marriage.'

'Yes, you do seem to be his nemesis, don't you? Well, I'm having a day off tomorrow. If they discover anything interesting on the security tapes they can phone me. But not during matinée hours.'

'You're going to see a show?'

'Yes, *Peter Pan*.'

'Really? Appropriate.'

'How do you mean?'

'Well, that's what Harry's trying to be, isn't it?'

Brock wasn't too impressed by that observation, and decided to change the subject. 'I heard a rumour that you and Leon are going up north for a couple of days. Is that right?'

He noticed Kathy's grip tighten abruptly on the steering wheel, and followed her eyes flicking down to the car clock. He felt the car give a little swerve on the road.

'You all right?'

'Oh . . . yes,' she said. 'I just forgot something. Doesn't matter. What were we talking about?'

'About you going up north.'

'No, I don't think so. Not this week anyway.'

Brock looked over, curious, but she said no more, her face giving away nothing of what was going on inside her head.

When she got home to the deserted flat she still couldn't really believe that it could have happened. He hadn't phoned. Presumably he had assumed she'd deliberately not come. Well, of course he would. What else could he think? That she'd *forgotten*? The idea was absurd. DS Kathy Kolla didn't forget appointments.

She looked at the time yet again. The train would have reached Liverpool long ago. Reluctantly she tried his mobile number, but got the message that it was switched off. Then she got the number of the Adelphi Hotel and rang that. She asked reception if they had a room in the name of Desai and the woman said yes. She imagined him in the room, tired and angry with her, and her courage, or perhaps it was her stamina, failed. She rang off before she could be connected, and turned to a small pile of mail. Among the junk was a Christmas card from her aunt and uncle in Sheffield, and a separate small package containing a Christmas present from them which she didn't open. She winced, realising that that was something else she'd forgotten. There was also her credit card statement, the size of which gave her a small shock.

On the other side of London, as far to the south of Eros as Kathy was to the north, Brock was working his way through his house, tidying stuff away and putting potentially dangerous things — the toasting fork, the carving knife, the can of rat poison — and fragile things — the sole artwork (a Schwitters tram ticket collage), the laptop, the wine glasses — out of reach of small children, and wondering as he did it if all this was really necessary. He discovered, when he finally sank below the surface of a hot bath, that he really was looking forward to being invaded.

17

Brock woke the next day with somewhat less confidence, and grew more apprehensive as the time of his guests' arrival drew closer. It wasn't a bad morning, with a bit of sun breaking through the clouds, but still, day showed Warren Lane in a colder and more realistic light than night, and there was no avoiding the fact that this was not Disneyland.

The party arrived on the dot of nine, as promised. It was one of the things he liked about Suzanne, her determination to stave off slack timekeeping and other symptoms of chaos. And as he helped them in, each carrying a piece of luggage, he recognised immediately that this was exactly what the children needed and responded to. They were a team, each secure in playing their part.

And he realised too that he needn't have worried about the place not being interesting enough for them, as they followed him, wide-eyed and observant, exchanging whispered comments, up through the house, from the winding stairs and landings lined with books to the living room with its hissing gas fire and bay window projecting out over the lane and the long bench with computers, out to the kitchen with its eccentric collection of gadgets and air heavy with the smell of coffee, then upwards again to their room under the roof. He and Suzanne left them there, marvelling at the height of the beds off the floor, which grandly raised them up and gave them views out of the dormer window, over the little courtyard at the back of the house and beyond the rooftops towards the very distant prospect of Dulwich Park.

They had had an adventurous journey, Suzanne explained over the cup of coffee which Brock had ready for her. Leaving well before dawn, they had, against her better judgement, breakfasted on the road on generous helpings of sausage and eggs. Ten minutes later they had watched the sun rise in a golden blaze through the eastern mist while Miranda brought up her breakfast on the grassy verge. She had done it uncomplainingly, and Suzanne hadn't had the heart to remind the little figure, grey and heaving, that she had warned her that precisely this would happen if she had a greasy meal while travelling in the car. After that they did the journey in hops, stopping regularly to avoid further incident.

As she explained all this, Brock was further reassured. With her competence and the kids' resilience, everything would be fine.

'I feel like a truant,' Suzanne said. 'The shop's so busy, and I've just walked out and left them to it, and it feels great.'

'Me too.' He smiled.

'Your case? You're sure we're not in the way? The children have been following all the gruesome details on TV. I'm afraid you're going to get a request for a guided tour of the murder sites.'

Brock laughed. 'They'll probably enjoy Silvermeadow. There's a volcano, you know. Erupts on the hour.'

'Yes, I'd heard.'

'We both need a break,' Brock said. 'You're looking tired.'

'Is that a polite way of saying haggard?'

'Never.'

He went to her and gave her a kiss, interrupted immediately by the sound of children's footsteps on the stairs. They assembled side by side in the doorway and the boy asked solemnly, 'We wondered if we could visit your courtyard, Uncle David.'

'Of course,' Brock said, and led the way.

There wasn't much to see: several large terracotta pots supporting the scruffy remnants of unidentifiable plants, and a wooden bench placed in the corner most likely to catch a little sun. Next to this bench stood the most impressive object in the yard, to which the children were drawn.

'What do you think that is?' Brock asked.

'A bush,' Miranda said immediately.

'No,' Brock said. 'It's a tree.'

'A baby tree?' she said.

'A grown-up one. It's about the same age as me.'

She frowned dubiously, peering more closely at the twisted roots writhing out of the moss in the shallow blue-glazed bowl, the gnarled branches, the layered foliage of pine needles.

'Well, it looks old, but it can't be, cos it's only little,' she said.

'About ninety centimetres tall,' Stewart suggested.

'It's like it's been shrunk,' Miranda said.

'Like looking through the wrong end of a telescope,' her brother offered. 'Is it a dwarf?'

'That's right,' Brock said. 'Would you like to know how I did it?'

'*You* did it?' Miranda said, eyes huge. 'You made a dwarf?'

He took them into the kitchen, where he hunted through the drawers until he found his roll of bonsai tools, the Japanese branch cutters and root shears and scissors and potting stick and binding wire, and told them how he was able to shrink everything about the tree to scale, except for the needles and cones, which tried to grow to normal size.

'Isn't that cruel?' Miranda asked grimacing. 'Cutting their roots? Isn't that like cutting their toes off?'

'It doesn't hurt,' said Stewart dismissively. 'Trees can't feel things. They don't have nervous systems.'

'How do you know it doesn't hurt?' she protested. 'Just because it can't scream!'

Brock saw the tear begin to swell into her eye and said gently, 'That worried me at first, Miranda. But there is a way you can tell that the tree doesn't mind.'

'How?' She sniffed.

'Because it grows perfectly. It's as healthy as an ordinary tree, and will live just as long, if it's looked after. Unhappy trees don't do that.'

'Don't they?' She looked as if she wanted to believe him, but wasn't quite convinced.

Kathy phoned the Adelphi again first thing and made her abject apologies to Leon. She wasn't sure if he really believed her when she said she'd totally forgotten about the train until it was too late, because he said little.

'I could get a train up there this morning,' she suggested.

'Yes.' He didn't sound enthusiastic.

'Well, do you want me to?'

'What'll you do if you don't come up?'

'Oh, work. I've got some things to follow up.'

'I think you'd better do that, Kathy. You've obviously got a lot on your mind.'

They hung on in silence for a moment, then she said, 'I'll meet you at Euston tomorrow evening, then. What time does the train get in?'

He told her and they rang off. For a moment Kathy was inclined to get on a train anyway and surprise him, but then she got cold feet and decided against it.

She drove to the Herbert Morrison estate, parking on the high street and walking to Crocus Court. Naomi's grandmother answered the door and invited her in, though Naomi, whom she wanted, wasn't at home.

'She's working at Silvermeadow this morning, Sergeant. Is there anything we can do?'

There seemed little point, but Kathy showed them the photographs of North and the others anyway. They recognised none of them.

'Never mind,' Kathy said. 'I suppose Lisa is at work too, is she?'

'Oh no. Lisa gave up her job at the mall. She won't go back there now.'

'Not as tough as our Naomi,' Mr Tait put in with satisfaction.

'Naomi isn't insensitive,' his wife said quickly. 'I wouldn't want you to think that. But she's more mature than Lisa, better able to face up to reality. Well, she's had to be, poor little soul. Whereas Lisa is a very sensitive girl. She's really taken things to heart. Her mum's quite concerned about her, I think.'

'Well, I might call round there and check on her,' Kathy said. 'Thanks for your help.'

She set off again along the deck, stepping aside for two women with toddlers in pushchairs returning from the shops, and felt suddenly despondent. She'd told Leon that she had a life. What a joke. Everyone else was getting on with theirs, while she wandered round this bleak and sodden housing estate like a stubborn saleswoman peddling something that nobody wanted and in which she herself no longer believed. Yes, that was true, she thought, accusing herself coldly. She wasn't doing this because she really believed that Kerri's death was connected to North's crime; she was doing it because she wanted to make a point to Bren and Leon.

Lisa seemed even more timorous and nervous than the last time. Her mother didn't introduce Kathy to the man who shuffled away to a bedroom as she came in, clearly not interested in taking part in her conversation with the girl.

'Sorry to bother you again, Lisa,' Kathy said, noting the redness round the eyes against the pale complexion. 'How've you been?'

The girl whispered, 'Okay.'

'Good. Look, I just wanted to show you a few pictures. See if you can remember seeing any of these people.' She opened the envelope and took out the photographs once again. Definitely the last time, she told herself.

'Why?' Lisa said doubtfully, seeing the men's faces. 'Who are they?'

'They're just people we want to contact. You may have come across them. Take your time.'

Lisa went through the sheaf slowly, listlessly. 'No,' she said when she reached the last one. 'I don't know any of these men.'

'Oh well, can't be helped.' Kathy shrugged and began to gather them up again.

'I know her though,' Lisa said tentatively, pointing to one of the enlargements from the security cameras in the mall. It showed North as he had been caught on film ten days before, holding the hand of a child.

'You know the little girl?'

'Yeah, she lives here, on the estate.'

'Are you sure?' Kathy said doubtfully. 'The picture isn't all that clear.'

'Well it looks like her. Kerri . . .' She hesitated, biting her lip. 'Kerri used to baby-sit her.'

'Kerri knew her? Have you any idea what her name is?'

'Mandy, I think. Yes, Mandy. I don't know her other name.'

'Where did you see her?'

'I went with Kerri one evening. We stayed there with Mandy till her mum came back from the movies.'

'Did you meet the girl's mother? What was she like?'

'I don't remember really. Like you, I think. Yes, fair hair, like Mandy.'

'About my age?'

'Maybe.'

'Was that the only time you saw the girl?'

'I've seen her around, with her mum. I do remember what she looked like.'

Kathy looked hard at her, becoming more convinced, aware of her heart thumping. 'That's good, Lisa. Very good. Did you ever see her with a man?'

'Don't think so.'

'And you say she lives on the estate?'

Lisa nodded. She was sounding reluctant now, and Kathy realised that she was leaning forward in her eagerness to hear the answers, making the girl anxious. She forced herself to sit back and appear relaxed.

'Well, that's interesting. Don't suppose you remember where exactly?'

'In one of the other courts. Tulip, I think.'

'You still eating chocolate bars?'

The girl nodded.

'How about if we went down to the corner shop and I bought you some as a reward for helping me?'

The girl glanced towards the kitchen where her mother was doing something, the radio on. 'Okay.'

'And on the way you could show me where Mandy lives, eh?'

From her car, Kathy called Brock's home number. When he answered he sounded out of breath.

'Kathy? What's up?' She could hear children's laughter in the background.

'Sorry to intrude, Brock.'

'We're just on our way out. What is it?'

'I think . . . It's possible that I've found the little girl North took with him to Silvermeadow two weeks ago.'

'What!'

'I showed Lisa some pictures. She identified the girl as someone that Kerri used to baby-sit. Someone who lives on the Herbert Morrison estate.'

'*What!*' This time Brock's voice was a bellow. 'Kathy . . .' He recovered himself. 'You're making a habit of this, aren't you? Dropping bombshells.'

'I hope this one's more productive. I wouldn't have bothered you until I'd checked this out, but then I thought, if there's any chance that North is with them—'

'Yes! Quite right. Where are you now?'

'On the high street, parked outside the estate.'

'I'll meet you at the incident room in Hornchurch Street as soon as I can get there.'

As she made her way there Kathy reflected that if North was in Tulip Court then they had been coming and going within yards of him all this time. And, whether he had murdered her himself or not, he must surely be the reason that Kerri Vlasich had died.

It took several hours to secure Tulip Court without the residents realising what was happening. During this time the tenant of the flat was identified from council housing department records as Sophie Bryant, a single woman living with one child, a five-year-old girl. Once Brock was satisfied that the area was secure, a policeman in a postman's uniform went up to the flat with a registered parcel marked for a Mr Brown at that address, and rang the bell. After getting no reply he rang the adjoining flats, and learned that nothing had been seen of the Bryants for several days. Their visitor, a middle-aged man known as Keith, hadn't been noticed for a week.

Later that evening Brock, Kathy and two detectives entered the flat using keys supplied by the housing department on production of a search warrant. It was clear that Mrs Bryant and her daughter had taken most of their clothes and personal belongings with them. The whole apartment had been carefully wiped clean of fingerprints.

When he got home to Warren Lane that night, Brock found that Suzanne had a cooked dinner ready for him. The smell of it, beef bourguignon, percolated deliciously through the house and lifted his spirits as soon as he stepped through the front door. He opened a bottle of burgundy and they ate a companionable meal, telling each other about their day. The pantomime had been a great success, and further expeditions had been planned for the following day.

'I'm really sorry I missed it, Suzanne,' he said.

'Oh, it doesn't matter.' She patted his hand.

'Yes it does,' he said, and meant it. The chance wouldn't come again. He took hold of her fingers and gave them a squeeze. 'I was really looking forward to it, the atmosphere, the children's faces. Was Captain Hook good?'

'Terrifying. And the crocodile. The kids were absolutely captivated. Do you know, it was the first time they'd seen live theatre? I'm just worried I might have got them stage-struck and blighted their little lives for ever.'

'Would that be so bad? Miranda's got stage presence, I reckon. Tragedy, though, not pantomime. Lady Macbeth rather than Cinderella.'

'She can be rather intense, can't she? Coming back on the train she asked if you were very lonely, living on your own.'

'What did you say?'

'I said she should ask you, if she could catch you in.'

Brock laughed. 'Tomorrow, I promise. Where are we going?'

'The zoo, but don't make promises, David. Sergeant Kolla may ferret out another lead. Now she *does* sound intense.'

'Determined, certainly. But I thought she was becoming a bit more relaxed recently.'

'Does she have a man?'

'Not sure.'

'Don't you know? Don't you discuss such things with your colleagues?'

'No. And I'm not sure in the sense that I thought I'd detected some mutual interest between her and someone, but now I don't know.'

'Another copper?'

'Yes.'

'Is that a good thing?'

'Probably, yes. Why not?'

'I just thought life might get a bit in-bred, you know. Anyway, how can I say? I've never even met Sergeant Kolla.'

'Do you want to?'

'Yes, I think I do. Then I can stop being jealous of her.'

'Eh?' Brock lowered his fork to his plate in surprise.

'Yes, of course. You obviously have a lot of, well, respect for each other.'

'I should think so.'

'Don't get huffy, David. Tell you what, why don't you invite her and this possible mutual admirer over for a meal, and I'll tell you whether they're made for each other or not. Make it tomorrow evening. I'll cook something nice.'

'Are you sure?' Brock looked doubtful.

'Why not? Unless you're trying to keep me a secret?'

'No, no . . .' He frowned at his plate. 'Why would I do that?' But it was true, he realised. He didn't want . . . what? To have to define their relationship to people who had nothing to do with it? Was that it? Or to have to explain when, if, it came to nothing.

Suzanne burst out laughing. 'Oh, David. I hope you lie better than that to your villains.'

He grinned back. 'They're not usually as perceptive as you.'

They held each other's eyes, smiling, then leant towards one another across the corner of the table and shared a gentle kiss.

'Let's go to bed,' Suzanne suggested, and they got to their feet and carried dishes through to the kitchen. Brock watched her at the sink, rinsing plates, and was filled with a sense of gratitude. He took hold of her again, and again they kissed, longer and deeper.

They were disturbed by a small shuffling sound at the door, and looked over to see Miranda there, face puffy with sleep, staring fixedly at them.

'Are you all right, darling?' Suzanne said, going to her.

'I had a bad dream,' the little girl muttered, and rubbed at her eyes. 'I saw a monster.'

'Don't worry, my darling.' Suzanne gathered her up in her arms. 'There are no monsters here. Uncle David would never allow it.'

Miranda stared across at Brock with the same uncertain look he'd seen on her face before.

Suzanne stroked her hair and said, 'Probably it was the crocodile in the pantomime that gave you the dreams, darling.'

The little girl pressed her face against Suzanne's cheek and whispered something.

'What, darling?'

'The monster turns people into dwarfs, and eats them for his dinner,' Miranda whispered, and again stared at Brock, then at the dinner plates on the kitchen table.

18

Kathy was at Euston in plenty of time the following evening, Thursday the twenty-third of December. The train was late and her feet were frozen by the time it arrived. She felt her heart give a lurch when she saw him, and she thought, That's how you know, isn't it?

He walked steadily towards her through the milling people, the slamming doors and baggage trolleys, his eyes on her, the barest smile, and they embraced and kissed each other on the cheek.

'You're cold,' he said.

'Freezing. How was your trip?'

'Pretty good.'

'Tell me all about it in the car.' She turned towards the exit.

'Kathy, wait. I'm not going back to the flat.'

'What?' She thought she'd misheard him in the noise of the station.

'I'm getting a taxi to my parents' house. I've arranged to spend Christmas with them.'

The roar of people and banging doors seemed to fade to a buzz in Kathy's head. She stared at him.

'I'm sorry. I just decided this afternoon.'

'What then?' she asked.

'Then?'

'After Christmas.'

'Oh. Well, we'll see, I suppose.'

He took a step towards her, and brushed his mouth against her cheek again. 'Sorry. Best this way.'

She stood immobilised as he walked past her and away.

Later, when she got into her car, she remembered Brock's unprecedented invitation to them both to dinner that evening, and swore under her breath. She didn't want to call it off. She wanted to meet the mysterious Suzanne, and her children. *His* children?

As some kind of compensation, she had bought not one but two ridiculously expensive bottles of wine. She stood clutching them on Brock's doorstep, the wind whistling round her upturned coat collar, turning her nose red, and listened to the heavy footsteps coming down the stairs inside.

'Kathy! Hello. Come in out of the cold.' Brock looked over her shoulder. 'Did you come separately?'

'Leon's not coming, Brock. Sorry.'

'Oh dear. Everything all right?'

'Not really, no. Bit of a misunderstanding.'

'You sound glum,' he said, closing the front door behind her and taking the bottles so that she could take off her coat. He looked concerned, but then a thought seemed to strike him and his expression changed to a little smile.

Kathy regarded this with surprise and some irritation. She didn't enjoy the idea of him finding her and Leon a joke.

'These are very good,' he said, examining the labels on the bottles, and the little smile broke out again.

Kathy wasn't in the mood for private jokes she didn't understand, especially if, as seemed likely, they were at her expense. 'What's funny?'

'Oh . . . just that I've been trying to figure out how to tell you and Leon that I'm on my own too.'

'You are?'

'Yes. Suzanne and the children have gone, I'm afraid. Sorry. As you say, a bit of a misunderstanding.'

'Oh dear . . .'

Kathy didn't know what to say. Neither of them did. They stood there in the small hallway looking uncomfortable. The more she thought about it, the more awkward it became. They saw each other continually at work but rarely outside, and here they were forced into a social intimacy that probably neither of them welcomed, because of partners who had now abandoned them.

'They weren't ill, were they?' she asked, for the sake of something to say.

'No, nothing like that. Leon?'

'No, no. Actually I never even had the chance to tell him you'd invited him. It's not his fault. I'm sure he would, er, want me to apologise . . . for him.'

'Fine, fine.'

She was beginning to understand his smile. What else could you do? She grinned back.

He led the way up the stairs and into the kitchen where he uncorked and poured the wine. She couldn't see any signs of food preparation.

'Absent friends,' Brock said. 'Mmm, this is good. Bad luck on them. Here, let me show you something.'

He picked up the bottle and led her up the next half flight to the living room. It was exactly as Kathy remembered it, except that in the centre of the room, on the rug in front of the hissing gas fire and surrounded by the sofa and armchairs, on the very spot where she had once stabbed a man to death, was a small pile of garden rubbish. She shuddered and turned away.

'Ah,' she heard him say. She realised he must have noticed her reaction. 'The spot, yes. I'd almost forgotten. You haven't been back since, have you? Are you all right? Sit down.'

She wasn't all right, she discovered. She could feel the blood draining from her head, and sat down firmly on one of the armchairs, willing herself not to pass out in front of him. She was startled by the force of her reaction to seeing the place again.

She forced herself to speak, the blood buzzing in her ears. 'Don't you mind? I really thought you'd have sold this house after it happened.' She was glad now that the others weren't here. She wouldn't have wanted to have to explain.

'No need. The blood didn't stain the polished floorboards. I only had to buy a new rug.'

He was being deliberately prosaic because he had seen now that she was having trouble, and this was his way of helping her. She grimaced in acknowledgement. She had killed the man, but in self-defence, when she disturbed him after he'd half-killed Brock. He'd had a blade – she pictured it now, glittering in his hand – and she'd been unarmed. The only weapon available had been the long fork with which Brock toasted bread and crumpets on the gas fire, and with which she had finally, unavoidably, stabbed the man in the throat.

Her eyes turned to the mantelpiece above the fire, and it was hanging there.

'Christ, Brock,' she whispered. 'You've still got the bloody toasting fork.'

She took a gulp of her wine, the glass trembling wildly in her hand. 'You didn't tell the children, did you?'

'No. Are you sure you're all right, Kathy? Maybe a brandy would be better?'

She shook her head, trying to find words of conversation. She wanted him to talk, about anything else. 'So, what's with the compost heap?'

'Ah yes, I've been sitting here for much of the day contemplating that' – he waved a hand at the debris – 'trying to learn the appropriate lessons.'

Kathy noticed a half-empty bottle of whisky and an empty glass on a side table, and wondered just how much help he'd had in his contemplation.

'What is it?'

'It is, or was, my prize bonsai. *Juniperus chinensis*, Chinese juniper. It was started from advanced stock on VJ Day, nineteen forty-five, by my father. About the only thing of his that I still possessed, that and the bonsai tools. He was an enthusiast, a great admirer of Japanese culture.'

'So what happened to it?'

'Two children by the name of Stewart and Miranda. They thought I was getting a bit too pally with their grandmother—'

'Suzanne is their grandmother?'

'Yes, of course. You didn't think they were ours, did you? Anyway, they decided to terminate their visit by doing something so unspeakable that I'd be forced to kick them all out. Quite smart really, for eight and five years old respectively.'

'And did you? Kick them out?'

'No, of course not. But the plan worked anyway. Suzanne was so mortified that she insisted on taking them away. I told her not to be so daft, but she wouldn't stay. I think it was the cold-blooded way they did it that bothered her most. I'd told them about the tree, and they knew it meant something to me. They got up very early this morning and went out to the yard, uprooted it, brought it in here and systematically chopped it up with the bonsai tools. Quite an effort. They owned up to it straight away. Wanted me to see how incorrigible they would be.'

He reached over with the bottle and refilled Kathy's glass.

293

'I wish they hadn't chosen that spot to do it,' she said. 'But why were they so upset at the idea of you and their gran?'

'Their father ran away with some woman a couple of years ago, and then their mother went off the rails a bit. You know, feelings of rejection, depression, guilt . . .'

'Yes . . .' Kathy sipped her wine.

'Then some rich bloke came along. Offered her a great time on some Greek island, but kids not welcome. So she got her mum to take them, just for a week or two. That was a year ago.'

'Oh.'

'Yes. So men are very bad news. They break up the family. Destroy their security. It had happened twice, and they weren't going to let it happen again. They were going to hang on to their gran at all costs. Can't really blame them, can you? Poor Suzanne. She tries so hard to do the right thing.'

'You're not going to give up, are you?' Kathy said, surprising herself with the force of her question.

'Give up? No. But I'd better let things calm down. Be patient.'

'Maybe you can be too patient . . .' she said, then stopped herself. 'Anyway, that's sad. And you've been sitting here working this out.'

'Oh, it didn't take long to work it out. No, mostly I've been sitting here wondering what else it can tell me.'

'What else?'

'Well, their story is Naomi's story, isn't it? Parents don't cope, grandparents have to take over. It's not uncommon. There's a lot of it about these days.'

Kathy said nothing. In a way it was her story too.

'But it brought it home to me what it does to the kids. They took quite a risk, after all. They could have alienated their grandmother and made her side with me. But they had to trust that they weren't too late. They were prepared to do almost anything to hang onto her, what was left of their family.'

'And Naomi?'

'Yes, Naomi . . . A very determined young woman, wouldn't you say?'

'Tough, her grandparents called her.'

'Tougher than them, certainly. They're quite frail, aren't they? While Naomi goes out to work to buy them lottery tickets, to keep alive their impossible dream of getting out of that estate and living in a cottage by the sea.'

'I'm not sure . . .' Kathy said tentatively. The wine and the shock on an empty stomach were making her feel dizzy, and she was becoming increasingly uncertain that she was following Brock's train of logic, or even that there was one.

'Where it takes us? Well, it took me somewhere I should have gone long ago. Do you remember the picture of Naomi's elder sister on the wall of the Taits' sitting room?'

'Er . . . with the two dogs?'

'Yes, that's it. I got to wondering about the dogs.'

'The dogs?' Kathy stared at him, quite lost now.

'Mmm. Goodness, we've nearly finished this bottle already, and I haven't got a thing for you to eat. I was going to take you and Leon out to dinner somewhere. What do you think?'

'I'm not sure I could get up from this chair and go out into that cold night again,' Kathy said.

'Pizza?'

'That sounds good.'

'Excellent.'

Brock got to his feet and went over to the phone. The pizza delivery number was on one of a number of cards pinned above it. It looked well thumbed, Kathy noticed.

'So . . .' Brock settled himself again in front of the fire. 'The sister, Kimberley, I looked up her record.' He waved a hand at the computer.

'Drugs, wasn't it?'

'Yes, possession and supply. Also theft, from her employer, a veterinary practice.'

'A vet?' Kathy looked up sharply.

'Hence the dogs, presumably. Perhaps the picture was taken at her work.'

'Not the ketamine?'

'Exactly. As well as cash, her employers accused her of stealing certain animal drugs: Stenbolol, an anabolic steroid, as well as a consignment of Ketapet which was never traced. She was also found to have supplied amphetamines and Ecstasy to two other employees.'

'You think Naomi took over her sister's drugs and sold them at Silvermeadow?'

'I'm getting the batch numbers checked. If it is the same stuff, it's just possible that Kimberley herself supplied Speedy before she was caught, but Naomi seems more likely. We know that she knew all about ketamine, and she knew Wiff.'

'Yes.' Kathy remembered how shocked both Naomi and Lisa had been when she'd told them the name of the drug they had found in Wiff's den. 'She told me that Wiff was selling ketamine for someone else.'

'Maybe he was *buying* it for someone else, from her.'

'Naomi was supplying to Wiff and Speedy? And Kerri too?'

Brock stared at his glass. 'That was the other reason I was feeling glum when you arrived, Kathy.'

They went over it again and again as they worked through the pizza and the second bottle, but got no further than the conviction that Naomi knew more than she'd let on. Finally Brock wiped his mouth and said, 'I was sceptical at first, Kathy, but now I'm prepared to believe that you may be right, that everything is connected to everything else. That place . . . Bo Seager described it as a dream that had turned sick, and it is a bit like that. Like one of those buildings that gets legionnaires' disease in its air-conditioning, or golden staph in its plumbing. Only this isn't a virus. Once upon a time they'd have probably called in an exorcist to purge it. Now they give it to us.'

'Mmm.' Kathy felt her eyelids drooping. 'Sorry I didn't get to meet Suzanne.'

'Another time . . . hopefully.'

'At least you must have plenty of spare beds here now.' She remembered crisp white sheets from an earlier visit.

'Absolutely. And I can manage to supply breakfast. But I make toast in an electric toaster these days.'

'Thank goodness for that.'

19

'It's about the photographs, is it?' Mrs Tait asked. 'You wanted to show them to Naomi?'

'That and one or two other things, Mrs Tait. You remember Detective Chief Inspector Brock, don't you?'

'Course. Come in and sit down.'

Her husband straightened himself in his armchair as they came into the sitting room. He looked out of sorts, as if he'd just lost an argument. 'Blimey,' he muttered. 'How many coppers does it take to change a bleedin' lightbulb?'

'Jack!' his wife hissed, and said to Kathy, 'Did you want to speak to Naomi in her room?'

'We'd like you to be present, if you don't mind, Mrs Tait,' Kathy said, although of all the interviews with juveniles she'd conducted, she suspected that this one would have been a lot easier if they hadn't had to have the relative present.

'Sit down and I'll fetch her then.' She shot a warning look at her husband and hurried out.

'Goin' to snow, then, is it?' he asked belligerently.

'Could be.'

'Last time it snowed the central heating packed in. Sod's Law, innit?'

Kathy smiled. 'Has Naomi got to go to work today?'

'Yes. All weathers. She's not put off by a bit of weather.'

'Do you and Mrs Tait get over to Silvermeadow to see her when she's working?'

'The wife goes sometimes. Not me. Can't be bothered, waiting for a bus.'

'No,' Kathy said, looking aimlessly round the room, at the new lottery ticket on the mantelpiece, the photo of the other sister. 'Must have been easier for you when Kimberley was around. I suppose she had a car.'

Jack Tait frowned suspiciously at Kathy, then looked up as his wife and Naomi came in.

'What was that?' Mrs Tait asked. 'Who had a car?'

'We were talking about getting to Silvermeadow,' Kathy said. 'I suppose it was easier when Kimberley could take you there in her car.'

'Oh, yes, she had a nice little car. What was it, Jack? A Renault, wasn't it? But she didn't go to Silvermeadow. She worked down Barking way, and if she wanted the shops she would go to Thurrock. She took me there several times. Jack didn't come.'

'Did she never go to Silvermeadow?' Kathy asked.

'I don't think that she ever did. Did she, love?' She turned to Naomi, who shrugged indifferently. 'Anyway, how can we help you?'

Kathy showed Naomi the photographs. She studied each one slowly before shaking her head.

'What about the little girl?' Kathy asked, pointing at the picture, but again the answer was no.

'So what's this in aid of then?' Jack Tait said. 'I thought you'd found the bastard who was responsible for Kerri. The papers said he topped himself.'

'There are still some loose ends, Mr Tait.' Brock spoke for the first time, very deliberately. 'And we're pretty sure that Naomi can help us sort them out.' He looked at the girl, who slowly raised her eyes and met his.

'Like what?' her grandfather demanded.

'The man you just referred to, he died from an overdose of a drug.'

Mr Tait snorted with disgust. 'Figures.'

'This drug is manufactured as an anaesthetic, for animals.'

Kathy sensed both grandparents stiffen as this sank in. But Naomi, still and attentive, her eyes fixed on Brock's face, showed no reaction at all.

'It's known as Ketapet, and it's used by vets. In fact it's one of the drugs that Kimberley was accused of stealing from—'

'Now just wait a minute!' Jack Tait half rose out of his seat, face reddening with anger.

'Jack!' his wife interrupted sharply. 'I'm sure they're not suggesting there's any connection with Kimberley.'

'Well, yes, I'm afraid there is, Mrs Tait. We've established that it was exactly the same batch of that drug that Kimberley took. Isn't that right, Naomi?'

'Naomi?' her grandmother cried, horrified. 'What's it got to do with Naomi?'

'I'd like her to tell us,' Brock insisted.

The girl continued staring at him for a moment, then lowered her eyes. 'I don't know,' she said softly. 'I don't know anything about it.'

Jack Tait immediately said, 'There!' His wife just stared at Naomi for a moment, then got up and went and sat by her side, putting an arm round her shoulders.

'Naomi,' Kathy said, 'please tell us everything you know. It's very important. You remember when I told you about the drug we'd found in Wiff's den? And you asked what the drug was? When I told you ketamine you were shocked and upset. You *knew*, didn't you? Well, we found Wiff later that night, and Speedy. Both of them were dead, from overdoses of ketamine, the same stuff your sister had.'

Mrs Tait put a hand to her mouth, looking as if some familiar horror was revisiting her, but Naomi was as unmoved as before. 'No,' she said calmly. 'I told you what I thought. I knew that Kerri had tried K, and I thought Wiff might have been killed by the same man as gave it to her.'

'But how could it possibly be the same batch as your sister had?'

'I dunno. I s'pose she must have sold it to someone, and they sold it to someone else. How would I know? You can give me a blood test if you like – I've never touched that stuff.'

'But your gran just told us that Kimberley never went to Silvermeadow. Whereas you—'

'You tricked me into saying that!' Mrs Tait said indignantly. 'I don't know whether she went or not. She may have done, without telling me. But Naomi's a good girl. She wouldn't get mixed up—'

Her husband raised himself unsteadily to his feet, face furious. 'I've 'ad enough of this.' His voice choked with phlegm and he fought to continue, his good hand pointing at the door. 'You get out, you hear? Get out!'

Brock got to his feet. 'No need to get upset, Mr Tait. We're going. We had to ask these questions, you understand. Last thing we want is to cause you more upset, especially at this time of year.' He looked again at Naomi, giving her a kindly grin when she looked up. She made a sad little smile in return, and Mrs Tait, somewhat mollified, showed them to the door.

As they made their way along the deck, Brock muttered, 'Yes, she knows.'

'You think?'

'I'm sure of it. She had the same look that those two kids had when they showed me their handiwork with the tree. She knows exactly how her sister's Ketapet got to Silvermeadow. But she's thought her story through, and she's very cool.'

He stopped at the stairs, resting his hands on the concrete wall as he thought about it. From below they could hear the footsteps of someone climbing up.

'Her friend Lisa isn't so tough,' Kathy said.

'That's what I was thinking.'

The figure of a man emerged out of the gloom of the stairway. He glanced up and they recognised Gavin Lowry, looking even paler and more pinched than usual.

'They told me you'd be over here,' he said, slightly out of breath, vapour rising from his mouth. 'Thought I'd see if I could help.'

'Thanks,' Brock replied. 'How are things with you?'

Lowry shrugged. 'Oh, you know, sir. Pretty shitty.'

'Yes, I can imagine. Have you been talking to Connie?'

'She won't have it. Taken the kids to her parents. Told me to move out so she can come back.'

'Maybe when the dust settles, Gavin,' Brock said. 'Sometimes it's the secrecy that holds people together. Now it's all out in the open she may have second thoughts.'

'But is that what I want?' he replied bitterly. 'Way I feel right now, they're welcome to each other. Anyway, I want to get stuck into some work, take my mind off things.'

'Okay. You know Naomi, don't you? She lives at the other end of this deck.'

Lowry nodded. 'Yeah, I know her.'

'We suspect she may have supplied Speedy with the ketamine, flogging him her sister's drugs. We've just interviewed her, and she denies it, but we're not convinced. You could keep an eye on the place for an hour or two, until we check a few things out, see she doesn't try to dispose of any evidence.'

'Sure. While I'm here I might catch the little toe-rags that tried to bomb me with the TV set.'

'If you do, old son,' Brock said, patting his shoulder, 'just remember that they're not Harry Jackson, okay?'

Lowry grinned and dug a pack of cigarettes out of a pocket. 'Started again,' he said ruefully.

Lisa's mother groaned as she saw them standing there at her door, and asked them in reluctantly. 'I'm on my way out,' she said. 'Sorry about that.' She was wearing a short black leather skirt with matching jacket and boots, and enough make-up, Kathy noted, to light up Oxford Street.

'This is very urgent. We need to speak to Lisa again.'

She sighed. 'Well, if my friend comes you'll just have to speak to her on your own.'

'That's not possible, I'm afraid. There has to be what we call a "responsible adult" present while we talk to her. If you prefer we can take her to the police station and get a social worker to sit with us.'

She wasn't sure about that. She puckered her scarlet mouth and said, 'Won't take long, will it?'

'That rather depends on Lisa,' Kathy said, looking at the pale face watching them through the gap in a bedroom door which had just opened a few inches. 'If she can tell us what we need to know, we won't be long at all.'

'Well, come on then. Lisa! Come out and answer their questions. Hurry up.'

They sat down, and Kathy said simply, 'We've discovered where the ketamine came from that killed Wiff and Speedy . . . and Kerri,' she added, watching the girl's eyes grow large. 'It's time you told us what happened, Lisa.'

The girl's lips set in a tight line, and for a moment it seemed that she would defy them as Naomi had done, but then the line curled down at the ends, tears appeared at her eyes, and her whole body began to shake.

Perhaps the secret of telling the difference between false and true confessions, Kathy thought, lay in the fact that the first were designed to prolong matters, whereas the second were made to bring things to an end – an end long avoided, long postponed and now desperately sought. And she had no doubt that Lisa's confession, when it eventually came, was of the second kind. It came out with an almost physical force, making the girl's face grimace in pain, as if it were something bad she'd swallowed some time ago which had been sitting like a cold stone in her stomach, and now at last could be brought up.

It was very short, just three words.

'We killed Kerri.'

Then she burst into tears.

Her mother stared at her with a look of astonishment, the two detectives with something like regret.

The tension was broken by the front door bell, absurdly playing the opening bars from 'Teddy Bears' Picnic'. Lisa's mother jumped to her feet, muttering, 'Bleedin' heck,' and raced out to answer it. The others waited without speaking while there was a short exchange on the doorstep, punctuated with expletives. Then the front door slammed and the woman returned to the room, her heels clacking on the plastic tiles in the hallway.

Now that the words had been said, the awful words she must have had to bottle up inside herself for almost three weeks, Lisa let the rest pour out, interrupted only by her sobs and moans.

The trouble with Kerri was that she had become unreliable and greedy. In the beginning, after Naomi had found where her sister was hiding the drugs, and had begun to steal them and sell them in a small way to friends, and then through Lisa and Kerri to friends of friends, they had worked together like a team, a small business venture, as Naomi had put it, for a modest but regular commission. After Kimberley was arrested and put away they thought their venture would come to an end, but Naomi seemed more determined than ever to keep it going. She managed to contact her sister's sources and persuaded them to deal with her. Instead of fading away, their business flourished, their network of customers at the mall increasing month by month. It didn't seem wrong. As Naomi had said to them, they were supplying a need, a market, just like all the other traders in the mall. And the mall people knew about it, or at least Wiff's patron and protector, who saw everything going on at Silvermeadow, knew about it, and he was paid a regular fee in kind for his co-operation. Early on he became interested in K, and took it on a regular basis. He had also requested Ecstasy, speed and poppers at various times.

'And you have no idea who this was?' Kathy pressed her. 'Wiff never mentioned a wheelchair?'

Lisa shook her head, wiped her nose and continued.

Kerri was becoming unreliable, she said. She was taking stuff herself with increasing regularity, especially Ecstasy, and when she became fired up she would say things she shouldn't, showing off to the boys. She had fights with Naomi over this, and then they discovered that she was stealing from their stock for her own use. When Naomi confronted her they had a big row, and Kerri made her threat. She said that one day soon she would be out of there, going to live with her dad in Germany, and when she did she'd blow the whistle on Naomi's ring, and make sure she went to jail just like her sister.

Naomi said they had no choice. She spoke to Wiff, who had told them stories in the past about girls disappearing from the mall. They weren't fairy-stories, he'd assured them. In fact his boss, who saw everything, knew who was responsible but didn't interfere because the girls were rubbish, causing trouble. Naomi said that Kerri was trouble too, and that she had threatened to expose them all, which wouldn't suit Wiff's boss. She told Wiff that Kerri was a danger to them all, and that he should tell his boss, and have him arrange for Kerri to disappear like the others.

That was how they'd killed Kerri.

Later, at Hornchurch Street, in the presence of a solicitor and a psychologist, Lisa repeated her story in a more coherent version, her tears exhausted now.

When Brock and Kathy were satisfied that they had heard as much as they were likely to get from her, they joined a waiting group of detectives, collected the warrants and returned to Crocus Court. Gavin Lowry was in the same place, a scattering of cigarette stubs at his feet. There had been no movement from the Taits' flat.

When they knocked on the door it was as if they were expected. Brock explained that he had a warrant for the arrest of Naomi on suspicion of possession and supply of a class B controlled drug, and a second warrant to search the Taits' flat.

During her formal interview at the station, Naomi began by repeating her earlier denials. When they told her something of what Lisa had said she replied that her friend lived in a fantasy world and made up ridiculous stories. Even when they told her that they had found an assortment of controlled drugs hidden inside the base of the bed in her sister's bedroom, she maintained her innocence, claiming that they must have belonged to Kimberley.

Her performance was impressive, and some of those listening to the interview were convinced by it. It was only when Brock told her that they had opened up the portable radio/CD player in her room, and found the banknotes packed tight in the back of the speaker compartments, and told her the exact amount – £31,548 – that she broke down.

The money was the thing, the beginning and end of it all, the profits that she had been patiently accumulating for over a year, the lottery win with which her grandparents would buy their dreamed-of cottage and take them all away from Herbert Morrison and London for ever.

Her account, when it finally came, tallied closely with Lisa's, but with one dramatic additional piece of information. At one point, when she had been talking to Wiff, she had expressed doubts about the tale of the monster of the mall who made people disappear, and had suggested that this was a story his boss had invented to keep him frightened and obedient. Wiff had been affronted and had told her things about the man. Naomi said she hadn't told Lisa about this, because she was frightened about what she was told, and was worried about Lisa keeping it to herself.

He had a special room, Wiff said, a secret place, a den, where he took the women and kept them before he got rid of them. And Wiff knew who the man was. His boss, who was also scared of this man, had video tapes of him, which he called his insurance. From these tapes he had made some still photographs, one of which Wiff had acquired, as *his* insurance. Naomi said that he had shown her the picture.

'You've seen a photograph of this man?' Kathy queried.

Naomi nodded, eyes down. 'He was with one of the girls who disappeared.'

'With her?' Kathy repeated carefully.

'Yeah, you know, on top of her, doing it to her.'

'Can you describe the girl?'

'Black hair, thin face, pale, bit older than me. I didn't recognise her. She looked as if she was asleep, or dead, even though he was on top of her.'

'And the man, can you describe him?'

'Oh, I knew who he was.'

They weren't conscious of it, but everyone listening held their breath for the moment she hesitated before saying the name.

Later, any lingering doubts were dispelled when she was given a file of photographs of missing women, and picked the portrait of the dark-haired girl that Kathy had found among Velma's belongings at the hospital.

'This is her,' she said. 'This is the girl Mr Verdi was fucking.'

20

Bruno Verdi shook his head sadly when they confronted him with the story, as if now he'd heard just about everything.

'You're not serious?' he said. 'My God, if it wasn't poor Kerri they were talking about I'd be laughing. Instead I just feel sick. Where do kids get these ideas? Watching too many movies, eh? Too much TV. Drug rings? Serial killers? Perverts? What kind of fantasies are these? Whatever happened to childhood innocence, eh?'

'It went out with Mr Kreemee,' Kathy said.

'Now, now, now. If you're going to be nasty I'm simply not going to say another word till I have a solicitor present.' He stroked his moustache with an air of complacency.

'You deny these allegations then, do you Mr Verdi?'

'Of course I deny them!' he said, angry now. 'They're ridiculous. Nothing but teenage fantasies. I'm really quite shocked, Chief Inspector,' addressing himself entirely to Brock now, 'that you would give them a second thought. Where is the evidence, eh? Where is this secret room, this photograph, these video tapes? These are the sick imaginings of two young drug dealers who maybe think that if they give you a good story you'll go easy on them! Eh? I'm right, aren't I? You must see this.'

They questioned him for almost three hours, until there was no more to say. Never once did his confidence falter.

After they released him, Kathy spoke again to Naomi.

'The room that this man had, his den, did Wiff say anything about it? Did he know where it was?'

She thought for a moment. 'I think he said it wasn't far away. That's all.'

'Did he give any idea of how big it was, what it looked like?'

'No, nothing.'

'What about the photograph he showed you? What sort of room was that taken in?'

Again she frowned in thought. 'It was quite a big room, I think. You could see a wall in the background, and a chair.'

'Wallpaper? Curtains?'

'No. Bare blocks, like a garage, or a factory.'

'Anything else? Close your eyes and try to see the scene again. Is there a light fitting or furniture?'

'I assumed they were on a bed. I don't really know. I can't picture anything else.'

'But you're absolutely convinced the man was Bruno Verdi, the man who runs the ice-cream place? It couldn't just have been someone who looks like him? With a moustache?'

'No, no. It was definitely him. He was looking straight at the camera, with his teeth bared.' She shuddered. 'You mustn't tell him that I told you this. He'd kill me if he knew.'

'I'm afraid he already knows, Naomi.'

'What?' The girl said it with a yelp of fright. 'You told him about me and Lisa?'

'We told him that friends of Kerri were helping us. He'll be able to work it out. He denies it all, of course.'

Naomi had begun to rock with agitation in her seat. 'Then you mustn't let him go until you've got proof! Don't you see?'

'I'm afraid we've had to let him go. We have no evidence to back up your story. Don't worry. You'll be staying here for a while. He can't hurt you here.'

'And then what?' she moaned. 'You don't know. You don't know what he's like. Wiff warned me.'

Her words bothered Kathy, especially when Naomi was released into her grandparents' care, in view of her age and the proximity of Christmas. Kathy didn't think the proximity of Christmas would inhibit Bruno Verdi if her story was true, and Brock agreed that he should be kept under twenty-four-hour surveillance for the time being. A search was begun of industrial buildings and garages around Silvermeadow and in the neighbourhood of Verdi's home, but no den was found.

Kathy, meanwhile, had heard nothing further from Leon. Several times she almost rang him, but then stopped herself with the thought that it would be a weakness, and that Christmas was itself a kind of a test, and once that barrier was passed then perhaps . . .

As she'd left his house that morning, Brock had made some comment about sharing a Christmas Day lunch if she wasn't doing anything else, but they didn't speak of it again and she assumed he'd forgotten.

As evening drew on, Kathy found herself in a deserted office in the Hornchurch Street station, listening to the sounds of a party somewhere far away in the bowels of the building. It was Christmas Eve after all, and the whole building had experienced a sudden excrescence of glittery decorations and tipsy bonhomie.

She didn't want to go home to her empty flat, and the thought of her large bed and glossy appliances struck her as ridiculous. Since her credit card statement had arrived she'd found it impossible to recapture the mood in which she'd splashed out, and she thought of herself as having suffered a crazy spell, a black-out, yet another victim of the Gruen Transfer.

But it wasn't just that. He had been there too, part of the transaction. It had been a signal to herself, and maybe to him also, of where she thought she was heading. Perhaps that was part of what had gone wrong.

Anyroad, she said to herself, in her Aunt Mary's flat Yorkshire brogue, and immediately winced with guilt. She had still done nothing about their Christmas presents. In her head she heard Uncle Tom's gloating: *Told you so! So wrapped up in herself she's forgot us.*

And to what purpose? North had got clean away, and so, in his own way, had Verdi. She couldn't believe that Naomi's vivid description of the photograph had been invented, yet they had nothing. Again and again they had uncovered lies: Verdi, Testor, Harry Jackson, Lisa and Naomi. The ground had been thick with them and they had duly unearthed them, one by one, like diligent archaeologists scraping back the layers, finding shards which in the end amounted to nothing. She remembered her training, the law lecturer who had kept on at them, nagging: *There are only three kinds of admissible evidence: forensic, witness and confession.* Now they had ended up with no confession, no witness, and the only useful forensic evidence likely to be in a room that they couldn't find, and perhaps didn't even exist.

By rights, she thought, there was only one place it should be, this hidden room, and that was at Silvermeadow itself, the focus of everything. Yet this was the one place it couldn't be, surely, the place that had been searched not once, but twice.

She suddenly found the idea of Silvermeadow, its lights and warmth and bustle, rather appealing, which was a measure, she assumed, of how depressed she must be feeling. A shriek of drunken laughter echoed from the corridor. Better there than here, anyway. She would get a card and present for the relatives, and a single cracker, funny hat and microwave Christmas dinner for herself.

21

The mall was packed with a seething, anxious mob. The customary trance-like atmosphere had given way to a mood of urgency, as last-minute shoppers, heads down, frowning, rushed from shop to shop, scoring names off lists. The carols sung by a local school choir, amplified throughout the centre, had to compete with the wailing of over-excited children and the furious hubbub of raised voices.

Halfway along the mall Kathy spotted Harriet Rutter seated at a café table. Her heart sank, and she stopped. At that moment the phone in her bag began ringing. She turned against a shopfront to answer it, putting a hand to her other ear. Through the glass she could see a child strapped into a pushchair angrily battering a rack of wrapping paper with its tiny red boots.

'Kathy? Brock here. What on earth's that noise?'

'The roar of rampaging shoppers. I'm at Silvermeadow.'

'Really? What are you up to there?'

'I forgot to get presents for my relatives in Sheffield.'

'Aunt Mary and Uncle Tom? You'll be in deep trouble.'

'Yes, I know.'

'What? Can't hear you. Look, the reason I called was to check you were still all right for Christmas lunch tomorrow.'

'Really?' Kathy brightened. 'Is it still on?'

'Of course. Unless you've had a better offer?'

'No. You neither?'

'No. We can call it the Rejects' Lunch. The Salon des Refusés.'

Kathy laughed. 'What can I bring?'

'Well, since you're at the shops, you could see if you can find a Christmas pudding. I've already got the duck.'

Kathy rang off and smiled to herself. A duck. So he'd been shopping too.

She continued along the mall, and reached Harriet Rutter. She seemed to be alone, only one plate and cup in front of her, her gaze aimlessly scanning the moving crowd. Kathy paused reluctantly and said, 'Hello Mrs Rutter. How are you?'

The other woman turned with a vague smile that chilled as soon as she realised who had addressed her. 'Ah . . . Sergeant.'

'Are you on your own? Is Professor Orr not with you?'

Harriet Rutter shook her head abruptly. Kathy noticed that she seemed to be holding herself stiffly upright, like a widow at a funeral. And now she looked more closely, she was almost sure that there was moisture gleaming in the corners of the woman's eyes.

She really didn't want to stop and hear the story, whatever it was, but she felt compelled to ask. 'Is something the matter? Are you all right?'

Mrs Rutter shook her head, speechless, and this seemed so completely out of character that Kathy was taken aback.

She took the other seat at the table. 'What is it?'

'Robbie and I . . . have had a falling out. That's all.'

'Oh. I am sorry. Do you know, I think it's Christmas that does this. Everybody seems to have the same problem.'

The other woman looked at her doubtfully, as if to see if she was making fun of her.

'It's got nothing to do with Christmas. It's my fault. I should have been more patient . . . more sympathetic.'

'Oh dear. Do you want to tell me? Is there anything I can do?'

Mrs Rutter's eyes widened. 'You!' she whispered, and turned abruptly away, behaving almost as if it was all Kathy's fault.

Kathy was puzzled. 'What do you mean?'

Mrs Rutter slowly turned back to face her, mouth set defiantly. 'I mean that Robbie was devastated, utterly *devastated*, by the treatment he got from you people.' She spoke in an uncharacteristically low tone, almost a whisper, as if she didn't want anyone else to hear. 'You have no idea what I'm talking about, have you?'

'No, no I don't.'

'I suppose you deal with hardened criminals all the time, don't you? And you assume that everyone's the same. Well I can tell you, by the time you and that Sergeant Lowry had finished with Robbie, the poor man was a wreck. He hasn't been able to sleep, or eat. And he's not a weak man . . .' The tears were flowing freely now. 'He was in the army, long ago, and he's coped with all the usual trials of a long and useful life. But you *humiliated* him. You made him out to be *rubbish*. You *hurt* him.'

Kathy was stunned, and felt herself wilting before the ferocity of the woman's outrage. 'Mrs Rutter, Professor Orr seemed quite all right when I last saw him. He didn't like being questioned, of course, but he was co-operative, and didn't seem too distressed.' But that was before Gavin Lowry had had a go, and she remembered how angry Lowry had seemed afterwards.

Mrs Rutter wasn't interested. She turned away and wiped her eyes and nose with a small handkerchief and recomposed herself. 'What's really galling is that that awful man has got away with it. That's what Robbie can't abide.'

'DS Lowry?' Kathy asked.

'No! *Bruno Verdi!*' She curled her lip as she pronounced the name like an obscenity. 'He put those things in Robbie's filing cabinet. Any fool could have worked that out in one minute. Even the police. He's an evil and spiteful little man . . . But, I'm afraid.'

'You're afraid of Verdi?'

'Of what Robbie may do. That's why we quarrelled. I wanted him to put it out of his mind, forget about it, but he can't. He says he's going to expose Verdi. He's become obsessed by the idea.' She shook her head hopelessly. 'How can he?'

Kathy had the sudden notion that Orr's outrage at being accused of possessing a dirty video might just be because it had touched a nerve, and perhaps one that Mrs Rutter might have recognised. Maybe she had had her own suspicions about the great man's proclivities. Didn't they used to chat up the young people in the malls together? And then there was the matter of the coins.

Kathy mentally kicked herself; she had forgotten about the coins. What was happening to her memory? Maybe sex and shopping affected the brain.

'Do you think, if I spoke to him, apologised?'

'Oh, I really don't think that would do any good. Not now.'

'Is he at home?'

'No, we came here together. That's when we quarrelled.'

'He's here, is he?'

She nodded. 'I think he's gone to that hut.'

'Well, I might call in on him and see if I can calm him down.'

Mrs Rutter looked doubtful, then relief began to soften her face. 'Would you? It might help.'

As she continued along the mall Kathy passed a deli, and selected one of the small gourmet Christmas puddings they had on offer, and a box of mince pies. She also noticed a sign advertising a delivery service to anywhere in the UK, and with relief ordered a presentation box of delicacies to be sent up to Sheffield, with a hurriedly written card which she backdated to the twentieth. She had a moment of anxiety as the machine scanned her card, but some residual credit still apparently remained, and she emerged from the shop contented.

The icy wind caught her breath as soon as she stepped out of the shelter of the east entrance. She lowered her head, turned up her collar and strode towards the top of the grass bank that separated the upper and lower carparks, where she could see down the bare flank of the centre to the two steel containers in their water-logged compound at the far corner. It occurred to her that Orr couldn't be in his hut, because they had put a new padlock on the door, one to which only the police had a key. And yet, screwing up her eyes against the wind, Kathy was almost convinced that she could see a glimmer of light reflecting from the puddle at that end of the container. Puzzled, she began the tricky descent down the slippery grass slope and across the muddy ground below.

There was definitely light coming from the bottom edge of the door, and when she reached it she was able to make out the hasp that secured the door dangling loose, and still locked by the padlock to the staple which had been forcibly wrenched from the jamb. Robbie Orr had obviously come prepared.

He literally jumped into the air when she pulled the door open and said hello. Coat flapping, arms flailing, he scrambled to hide whatever he had been examining on the table as he turned to face her.

'What do you want?' he barked.

He was certainly the worse for wear, she saw. He looked older, clothes dishevelled and splashed with mud.

'I bumped into Harriet in the mall. She said you might be down here. Can I come in?'

She stepped in before he could reply, and swung the door to.

'I'm busy,' he said angrily, and she caught a whiff of whisky. 'I don't want to be disturbed.'

'What are you doing?'

She stared at the tabletop behind him, and he shuffled sideways to block her view. She was startled to see what looked like copies of the computer plans that Allen Cook had provided for their search. Even more disconcerting was a glimpse of what looked like several fat brass cartridges. He began feeling along the edge of the table with the long, bony fingers of his left hand towards the jemmy he'd presumably used to force open the door. His right hand was plunged deep in his coat pocket, and he seemed reluctant to take it out. The coat was dragged down on that side of his body, as if the pocket contained something heavy.

'DS Kathy Kolla,' Kathy suddenly said with a big smile, and stuck out her hand. 'Remember me?'

He jerked back from her hand, then flushed when he realised she was offering it to shake. 'Of course I do!' He flapped his left hand at her, while his right remained firmly in the pocket. 'Please go away.'

'I thought maybe we could talk things over. I think we could help each other.'

He leant forward, eyes glittering with anger. 'Don't try your soft soap on me, lassie,' he said. 'I know why you've come.'

'Do you?'

'Aye. To save your corrupt friends. To have me take the blame for your bungling. What have you got in your bag, eh? What did you bring to hide in my drawers this time? More filth? Perhaps you'd like me to tell you what an attractive wee girl she was? How she liked to tease old men like me for a pound or two? Is that what you want to hear?'

'I want to hear the truth, Robbie. Did she tease you?' Kathy searched his face, trying to read it. Inside the pocket of her coat her fingers found the small black disc she had taken from the box on Kerri's desk, and she held it up for him to see. 'You did give her old coins, didn't you? What were they? Gifts, tokens?'

Orr stiffened. 'I gave coins to many of the young people in the mall,' he growled.

'Why?'

His lip curled at her with contempt. 'Not for the reason your sordid police mind imagines, I dare say. I wasn't trying to buy them, Sergeant. They have far too smart an estimate of their own worth to sell themselves for trinkets. I wanted them to learn a different lesson about money. The coins came from this hillside. I found them near the bones of the Saxon children. Small change. Part of the hoard the Vikings were looking for. I wanted them to know that children like them were murdered for these coins. That the coins survived, but the children did not. But I was naïve. Today the children are more greedy, and the people that hunt them more evil.'

He rocked back on his heels, and reached behind him with his left hand to grip the table, as if running out of steam.

'I didn't come here to trap you,' Kathy said quietly. 'If you know something, let me help you.'

He looked at her sadly. 'Have you arrested Verdi?'

'No.'

'Have you found his lair?'

She shook her head, startled.

'Then you can't help me.' He turned away dismissively.

'What do you know about a lair?' she asked. 'We've been looking—'

'In all the wrong places, no doubt.' He turned to her again, a smile of patronising superiority twitching his whiskers.

He's been a teacher for years, she thought. He can't help turning every conversation into a seminar. 'Well, I don't know. We know its walls are bare concrete blocks—'

He looked sharply at her. 'Oh yes? How do you know that?'

'A witness says she saw a photograph of Verdi in a bare room, with a girl.'

He nodded. 'But *where* is it?'

'We don't know. We've been searching disused factories, garages –'

He made a scoffing noise. 'Pathetic!'

'It was the best we could come up with.'

He pondered, and she thought, Come on, you can't resist telling me something.

'Are you familiar with the legend of the Minotaur, Sergeant?'

'Not really. It was a monster, wasn't it?'

'Aye, half man and half beast. It lived on human sacrifice, the youth of Thebes.'

'And where was its lair?'

'In the labyrinth at Knossos, on the island of Crete. I spoke to your chief inspector about my time there, you may remember. The labyrinth was within, or some said beneath, the palace.'

Kathy thought about that. 'If you're suggesting that Silvermeadow is the palace . . . We've been all over it, and beneath it. That's where we found –'

'Aye, I heard. The remains of human sacrifice.'

'But no lair.'

He said nothing.

'Did they catch the Minotaur?'

'The hero Theseus slew it, yes.'

'How did he find it?'

'A young woman showed him the way. Ariadne. Alas, I fear you will not be my Ariadne, Sergeant. Too bad. Now please go away.'

Kathy felt her patience ebbing. His dismissal reminded her of every dismissal she'd ever experienced at school. 'Sorry,' she said briskly. 'I can't do that. It looks as if someone's forced that lock. I'll have to get security.'

She reached into her bag and took out her phone.

'Don't do that!' He spun round and shouted at her, his earlier agitation flaring up again.

She glanced at his right hand, still jammed in his coat pocket, then began to press the numbers.

The hand suddenly lurched into movement as if of its own accord, hauling out of the pocket one of the largest and heaviest-looking handguns Kathy had ever seen. He pointed it at her, the barrel wobbling alarmingly, and lifted his other hand to try to steady it.

'Bloody hell!' Kathy breathed. 'What is *that?*'

'The phone!' he barked, flecks of spittle on his lips. 'Put it down! Put it down!'

She shrugged and slipped it back in her bag.

'No, no! Put it on the floor! Put it on the floor and step back!'

Kathy did exactly as he said, her eyes on the trembling fingers that held the swaying ordnance.

He stepped forward and swung a clumsy kick at the phone, missed, tried again and connected, sending it spinning away. 'Foolish woman!' he gasped. 'You foolish, foolish—'

'Where on earth did you get that?' Kathy asked, trying desperately to sound completely calm and unconcerned by his obvious incompetence with the gun.

'The very place,' he said, and gave a rather wild little laugh. 'Knossos, Crete. The island was full of small arms after the war. I bought this from a village boy for two packets of cigarettes – two more for the box of ammunition.'

'Over fifty years ago? Have you ever fired it?'

'I tried it once after I bought it, on the beach. Nearly deafened me.'

'Are you sure it still works?'

'We'll have to see, won't we? Sit down.'

He nodded towards the chair. Kathy moved carefully towards it, and he matched her steps in a slow-motion ballet to position himself between her and the door. When he was satisfied, he lowered the gun to his side, much, Kathy suspected, to the relief of them both. She tried to read the expression on his face. Not anger, she thought, nor fear. More like perplexity.

'This is awkward, isn't it?' she said slowly. 'You can't lock me in here because the lock is broken, and you can't let me go.'

He nodded sharply, as if this was exactly what he'd been thinking.

'Would it help if I were to say that I'm as anxious as you are to find this room, if it exists?'

'It exists,' he said flatly.

'How do you know?'

'I've found it.'

'You've been there?'

He shook his head. She followed his glance over to the table, covered by the sheets of plans. She noticed coloured pencil marks.

'Those are the plans we worked from,' she said, puzzled. 'What could we have missed?'

A hint of the smug tutorial smile crept back onto his face. 'They have been tampered with.'

'How do you know?'

'Because when I first arrived here, when the construction of the building had hardly begun, they gave me a set of the plans so that we would know where to concentrate the digging. I still have them.'

'We know those plans have been modified since then—'

'I know that. But they've also been tampered with. A room has been removed. A special room. I saw them build it.'

Kathy stared at him, not sure what to believe, and then Allen Cook's comment came into her head: *Harry Jackson has a lad who's a bit of a computer whiz, and I pay him to work on it from time to time.* Speedy Reynolds of course. He could have done anything to the plans and nobody would have been the wiser.

'You saw this room being built? What was special about it?'

'It was right in the middle of the food court, shaped as an octagon, a pit containing a stage that could move up and down for spectacles and events. But it was too large, too ambitious, the costs got out of hand. Then one of the directors had a holiday in Hawaii, and when he came back they changed their plans. They sealed off the pit and built that ridiculous volcano on top. I was on good terms with the site foreman. He told me all this. The workmen thought it was a great joke.'

'But the room is still there, under the volcano?'

Orr nodded.

'But if it was sealed off . . .'

'It was connected to the main plenum duct by a short corridor and a door – you can see it on the original plan – so that they could get to the machinery under the stage. But that's been removed from the plans too.'

'So you think you can reach it from the plenum?'

'Yes.' Orr looked unhappy, and Kathy thought she could guess why.

'But how can you get into the plenum? The only way is through the security centre. Christ, you weren't going to hold them up with your blunderbuss, were you?'

He lowered his eyes guiltily and muttered something indistinct.

Kathy looked at him sadly. He was just a pathetic old man, bruised, almost casually, by Verdi's malice and Lowry's bullying. Thank goodness she'd come down here before he'd tried to carry out his plan. She could disarm and arrest him now without difficulty, but what would that achieve? Verdi and Lowry would find it all very amusing, no doubt.

She didn't hold much store by his theory. She could imagine him poring over the plans, the revelation when he noticed the discrepancy that allowed him to pin-point the missing room, the old instincts aroused by the promise of a hidden, buried chamber of horrors. Under the volcano, too. Really, he had been planning his last great expedition, Orr as Theseus as Indiana Jones, archaeologist-hero, complete with antique revolver.

They had searched the plenum thoroughly and seen no sign of the door. Yet he had watched the octagonal room being built. They probably should have another look, although she could imagine the scepticism if she suggested it. One thing at least was sure: if Verdi did have a den down there, he wasn't there now, for the surveillance team had reported that he had gone home early that afternoon, leaving the gelato parlour in the charge of two assistants.

'It's a funny way to spend Christmas Eve, Professor,' she said at last.

He was lost in thought, and looked at her vaguely. 'What?'

317

'Suppose I agreed to be your Ariadne, and get you into the plenum.'

'Would you?' he asked suspiciously.

'On strict conditions. No guns, and I phone in and report what we're doing.'

He frowned at her, then at the phone lying by his foot. Without a word he lifted his boot and stamped on the phone, then again. It splintered with a loud crack.

'No gun and no phone,' he said simply. He went over to the filing cabinet and placed the gun inside.

Kathy shook her head in exasperation. 'Show me your map, then.'

They stood together at the table and Orr showed her where the missing room was located.

'Have you got torches?' she asked.

While he went back to the cabinet and searched through the drawers, she took a page from a notepad on the table and wrote 'Please advise DCI Brock NOW' and added his mobile number. She slipped the paper into her pocket and began folding up the plans to take with them.

They trudged together across the mud to the lower carpark, and into the mall at the first entrance they came to. They passed briefly through the still frantic crowd until they reached a side corridor, where Kathy led the way to the security door at the end. She used her code to pass through and into the service corridor beyond, leading to the service road. It was deserted now, no deliveries at this late hour on Christmas Eve. They walked on in silence until they came to the lighted window of the security centre at the foot of the entry ramp.

Kathy was relieved to see Sharon's face illuminated inside, doubting whether she would have been able to talk their way past Harry Jackson. She waved to her and opened the door.

'Hi, Sharon. Still hard at work?'

'I'm just about to knock off, Kathy,' she replied, looking doubtfully at the old man following at Kathy's back.

'You know Professor Orr, don't you?' Kathy said. 'He's helping me clear up one or two loose ends in our investigation. He was here when the building was being constructed, you see. We just need to take a quick look down below in the plenum duct.'

'You want to go down there now?'

'Yes, that's right.' Kathy began to walk towards the rear of the office.

'I'd better check with Harry first,' Sharon called after her. 'I couldn't let you through otherwise.'

'That really won't be necessary,' Kathy said firmly. 'And it'd hold us up – and you too. Harry might feel he has to check with my boss, and that might take hours, finding him. We only need five minutes, ten at most. If we're not back then, contact Harry and tell him I insisted.'

Sharon wavered, then capitulated. 'Well, just make sure you do get back before he comes down here, Kathy. He'll give me hell.'

She took them to the door at the back of the unit and gave them a hard hat each. As she took hers, Kathy gave her the piece of paper on which she'd written Brock's phone number. 'Just in case there's a problem, okay?' she whispered.

As they descended the long ramp, Kathy was aware of appreciative little noises from Orr behind her. 'This is really very good,' he murmured. 'It feels very like the passageway down into one of the tombs of the New Kingdom. Did I tell you I was with Emery at Saqqara?'

The illusion became even stronger when they moved from the chamber at the foot of the ramp into the unlit plenum duct itself, with its low ceiling and whispering darkness. Orr stumbled as he stepped inside, banging his helmet against the ceiling just as Leon had done. The memory gave Kathy an unexpectedly sharp jab of regret. She put out a hand to steady Orr, and flinched as his coat swung against her and something heavy and hard banged against her knee.

She swore softly and turned the light on him, seeing the bulge in his coat pocket. 'That bloody gun!' she hissed. 'You promised!'

'I'm sorry, Kathy.' His voice was plaintive. 'I felt obliged . . . in case I led you into any danger.'

'The only danger I'm in is from that damn thing going off by mistake!'

'No, no. I was in the army, you know. The safety catch is on. What in God's name is that sound?' Orr breathed. 'It's like the voices of ghosts.'

'It's only the machinery,' Kathy said, and turned away, irritated. 'The extract fan's at the far end. Come on.'

They passed evidence of where workmen had begun replacing the missing grilles in the incoming ducts, and came to the place where Wiff's nest had been, still cordoned off with police tape. Here they examined the original plan, orienting themselves. If the door to the octagonal room existed, they realised, it must be quite close.

They moved on down the main plenum to the next short branch to the left, which they followed to its end, closed by a panel of louvres. This, they decided, talking for some reason in whispers, was where the door should have been. But there was no sign of a handle or hinges in the louvres, which appeared firmly fixed. Orr rattled them in frustration, pushed his shoulder half-heartedly against them, then stepped back in astonishment as they swung soundlessly open.

Their torches showed another corridor beyond, its walls formed of grey concrete blockwork. It ran forward for about twenty yards, then turned left and stopped at a door. Kathy told Orr to wait and tried the handle. It turned, and she opened the door into a darkened room. The air was suddenly much warmer and had a strong human smell, of urine and sweat. She pointed her torch into the dark space and picked out a chair, an electric fan heater and a pair of wellington boots. As the beam swept slowly across the room she saw a mattress on a steel-framed bed. From the headframe hung a pair of handcuffs.

'Oh God . . .' she breathed. 'You were right, Robbie. Just stay where you are please. Don't come in here.'

She shone the torch back along the wall towards the door and found a light switch. A harsh white fluorescent light flickered into life overhead, and Kathy stepped cautiously into the room. There was a suitcase near the bed, open, with clothes heaped untidily inside.

At her shoulder, Orr whispered, 'I knew it, Kathy. I knew I was right. The Minotaur's lair, eh?'

'Yes. And I told you to stay outside. For goodness' sake don't touch anything.'

She was staring at the mattress. There was a sleeping bag heaped at one end, a pillow at the other, magazines scattered in between. Behind her she heard the door click shut. She turned, assuming Orr had followed her instructions and left, but he was still at her back, staring towards the door. Then she saw the man standing there and her heart gave a violent jolt.

'Who the blazes are you?' Orr demanded.

The figure didn't answer, but Kathy knew who it was. She had seen the face on video and mug shots, and once in the flesh.

Gregory Thomas 'Upper' North.

22

Kathy spoke slowly and clearly. 'I'm a police officer. I'll show you my warrant card.'

She made to reach into her pocket, but North raised a warning hand and she froze.

'What's your name?'

She had heard people mention the soft, sibilant voice that reinforced the impression he was under the influence of something even when he wasn't.

'DS Kolla.'

'Division?'

'Serious Crime. With DCI Brock.'

Without the heavy-rimmed glasses he looked much more like the North of the earlier pictures, slightly dreamy eyes pinched together, cruel mouth. At the mention of Brock's name he blinked and stared more fixedly at Kathy.

'Is he here too?'

Kathy hesitated and saw the eyes focus threateningly.

'No, he's not here at the moment.'

'Who else is with you?'

'No one. Just us. At the moment.'

'What does that mean?'

'It means I'm supposed to report in.'

The mouth formed a thin smile. 'Sure. Who's he?'

'He's—'

'Now look!' Orr interrupted, becoming incensed that someone he took to be a maintenance mechanic, dressed in tracksuit and trainers, should have the presumption to question a police officer in this way. 'You show a bit of respect, sir!'

'Robbie . . .' Kathy said warningly, remembering all she had been told about North. If she could just keep things calm for ten or fifteen minutes, Sharon would have told Brock, who would surely come. But Orr was waving his hand imperiously at her as he continued to address North in his most pompous classroom manner.

'I am Professor Robbie Orr, and I am an archaeologist assisting this officer in her investigations. We have no interest in you, and I suggest you leave now before—'

'Tell him to keep his fucking mouth shut,' North hissed.

Orr, unlike Kathy, had not noticed the black object dangling from North's right hand.

'How dare you speak to us in that manner!' Orr exploded. 'If you can't show a little respect—'

North brought his right hand up until it was pointing at Orr's chest. Orr blinked in astonishment as he made out the automatic and silencer.

'Robbie, please keep quiet and leave this to me,' Kathy said, with some intensity. She tried to glance unobtrusively at his hands, terrified that he would try to pull his antiquated gun from his coat pocket. 'Don't move or say a word, and everything will be perfectly all right.'

Orr swallowed, then drew himself up straight. 'No, Kathy. I refuse to be intimidated by some loutish thug. Does your employer know you have that thing?' he challenged North. 'Good God, sir! I'm not frightened of the likes of you. I was with Templer in Malaya!'

There was silence for a moment. North was frowning, as if trying to work out what the hell Orr meant, and Kathy began to say something to try to divert his attention. But before she could get the words out, North said, 'Yeah? Well I was with Ronnie Kray in Pentonville,' and the gun jumped twice in his hand, with two vicious thumps.

Orr toppled abruptly backwards, lay felled on the floor, a look of blank amazement on his face. North stared down at him for some seconds, as if contemplating a fine piece of work, then swung the gun to point at Kathy's head. Instinctively she closed her eyes, waiting for oblivion.

A long silence, then she heard his voice. 'Take the coat off, very carefully, darling.'

As she eased it off and handed it to him a hissing, gurgling noise came from the figure stretched out on the floor beside her. She glanced down and saw pink foam on Orr's lips.

North backed over to the bed and emptied the pockets of Kathy's coat without taking his eyes off her, spreading out the purse, handcuffs, wallet with warrant card. Then he told her to turn and stand over against the wall, hands and feet spread. She felt him come close against her back, the end of the silencer press against her temple, then his free hand feeling in the pockets of her jeans, then round under her sweater to the front of her shirt, unbuttoning it and feeling inside to her skin. The hand slid up to her breast, pausing there a moment, his breathing heavy in her ear, then continued feeling her front, her belly, then round to her back, tugging the shirt out of her jeans so that the fingers could feel over her skin, up to her shoulders, then through her hair.

The hand went round to her front again, to the belt and zip of her jeans, undoing them. She said, 'No,' and tried to twist round, but he grabbed her hair and banged her face against the concrete block wall, pressing the metal tube harder against her temple. Then he returned to what he had been doing, unfastening her jeans, pulling them down to her ankles and feeling up and down her legs. He pulled off her shoes, threw them aside, and stepped back.

'Hands behind your back,' he said.

She obeyed, and felt the handcuffs on her wrists.

'Turn,' he said. 'Sit.'

She squatted against the wall, jeans still round her ankles. The blow to her head had dazed her; her brow throbbed painfully. She fought to control the trembling that threatened to take her over, and tried to concentrate on things outside herself – on Orr, lying a couple of yards away, wheezing and bubbling faintly.

North was sitting on the bed, examining her wallet again, when she heard something, a faint metallic clang, from outside the room. The metal door of louvres, she thought, and imagined someone making their way slowly along the connecting corridor to the door of this room. Please let it be Brock, not Sharon, she thought, staring transfixed at the door handle as it began to turn.

She glanced at North, still preoccupied with her wallet, then back at the door. It opened a few inches, then a few more, and she recognised Harry's profile in the gap. She wanted desperately to call out to him, tell him to run, get help, but she guessed that North would start blazing away indiscriminately if she startled him, so she bit her lip and watched Harry in silence as he slowly took in the scene in the room, his eyes widening at the sight of Orr stretched out on the floor, Kathy against the wall. *Run!* she silently urged him, as he stood staring at her, then at North, seemingly unable to decide what to do.

Finally she couldn't stand it any more. Terrified that he'd say something, she gave a little sharp warning shake of her head. But the movement registered with North, who looked up suddenly, first at Kathy, then at the doorway, and took in Harry.

'Run, Harry!' she finally blurted. 'Get help!'

But instead of running, he began to walk slowly into the room.

Incredulously, Kathy watched him crouch beside Orr. Then she was aware of North picking up his gun at last. He waved it in the general direction of Harry and said simply, 'He's dead.'

Harry looked up, face grim, then got to his feet and stared at Kathy. He took in the livid mark on her forehead, the dishevelled clothes, bare legs. 'Christ, Greg,' he said. 'You didn't have to—'

'What? You think I screwed her?' North gave a short laugh. 'I was looking for a wire. She's clean. She doesn't even have a gun.'

Jackson looked over at the contents of her pockets spread out on the bed at North's feet, then in puzzlement at Kathy. 'No radio? No phone? What do they teach you kids these days?'

Kathy felt a wave of panic and despair rise inside her as she finally understood. She saw that he was holding in his hand the note with Brock's phone number that she had given Sharon, and wondered desperately if she had made the call.

She took a deep breath, trying to make her voice sound strong, in control. 'We've got an operation going, Harry, searching for hidden rooms. It's only a matter of time before the others move down here. I left my phone upstairs. I should have checked in ten minutes ago.'

He studied her thoughtfully, then shook his head. 'That wasn't what you told Sharon, Kathy. And it doesn't make any sense to me. An operation? With this old geezer? And not even a can of capsicum spray on you?'

He turned back to North. 'You been checking the radio traffic?'

'Earlier, yeah. Nothing special.' He reached down from the bed and switched on the radio on the floor nearby.

After a moment the unmistakable sound of a police radio exchange came through: 'Oscar Lima, receiving seven one five,' and the reply, 'Seven one five, go ahead.' The voices were flat and untroubled. 'All quiet on Nelson Road, Oscar Lima . . .'

Harry Jackson turned back to Kathy. 'Sounds more like you had one of your little brainstorms, Kathy. What, decide to crack the case single-handed, did you? Christ . . .' He shook his head sadly. 'Haven't you got anything better to do on Christmas Eve?'

'She's one of Brock's,' North said.

'I know.'

'So she's not good to have around.' He said this pointedly.

Kathy looked up at Jackson's face, trying to read his reaction. He met her eye briefly, then turned away.

'Let's think about it.'

'What's to think about?' North said. 'Don't worry, Harry. I'll do it. My pleasure.'

'We don't know for sure what's going on out there.'

Jackson went over to North and began speaking to him urgently in a low voice that Kathy couldn't hear. She watched their expressions as the discussion went backwards and forwards. At the end of it, when Jackson got up from the bed and walked away, head lowered, hands in pockets, she couldn't tell for sure which way it had gone, but it didn't look encouraging.

'I'm hungry,' North said, casually picking up a magazine. 'Get us something, will you, Harry? Nothing spicy; my gut's playing up, stuck down here in this hole. Something with chips − fish or burger or something. And a decent bottle of plonk. It is Christmas Eve, after all.'

'Sure,' Jackson muttered. He turned to the door without looking in Kathy's direction.

'Don't I get a last meal?' she said.

North smiled, but said nothing.

Harry looked back reluctantly over his shoulder. 'What do you want?'

'I want you to get help for Orr,' Kathy said. 'Please, Harry. You can't just let him die. Take him out of here and leave him somewhere and call an ambulance. If he survives he won't be able to talk for days. Come on, Harry. It's no risk to you.'

He smiled uncomfortably at her. 'Nice try, Kathy.' The tone of his voice chilled her. It was sympathetic, regretful, as if he didn't expect to be talking to her again.

North said, 'There's some car keys in her bag, Harry. Maybe you'd better get rid of it.'

Jackson came back over to the bed and picked up her keys. 'Yeah, I'll bring it down beside mine, then I'll close the service road for the night. Where is it?' he asked her. 'I know what you drive.'

'Go fuck yourself, Harry,' she said.

'Suit yourself.' He turned and made for the door.

As his footsteps faded away, North got to his feet and stretched, and for the second time Kathy braced herself, feeling sick in the pit of her stomach.

'So, Kathy, is it?' he said. 'Your name?' He began to stroll towards her, a little smile playing on his lips.

'Yes, that's right. A bit like Mandy.'

'Eh?' He stopped dead. 'What did you say?'

'I said my name is a bit like Mandy – two syllables, five letters—'

'What do you know about Mandy?'

'Which Mandy are we talking about? Mandy Rice-Davies? Or Mandy Bryant of twenty-three Tulip Court?'

'Don't get fucking smart with me, bitch. How do you know about Mandy?'

'And Sophie. Well, how would we know? I mean, who do *we* know that knows about Mandy and Sophie? Now Sophie is two syllables and six letters. Like Connie. That's a coincidence too, isn't it?'

He was standing right over her now, glaring down, and Kathy smiled sweetly back up at him, feeling like a swimmer floundering through crocodile-infested waters. She watched him raise his hand and bring it down across her face once, twice. He seemed to like to work in twos, she thought: two bullets, two blows. One just wasn't enough for Upper North. She heard his voice talking angrily, to her presumably, but she couldn't make it out, what with the roaring in her ears and the shock of the pain where his rings had split her mouth.

He squatted down beside her and gripped her by the hair and spoke distinctly into her ear. 'Tell me, you fucking bitch, or I'll cut your fucking tits off. Who's Connie?'

So he didn't know about Connie. She wondered where the knife was. She hadn't noticed one so far.

'She's Harry's girlfriend, of course,' she mumbled through lips that seemed to be inflating as she spoke. 'Who also happens to be DS Lowry's wife.'

'And she told you about Sophie and Mandy?' he hissed.

'That's what DS Lowry said.'

He pushed her head away so hard that she sprawled sideways onto the floor, arms trapped painfully behind her. From this position she watched his trainers stride away, then begin pacing backwards and forwards across the room. As they passed Orr, the prostrate figure groaned feebly and tried to raise a hand. North stopped, launched two vicious kicks at the old man, then continued on his way.

It seemed a very long time before they heard Harry Jackson's footsteps again. Long enough for North to calm down and sit on the bed, and long enough too for Kathy's hope that Sharon had phoned Brock to fade. At one point Kathy heard a faint rumble and creaking coming through the plywood ceiling of the room, and imagined Mount Mauna Loa erupting overhead for the benefit of the final shoppers, though the construction was sufficiently solid that they would never have heard any cry from her.

When Jackson came in, North waited while he put his burden of carrier bags down on the table, then got easily to his feet, walked over to Jackson and threw him against the wall. Jackson was a big man, six foot two and a couple of stones heavier than North, but he lacked the other's violent energy, and was caught completely by surprise.

'Wha—?' he gasped, as North rammed a forearm across his throat and began haranguing him in a hoarse undertone. Kathy picked up the odd word, mainly obscenities and names: Connie, Sophie, Lowry . . .

Finally the angry monologue became a conversation, Jackson struggling to get the words out. She couldn't hear exactly what was said, but the gradual shift of North's tone, from fury to doubt to acceptance, was clear enough. She closed her eyes and waited for the retribution.

Footsteps — the click of Jackson's boots coming towards her. She opened her eyes as he bent down and took hold of her by the arms and hauled her into a sitting position, then up onto her feet. He reached down and pulled up her jeans, yanked up the zip and stood in front of her with arms braced against the wall on each side of her head.

'I don't blame you for trying,' he said, voice low, 'but that was *really* stupid. Have you any idea what he's like when he loses it?'

She looked past him at North, now ripping open the paper bags and taking handfuls of fish and chips while he fiddled with the controls of a small portable TV. It blared into life with the music of a cartoon programme.

'How did you ever put your life in his hands, Harry? I did it by mistake. What's your excuse?'

He held her eyes and said, 'I got a letter today, Kathy, Christmas Eve. Me and Bo Seager, both. Our services are no longer required.

The company would appreciate it if we would clear our desks and piss off.'

He glanced back over his shoulder at North, who was now humming to himself as he ate.

'Now I'm a slow learner – it took me fifty years to figure it out – but I'm not so slow that I had to wait for them to tell me. You only get one shot at life, this is not a dress rehearsal, seize the day – all those old lines, they are *true*. You don't understand because you're young, Kathy. You think you have time to spare. Well, you don't. None of us does. I finally understood that when Connie told me she wanted to leave Gavin for me, and I realised that this was my very last chance, and after this was nothing. And I looked back over my life, and saw it for how it had really been: fifty years fretting over pennies, stuffing around, making do. And I thought, No more, *no more*. I didn't know what I was going to do about it, but I was going to do something.

'That afternoon I walked through the mall, smiling at the shoppers, passing the time of day, and thinking, What a load of fucking zombies. Don't you realise how utterly pointless you are? I've wasted most of my life trying to keep you safe – for what? And it was then I spotted Upper North.'

Perhaps North picked up his own name above the sound effects from the TV. He called over, mouth full of food, 'What you talking to her about?'

'I'm just putting this one straight on a few matters, Greg.'

'What's the point?'

Jackson eased back slowly from the wall. 'Yeah, you're right. There is no point.'

But there had been a hint of regret, and Kathy guessed he still wanted to tell her how it had happened.

'Why didn't you just go for the reward?' she said quietly.

He looked her in the eye. 'I checked that later. Ten thousand quid. About what I expected. Pennies.'

'Honest pennies.'

He snorted and began to turn away.

She said quickly, 'I can see how you were able to fool everyone else, Harry. I just can't understand how you managed to fool yourself.'

He turned back, about to say something, but she cut in, 'Murder isn't like other crimes. You can't balance a human life against cash. *He* can, but that's what makes him different. You've persuaded yourself you can live with it, but you're wrong.'

Jackson shook his head slowly. 'No. We don't have a choice between life and death, Kathy, only between death today and death tomorrow. Enough of my friends have passed away over the years for that to finally sink in – everybody dies. Once you really accept that, that it's not a matter of *whether* but of *when*, it puts everything else into perspective. Him' – he nodded down at the figure on the ground – 'he's dying a couple of days or a couple of months before he might have done. So what? He'd only have wasted the time anyway. I can make better use of it than him.'

'What makes you think North isn't looking at you in the same way?'

He smiled at her. 'That's why the money is already deposited equally in two Swiss bank accounts, one in his name and one in mine. That way neither can steal from the other. Don't worry, I've thought a lot about this. It's a finely balanced arrangement.'

'He needs you to hide him here . . . and you need him . . . ?'

'I need his silence, Kathy. Because unlike him I'm not going to be on the run for the rest of my life. I'm going to retire quietly with my new family, buy a villa overlooking a Mediterranean beach, and live like a king.'

He seemed quite unconscious of what Kathy would have to conclude about her own future from his sharing this rosy vision with her.

She pretended not to notice, and said, 'So you did it all between you? Just the two of you?'

'That's right.' Although he tried to sound cool and off-hand, Harry was clearly still somewhat in awe at what they'd done.

'To North's plan?'

'No,' Jackson leant forward to Kathy's ear, '*my* plan. When it comes to planning, ex-coppers make excellent villains. Greg North's expertise is more in the—'

'Execution.' Kathy finished the sentence for him. 'Yes, I've gathered that. Still, it must have been his idea, originally?'

'Uh-uh.' Jackson shook his head, pleased by her look of disbelief. 'I'd worked it all out long before I saw him in the mall that day. Bo got me started, actually. She told me, early on when we first began working together, about this hold-up at a mall in Canada, and after that I used to think about it sometimes, just for my own amusement, working out how it could be done.'

He stopped at the sound of North's laughter from the other side of the room as he watched the cartoon film while the police messages continued on the radio.

'Turn the small light on, Harry,' North called out suddenly. 'This one reflects in the screen.'

He got up and switched off the bright overhead fluorescent while Jackson turned on a small desk lamp on a chair beside the bed, creating a pool of light in a now darkened and shadowy room, the far end illuminated by the flickering screen to which North returned.

Harry came over and began to lead Kathy towards the bed. She stumbled, then, as he grabbed her arm, she whispered urgently, 'Harry, please, let me try to help Orr. Let me at least sit with him.'

He glanced over at North's back, then shook his head. 'Forget it, Kathy. Just sit down on the end of the bed. You'll be more comfortable.'

Kathy stared at the old man on the floor, unable to detect any sound or movement from him now, while Jackson searched among her things for the key to her handcuffs. When he found it he unfastened the cuff on her left wrist and clipped it to the bed frame, then sat down at the other end of the bed and gathered her possessions together. He picked up her notebook and put the rest of the things down onto the floor out of her reach.

'So, you worked out how it could be done,' Kathy prompted. She no longer really cared how they'd done it, but knew she must try to keep him talking to her.

Jackson, reading her notes, didn't reply at first. Then he said, 'How much do you know about Bruno Verdi?'

'Know, or suspect? I suspect that he murdered his niece, Kerri Vlasich, and before that two other girls, maybe more.'

'Hmm.' Jackson returned his attention to the notebook, turning the pages slowly.

'Do you know?' she prompted.

'Some time ago we had a bit of a problem with a girl called Norma Jean. You know about her?'

'Yes.'

'Yeah. Vagrancy, thieving, soliciting, dealing, shooting up in the toilets. Not unique by any means, but more persistent than most. Nobody seemed prepared to deal with her.

'Well, one day I was down the gym with Bruno and Speedy and we were talking about Norma Jean. Bruno was complaining about how we weren't solving the problem, and how it was beginning to affect business. I said I'd love to get rid of the girl, if anyone could tell me how, and Bruno said, if I really meant that, he could take care of it. When I asked what he meant, he looked kind of sly, you know, and said he could arrange to have her taken to Birmingham.'

'Birmingham?'

'He said he knew of a refuge there. Once there, he was sure Norma Jean wouldn't want to come back. I said that sounded good to me. He said the only problem was that she wasn't likely to go voluntarily. So it was a matter of finding some way to persuade her, for her own good of course, and ours. He said he could arrange this, if security would turn a blind eye, and if necessary cover up for him afterwards.'

'You agreed to this?' Kathy said, incredulous.

'I didn't know about his earlier history with the ice-cream van then, and he seemed genuinely concerned for the girl, wanting to help her start again. Honestly, Kathy, I thought he was doing us all a big favour.'

'What changed your mind?'

'Few months ago I had a run-in with Speedy. I'd caught him before taking drugs, or under the influence, but I'd always given him the benefit of the doubt. I knew he was on pain-killers, and I thought that was what was making him groggy. But this time I caught him red-handed with speed, and I said he was out. So then he told me a few home truths about what was going on in this place, things I didn't know about.

'He told me that after our conversation in the gym, Verdi had asked him if there was anywhere at Silvermeadow where he could keep Norma Jean for a few days, to frighten her, so she'd know not to come back. They'd looked at the building plans together, and found this room at the back of the plenum that wasn't used, because it was practically inaccessible. So Verdi did some work on it, fixing it up with a solid door and moving in furniture, and Speedy removed it from the computer plans of the building. Part of the deal was that Speedy wanted a CCTV camera installed, so he could watch what went on in the room from his control console.

'So he was able to tell me exactly what Verdi did to the girl. I'm not sure she knew too much about it – she was doped with some stuff Speedy was experimenting with. Then after three or four days, Verdi "took her to Birmingham". That was the phrase he used for dumping her in the compactor. And the problem was, I was implicated in it. They could say I'd put them up to it, encouraged them from the beginning. And not just in that one case, either. Some time after Norma Jean we had a similar problem with another difficult kid, a foreign girl, and I said to Verdi, sort of joking, that I wished she'd sod off to Birmingham too, and he smirked and tapped his nose and said he'd see about it.'

He paused, and Kathy saw that the pages of the notebook he held in his fingers were trembling.

'Speedy knew Verdi was killing the girls?'

'Yeah. He'd seen him do it on camera, and he had the evidence on tape.' He glanced back over his shoulder at a holdall at the side of the room.

'You got the tapes from Speedy's house,' Kathy said. 'You murdered Speedy and Wiff.'

'Greg did it,' Jackson said softly. 'It had to be done. They were in the way, and we needed to get you lot to leave Silvermeadow.'

Kathy tried to take in the implications of this. Her head was buzzing and sore, the noise from the TV and radio distracting. 'And Kerri? Did Verdi kill her too?'

Jackson didn't answer. He looked away, then North's voice called from the other end of the room, 'News,' and Jackson got to his feet and went over to the TV.

While they were occupied, Kathy tried to explore what she could of her surroundings. She couldn't reach the suitcase or other things at the top end of the bed, nor could she get anywhere near Orr. The bed frame was surprisingly heavy, and gave a loud creak when she tried to move it. She hesitated, tried again, but could only shift it with difficulty, an inch or so at a time. She felt under the mattress and sleeping bag, hoping for something she might use as a weapon, or to prise open the handcuffs, but without success.

After ten minutes Jackson returned, carrying two glasses of red wine. 'Nothing on the news,' he said, handing one glass to her.

'Doesn't he mind sharing?' she asked, nodding at North, engrossed now in some soccer.

'His taste runs more to the chemical than the grape,' Jackson muttered.

Kathy sipped at the wine. It burned her split lip and the taste reminded her of her evening drinking with Brock. The thought filled her with a sense of loss and despair. He wasn't coming to rescue her. No one was. Jackson was right: this was a truly stupid way to spend

Christmas Eve. She didn't want to listen to more of his story, yet she knew she must keep him talking.

'So this was the room,' she said.

'Eh?'

'That Verdi used.'

'Oh, yes. When Speedy explained it all to me, I went and had it out with Verdi. I told him I didn't want to know about Birmingham, or what he'd done with the kids. As far as I was concerned he'd taken them to a refuge, and that was that. I told him the basement room was off limits now, the locks changed, and there were to be no more disappearances.'

'How did he take it?'

'The way he takes most things, with that big operatic smile that means nothing.'

'When was this?'

'Maybe three or four months ago.'

Long before Kerri disappeared then. Kathy had the feeling she didn't want to hear about Kerri.

'It was some time before I put the basement room together with the perfect robbery. The problem with the Canadian hold-up Bo had described wasn't the heist itself, but the getaway. There isn't going to be much time between robbing a security truck and having the alarm raised, and when the robbery takes place in an out-of-town shopping centre there aren't any surrounding city streets to get lost in. There's great access to the motorway, but it's covered with cameras.

'But suppose the robbers could disappear into the centre itself – the last place people would think of looking for them. I thought it was a neat idea. I looked closely at the way Armacorp did their collections, and I reckoned I could see how it could be done, using that hidden room.'

'But how did North get down here after the robbery? Not through the security centre door into the plenum.'

'Same way the kid Wiff got in and out of the plenum, through the drop ducts. There's one in each of the stairways. North climbed down the last one with the uniforms and cash, and I replaced the grille after him and spent a couple of hours locked in a toilet cubicle, out of the way.'

Harry Jackson drained his glass and glanced at his watch. Kathy didn't want him to leave, certainly not until she had found some way to hold North at bay.

'But why on earth involve a madman like North, Harry?' she said.

'Because I'd never have done it otherwise. I had a plan all right, and I was beginning to feel desperate enough to dream about the money, but I was no hold-up merchant. I'd never done anything like that before. In my heart I didn't believe I *could* do it. It was only when I recognised him in the mall that day that I thought, for the first time, that I might actually go through with it.'

He glanced at her glass. 'You're not drinking.'

'No. I can't face it.'

'You should drink. It'll make you feel a bit better.'

Kathy laughed. 'It'd take more than a glass of wine to make me feel better, Harry.'

'I could get you a bottle of something else. What do you like? Vodka? Scotch?'

He is feeling guilty, she thought. He'd feel better if I died with a smile on my face. Some hope. This was why he was talking so much – his guilt, and presumably because there was no one else to confess to, apart from North, who wouldn't have understood his need. Kathy doubted if Connie knew much of the real story.

'I don't think so, Harry. Here, you have the wine.'

He shrugged and took the glass. 'Look,' he said, so softly she had to lean over to hear, 'I'll do what I can to help you, okay? Don't worry, and for God's sake don't annoy him.'

'Are you a Catholic?' she asked.

'Lapsed,' he said, surprised. A sudden look of consternation appeared on his face, as if he thought she might be about to demand a priest to give her the last rites. 'Why?'

'Just wondered. So you walked up to North in the mall and said, I know who you are, did you?' Kathy asked. 'He must have been pleased.'

'Not quite like that. I followed him out to his car and we had a conversation. I told him who I was, and said that before I decided whether to turn him in, I had a proposition to put to him. I said I was looking for a partner to help me steal a few million quid, if he was still in the business.'

'He believed you?'

'After a while. He told me he'd come back to the UK to see his girlfriend, Sophie, who had had his kid while he was abroad. He'd never seen the little girl, and he wanted to persuade Sophie to come away with him. His funds were running low, too, and he'd been talking to one or two old mates about doing another job. Only he was finding that people weren't so pleased to see him, after all the publicity he'd got the last time.'

'The bank job in the City. He killed two coppers. Didn't that bother you, Harry? Or did your amazing discovery that everyone has to die one day make that all right?'

Kathy had resolved not to antagonize him, but there was something so self-absorbed about the way he was going on that she hadn't been able to hold back the bitter words.

Jackson looked sharply at her. 'I'd watch that tongue, Kathy. You won't find North as patient as me.'

She bit back a reply.

He looked away, as if he was losing interest in talking further with her, and she came in quickly with the question she most needed answered, but dreaded most.

'You didn't answer my question about Kerri Vlasich. Did Verdi kill her?'

He looked down at his shoes, then rose slowly to his feet. 'I think we've talked enough.'

'Who did kill her, if he didn't?'

He was checking his watch again. For a moment he seemed about to say something, but then shook his head and began to walk away.

'You did, didn't you, Harry?' Kathy said. 'Kerri used to baby-sit for Sophie Bryant, and one time she saw you there, with North, and recognised you from Silvermeadow. That's why she had to die.'

Jackson stopped and looked back at her, his face expressionless.

It had been a guess, but the only way Kathy could see that Kerri could have put herself at risk was by baby-sitting for North's girlfriend. Seeing North alone would have meant nothing to her, but seeing Jackson with North would mean something once the robbery had been carried out and North's picture was in every newspaper. Then Jackson's dream of a quiet retirement with Connie would be blown, and, like North, he would be on the run for ever more.

And it meant that Jackson was prepared to kill for that dream; that he hadn't just tolerated North's murdering, but had himself killed in order to protect himself. Which was why his words of reassurance to Kathy, that he would do what he could to help her, were meaningless.

'Come on, Harry,' she whispered. 'You didn't seriously think you were in the clear, did you? We've had you in our sights for over a week now. That Mediterranean villa just isn't an option any more.

We're still short of proof to pin you for Kerri's murder, but if you kill me too, Brock will never let you rest. There won't be the remotest corner of the world you can hide in. Your one chance is to use the fact that you've got me to do a deal with Brock. Go to him, tell him you never intended anyone to get hurt in the robbery, that North did all the killing. I'll confirm that he shot Orr in cold blood, with you not here. Tell Brock to do the best he can for you, and tell him where I am. He'll be grateful, Harry. So will I. This is the only chance you've got.'

'You two are doing a lot of talking.' North's voice, harsh and suspicious, emerged from the shadows.

Jackson jumped, turned round quickly. 'Yeah.'

'What have you got to talk about, for fuck's sake.' North's voice definitely was more slurred than before. 'You look red, Harry. What's the problem?'

'No problem. The bitch has been working on me the same as she was on you, Greg.'

'Yeah, right. Let's do the bitch, get it over.' He drew something from his pocket. With a sharp click the blade snapped open.

'Hang on, Greg!' Jackson said with alarm. 'Brock knows more than we thought. That's what I've been getting out of her. Looks like we may need her as a hostage.'

'You reckon?' North licked his upper lip, disappointed and suspicious. 'I want to send Brock a message, when he finds her. Something he'll remember.'

'Sure, Greg, sure.' Jackson was looking rattled, and Kathy thought she should try to ease North off this line of thought.

'Why are you still here?' she asked him. 'That's what I don't understand. Why haven't you made your move already?'

He looked at her with a sly, dangerous smile. 'Safest place, darling. Tomorrow, Christmas Day, I become a pilgrim.' Sniggering at this thought, he reached down into the suitcase and pulled out a priest's dog collar. 'Special trip for the God squad. Dawn charter flight from Luton, Christmas lunch in Bethlehem, afternoon in the Holy Land, Christmas dinner on the evening flight back, minus one pilgrim.'

'Optimum timing, right?' Jackson said, his voice mechanical, talking to make time while he tried to get his brain to work. 'Robbery on the peak Saturday before Christmas for maximum takings, and getaway on Christmas Day when the search has died down and security's thin on the ground.'

Kathy thought about that. The accidental finding of Kerri's body must have rattled them, bringing dozens of police to Silvermeadow at just the wrong time. Killing Speedy had been a desperate improvisation to persuade them to close the case and leave before the planned day of the robbery.

North had turned and wandered back to the other side of the room, folding the blade of the flick-knife back into its handle. A toilet bucket had been improvised over there, and they heard him peeing, loud and long.

Kathy looked carefully at Jackson, wondering if she'd made any impression at all. His complexion had washed out to a sick grey, a film of sweat on his brow.

'Must be just like home from home for him in here, Harry,' she said. 'He's spent half of his life in prison. What about you? How long will you last inside?'

'Give it a rest,' he muttered. 'And for Christ's sake don't wind him up again this time.' He got to his feet.

'You're leaving?' she asked in alarm.

'I've got to close up the mall. Don't worry, he won't touch you as long as we might need you for insurance. I'll be back later.'

'Then what?'

'I told you, I'll do what I can.'

'Somehow that doesn't reassure me, Harry.'

'I'm not giving this up, Kathy,' he whispered angrily. 'I've come too far to do that.'

Kathy felt a stab of panic. It was true: he had come too far. There was nothing she could say, no angle she could work.

'The thing you've got to ask yourself, Harry, is what's the best outcome you can get for yourself?' she said desperately. 'Do you think Connie will agree to spend the rest of her and her kids' life on the run with a wanted killer? When I walked in here your options narrowed very sharply. You'd better do some hard thinking up there. You've got Brock's mobile number, remember? Do yourself a favour and use it.'

It was the best she could come up with. For a moment there seemed to be a glimmer of doubt in his eyes, then the hard look snapped back and he turned away with a dismissive snort.

'Harry!' she called after him. 'Get me a drink of water. Please.'

He hesitated, then poured water into a glass on the table and brought it back to her. Kathy took a gulp of water, then said hoarsely, 'What are you going to do?'

'There's nothing I can do, Kathy. I'm sorry. Really. What's done is done. I have to live with it. I can't change it now.'

'Suppose you could?' she whispered. 'Suppose you could go back a month, and forget about the hold-up, and Kerri, and Speedy, and everything.'

He shook his head. 'Christ . . . life isn't like that.'

'There's no hard evidence linking you to the hold-up or North, or to Kerri's death either.' She lifted her face closer to him, straining to make him understand. 'If you were to stop North right now, a citizen's arrest, and rescue me, who's to say you're not a hero? Me? Not likely. North? Everyone knows that he'd sell his mother for tuppence.'

'You'd look after me, I suppose?' he said. 'Oh sure.'

'Yes, Harry, I promise. You've got a good record. Why not? You can start again, with Connie.'

He smiled, looking sick. 'You're a trier, Kathy. Got to hand it to you. But you know I couldn't, even if I wanted to. You've seen what he's like. He's got that gun. I couldn't take him.'

'If you had a gun, I could distract him, Harry.'

'If . . .'

'There's one in the pocket of Orr's coat.'

'Eh?' He looked at her as if she were mad.

'In the right-hand pocket. An old service revolver, loaded. He brought it to shoot Verdi. Unfasten my handcuffs, and wait until he comes towards me.'

He shook his head and backed away from her. 'God, you never give up, do you?' He turned and went to the door.

North watched TV for the best part of an hour. At times Kathy thought he might have fallen asleep, but then he would sit up and look over to see what she was doing. Whenever he seemed absorbed in the screen she would continue with her attempts to ease the bed to which she was handcuffed away from the wall and closer to Orr. After a long, suppressed struggle that left her sweating and aching, she discovered that it would budge no further, and when she looked under it to see what the problem was she discovered that one of its legs at the head was chained to a bolt in the wall. She had been wasting her time. In desperation she tried stretching out on the floor, reaching out as far as possible towards Orr. Straining on her handcuffed wrist, she was just able to get a foot to within a couple of inches of the top of his motionless head, but no closer.

She was sitting crouched on the end of the bed, shivering with frustration and chill, when North yawned, stretched, jabbed the TV off and turned to stare at her.

'Like *The Bill*, do you, Greg?' she asked as he came towards her, not liking the look in his eyes one bit.

'Yeah, always used to watch it. Didn't think it would still be on when I came back, but there they were, the same old characters. Well, some had changed. June, for instance. I understand she had a spot of bother. I was sorry to hear that. I always had a soft spot for June. Being a blonde, maybe, like you.'

He contemplated her with a slightly dreamy look, then squeezed his nose and sniffed noisily. He seemed suddenly voluble, and she guessed he'd been snorting something.

'I should have let you watch it, darling,' he went on. 'Special Christmas Eve episode. Reg played Santa at the children's hospital with a raving paedophile on the loose. You'd have enjoyed it, the way they all back each other up, and the villains always get caught in the end. Would you say that's realistic, darling? From your perspective, as a serving officer, in the flesh, like?' He stared down at her legs. 'How did you get your jeans on again?'

'Harry—'

'Oh, good old Harry.'

'I don't know about good, but he's certainly smart.'

'Oh yeah?' he said vaguely.

'Smarter than you, anyway, if you haven't figured out what he's going to do tonight.'

North grinned at her tolerantly. 'Don't try it again, darling. I thought I taught you about your lip.'

Kathy shrugged and looked away. 'Suit yourself.'

There was a short pause.

'Go on then, I could do with a laugh. What's he going to do?'

'When he's finished, there's going to be three dead in here.'

'Oh yeah?'

'Yes. The old man and me shot with your gun, and you dead of an overdose, same as Speedy.'

'Is that right?' North sniggered. 'You amaze me, you really do. Now why would he do that?'

339

'Because he has no choice. My coming here doesn't make much difference to you – you're going to be on the run anyway. But for him it's a disaster. He doesn't want to go on the run. His new girlfriend won't stand for it. His whole plan was to retire in respectable comfort with her, a free man. Hasn't he told you about the villa overlooking the Mediterranean?'

North nodded, more cautious now, looking as if he resented having to get his nicely mellowed brain to work.

'We already had our suspicions about Harry, and if you two kill me Brock won't rest until he's put him away. That's not Harry's plan at all. That's what he and I were talking about while you were watching Bart Simpson. So now he only has one option. He has to make you responsible for everything, and he has to have you and me both dead so we can't tell the truth. It worked with Speedy, maybe it'll work again. My guess is that at this moment he's desperately trying to figure out a way to do it that won't look too suspiciously much like the way Speedy died. That's really his only problem. Then, when he's done it, he'll help Brock to find this place, and clear up the case. After a decent interval he'll go off with his half share, confident that Greg North will never come crawling out of the woodwork one day to give him away.'

North stared down at her, silent, and with a sense of dread Kathy watched his doped smile fade and black fury flare in his eyes.

He bent down and grabbed her left arm and leg, lifted her up and threw her bodily across the bed. Her right arm jerked taut and twisted on the handcuff, and Kathy screamed as she felt the muscles in her shoulder tear. He was on top of her, on her back, spitting as he shouted into her ear.

'Nice try, bitch! You're a fucking comedian, know that? Now I'll tell you *my* fantasy. You're a copper, see? Let's call you *June*, eh?' He began pulling at her clothes. 'Yeah! And June is going to die, right? Just like on *The Bill*. Only this time, when you're dead' – he was gasping with effort and rage, tearing at Kathy's clothing – 'and they open you up on the stainless-steel table . . . inside of you . . . they'll find a message . . . a personal message, from me . . . to Brock.'

Beyond his hoarse shouting in her ear and the pain screaming in her shoulder, Kathy heard another voice calling out, telling him to stop. Jackson, she decided. Finally North heard it too, and he paused long enough in his struggle with her jeans to tell him to fuck off.

Then he went abruptly still.

Kathy twisted her head up and saw his face inches away, saliva dribbling from his mouth, and the barrel of Orr's gun pressing up under his chin.

'I said' – Jackson's voice came from somewhere beyond – 'get off her, Greg.'

'What are you doing?' North was genuinely astonished. 'What are you fucking doing?'

'She'll have to come with us to the airport, in case we run into trouble. We'll need her to be able to walk. Just leave her alone.'

'Okay. Sure, Harry. Take it easy.'

North's voice had become steady, calm, but Kathy could see the look in his eye, which Jackson couldn't. He slowly got to his feet, still with Jackson at his back. Harry began to lower the heavy gun, and in that moment North uncoiled like an eel, the flick-knife blade opening in his hand and slamming into Jackson's side.

'Too old, Harry,' he hissed. 'Too slow.'

Jackson staggered back against the wall, and as his knees buckled he lifted the heavy revolver and pulled the trigger. There was a loud clunk as the hammer struck. He sank onto his knees, face screwed in pain, and lifted the gun again, struggling to thumb back the hammer.

Another clunk. This time North gave a wild whoop of mocking laughter. A jet of scarlet spurted from Harry Jackson's mouth and he began to topple forward, and as the gun hit the floor a great explosion shattered the air.

It was a moment before Kathy realised what had happened. She took in Jackson spreadeagled on the floor, face down, and North slumped back against the end of the bed, facing him. His knife had dropped to the floor, there was a puzzled look on his face, and the top of his head, above the eyebrows, was gone.

The barking dog roused her. Far away at first, she gradually allowed herself to believe that it was coming closer. Not much time had passed, she thought, for her ears were still ringing from the explosion. She tried to shout, but her throat was dry and she could barely raise a cough. Then the door opened and the German shepherd bounced in, dragging a dog-handler behind it, closely followed by Lowry and Brock.

They all stopped dead, even the dog, at the shock of the scene in the room: four corpses, blood splashed everywhere, on the walls, the floors . . .

Kathy realised that one of the corpses was her. She lifted a pale face and muttered hoarsely, 'About bloody time.'

Brock stared at her. 'Oh, Kathy,' he whispered. 'You don't do things by halves, do you?'

23

On the way to hospital Brock confirmed that Sharon hadn't phoned him, and explained that Lowry had been the one to raise the alarm. He had spent Christmas Eve drinking alone, until he reached the point of deciding to beat the hell out of his old mate Harry Jackson. He had driven to Silvermeadow, arriving after the centre had closed, and gone down to the service road. The security grille was pulled down for the night, but through it he had been able to make out both Jackson's car and Kathy's parked near the security centre window, in which a light was showing, but no sign of any staff on duty.

'This'll strike you as odd, Kathy,' Brock continued, as the ambulance swayed down the motorway, 'but for some extraordinary reason he decided to check with Hornchurch Street, and then with me, before he did anything.' But his sarcasm was lost on her, he realised, lying there pale and withdrawn, and he decided to save it for later.

Actually, Leon Desai had already phoned Brock before Lowry's message came in. Kathy wasn't answering her phone at home, and her mobile number was reporting a fault. He just wondered if Brock knew that she was all right. Kathy didn't react to that either, so Brock said no more.

At West Essex General they gave her immediate treatment for her damaged arm and face, and decided to keep her in for observation for the night.

The following day Brock picked her up and took her to Hornchurch Street where she made a full statement to him and a senior woman police officer, and then disappeared from sight.

The Christmas Day shifts were staffed mainly by men and women who either had no family to spend this special day with, like Brock

343

and now Lowry, or else found it so stressful that they were pleased to volunteer for work. For those involved, clearing up after Kathy's spectacular mess was a welcome chore.

There was Verdi to be arrested, on the basis of hard evidence at last, both the collection of sickeningly graphic tapes which were discovered in Jackson's holdall, taken from Speedy's house, and also the forensic traces they found in the octagonal room. And then there was the question of the girls, Naomi and Lisa. The fact that their testimony was no longer required either to incriminate Verdi or explain the fate of Speedy, Wiff and Kerri Vlasich raised something of a quandary. The only concrete evidence of their illicit drug business in the food court was their own confessions, and confessions could be retracted, especially by the young and vulnerable. How much effort was worth expending to make charges stick? Naomi's grandmother seemed to have worked this out for herself when Brock spoke to her later on Christmas Day.

'If it weren't for the money,' she said cautiously, 'we might almost be prepared to forgive our Naomi. But you can't just turn a blind eye to nearly forty thousand quid, now can you, Chief Inspector?'

Brock agreed that that was a problem.

'I mean, we might say that Jack had had a windfall at the dogs, and it was nothing to do with Naomi at all. We *might* say that, but we'd never be able to take advantage of it, not knowing what we do. But supposing . . .'

She paused and looked wistfully at the little portrait gallery of her drug-blighted family on the wall.

'Yes?' Brock asked sympathetically.

'Well, supposing it were given away, to a good cause, something to do with drug rehabilitation or something, as a memorial to Naomi's poor mum, who passed away on this very day two years ago.'

'Ah. Interesting thought,' Brock said, scratching his beard.

'Do you think so, Mr Brock? Do you really think so?'

Brock promised to consider it. In a few years, he thought, Naomi would have Nathan Tindall's job, or own a satellite TV company, and he had no desire to blight the future career of such a promising young capitalist.

Late on Boxing Day, Brock sat down in front of the roaring gas fire with a cold snack and a bottle of excellent red, and resisted the impulse, yet again, to phone Suzanne. Instead he picked up the little book that she had brought for him, which he had not yet opened. Émile Zola, he read, turning over the fly-leaf; *Au Bonheur des Dames*, or *The Ladies' Paradise*, 1861.

He closed it again and took a sip of the red, the same as the one Kathy had brought. It was difficult to concentrate on anything else. If it was closure you wanted, he thought, it was closure Kathy gave you. All the villains dead or sorted. Everything resolved – except, of course, Kathy herself.

Leon Desai, whom she had refused to see during the medical procedures and debriefing on Christmas Day, had turned up in some agitation on Brock's doorstep this morning, thinking she must be sheltering there. But after accepting a Christmas drink and some words of advice he had returned to his parents' home none the wiser.

After he had gone, Brock had driven over to Finchley and taken the lift to the twelfth floor of the block of flats where Kathy lived. Her neighbour, Mrs P, stuck her head out of her front door when she heard the key in Kathy's lock, and Brock had given her a bottle of gift-wrapped port which he said Kathy had asked him to give her. She would be away for a while, he had explained, if Mrs P wouldn't mind keeping an eye on her flat.

Inside the flat he had found the credit card statement from the bank, with its accompanying letter warning that her limit had now been exceeded. He had put it into his pocket and returned to his car, where he wrote out a cheque and put it into an envelope with the payment slip and posted it on the way back.

He gave a little start as the phone at his elbow began to ring.

'Hello, David.'

'Suzanne! How are things?'

'Fine. What are you eating?'

'Duck sandwich. How's the patient?'

'She's not too bad. Enjoying a bit of hero worship, I think. I'm afraid you've lost your status as number one cop.'

'Kathy has several advantages over me,' he said. 'She's black and blue from head to foot, and she's not likely to run off with their gran.'

'Yes. I'm sorry. Their confidence is so fragile. It would take so little to shatter it.'

'Hmm.'

He wasn't too sure about that. For all her tears at the thought of him pruning the bonsai's toes, little Miranda had been quite prepared to murder it when that became necessary. He rather felt they were every bit as tough as yesterday's duck.

They chatted for a while, then Suzanne said she would have to go and do something in the kitchen, and added, 'Have you tried the Zola yet?'

'It's right here on my lap. I was just about to open it.'

'I marked some passages for you. Have a look.'

She rung off. He refilled his glass and opened the book. The passages were marked by slips of paper, and he turned these over, reading. Some described the incredible new department store which was the central character of the book, its vast size and glittering interiors, its irresistible attraction to the fashionable consumers of Paris, its devastating effect on the old businesses around it, and the underpaid, desperate humans who worked within it.

Then he came to a page which Suzanne had doubly marked for him, describing the philosophy that had inspired Mouret, the creator of this phenomenon:

Mouret . . . finished explaining the mechanism of modern commerce. And, above all that he had already spoken of, dominating everything else, appeared the exploitation of woman to which everything conduced – the capital incessantly renewed, the system of assembling goods together, the attraction of cheapness, and the tranquillising effect of the marking in plain figures. It was for woman that all the establishments were struggling in wild competition; it was woman whom they were continually catching in the snares of their bargains, after bewildering her with their displays . . . And if woman reigned in their shops like a queen, cajoled, flattered and overwhelmed with attentions, she was one on whom her subjects traffic, and who pays for each fresh caprice with a drop of her blood . . .

Now the baron understood . . . His eyes twinkled in a knowing way, and he ended by looking with an air of admiration at the inventor of this machine for devouring the female sex. It was really clever.

Brock put down the book and pushed away the inedible duck sandwich. He got to his feet and went over to the bay window that projected out over the lane. The snow had finally begun, falling in big, lazy flakes through the still, cold air.

He lifted the glass of wine to his mouth and repeated aloud the words he had just read.

'With a drop of her blood . . .'

346